Jane Wenham-Jones

Mum in the Middle

A division of HarperCollins Publishers
www.harpercollins.co.uk

Harper*Impulse* an imprint of
HarperCollinsPublishers
1 London Bridge Street
London SE1 9GF

www.harpercollins.co.uk

This paperback edition 2018

First published in Great Britain in ebook format by
HarperImpulse 2018

A catalogue record for this book is
available from the British Library

ISBN: 9780008278670

This novel is entirely a work of fiction.
The names, characters and incidents portrayed in it are
the work of the author's imagination. Any resemblance to
actual persons, living or dead, events or localities is
entirely coincidental.

Printed and bound by CPI Group (UK) Ltd, Croydon, CR0 4YY

For Karen with love – I wish you were here to read it.

Chapter 1

To a Wonderful Mother on Mother's Day.
Mum, I want to tell you
On this your special Day
How much I do appreciate
You in every way
I may not always show it
I may forget to phone
But today I just want you to know …

Ahh. They may fleece you, your kids. They may fill your spare bedroom – the one you need to turn into an office – with their junk and unstrung guitars. And empty a fridge in one sitting and spill cider on the new rug. But when push comes to Mothering Sunday shove they come up trumps. A small sentimental lump rose in my throat as I turned over the card from my darling youngest son:

… I need another loan!

Ho ho ho! Ben had scrawled, next to a large smiley.

Ha, Ha, Ha! *You and me both, sonny.*

I put the card on the kitchen dresser, with the one from

Tilly and the florist's greeting from Oliver, who'd sent an extravagant arrangement of creamy roses the previous day (no doubt arranged by his girlfriend, Sam, but gorgeous of him nonetheless) and surveyed the line-up.

My three lovely children – still costing me a bloody fortune but caring enough to remember what day it was. Even if they couldn't be here. I allowed myself a small pang of self pity.

'You time,' Caroline, my best friend and one-time sister-in-law, had said at our last drink, before I'd got the train from London back to Northstone. 'Time to get *your* life back.' She had wagged a perfect ruby nail in my direction. 'Kids gone, new house, new town, all sorts of fresh opportunities.' By the back door was the final remaining black sack stuffed with detritus from Ben's bedroom.

I missed him crashing and banging his way around the kitchen, leaving trails of sweatshirts and unwashed cups. And not simply because my boss had dropped a bombshell at Thursday's meeting and put me in charge of the company Facebook page and I didn't have a clue where to start.

Feeling a twinge of anxiety rising – Instagram had been mentioned too – I looked at the clock, grasped keys, handbag and Ben's unwanted junk and went outside to peer into the bins. Not having yet got the hang of what was collected when, I'd left both wheelies on the pavement. The blue one was full of beer cans and last week's newspapers. The black one was empty.

I dumped the sack inside it and began to pull the bin back up the drive of Ivy Cottage. A misnomer if ever there was one, since the only ivy in the entire place was wrapped around an old sycamore tree at the bottom of the garden of this decidedly non-cottagey, rather lumpen-looking semi, with an incongruous extension on the back. The estate agent had called it quirky.

'Quaint,' he'd added, waving his arm at the way the front door opened straight onto the square sitting room – a feature which still slightly took me by surprise if I came home post-rosé – and the steep stairs that ran up one side. The kitchen beyond needed updating. The whole place cried out for paint. But it had a garden and a pond and a walk-in larder. And after too many years of living in a house still half-owned by my ex-husband, it was all mine.

'Living the dream,' Caroline had called it. Away from the rat race in a gorgeous little town I'd always hankered after. 'The next chapter,' she'd declared, topping up our glasses with celebratory fizz and ticking off the excitements. The home to do up exactly as I wanted, the cool new friends waiting to be made, the space I'd now have in which to take stock and plan the rest of my life.

It was only because I was tired, I told myself now. Wrung out by moving and work and scrubbing and hauling furniture about – more drawn to a long lie-down than adventure. That's why I found myself looking around at my unnaturally tidy sitting room, unsullied by a single lager tin or take-away container, thinking wistfully of that other perpetually messy, noisy abode where there was always a starving teenager sprawling, a manic cat killing something and washing piling up.

All the things I used to complain about, really, I mused wryly, as I went back for the other bin, making a mental note to write in my diary it was bottles next time, and then jumping when a piercing voice cut through my thoughts.

'Hey! OY!'

I looked around for a wayward dog, very possibly chewing on a small child, only to find that strident tone was directed at me.

'Tess! How you doing in there?' My opposite neighbour was standing by her gates, dressed in a quilted jacket and wellington boots with flowers on. 'SURVIVING?' she yelled.

I'd met the striking-looking Jinni before – she'd hollered at me when I first moved in – and I had her down as an interesting mixture of bohemian creative and woman of formidable capability. She was renovating the big old rectory over the road, and I'd seen her both floating around in a kaftan, apparently reciting poetry to herself, and up on the roof with a hammer.

'All straight, then?' she demanded, crossing the street and surveying me. 'I hate bloody Sundays, don't you?' she continued, clearly not caring whether I was 'straight' or not. 'Can't get on with anything till the bloody plumbers turn back up tomorrow. If they do ...'

'How's it going?' I nodded towards the beautiful grey-stone house with its mullioned windows and creeper.

'Want to see?' Jinni jerked her head towards her front door. 'Fancy a drink?'

I looked at my watch. 'I'd love one,' I said, thinking that a spot of lunchtime alcohol was exactly what I could do with. 'But I've got to drive to Margate. To see my mother,' I added, as Jinni raised her brows.

'I'm an orphan now,' – she gave a loud and not entirely appropriate-sounding laugh – 'so I don't have to do all that Mother's Day crap.'

I rather wished I didn't have to either, but Alice had spoken. My sister does not believe in 'me' time – especially if it's mine.

Jinni pointed down the road. 'Seen all the kids scuttling to the church to get their free flowers? Never go any other time. Little buggers ...'

'Do you have children?' I asked.

Jinni nodded. 'Dan's in Australia, working for a surf school, and Emma's teaching up in Nottingham.'

She did not look at all sad about this. In fact she was smiling widely. 'Haven't seen either of them since Christmas,' she said cheerfully. 'But Dan's back in the summer and Emma will roll up at some point. What are yours doing?'

I tried to sound as pleased as she did. 'They're all in London. Oliver is a trainee surveyor, Tilly's finished drama school and is working in a diner while she tries to get auditions and Ben's at uni doing computer science with music.'

'Off your hands, then,' Jinny said.

'Yes.'

I thought about telling Jinni that, as odd as it sounded, it was the first time in my 47 years I'd ever lived alone. That since Friday when Ben had abandoned his sensible plan of saving money by living with his mum while studying in the capital, for the much better one of taking up a box room near the Holloway Road and disposing of his student loan in a variety of bars – I was not finding it very easy.

I'd been lucky to have him here at all. How could a small

market town, known for its pottery and teashops, with four pubs, a tiny theatre and a KFC – deemed such a potential den of iniquity, it had by all accounts had the locals up in arms – compare with life in the city?

But I didn't know Jinni well enough to start bleating. Instead I forced my face into bright smile. 'And what about you? What do you do – or did you do? I can see this must be a full-time job ...'

'Bloody nightmare,' said Jinni merrily. 'I was an actress too, if your Tilly needs warning onto a better path. Did you ever see *Maddison and Cutler*?'

'Er, I may have seen the odd episode, I remember it being on ...'

Jinni laughed. 'It's my only claim to fame – unless you count playing a prostitute in *Casualty*. I was Maddy!'

I stared at her dark eyes, defined cheekbones and red lipstick and had a sudden flash of recognition. Remembered Rob watching appreciatively as the hot young TV detective – always dressed in tight black leather and invariably waving a gun about – strutted her stuff.

'Oh my God,' I said. 'My ex-husband fancied you rotten!'

Jinni laughed again. 'It made me a fortune, well, enough to eventually buy this place, anyway. And I married well.' She laughed again. 'And divorced even better. He was the producer', she added. 'Egocentric bastard ...'

She talked on, telling me her plans to open a boutique B&B, dropping in details of her past, her hands waving about expressively, her glossy dark hair tossed back over a shoulder, kohled eyes fixed on mine. She had an energy and passion about her that made me feel dull and mousy.

She'd just finished a diatribe about how men were all largely useless but she did miss it if she didn't have one to go to bed with occasionally and had moved onto the sort of bathrooms she was planning.

'They are going to be really sleek and classy,' she was saying, 'with rain showers and power baths, but I want to give each bedroom a totally different style with a mix of contemporary and vintage.' She stopped and gave another of her strange honks of laughter. 'In other words, I'll be round the junk shops and ... Oh Lord, here we go!'

A small thin woman in her sixties with cropped grey hair and sharp, pretty features was coming along the pavement in jeans, dark donkey jacket and a red patterned scarf. Her dark eyes looked us both up and down.

'Hello, Jinni,' she said coolly, before holding her hand out to me. 'I don't think we've met,' she added, her voice low, but with an edge.

'How remiss of you!' Jinni's tone was dry. 'Not harangued Tess with one of your many petitions yet? Not even the one about me?' Jinni turned back to me, unsmiling. 'Ingrid is against what I am doing here. She thinks if I am allowed to open a B&B it will bring ruin and devastation on the town and all who live here ...'

Ingrid released her grip on my fingers and gave a chilly smile. 'I am concerned,' she said in her cultured tones, 'about extra traffic and congestion in this narrow road.' She held out a flyer. 'We are already seeing a greater influx of Londoners using this as a weekend base and contributing nothing to the local economy Monday to Friday. And now, with the high-speed rail link bringing in new residents who can comfortably commute from here,' she paused and raised her eyebrows at me, 'the housing stock is shrinking and local people are being priced out of the market.' She gave an extraordinarily sweet smile that was framed in steel.

'Tess is my newest neighbour,' Jinni told her. 'Ingrid is Northstone's foremost agitator,' she said to me. 'No issue too small! The local council adore her.'

'I prefer the term "campaigner"' said Ingrid, with another sugary-tight beam. 'It's nothing personal,' she finished. Jinni made a small snorting noise.

'Well, nice to meet you,' I said uncertainly. 'I must get going. Jinni, I'll um—'

'Come over soon,' Jinni finished for me shortly. 'And shout if you need anything.' She turned abruptly and strode back over the road towards her house.

As I moved back towards my car, Ingrid fell into step beside me. 'Do you have a view on this ... development?' she asked, enunciating the final word as if it could do with a dose of antibiotics.

'Well, the plans sound lovely,' I said, trying to sound friendly and reasonable. 'And Jinni seems very nice to me.'

I shivered. It had got cold while I was standing there. Ingrid looked at me with a pitying expression and then gave an odd little laugh. 'Yes,' she said. 'Things aren't always what they seem.'

Chapter 2

It seemed like a stroke. That's what her best friend Mo said when she phoned to say my mother had been taken to A&E. The patient, discharging herself in a matter of hours, insisted it was a fuss over nothing much.

'Gerald's taking me away for a few days,' she'd announced, moments after I'd cancelled work to rush to her bedside. 'We're going to see Sonia in Dorset. Well he is. I'm going to the pottery if it's still there. Not been to Poole for donkey's years.'

'Shouldn't you be resting?' I enquired, knowing I'd have more luck suggesting a little light pole-dancing or a ride on a camel.

'What for? They can't find a thing wrong with me. It was likely migraines with what do you call it?'

'I don't know.'

'Yes you do – migraines where you can't speak.'

'I really don't know anything about them.'

My mother had sounded impatient. 'I wish you wouldn't be deliberately obtuse.' While I was spluttering she swept on. 'I've just looked it up and already it's gone. So annoying. That word to do with light – they take pictures of it.'

I felt a frisson of unease. 'Mum, what are you talking about?'

'Migraines! It's not that I mind Sonia, you know I don't, but I don't want to sit there all afternoon, when there's the harbour to see.'

'Well you don't have to, do you?' I said, struggling to keep up with my mother's conversational switchback technique. Was she usually as scattered as this? 'Sonia won't mind if you go for a walk. She can catch up with her dad.'

'We're not staying there. Gerald's got us a hotel.'

'That's nice. Can I speak to him?'

'He's gone home to pack.'

I listened while she talked on, covering a myriad subjects ranging from the problems of deciding what to take when March was cold one minute and sunny the next, Mo's dog's possible gallstones and the squirrel in her garden who'd eaten all the bulbs.

She did sound okay – her voice was strong enough and she appeared to be wandering about the house as she told me about the nice staff at the hospital, who were forced to work such long hours with little thanks from this government, and how the doctor had been impressed with her blood pressure.

Keeping her to the point was no easy task, but then again, as I wrote to my sister, that was nothing new.

Mother's made of stern stuff, I typed, as much to reassure myself as Alice. And it was true. She was rarely ill, still gardened and her gleamingly clean house put mine to shame. She travelled, went to galleries and the theatre, was a sterling member of Margate Operatics and had more friends than I did. Seventy-four was no age these days. *Even if she has had a TIA and is keeping it quiet*, I concluded, knowing that Alice would immediately Google the full implications of a Transient Ischaemic Attack and be an expert on it by the next time she wrote. *It will take more than a few microscopic clots to finish her off.*

I pushed away the memory of Tilly saying that when she'd last phoned, Granny sounded even more bonkers than usual and the way my mother had suddenly sounded vague and distracted and appeared to temporarily struggle to recall Ben's name. Was she feeling unwell more often than she was letting on?

I'd been phoning daily, I told my sister instead, as I tried to still the anxious fluttering in my stomach as I imagined my seemingly indestructible parent suddenly helpless and frail. Her dear old friend Mo was there a lot; Gerald as often as he was allowed to be.

Alice was having none of it. No amount of explaining that our mother herself had actively discouraged me from going down this weekend, saying the traffic would be bad with all those other mothers being towed out to lunch, that I had a long list of household tasks to complete and a presentation to finish before Tuesday, would sway my elder sister. *You need to see for yourself,* she instructed. While actually numbering my duties: *1) get a proper list from Mother of all symptoms. NB What exactly was said by medics? (suggest you take notes). 2) double-check with Mo for accuracy. Have noticed Mother can be woolly of late. 3) Speak to Gerald (do not be fobbed off by Mother. I do not have a number for him. Make sure you obtain. 4) I think it would be best to phone her GP on Monday and you'll need to be fully armed with the facts …*

I growled and sighed. Years of experience have taught me that when a diktat arrives from the US, it is quicker in the long run to follow it. Alice may be three thousand miles away in Boston. But her sheer will can still fill a room.

Thus on an afternoon when I would rather be perusing my sample pots and deciding which shade of foodie yellow – I am hovering between autumn honey, golden sugar and lemon delight – to use on the dining-room walls, drinking wine with Jinni or even wielding the Shake n' Vac in Ben's bedroom – Tilly has complained it smells of hamsters – I am crawling around the M25, with a potted azalea and the gnawing suspicion that by the time I actually have the opportunity to start this brave new life of mine, I'll be on a mobility scooter.

Then I hear Alice's voice reminding me it's the least I can do on Mother's Day when I haven't seen our mother since before I moved – even if she was away with Gerald on an art appreciation cruise and then spending every spare minute rehearsing H.M.S. *Pinafore* – when she, Alice, is sitting on the other side of the world, worrying.

'Get on a bloody plane, then!' I say out loud, looking at the line of traffic snaking ahead and braking sharply as the van in front abruptly stops.

'Arse!' I shout, as I inch forward again, shot through with guilt and resentment.

My mother's not overly thrilled, either.

'He's a very clever man,' she says, as I step across the

threshold of her neat chalet bungalow. 'But I do wish he wouldn't go around in that dress.'

She has been to an exhibition by Grayson Perry at the Turner Contemporary, where she has admired the pots and 'those wooden ones' but still isn't convinced the artist needs the frock and wig.

'It's the children I think about,' she says. 'They'll get teased at school.'

'I don't think so, Mum.' I say, handing her the plant and throwing my coat over the bannister. 'As far as I know, he's only got one daughter and she's grown up now.'

'Hmmm,' my mother looks as though she doubts this. 'Sonia hasn't got any better either.' My mother has always believed in the non sequitur to keep conversation zipping along. While I am still making the mental leap from the famous artist to Gerald's rather dour daughter, she has moved on to her geranium cuttings having died in the frost.

'You don't expect it in March,' she says. 'Though Mo will say that May thing about casting the clout.'

'How is Mo?' I enquire, trying to analyse what is even odder about my mother than usual.

'Still likes her tea.'

It is then that it hits me. My mother hasn't moved. Usually by now I'd have been offered three different sorts of hot beverage and very probably a sandwich. But I've been in the house a good five minutes and she is still in the hallway in front of me.

'Shall we go and make some?' I suggest.

'Some what?'

13

Everything in the kitchen looks as always. The surfaces shine, the sink is scrubbed, the storage jars arranged in formation. The floor is speck-free, the tea towels folded with regimental precision and the mugs lined up along the shelf have their handles pointing in the same direction.

But as I watch my mother, watching me filling the teapot, the low-level dread that started when I hit the Thanet Way, deepens further. 'Are you okay, Mum?' I ask, disturbed by her stillness.

She looks back at me, her face troubled, the skin on her cheeks seeming to sag. I see how old she looks and how tired.

'Not really,' she says.

I carry the tray to the sitting room and wait while she settles herself in her usual chair. The book on the table is the same crime thriller she told me she was reading weeks ago. A bookmark pokes out of it, barely a quarter of the way through.

The air in here feels slightly stale and the irises on the pine cupboard are curled and faded. My mother flings open windows in deepest February, will sense a dead petal at ten paces.

'What's happened?' I ask. 'You're not well, are you?'

She shakes her head slowly. I am clutched by fear.

'It wasn't a migraine, was it? When they took you to hospital?'

She sits up straighter. 'Oh yes, they think it was,' she says, sounding stronger. 'A migraine with auras,' she adds firmly. She smiles at me now. 'I thought it was a stroke too ...'

She lifts up her tea and takes a small sip. 'I didn't want to say it on the phone'.

My heart is thumping as she tells me.

She'd been in the garden, trying to pull out the dandelions from among her sprouting forget-me-nots, when she'd started to feel a bit sick. So she'd come indoors to get some water and then her vision had started to go hazy and she was seeing wavy lines. Recognising this as classic migraine, after having them for years, and feeling her head start to ache, she'd called Mo to put her off coming round for supper. But when she tried to speak to Mo, her words came out backwards.

Mo called an ambulance and came straight round. They both now thought my mother was having a stroke, and the paramedics clearly agreed as she was whisked off to A&E – 'such nice young people, couldn't have been kinder' – where she had various tests and a CT scan, which showed that in fact she hadn't had a stroke, and they concluded, according to my mother, that it probably was just a migraine after all.

By now she could talk normally again and they told her migraines could affect speech and that if she hadn't tried to make the phone call she might never have known. The relief made my mother feel better immediately and she went home, took painkillers and had a better night's sleep than she usually did, feeling fine by the next day, although the hospital wanted her to have a second, different, sort of scan, just to make sure, so she had gone for that when she got back from Poole, and seen a neurologist.

'And?' I prompt as she is silent again. 'What did he say?'

The room is getting darker and my mother rises from her chair and walks slowly across the carpet and turns on the standard lamp she's had all my life. Then she sits down again and I see the distress in her eyes. 'I had wondered,' she says. 'But it was still a terrible shock.'

'What?' I ask softly, my mind racing through the possibilities. *A stroke the first scan had missed? Cancer? A brain tumour?* 'Tell me.'

'Oh Tess,' my mother says, with tears in her eyes. 'I've got some sort of dementia.'

Chapter 3

'My uncle had Alzheimer's.' Jinni opened a cupboard with one hand and reached into the tall fridge with the other. 'It's an absolute bastard.'

I sat at the enormous table in her vast stone kitchen, looking in awe at the battered range, deep butler's sink and numerous drawers, as she deftly uncorked a bottle and put a generous white wine in front of me. I swallowed.

'It's not necessarily that – the damage is frontal-temporal only but I've been Googling and it doesn't sound good. I don't know how quickly ...' I stopped. 'We're waiting for an appointment with the consultant.'

Jinni looked back at me. 'And she's okay at home on her own?'

'Her friend Mo is going in and out. And her partner, Gerald. Not that we're allowed to call him that!'

I didn't add that Mo had said she thought the days of my mother being left alone were numbered. I was still getting my head around it. Mo, sworn to silence until my mother had told me herself, had been on the phone for over an hour.

She'd been worried about my mother's forgetfulness, peculiar statements and occasional lack of coherent speech for some time. But Gerald had appeared unbothered ('typical man! They don't notice anything unless it's in a mini skirt') and my mother had dismissed her concerns, while insisting I was due to visit any day, so Mo had hoped I'd turn up soon and pick up on it myself.

'I'm so sorry,' I'd said guiltily.

'Nothing to be sorry for, Pet,' Mo interrupted me. 'Wouldn't have made a ha'pence worth of difference'

It seemed nothing would. I was hanging onto the word 'slow' I'd found on the internet. A slow, degenerative neuro-logical condition. Perhaps it would take a long time and my mother would stay at this stage, where she lost her train of thought and stood staring. Maybe all the other horrors I couldn't bear to imagine, listed under symptoms and outlook, happened to other people's mothers and not mine.

I hadn't told the kids yet. I told myself it was best to wait till we'd had the full prognosis, but really I couldn't bear to say the words out loud.

I wouldn't have told Jinni if she hadn't looked at me so directly and said I seemed upset.

'She looks normal,' I said. 'She sounds the same, but there's this ...' I stopped, struggling to put my finger on it. 'Lack of interest ...'

I'd shown her photos of the house, suggested dates for her to come and stay. Usually she'd have been on her diary like a tramp on a kipper.

Now she nodded with distance in her eyes.

'She's afraid too,' I said. 'I don't know what will happen.

Alice is already talking about carers but Mum says she just wants to keep everything normal for as long as she can ...'

I'd read about people with mothers who'd simply gone a bit doo-lally and couldn't be trusted with a gas supply, but who were happy enough in their own little world. I'd tried to picture my mother like this and failed.

Then I'd found horror stories of aggression and incontinence and smashed furniture, and switched off the computer, unable to bear the tales of rage and tears and family breakdown.

'But I don't know how long that will be ...' I said.

Jinni shook the plaster dust from her hair. 'Come and see a fireplace.'

I followed her obediently up a wide staircase to a bare back bedroom overlooking her tangled garden. A large chunk of ceiling was missing.

'Look!' She waved an arm at a pretty iron grate surrounded by flowered tiles. 'Victorian! Been boarded up.' She kicked at the sheet of painted hardboard she'd hacked away from the chimney breast. 'Philistines!'

She threw open one of the cupboards either side of the chimney breast. 'It's the third one I've uncovered. Don't you just love all this storage?'

'It's going to be gorgeous,' I said, looking around at the long windows and cornice work, grateful to be distracted.

'Yeah,' Jinni pulled a face. 'If I don't drop dead of exhaustion first. I'm knocking through here to make an en suite.' She slapped a palm against the wall. 'If you ever want a stressbuster, grab the sledge hammer.'

Back downstairs, my fingers curled around the leaflet in my pocket. The reason I'd plucked up the courage to bang on Jinni's door.

'Did you get one of these?' I held out the flyer for a Wine and Wisdom evening for the local theatre group. *Individuals welcome!* 'Do you fancy going?'

Jinni stiffened. 'Eurgh. Those am-dram types get on my wick – all emoting and "getting in the zone" as if they're Dench or Olivier – and if I see Ingrid once more this week, I might swing for her.'

She took a large mouthful of wine. 'She's the bane of my bloody life. Still objecting to my change-of-use application on all sorts of insane grounds and she's been up and down the street trying to get everyone else to protest as well.'

'She put a note through my door about it,' I told Jinni uncomfortably. 'Said she was worried about extra vehicles and you chopping down trees.'

Jinni scowled. 'Don't listen to that environmental crap,' she said. 'It's sour grapes. Her creepy son tried to buy it before I managed to. I outbid him. That's the real reason the old witch is so bitter and twisted.'

'Oh!' I waited while Jinni took another swig from her glass. 'What was he going to do with it?'

'Turn it into flats probably. Or demolish it – one of his mates owns the place behind me so I expect the plan was to flatten the lot and build a whole new cul-de-sac. Even more cars, even more of the dreaded DFLs tempted here. Not that they need much tempting now we've got the fast train. And a whacking great profit for him. Wanker.'

She poured some more into her glass and pushed the bottle towards me. 'I wouldn't mind if she was honest about it. But it's so damn hypocritical. I'm making this place beautiful again, bringing out all the original features. I've been advised to take out one tree because it's diseased and it might bloody fall on me. I've got huge plans for the garden. It's going to be stunning. And if I had his money, yes, I'd keep the whole place just for me but I'm going to have to do B&B to afford the upkeep.'

She stopped and took a deep breath. 'Sorry to rant on.'

'He's a builder, is he?'

'David?' she said, with a comical sneer. 'He's an architect. Got some flash practice in town. But fingers in all the local pies. Ingrid's always storming the council offices talking about all the new commuters ruining the area and there not being enough affordable housing, while her precious boy is the first one to mop up any bargains and make a fast buck. They both make me sick.'

I looked at her, startled by the real venom in her voice. I made myself smile. 'So that's a no, then?'

Jinni grinned back.

'Sorry hun – you'll have to be brave and go on your own.'

'Bravery's not my strong point.'

It was held in a function room at the back of a pub called the Six Pears. I walked the half mile there, looking in the old-fashioned shop fronts, as I crossed the cobbled market square onto the High Street, still finding it hard to believe this was now home.

The town had changed and spread over the years since I'd first come here to visit my friend Fran. There were rows of houses where once there were fields, more traffic and speed bumps and the lovely old ironmongers had closed down now. But Northstone always kept its charm. Even in the years when Fran was in Italy, we'd got into the habit of stopping off on the way back from the coast for coffees or ice-creams, to poke about among the antiques or simply find a loo, and I'd often imagined living here.

The fantasy had grown legs the moment I'd read about the new high-speed link to the city. House prices were rising sharply and already the bookshop had become an emporium of scented candles and high-end bath oils and our favourite pub, with the bar billiards table, a raw-food restaurant. When we got a buyer for Finchley, I moved fast. I loved the idea of a small community and a proper local, quiet streets and the river nearby. With London now under an hour away, it seemed meant to be. I'd thought about Ben getting to uni and me getting to the office, and having somewhere to park and a garden. But somehow I'd overlooked the day-to-day reality of making new friends and who I'd talk to ...

The wind was cold and I could feel the make-up running from my streaming eyes as I reached the door, suddenly wishing I'd stayed at home with some biscuits and the box set of *Downton Abbey*.

But, I reminded myself as I shoved my body across the threshold, I needed a social life.

Visions of painting the place red with Fran had faded fast – the last time I'd dropped in, it was all baby yoga, organic dishcloths and making sure her four children got their ten-a-day. Apart from Jinni, the only person I'd spoken to at any length since I got here was the chap in the corner shop and that was only a thrilling exchange about my newspaper delivery and why he was fresh out of washing-up liquid.

A woman with grey-blonde hair and some rather nice silver jewellery was sat at a table next to a cash box.

'Wicked Wits?' she enquired, consulting a list.

'Sorry?'

She repeated it, mouthing the words carefully as if I were in need of learning support. 'Are you on a TEAM?'

'No, I'm on my own ...'

She rustled the paper. 'The Wits said they were waiting for one more.' She beamed. 'But if you're a one-off I'll give you to Brigitte ...'

Brigitte, a dramatically made-up lady with highly defined eyebrows, was, as she immediately introduced herself, chair of the Northstone Players –for which the evening was raising much-needed funds – and currently rehearsing Madame Francine for their forthcoming production of *A Frenchman in Disguise*.

'Do you know the play?'

I shook my head.

'Ever done any acting?' I shook my head again. She patted my arm. 'We're always looking for help with the scenery ...'

She led me across a room filled with round tables adorned with paper, pens and bowls of peanuts, through small groups of people holding glasses, to the far corner. A broad-shouldered, grey-haired man in his late fifties sat with a younger, bearded chap and a blonde girl of about twenty.

'One for you, Malcolm,' Brigitte said. 'This is Tess – she's new to Northstone and could be your secret weapon.'

'I don't know about that ...' I squeaked, embarrassed.

Malcolm looked me up and down. 'Neither do I,' he said gruffly.

Malcolm was the editor of the local paper, the *Northstone & District News*, as well as other regional publications; the young girl, Emily, was one of his junior reporters and the man, Adrian, another of the town's thesps, who, he told me, had written a play he was hoping they would perform for their autumn production.

'We'll call ourselves the Odds and Sods, shall we?' said Malcolm.

When we'd got to the third round and I still hadn't known the answer to anything except who'd played Deirdre in Coronation Street, I could feel myself sinking in my chair.

My only consolation came from the fact that Emily didn't seem to know much either and Adrian had only contributed the names of three Olympic gold medallists and the symbols from the periodic table for lead, tin and pewter.

Malcolm, on the other hand, was grunting out answers like a one-man Wikipedia and was only seen to be flummoxed when a question came up about boy bands. 'You must know that,' he instructed Emily, who didn't.

By half-time we were sitting in third place. 'And we haven't done current affairs yet,' said Malcolm, satisfied. 'What do you do? And why did you move here?'

I was halfway through regaling him with the highlights of my enthralling career as an office space planner, when I saw Ingrid bearing down on us with a beer mug full of money and two books of raffle tickets.

'Hello again!' she said briskly to me before putting the tankard in front of Malcolm. 'How's that paper of yours? Going to be any decent news in it for a change?'

'You'll have to fork out and find out,' he countered. 'For a change.'

'I always do,' said Ingrid. 'Though why it doesn't have a bit more online, I don't know.'

'Because then nobody would buy it,' he said. 'As it is they all stand there reading it in the shop.'

'You want to cut out all the smut, then, and put in something worth paying for.'

'The smut is why the few do pay for it.'

Ingrid gave him a withering smile. I got the feeling this was a well-worn exchange. 'Are you going to buy some tickets?'

'No,' Malcolm said. 'I've already paid to do the quiz.'

'This is to raise more funds. Lovely prizes.'

'They won't be.'

'Go on. Another couple of pounds won't hurt you.'

'I like quizzes. I don't like raffles.'

Ingrid thrust the books towards me. 'A pound a strip', she said, surmising correctly that I wouldn't dare refuse her too.

'Settling in?' she asked, while I fumbled for coins. 'Despite the neighbours?'

I felt Malcolm's eyes on me. There was a small silence.

'Jinni's been very kind to me,' I said eventually, keeping my voice even and smiling at Ingrid.

Ingrid looked cynical. 'I'm sure she has,' she said shortly.

'I've got something to tell you,' she added to Malcolm. 'But it's off the record.'

'Then don't tell me,' said Malcolm. 'Come back when you've got something I can actually publish.'

Ingrid grimaced. 'It's about the council. If I have my way, I'll blow the lid off the whole lot of them.'

Malcolm's tone was dry: 'I'm surprised they can sleep.'

'Annoying woman,' he said, when she'd moved off.

'Do you want a drink?' I asked him, disconcerted. Emily and Adrian had disappeared.

'Not allowed to. Doctor's a miserable bugger who said I'd got to give it up. Orange juice only.' He looked woebegone. I laughed.

'Shall I get you one of those?'

Malcolm peered into his empty glass as if searching for an answer.

'Why not.'

'Ingrid seems to be quite a character,' I said, when I got back.

Malcolm looked at his juice with ill-concealed disgust. 'Ingrid disapproves of me and the paper.' This seemed to please him. 'Calls it a filthy little rag.'

I raised my eyebrows. 'That's a bit strong.'

'She objects to page five and our Busty Barmaids. Though actually last week it was a busty librarian. Very fetching she looked too, glasses, hair up in a bun, pile of books in her hands and a stunning cleavage. Ingrid thinks it is degrading and demeaning to women. They're queuing up to be in it. And some of them are quite disappointed when I tell them they're keeping their tops on.'

I looked at him as I sipped my wine. I could imagine he'd been very good-looking when younger and he was handsome now in a craggy, lived-in sort of way. His shrewd eyes were still a piercing blue and he had a sharpness and vigour about him when he talked that was appealing.

He was looking back, intently. 'Do you disapprove too?'

I shrugged. 'Seems a bit last-century. But if the women are choosing to—'

'Sells newspapers.'

He lifted his glass. 'Nothing much else does – it's all about "digital content" these days and apps for your iPhone.' He shook his head. 'I'm the only regional newspaper that's still got the nerve. The media has been taken over by the fervent young all wanting to make a difference. Give 'em a story about a bishop and an actress and all they're interested in is historical sex abuse in the church and whether the actress is getting the minimum wage.'

I laughed. He shot a look across to where Ingrid was handing out tickets at another table. 'And it's a treat for our Pete. Makes up for all the time photographing fetes and sports days.'

'So how long have you been the editor, then?'

'Too damn long. Before that I was a sports writer on the *Sun*.'

'Ah.'

Whatever his background, his knowledge was staggering. By the time he'd sliced through the questions in current affairs we'd moved into the lead.

'Haven't we done well?' said Emily.

'You haven't,' growled Malcolm.

But she wasn't listening. I saw her flush and look simultaneously delighted and self-conscious. Across the room a rather beautiful young man – all blonde surfer curls and bright eyes – in a very white t-shirt and denim jacket was making his way towards us. His smile was wide and friendly as he reached the table. 'Did you win?'

'Did you get me a story?' asked Malcolm.

The young man shook his head. 'Very dull – no in-fighting.'

'Hmm. In my first newsroom we had a notice. If you don't come back with a story, don't come back.'

Malcolm waved a hand at me. 'This is one of my reporters, Gabriel.' He said it as if the name were a foreign word he was pronouncing carefully. 'And this is Tess. Tess has just moved here from Finchley.'

'Pleased to meet you.' Gabriel stuck out a hand. Emily was still gazing at him with adoration.

'And?' prompted Malcolm.

Gabriel grinned. 'And I do hope you are well?'

Malcolm rolled his eyes. 'Don't try to be clever – it doesn't suit you.'

Gabriel looked unabashed. 'I was going to make a bit of polite small talk first.' He took his jacket off and sat down next to me. 'I gather my editor thinks I should interview you.'

By end of the quiz, when I'd finally covered myself in glory in the food and drink round as the only one who knew what went into a velouté sauce – even Malcolm looked impressed – I'd learned Gabriel was new to Northstone too. His dream of being a top investigative journalist on the *Sunday Times* or *Panorama* was being delayed by the need to get some on-the-ground experience and he'd been told he was lucky to be working for Malcolm, who was old-school, one of a dying breed, who'd been properly trained and knew what was what.

So far it had involved a lot of council meetings – which was where he'd been tonight – and a great deal of turning up at charity events or the bedsides of mothers with the same birth plan as Kate Middleton. But now, finally, Malcolm had given him a feature to do.

'It's about the relationships between the locals and the DFLs' he'd told me. 'You don't have to be named, but it would help me if you were ...'

A woman on the outside of town had had her tyres slashed and was blaming it on the fact that she was Down from London, and her neighbours didn't like her buying up run-down cottages to rent out.

'Find out if it's fact or paranoia!' Malcolm had apparently barked and Gabriel was keen to impress him by doing just that. I didn't see how I could help and said so, but as Gabriel reminded me, with his big smile, of my lovely Ben, and I've always been useless at saying no, I'd agreed to him coming round in the week to question me on my experiences of living in the town to date.

'There is some bad feeling,' he explained apologetically.

'House prices have risen so fast that young people here could never buy anywhere here these days unless they had a fantastic job in London and even rentals ...'

He nodded at Emily, who gave him another adoring smile. 'Emily still lives with her parents because she can't afford anything else and I have a really tiny studio flat here. You can see how the locals could get fed up, with all the decent houses being snapped up by outsiders ...'

As I hurried along the dark High Street, head bent against the sharp wind, clutching the bottle of cherry brandy that Malcolm had thrust at me as my share of the first prize, I thought about Ingrid and her campaign against Jinni's project. But slashing tyres? Surely nobody would get that worked up. I shivered, hoping I'd left enough lights on to make the house feel safe.

As I came round the bend, a crowd of youngsters spilled out of the pub, laughing and jostling. 'You are such a loser, Connor!' one shouted with glee, pushing another boy along the pavement. The first boy, Connor presumably, responded by taking his friend's head in an arm lock and attempting to trip him up. There was more laughter, shouts of encouragement from the group and general shoving before one of them stepped back suddenly, nearly knocking me over.

As I gasped and steadied myself against the wall, another figure appeared amongst them.

'Oi!' said a loud and familiar voice, 'watch what you're doing, can't you!'

'Sorry,' mumbled the boy nearest to me, as I turned in surprise to the owner of the stentorian tones.

'Where've you come from?'

'The station,' said my daughter. 'Where do you think?'

'Danni is being a total nightmare!' Tilly spooned chocolate powder into hot milk and balanced a biscuit between her teeth. 'I couldn't stand her anymore.' She stirred the contents of her mug vigorously, put the half-bitten digestive down and opened the fridge. 'You haven't got much in here, have you?' She sighed at the largely empty shelves and picked up a packet of cheese. 'Not that I can eat anyway! I've got to lose half a stone before the next audition comes up.'

'You're fine,' I said, as I always did, smiling at my beautiful, sturdy daughter, who was always going to lose half a stone but never quite did.

'Do you know some catwalk models live on balls of tissue paper soaked in orange juice before a big show?' Tilly got a knife out of the drawer and began slicing through cheddar.

'Well, make sure you don't,' I said. 'Didn't you have to work this evening?'

'I did lunchtime and I'm not on till six on Sunday so I thought I'd stay here tonight and tomorrow. That's okay, isn't it?' She began to spread butter on crackers.

'Of course, darling. This is your home too.'

Tilly nodded. 'I've brought some washing ...'

I smiled indulgently, just glad to have her there. 'Get it, then.'

I walked through to the cramped little utility room at the end of the kitchen. 'This economy cycle is quite quick. If you–'

I stopped as the doorbell rang. I raised my eyebrows at Tilly, feeling a frisson of alarm at someone calling so late.

Tilly shrugged, unconcerned. 'I'll go.'

I followed her through to the sitting room as she swung back the front door, letting in a gale of cold air.

Jinni's eyes were wide and angry. 'Did you see anything?' she demanded, her gaze swinging from Tilly to me. We shook our heads stupidly as Jinni stepped inside and gestured back at the darkness behind her.

'It's all I bloody need, right now,' she said furiously. 'Some bastard's just smashed my window.'

Chapter 4

'Some bastard's also eaten all the Marmite.' Tilly waved the offending jar under my nose to indicate its cleanly scraped innards. 'That's Ben – he always puts it back when it's empty. He's done it to the jam too.' She gave me a stern look. 'That's what you should be investigating, Miss Marple. How he still gets away with it.'

'I think we'll need more coffee as well, after last night.'

Jinni had stayed through at least three pots' worth – liberally laced with the cherry brandy which I'd offered her for the shock! – and it was nearly two when Tilly and I had finally stumbled upstairs. I was still sitting up in bed in my dressing gown, yawning.

Tilly flopped down next to me. 'Is someone really out to get her? I still think it was those losers outside the pub – getting lairy on the way home.' My daughter rolled her eyes. 'You know what boys like Ben are like – can't take their drink and get all pathetic.'

I frowned at her. 'Your brother would never break windows.'

'No *Ben* wouldn't,' said Tilly with laboured patience.

'Because he's a lazy twat, for a start, but boys like him – *of that age* ...

She shook her head with the superiority of one four years their senior and wriggled her legs under the duvet. 'We need bread too. There was only one slice left.'

'You could see if Jinni needs anything as she'll be waiting in for the glass people.' I said as Tilly stretched out. 'I can't believe someone like Ingrid would do anything like that. But there has been trouble between locals and those moving in.'

I lifted my empty tea mug as if it might have magically refilled itself. 'Put the kettle on, darling,' I said hopefully, as Tilly settled herself more deeply into my pillows. I watched her eyes droop. 'Okay, I'll do it then.'

As I stood in the kitchen, curling my toes on the cold tiles, I hoped Tilly was right. Jinni's theories had grown increasingly wild with each brandy she'd chased down, and had concluded eventually that Ingrid or 'that wanky son' had been behind the smashed windowpane. She had regaled us with a number of run-ins she'd had with both of them and admitted she had herself put in an objection when his friend had wanted to build an extension David had designed behind her, so I supposed it was feasible they were annoyed with her ...

The young men up the road, on the other hand, had seemed full of good-natured high spirits, more likely bent on getting a kebab than embarking on vandalism.

But surely, Ingrid and this wealthy architect son of hers were too well-educated, too ... I searched for the right word as the water reached boiling point. By the time I'd carried two mugs back upstairs, my daughter was asleep.

'Civilised,' I said, two days later to Gabriel, who jotted it in his notebook. 'Would you like another biscuit?'

He gave me a flash of his beautiful white teeth, 'I'm good thanks.'

'So where do you come from originally?' I asked. 'Are you American? I can hear a slight accent. Does your mother miss you?'

Gabriel smiled. 'My father's a New Yorker. He met my mother here and she moved to the States. But we came back ten years ago. I left home ages ago – I did some travelling after uni.'

'You should still call her,' I said. 'Were you the last one to leave?'

'No, I've got two sisters. So, you think Northstone is generally genteel', he continued, trying to get me back on track. 'But what do you think about these outbreaks of violence?'

Gabriel sat back in one of my saggy armchairs and stretched out his jeaned legs. He was wearing another sparkling-white t-shirt and had obviously been brought up to iron. Ben's clothes all had that faded-out, crumpled air. Even Gabriel's boots were gleaming ...

I frowned. 'Well, it's not really violence is it? I mean a smashed window – could have been kids.'

Gabriel raised his eyebrows. 'What do you think of Jinni's theory that it's part of an orchestrated campaign to drive her out of town?'

'Well, I don't really think ... I mean it's easy to be paranoid, would anyone really ...'

'Has anyone been unpleasant to you, at all?'

'No, I said, shaking off an image of Ingrid's chilly smile. 'I don't really know anybody ...'

Gabriel shone a smile on me. 'You do now. Did you enjoy the quiz?'

'I was hopeless, but it was fun ...'

'Do you think the protesters' concerns are valid ones? Do people like you, moving here from the city and able to afford higher prices, push up the cost of housing?'

'I don't know enough about it to say,' I said guiltily.

'Well, do you feel you're contributing to the local economy? Are you using the local shops, for example?'

'Oh yes.'

'Would you say you have as much right to make your home here as anyone and nobody will frighten YOU off?' Gabriel looked hopeful.

I shook my head and looked what I imagined was motherly. 'I know you need your story,' I said kindly. 'But I just want to get on with life here and be friends with everyone, if I can—'

I cringed as Gabriel jotted this down. I'd sound like Pollyanna's grandmother. 'I use the shops, certainly,' I added, wondering how far a packet of ham and four loo rolls from the corner was going to boost the Northstone finances, 'and I only go to London once or twice a week. So although I'm a DFL, technically, I'm very far from being a weekender. This is my new home.'

As Gabriel's pen moved faster, I had a sudden pang for the house in Finchley. The jumble of coats in the hall. The kitchen with its crowded work surfaces and discarded coffee mugs. The radio playing over the sound of the television in the breakfast room and music coming down the stairs. Always someone there ...

'Which son is this?' Gabriel picked up the photograph of my youngest leaning back on the old sofa, guitar in his hands.

'That's Ben. He's really good.' I laughed self-consciously. 'But then I'm his mother–'

Gabriel nodded. 'He should come down to the Fox next time he's here – they have an open mic night. Tell him there's a Facebook page.'

'Do you play?'

'A bit – nothing special. I like to listen, though. So, what do you think of your neighbour Jinni, then?'

'I admire her. She's a bit barmy but ...' I clapped my hand to my mouth. 'Don't write that down! I mean she's eccentric in a good way – creative ... No, don't say that either ...'

Gabriel put his notebook down. 'No, of course I won't. We're just chatting now. I know she's crazy.' Gabriel laughed. 'I've spent quite a lot of time over there. I can't print most of what she says. Malcolm's always shouting at me to look up the laws of libel. Are you happy to have your photo taken?'

I pulled a face. 'Oh no – I don't think so. And I don't really want my full name ...'

Gabriel nodded. 'Okay, we'll just put Tess, and do you mind very much if I ask your age? Malcolm always wants to include it – you know, Tess, 38, said ...'

I laughed. 'I wish. My eldest is 24 – I didn't get started *that* early! I was 23.'

'Early enough!' Gabriel said. 'I'm 24 this year too. And I can't imagine having children right now ...'

At 24, I had two of them. And was married with a mortgage. I struggled to picture my offspring in the same position. Oliver was the most grown-up – he and Sam were looking for a flat together right now – but Tilly lived hand to mouth and Ben ...

'I'll email you the details,' Gabriel was saying, 'or come down to the office and I'll give you a leaflet. It would be great to see some new guys there ...'

'Sorry?'

'The open mic night. The next one's the Tuesday after Easter. You said Ben would be home then?' Gabriel was still smiling despite it being evident I hadn't been listening. 'Come into the office anyway. Have a coffee. I'm sure Malcolm would be pleased to see you again.' He paused. 'Perhaps you can tell him what a great interview we had. He isn't hugely impressed with my abilities right now,' he added ruefully. 'Told me I was useless this morning.'

'Really? Why?'

Gabriel pulled a face. 'I should have been here earlier. In his day there were proper journalists not – I quote – kids with their useless media studies degrees his dyslexic granny could have earned!' He shrugged. 'I did go to see Jinni on Saturday.'

'She said you were being very helpful about getting the glass fixed,' I said. 'She was ever so grateful.' I smiled and patted his arm.

Gabriel looked embarrassed. 'Oh, it was nothing.'

'It was bloody marvellous!' yelled Jinni, who had bolted over the road as soon as she'd spotted Gabriel coming out of my front door. She threw an arm around his shoulders. 'Your friend Sean has been and the window's all done. And guess who was passing as I said goodbye. I swear she stopped and smirked. Soon scuttled off when I gave her the finger, though.' Jinni wagged one at Gabriel now. 'You should put that in your article – the fact that she walks past my house all hours of the bloody day.' Jinni threw her hair back over her shoulder and snorted.

'I think my editor would say it's a free country and it doesn't prove anything,' said Gabriel apologetically.

'Bollocks,' said Jinni. 'Ingrid is obsessed with me, isn't she, Tess? You said yourself she's always going on about me – putting leaflets through your door.'

'She did put one through, yes,' I said awkwardly, feeling Gabriel's eyes on me.

'See! It's her or some loser she's whipped up into a frenzy!' Jinni was triumphant. 'Or the wanker son. He can't stand me either. And the feeling is mutual, let me tell you.'

She threw her hair even more vigorously over the opposite shoulder and gave a dramatic sweep of her arm. 'Still, what do I care? I've got a new window for nothing and when she sees her name in the paper she'll think twice about doing that again. You know how she likes to think of herself as a leading figure in the community for all her bloody agitating–'

'We won't be able to name her,' Gabriel interrupted. 'That would be defamatory.'

'Be bloody hysterical!' Jinni gave one of her great honks of laughter. 'Anyway, my darling boy,' she boomed, flinging an arm around his shoulders once more. 'I can't WAIT to see what you HAVE written ...'

The clock showed 4.07 a.m. when I decided I really *could*. I woke from a disturbing dream that involved Ingrid and a stunted, maniacally-faced son, who were both living in a tent in my garden. Gabriel and Jinni had sauntered in, arm in arm, and told me Tilly had been arrested for libel and had given the police my address ...

As I hastily pushed on the bedside light, anxiety gripped at my solar plexus. My mother had phoned at 1 a.m. convinced there was something wrong with her Sky box and asking me to talk her through which buttons to press to re-set it. I'd eventually persuaded her that we could deal with this much better by daylight and had fallen back into a fitful sleep dogged by fresh worries about my parent's strange little preoccupations and what they might herald for the future.

Last time it had been the tuner on her kitchen radio she said had packed up, although Mo had reported nothing wrong with it when I'd called back to try to help.

I was reminded of the mother I'd read about on one of the online forums, who had to go into a home when she kept turning the gas hob on and failing to ignite it.

All my usual middle-of-the-night agitations – and a few new ones – pressed in on me, squeezing my chest till it thumped. My mother, work, the unanswered emails, the half-painted walls and running repairs and –

Oh God – what *had* Gabriel written? I remembered my use of the word 'paranoid', my simpering about wanting everyone to be my friend, my protestations about using the shops ...

Jinni – only my second friend here – would be furious I hadn't backed her to the hilt. Everyone else in the town would give me a wide berth because I was clearly so needy and the owner of the corner shop would testify I only ever spent a tenner at a time and he'd seen me driving to Waitrose.

Gabriel might have written that I was complaining about Ingrid too, so then I'd get *my* windows smashed as well. In any event, I'd look like a complete prune and when my children came for Easter they'd be ashamed I'd given birth to them.

I lay listening to the *Shipping Forecast*, regretting the weak moment in which I'd agreed to forward Gabriel a small head-and-shoulders photo Ben had taken last Christmas. And trying to comfort myself with the fact that Tilly said it looked nothing like me, and ignoring that she'd added I looked as if I'd been admitted to Broadmoor. (I was carrying a tray of roast potatoes at the time and there was a hole in the oven glove.) Barely anybody knew me here anyway, I reasoned, and they'd hardly recognise me with that manic expression. (Would they?)

By six I'd come out in a light sweat. The paper wasn't out until tomorrow, so if I emailed Gabriel now he could probably make some minor adjustments. He was a nice boy – he wouldn't want me to worry.

I got out of bed, put on my dressing gown and fetched my laptop and the card Gabriel had left me, made a cup of peppermint tea and headed back beneath the duvet.

With the screen against my knees, I tried to keep my tone

light as I explained I was ever so slightly concerned about being misconstrued. If I could just see what he'd written, I suggested, I was sure I'd be completely put at ease, but if he had by any chance quoted me as mentioning paranoia or I'd sounded anything less than totally loyal to, and outraged by, the treatment of Jinni, then could he please amend accordingly, along perhaps with the fact that I found everyone in Northstone very friendly, rather than I wished everyone would be my friend, and if there were possibly room to mention it, that while I did go to the supermarket for major stockings-up, how totally appreciative and admiring I was of the local independent shops and how I intended to make sure I went to my own newsagent-cum-corner shop several times a week ...

I hope you are well, I finished. *And I will certainly tell Ben about the music night.* As a PS I added: *It was lovely to be interviewed by you and I hope to see you soon,* so he, Gabriel, could show Malcolm, if he wanted to, and he wouldn't feel that, despite my cold feet, he wasn't welcome to visit again.

As I pressed send, I felt as if a weight had lifted and I was simultaneously overcome with fatigue. I closed the lid of the computer, put it on the floor beside me and immediately fell asleep.

The next time I woke, it was half-past eight. In theory, I was supposed to be 'at my desk' by 9 a.m. in case the office needed me. And Paul – who insisted on landline contact with anyone working from home for this very reason – was not above calling at 9.01 just to see if I was.

I stumbled into the en suite and turned on the shower, taking a mouthful of cold tea on my way. It wasn't till an hour later that I was finally checking my mail.

There were two messages from @northstonedistrictnews. The first was an auto reply from Gabriel, informing contacts he was out of the office but if the message were urgent it should be forwarded to newsdesk@northstonedistrictnews or editor@northstonedistrictnews, who would be able to assist in his absence.

It seemed, however, that the message had already made this journey without me.

The second email was from Malcolm Priceman, Editor. And consisted of just two words:

TOO LATE.

Chapter 5

The newspaper offices were halfway down the High Street. I pushed open the door and crossed the floor to where a middle-aged woman sat behind a counter, looking at her screen. She looked up wearily as I came towards her and raised her eyebrows.

'I'm here to see Gabriel,' I said.

Her eyes swept over me, as if deciding. Then she jerked her head towards the stairs to the side of her desk. 'Go on up ...'

At the top I found myself in a large room with various desks and computers and people tapping at keyboards. A woman of about my age looked up and smiled. 'Do you want Malcolm?'

'Er, no Gabriel, please.'

'He's in with Malcolm.' She pointed to the back of the room, where double doors were open to another office beyond. I walked towards it feeling conscious of several pairs of eyes on me and rather wishing I'd ignored Gabriel's message.

He'd emailed at 8.30 a.m. apologising for not replying sooner and saying I had nothing to worry about. If I came into the office at lunchtime he would give me both a copy of the newspaper and the info on the open mic night for Ben.

I'd replied saying I would, then hot-footed it to the newsagent's to see the story right away. It was not too bad. The manic photo was small and the feature quoted Jinni at length and me not too much – and didn't mention anything about anyone being paranoid or otherwise, but focused on how upset and shocked I was that anyone could display such mindless aggression.

I didn't actually remember using this phrase, but it was better than sounding like a lonely hearts advert. The main picture was of Jinni pointing at a broken pane of glass beneath the headline 'Actress Fears Campaign to Drive Her Out', and above a report on how Northstone's top glazier had given his services free to replace the window.

I was Tess, 46 (either Gabriel couldn't do the maths or he was being kind), mother of three and a newcomer to the town and the only quote that sounded slightly cringy was the one about my finding it so handy to have a corner shop on the corner (where else might it be?). The online version was identical, except the photo of me was bigger, with a pop-up ad for greenhouses mostly obscuring it.

I heard Malcolm before I saw him. 'You don't make things up!' he was saying loudly, 'and you don't sneak rubbish about your mates into my newspaper AFTER I've seen it. Get it to the subs, I said. I didn't tell you to write a bloody fairy story first!'

'I didn't know it was ...' Gabriel was protesting.

'It's your job to know. You check the facts. Then you check

'em again, You don't put a load of bullshit in just because your crony in the pub gave it to you.'

I stopped outside the door, unsure what to do. The girl at the desk nearest to me was typing on, apparently unconcerned by the shouting.

Gabriel was saying something about helping Jinni, which seemed to infuriate Malcolm further. 'WE'RE NOT RUNNING A BLOODY CHARITY,' he roared.

His voice then dropped. 'And two tyres and one broken window is hardly "an orchestrated campaign",' he said sarcastically. 'By whom exactly?' I thought you said you wanted to be an investigative journalist. I'm surprised you can find your way out of bed ...'

Gabriel was still valiantly defending himself. 'You said I couldn't name names – I told you Jinni said Ingrid ...'

Malcolm gave a loud, disparaging snort, which seemed to echo around the office. 'Ingrid is a damn nuisance. She's not a complete imbecile.'

I stepped back as he strode through the doors. He saw me and stopped. 'If you're here to see me, I'm going for lunch,' he barked.

'I've come to see Gabriel,' I said. 'To say thank you,' I added, as I saw the crushed expression on the young man's face.

Malcolm looked sceptical. 'I can't imagine what for.'

'A great article,' I said boldly. 'I thought he did it very well.'

'Everyone's an expert today,' said Malcolm. 'Don't keep him talking too long – he's got work to do ...'

He marched on through the outer office. 'I'm going to Rosie's' he bellowed to the room in general.

The girl nearest us rolled her eyes. 'He goes there every day and has done for about twenty years. It would only be worth shouting about if he wasn't going to Rosie's.'

She pushed her keyboard away from her and opened a drawer, pulling out a foil package. 'It's your turn to make coffee, Gabe,' she said, unwrapping sandwiches.

Gabriel, who was still standing in the doorway shell-shocked, looked at me. 'Would you like a coffee, Tess?' he asked politely. 'I've got those things for you.'

He led me to a desk in the corner of the room and offered me the chair. 'Thanks for what you said.' He gave a small smile as he handed me a mug and fetched a second chair to sit next to me on. 'Sorry about the mess.' He pushed a pile of paper aside so I could put my coffee down.

I smiled back. 'No worries. It was a good article.'

Gabriel went slightly pink – looking touchingly pleased and grateful. Then he pulled a face. 'Not according to the big boss. I was only trying to help ...'

It seemed Gabriel had offered this bloke he knew, Sean, who had a replacement windows and conservatories company, a good mention in the paper if he replaced Jinni's broken glass and sorted out another rotten frame or two for her, to cheer her up after what had happened.

But Gabriel had taken Sean's word for it that Sean was the longest-established windows firm in Northstone, and one of Malcolm's friends had phoned him up this morning to complain, that in fact HE owned the oldest glazing company in the area and so Malcolm was furious because this friend was the chairman of the Rotary Club Malcolm belonged to, none too pleased at one of his competitors getting all those column inches.

'He says I should have checked,' Gabriel said ruefully.

'Well, has he?' I asked indignantly. 'He's taking the word of this Rotary Club chap, isn't he?'

Gabriel looked at me in admiration. 'I didn't think of that.'

As I got up to leave, I recognised Emily, the pretty young blonde girl who'd been at the quiz, coming towards us with a carrier bag. She stopped at Gabriel's desk and pulled out a baguette and a diet coke. 'I got you these,' she said, looking even more adoring than she had in the pub.

Gabriel smiled at her. 'That is really kind of you,' he said.

Emily flushed and looked at her nails, clearly not sure whether to stay or leave us. I helped her out.

'I'm off, then,' I said, putting my handbag over my shoulder and picking up the flyer for Ben and a booklet of Things-to-do-in-Northstone, which Gabriel very sweetly thought would help me make friends.

He kissed me on the cheek and I saw Emily look longingly at him. 'Thank you,' he said, with feeling – his slightly lost and emotionally battered look bringing out in me a surge of motherly concern.

It must have been the thought of how I'd feel if it was one of my boys being so unfairly judged because I am not usually given to bursts of assertiveness – not unless really roused – but the sight of Malcolm through the window of Rosie's Bistro opposite, tucking in without a care in the world, filled me with a flush of outrage on poor Gabriel's behalf.

The young man had helped Jinni out and brightened her up again and so what if he'd given a bit of a plug to the chap who'd done the work for free. It was a simple bartering system and what was wrong with that? It was really quite inventive and creative of Gabriel and weren't we, as a society, always complaining that the youth of today weren't sufficiently resourceful or self-motivated? The reporter's heart had been In the Right Place and it was completely unreasonable of Malcolm to shout like that. Where the whole office could hear too!

Malcolm looked up and saw me looking at him through the glass and waved. I might have left it if he'd seemed embarrassed at his earlier bad temper but he appeared quite pleased with himself. Before I knew it, I had pushed open the door and was standing in front of him, trembling with indignation, but preparing to make a calm, carefully thought-out speech about working practices, ethics and man management.

'I think you are bang out of order!' I said.

Malcolm finished the last mouthful of whatever it had been – clearly something with gravy – and put his knife and fork together. Then carefully dabbed at the corners of his mouth with his napkin.

'Excellent,' he said. 'Would you like a pudding?'

'The boy's an idiot,' Malcolm handed me a menu. 'The treacle tart is rather good or are you one of those annoying females who fusses about her food?'

'No, I'm not,' I said primly, wanting to refuse him but suddenly realising I was absolutely starving.

'Or the blackberry and apple crumble,' Malcolm added. 'I'm not supposed to, but I do.' He looked up as the waitress appeared. 'I'll have that. With custard.'

'It's not a case of "one of my friends",' said Malcolm when the waitress had gone again. 'He's one of our biggest advertisers. Whether I like him or not is irrelevant. I don't let friendships affect my newspaper. This other Johnnie-come-lately has apparently only been trading half the time Roger has, and as for being "award-winning", that's absolute balls. Never won a thing. He's a known bodger and Roger says half his business is putting right what this other cowboys got wrong. Of course, he's disgruntled to see him getting free coverage in an article full of inaccuracies.'

'How do you know that's all true, though?' I asked feebly, already knowing the answer.

Malcolm looked scathing.

'Because I Googled Companies House, read reviews online and asked Grace on reception what the general opinion was. She knows everything about everyone.' He leant back and scrutinised me. 'Why do you care?'

'I felt sorry for Gabriel – I'd hate it if someone shouted at one of my kids like that. He was only trying to use his initiative. And it was kind of him to help Jinni.'

'Kind?' Malcolm's tone was pitying. 'He's a journalist – it's not his job to be kind. He was just trying to pad the story out because he didn't really have one.' Malcolm sat up straighter as the waitress reappeared bearing two bowls. 'But he's not as clever as he thinks he is.'

He dipped a spoon into the steaming fruit and custard that

had been placed in front of him, put it his mouth and sighed with satisfaction.

'I'm trying to educate him,' he said when he'd swallowed. 'My trainees do things properly and go on to better things. I'm not going to let some silly American boy be any different.' He plunged his spoon in again.

As I took my first bite of strawberry cheesecake, I remembered what Gabriel had told me about Malcolm being very well thought of in the industry and how his last intern had landed a job on the sports desk of the *Daily Mail*, and decided Malcolm probably took a fatherly interest in Gabriel and was simply trying to teach him the ropes.

'Do you have children?' I asked after a moment's silence during which Malcolm munched.

'No,' he said. 'Don't like them.'

I smiled. 'Are you married?'

'Not anymore.'

'I'm divorced,' I offered, immediately feeling hot with embarrassment in case he thought I was making some sort of offer. 'I wouldn't get married again,' I added hastily, to show I wasn't in search of a husband.

'Neither would I,' he said with feeling. 'They were all mad.'

By the time we were on coffee, I'd learned he'd had two wives and a fiancée – the latter had left him because of his drinking and the fact that he was exceptionally rude to her mother. 'Dreadful woman,' he explained. 'Always "popping in" for something. I was relieved when that one packed her bags.'

'What happened to the other two?'

'One died and one went off with a woman she played

badminton with.' Before I could express sympathy at his bereavement, he leant forward with a sudden wolfish grin. 'I always knew there was something not quite right about her.'

I shook my head, knowing there was little point in protesting. And there was something quite refreshing about someone who didn't care what he said or how politically correct it was. I could see why he and Ingrid clashed.

He startled me by mentioning her name as I was thinking it. 'So what do you really think about this so-called hate campaign?' he asked, suddenly serious again. 'Coincidence or someone really so upset with incomers they'll resort to vandalism?'

'I like to think it's coincidence,' I said. 'There were some boys about that night – could have been them messing around and they broke it by accident.'

'Like you do,' said Malcolm dryly. 'Accidentally throw a stone ...'

'They might have been throwing something at each other,' I said, 'and one of them ducked and whatever it was sailed past the intended victim and straight through the window.'

Malcolm looked amused. 'Sailed past the intended victim, eh? Want a job?'

I laughed, feeling more comfortable with him now. 'You know what I mean. And the slashed tyres, well they were the other side of town, weren't they, and a couple of weeks ago? These things happen.' I shrugged. 'My next-door neighbour in Finchley got paint stripper poured all over his car.'

'And who did it?'

'Word was he owed money to some builders.'

'Never a wise move'

'But Ingrid seems to be the sort to make her feelings known with petitions, not physical damage.' Even as I said it, I had a picture of her steely gaze.

Malcolm nodded his agreement, his eyes still intent on mine.

'Oh! There she is.' I felt startled again as I spotted Ingrid on the pavement outside talking to a tall man.

Malcolm did not turn round. 'She gets everywhere,' he said.

'Thank you,' I said, when Malcolm had paid the bill and we were standing in the street again. 'That was very nice – and unexpected.' He nodded and strode off across the road.

I looked at my watch and followed. My plan to go to the butcher's – I was not only going to use the shops but was considering going the whole Easter hog and ordering a turkey – would have to wait. Ahead of me Malcolm lifted an arm as if to silence someone and I saw Ingrid was now right outside his office. I grinned to myself as Malcolm disappeared through the door and out of view – clearly having no truck with whatever Ingrid had to say – but it was too late to pretend I hadn't seen her.

'Hello, how are you?'

Ingrid appeared to straighten herself. 'Oh Tess –' She indicated the man next to her. 'This is my son, David.'

Ah The Wanky One. Telling myself I must keep an open mind, I stood up straight as well and held out my hand, looking directly at him, in the manner Caroline had instructed me to look at all males in her increasingly frequent collection of lectures with the umbrella title: 'Why you still haven't got a man'.

Even though this one would not be my type at all, being, according to Jinni, self-seeking and hypocritical with no moral scruples, but I was still momentarily shocked by how good-looking he was, with his dark hair and eyes, tall frame and defined features.

'How do you do?' I smiled.

He gave me a cursory glance. 'Pleased to meet you,' he said shortly, looking anything but.

There was a tense pause. I was still extending my hand. I dropped it to my side, embarrassed. Ingrid threw me an odd look, which I couldn't quite fathom and then David grasped her arm and propelled her away from me.

'Just leave it, will you!' I heard him say.

I stood for some moments watching their backs go ahead of me up the street, stunned by his rudeness.

Feeling horribly, almost tear-jerkingly, alone.

Chapter 6

'And you're complaining?' Fran swept a layer of colouring books, pens, iPads and beakers from one end of the table, so I could put my coffee down. 'The only time I ever get to be on my own is in the loo. And then one of them usually bangs on the door!'

She began to sift through sheets of paper. 'Freya brought home a list of all the stuff they need for their wild woodland project and now I can't find it.' She ran an exasperated hand through her short fair hair. 'It was right here.'

'Is the school good?' I asked, pulling some of the lists and envelopes towards me and beginning to flick through them too.

There was an order form for home delivery of paraben-free cleaning products, the guarantee card for a new washing machine, a programme of events put on by the Northstone Primary PTA and a letter home about head lice.

'Brilliant,' said Fran, distractedly. 'Northstone is great for kids. Jonathan was going on about moving nearer to London when he got his promotion but I said, no way.'

'Well, now there's the new train …'

'Precisely! And so what if the drive takes forever anyway, he should try being here. At least he could listen to the radio in peace – oh shit, the twins!'

There was a wail from above and Fran rushed from the room. Her three-year-old, Theo, appeared in the doorway and looked at me solemnly. 'Mummy is knackered,' he said matter-of-factly.

'Tired,' I corrected. I drew him towards me to give him a hug. He was wriggling away, wiping his cheek, as Fran returned with a toddler on each hip. She did look exhausted. I remembered her in her cottage near the High Street when my kids were young and she was working as a buyer for Harvey Nichols. And her expression if a sticky hand reached for any of the bright pots or crystal candle-holders she'd collected on her frequent trips abroad.

Now this stylish family house a couple of miles outside the town was adorned with fingerprints, childcare paraphernalia filled the hall and the tiles beneath the table were littered with crumbs.

'I've got Bella and Silas this weekend too!' she groaned, depositing eleven-month-old Jac on my lap and shifting his sister Georgia to her other side as she filled a red tumbler with water for Theo. He scowled. 'I wanted juice,' he said.

'Too much sugar,' said Fran, briskly. 'You can have some chopped mango and a carrot.' Theo scowled a bit more.

I looked at the three children and thought how gorgeous they were, with their big brown eyes and Fran's blonde curls. Of course she was worn out, with four kids and Jonathan's two teenagers from his first marriage staying every other weekend making six.

'I couldn't bear the thought of leaving those embryos in a deep freeze ...' she'd said when she'd told me she was going to have 'just one more' after Theo. Knowing the years of despair she'd gone through before IVF treatment and baby Freya, all the while having to be the yummy step-mummy to Jonathan's then-small children, I got that. But I was glad I'd done it early and mine were all grown up. So I could have, according to Caroline, the time of my life.

I jiggled Jac, who was grizzling and straining away from me towards his mother, still warm and fretful from his afternoon nap. 'Can you manage Georgia too?' Fran plonked the little girl on my other leg and began to chop vegetables. 'And I want a biscuit,' said Theo darkly.

Fran ignored this and pulled out a kitchen chair. 'Sit.'

Theo clambered on.

'Hands.' The small boy held them up obediently while Fran wiped them. Fastened to a blackboard behind her head was a page pulled from a magazine containing a list of the 'best brain food for the under-fives'. One of the photographs beneath the headline looked suspiciously like a plate of liver. Good luck with that one, I thought silently, as Theo poked suspiciously at his carrot – a bunch of which were also illustrated.

'Have you got a nutri-bullet yet?' Fran asked me. 'So much better for you than juicing because you get the fibre from the flesh and skin too. Slows down the fructose hit. I mix berries with frozen spinach, a pear and cherry tomatoes ...'

As she rattled on about the benefits of a daily avocado, beetroot and papaya paste, I glanced around at the granite work surfaces and the various stainless-steel lumps of gadgetry and thought about my own tired-looking kitchen with its wonky cupboard doors and chipped tiles. It was going to be my first project and I'd spent hours creating beautiful designs while I was waiting to exchange.

But since I'd moved in, my budget for home improvements was dwindling rapidly. I needed to ask Jinni's advice on where I might get a decent trade deal and find a fitter. She'd been over, in high dudgeon, when she'd discovered Ingrid had been on Twitter protesting against Jinni's planning application, keeping up a diatribe against the whole anti-DFL thinking, for which she held Ingrid entirely responsible, while I nodded and gave the dining room its second coat of Morning Gold. Until Jinni eventually drew breath and popped home for a tiny brush – with which she expertly touched in around the light switches – and a bottle of Rioja.

I filled Fran in on this excitement – I couldn't bring myself to talk about my mother – and enquired whether she knew either Jinny or Malcolm or Ingrid, but she didn't. Jonathan had met Malcolm once or twice and she knew Ingrid by sight after seeing her in the paper.

'She led all the fuss when they cut the bus service,' Fran said dismissively. 'And she runs some blog called Fight from Within about how we should all lobby the local MP for change.' She rolled her eyes. 'I'm a bit busy for all that, frankly.'

I looked at my old friend, tidying up the paperwork on the table as she searched for the elusive list, while her children shifted restlessly in my now-aching arms, remembering a time when she cared deeply about many issues. She'd banged the table and waved her wine glass at a bloke in a bar in Fulham, while rowing over international trading agreements, and then emptied the contents in his lap to illustrate her views on the falling pound.

'So you don't care about rising house prices and the DFLs taking over the town and pushing the youth off the property ladder?' I enquired.

Fran looked surprised. 'Not given it much thought,' she said, screwing up an envelope and making a pile of a few more. 'I know it's getting a lot more expensive to live here. Jonathan said house prices near the station have risen twenty-five per cent in the last year, but ...' she shrugged. 'That's happening all over the place. Who can afford London these days?'

'But you haven't seen any bad feeling – you know like that woman in the paper who had her tyres slashed?'

'The people here are great,' said Fran firmly. 'You get a few moaning of course – and that Ingrid likes a demonstration. She was at the school handing out placards when the swimming pool closed – but nobody cares that much.' She got a carton of almond milk out of the fridge and began pouring it into two lidded cups. 'Theo – don't mash it like that.'

The small boy scrunched his hand into a fist. Mango pulp oozed out between his fingers.

'Mainly we talk about our kids. When the twins are a bit older, I'll help more with the PTA–'

'So what have you been up to apart from the children?' I

asked. My opening gambit that I'd been feeling a tad isolated had been met with neither empathy nor any suggestion of a night out. 'Lucky you,' Fran had said dryly. Now she looked at me blankly.

'Do you go to a book group or anything?' I tried. 'I did in the old house,' I continued, recalling the complacent way I sometimes gave it a miss if it was cold out or there was something good on TV. 'I was wondering if there was one here ...'

'Have you Googled?' Fran said vaguely. Then as Georgia gave a piercing scream in my left ear, she held a piece of paper up in triumph. 'Found the damn thing!'

'Well no,' I said. 'I was wondering if we might–'

'Wellingtons, that was it. I knew there was something major I had to buy. You wouldn't believe how quickly her feet grow.' Fran shook her head. 'Small children cost a fortune.'

I thought about the credit card bill I'd opened that morning. 'So do big ones.'

'And I haven't got empty jars, they all go in the recycling. They ought to be taking plastic anyway – suppose they fall over and cut themselves. I'll suggest freezer bags.'

'Perhaps they're going to collect insects,' I offered. 'You can't put grasshoppers or earwigs in a bag. They'll get squashed.'

Fran looked alarmed. 'I was imagining wild flowers ... They're only year one.' She shuddered.

I looked at the clock. 'What time does Freya finish?'

Fran swung round. 'Oh God. Now! And then she's got her modern dance. I've got to go!' She grasped Georgia, who screamed again. Jac burst into noisy tears. 'Theo! Shoes!'

'Shall I fetch her? Or stay here with the others while you go?'

Fran was now darting about the kitchen scooping up children and changing bags, plastic cups and keys, looking wild-eyed.

'We've got tumble-tots while Frey's in her class,' she said breathlessly as she pushed Georgia's arms into a padded jacket and I tried to do the same to Jac, who went rigid and cried even harder.

'Sorry it's been rushed, Tess,' she said, when we were eventually strapping children into car seats. She came round to my side of the car and gave me a brief, hard hug. 'I miss you, I really do – I want to talk to you and catch up.' She looked at her watch and shot back towards the driver's door. 'Oh Christ, Frey's teacher will give me that look again!'

I blew the children a kiss. Theo, banging a shiny green alien figure hard against the rear glass, returned it straight-faced. 'We'll get together soon ...' Fran was calling through the open window, as she reversed out of their drive. 'When we've got more time ...' She stopped the car for a moment, stuck her head out and gave me a crooked smile. 'When *I* have, anyway ...

Chapter 7

I was beginning to need a few more hours myself. I'd been up since six and so far had achieved nothing but a lot of cleaning – there was still a fine layer of dust over the whole house from experimenting with Jinni's electric sander –the posting of a new office interior in Bromley that had only got three likes, and a chat with Meg and Jim next door I couldn't quite follow, about their problems with the water board.

I'd finally settled down to the latest job, when the bell rang. Jinni strode into my front room, a sheet of paper in one hand and her phone in the other.

'That FUCKING woman,' she yelled, by way of greeting. 'I shall wring her scrawny neck.'

I walked through to the kitchen and shut the lid of my laptop. Workstations for twenty in an office block in Cardiff would clearly have to wait. 'Coffee?'

'What's she done now?' I asked as the kettle boiled, pushing the latest missive from Ingrid – urging us to protest on the steps of the town hall about the state of the footpath through the allotments – out of sight before it inflamed Jinni further. Her hair was twisted up on top of her head and fixed with a turquoise scarf that matched her bright boiler suit. She undid it, shook her tresses about a bit, screwed them back up into a knot and retied it all.

'Well HE will have done it, of course – it's just the sort of sneaky, smarmy, underhand thing he would do. Anything to make life difficult for me.' She thrust the piece of paper at me, opened the back door, stepped out and lit a cigarette. A gust of cold air came in. 'Sorry!' she shouted, shutting the door after her and standing the other side of the glass, puffing furiously. 'I didn't know you smoked!' I called back, trying to make sense of the document I was looking at.

'I don't. Only when under duress.' She abruptly dropped the cigarette and ground it out under her foot, before carrying the squashed end back in with her. 'One of the plumbers left them behind. Bin?'

'Under the sink. So someone has put a tree preservation order on your horse chestnut.'

'Exactly! Now I've got to have this bloody "Mr Turner" looking at it. He's bound to be a wanker too and if I can't cut it down it's going to block out half the light in the back bedrooms, fuck up my plans for the garden, not to mention probably crash through the roof in the next big storm and kill me in my bed!!' Jinni glared. 'All because that bitter old bag and her weedy son can't stand to lose out to anyone else.'

'Weedy?' I asked, surprised, a fleeting image of the tall, masculine David popping into my mind. I cringed as I remembered my floppy hand extended into nothingness.

'Tosser, then', said Jinni, dismissively. 'Smug bastard.'

She picked up her phone, tapped at it and presented it to me with a flourish. 'And guess what I found on my doorstep at the same time?'

I looked at the screen. 'Is that what I think it is?'

'A turd!' Jinni confirmed.

I peered at the photo again. A small brown, sausagey-looking object lay on the stone slab. 'Could it be an animal?' I asked cautiously.

'Well, yes, obviously. Fox shit, I think,' said Jinni impatiently. 'Or a very small dog. But look at the position. Dead symmetrical.'

'I really don't think ...'

'I wouldn't put it past these zealots. God knows who Ingrid's wound up on social media. I emailed it to Gabriel – he thought it was suspicious too. He wanted to run something, but that miserable git of an editor–'

I stifled a smile at the thought of Malcolm faced with a picture of a fox poo and a conspiracy theory.

'We had foxes in the garden at my old house,' I said, reasonably, my face as straight as I could manage. 'Sometimes they'd leave mess right in the middle of the path up to the front door. Probably just how it came out.' The ludicrousness of this sentence made me giggle despite my best intentions. Jinni gave me a sharp look.

'Well, I think someone's been sniffing around my garden,' she said. 'I thought I saw someone the other night.'

At this, I felt a frisson of alarm. I had only just started to sleep better, without imagining an axe murderer lurking in every shadow.

'It might have been his tricky mate,' said Jinny. 'He doesn't like me either, since I got the size of his extension knocked back. But, bloody hell, it was bigger than the bloody house – and looked right over my garden ...'

'It might also have been a trick of the light,' I said, grasping the coffee pot and pouring the contents into two mugs.

'Have you got sugar,' asked Jinni. 'Or brandy?'

Visitors are like buses. No sooner had I packed a slightly glazed Jinni off across the road, suggesting that she left the knocking down of the next partition wall till she'd had an afternoon nap, than Gabriel appeared.

'I was just passing,' he said, 'and thought I'd say hi. Am I disturbing you?'

'Not at all.' I shut my laptop lid for the second time and put the kettle on again. 'How's it all going?'

Slowly, was the short answer. Gabriel reported a dull week in which he'd been scratching about for a decent lead story for Malcolm, who'd been more than usually grouchy. The revelation about the strategically placed poo had gone down particularly badly, with Malcolm bellowing that if it was the best Gabriel could come up with, he'd better go for a job in the chippy. Gabriel did not look traumatised about this – he grinned widely as he took off Malcolm's voice with impressive accuracy. 'And you'd probably mess that up too!' he finished loudly. We both laughed.

'A fox had done it,' I said. Gabriel nodded. 'I know. But there is some backlash going on. You know the woman with the holiday cottages who had her tyres slashed?' He looked serious again. 'She's had quite an unpleasant anonymous letter.'

'Oh?'

'Yes, I only found out when we were right up against deadline so I'm holding on to it till next week – in case anything else happens. I haven't even told Malcolm yet.' He lowered his voice. 'So if you can keep it to yourself ...'

'Of course.' I looked into his solemn face and once again suppressed the urge to snort. The whole thing had a bizarre village who-dunnit feel to it, and I couldn't believe Gabriel and Jinni were taking it so seriously.

'What are you doing for Easter?' I asked. 'Going home to see your parents?'

Gabriel shook his head. 'I've only got Good Friday off. He imitated the editor's gruff tones once more. 'News doesn't stop because it's a bank holiday!' Gabriel pulled a face. 'I've got to go to the Easter Fair on Monday – my punishment for the window company thing.'

I smiled. 'Well, my boys will be home for the whole weekend if you want to pop in and have a drink.' I was filled with a warm glow. All my children would be home ...

'I'd like that,' said Gabriel.

He gave me another kiss on the cheek as he left. I wondered if he had any friends to invite round to the tiny studio flat he'd mentioned. I guessed he was homesick and a bit lonely and I reminded him of his mum.

As I waved him off, I saw Ingrid walking slowly past the Rectory.

Jinni was right – she did come along this road a lot.

I hesitated for a moment, wondering whether to scuttle indoors or take the lead and call out hello.

But Ingrid's was staring straight ahead. She didn't look over at me at all.

Chapter 8

Shopping - done
House – cleaned
Downstairs loo - painted
Beds - made
Fridge - full
Washing – up to date (Ben and Tilly were bound to descend
    with bags of their own)
Ironing board – held together with tape. (See above) NB must
    get new one but do not let Ben use.
Turkey – collect Saturday
Work – shit!

I grabbed my office bag, throwing the last of my tea down
the sink. There was a key hidden under a brick in case Tilly
arrived early or Ben had forgotten his again. My train to
London left in twenty-two minutes and it took at least fifteen
to walk to the station. I'd asked for the meeting to be brought
forward so I could leave early. And I was seeing Caroline at
lunchtime. I really couldn't be late.

It was cold for April but by the time I turned the final

corner into the drab road that approached the station, I'd broken into a sweat. I pulled off my scarf and flexed my toes. The heels of my new ankle boots weren't that high but already the balls of my feet hurt.

As I walked through the double doors, I caught sight of my reflection in the booking office window. My face was red and what little style my hair possessed had disappeared in the wind.

Moving past the figures waiting, I started to make my way along the platform.

'Excuse me. Isn't it Tess?'

I turned round to see Ingrid's son David standing behind me. Last time he'd been in casual clothes. Now he was every inch the sophisticated gent, dressed in a clearly expensive suit and tie and carrying a brief case.

He was holding out his hand.

Even as my brain was telling me to ignore it and be as rude to him as he'd been to me, I was aware of my hot palm against his cool one.

He shook my hand firmly and kept holding it.

'I am SO sorry,' he was saying. 'My mother told me I was most terribly rude the last time we met. You were holding out your hand and I didn't even notice. I really do apologise. I'm not usually so discourteous.' He gave a huge and charming smile.

'I'm afraid you happened along at rather a fraught moment. My mother and I were having a slight *contretemps*. Not that that is any excuse for ignoring you.' He smiled again. He looked as though he were in an advert for the cloud of aftershave that drifted around me. All super-smooth shiny dark hair and crinkly eyes. I imagined he knew he looked like that.

I had to look upwards to hold his gaze. I could feel a crick in my neck but I wasn't going to be embarrassed this time.

'That's quite all right,' I said stiffly. 'I shouldn't have interrupted.'

'You weren't to know.' He bestowed another gracious smile on me. He really was very attractive.

No I wasn't, you dick.

'In the usual way, I'd have been delighted to meet you,' he said. 'I *am* delighted to meet you. I hope you will forgive me for the way we got off to a bad start. I promise I'll make it up to you ...' Those sexy eyes were still fixed on mine.

'It's fine really.' He was going over the top now and I felt awkward. I clumsily retrieved my fingers and looked at my watch.

'Are you going up to town too?' he asked, his tone solicitous.

I felt a twinge of alarm. Was he going to sit next to me? I thought wildly of pretending I was only going to the next station, getting off and getting on again at the other end. Except that was the plan that had gone so horribly wrong with Ben's geography teacher, who'd seen me again when she changed carriages herself – presumably to get away from somebody else.

'Yes – I have a meeting. I've got my laptop with me,' I gabbled. 'I have to prepare for it. I'm always so behind on everything. Lucky I've got the journey to catch up ...'

'Oh, I'm the same,' he said. And then he laughed. 'Don't

worry. I loathe being stuck having to make conversation too ...'

I stared at him. He raised an amused eyebrow. I felt myself flush.

'I didn't mean that.' I began, even though it was bloody obvious I had.

'I'm sure you didn't.' He was still grinning. 'It's been very nice to talk to you. I look forward to next time.'

With that he turned and strode away to the far end of the platform. I felt annoyed all over again. That was where I liked to sit too. As he reached the spot where I would have waited, he turned and gave me a wave. Then abruptly turned his back again. But not before I saw the pleased-with-himself smile plastered across his face.

Jinni was right. For all his apologies and hand-grasping, David was one smug bastard.

'Okay,' says Caroline. 'So, aside from Fran, who's knee deep in babygros, we've got the suave poser known as Smug Bastard, the mad actress, the even madder campaigner, a grumpy editor, the owner of the newsagent's and the butcher. And that's the sum total of your social circle in the entire town, is it?'

She crosses her elegant legs, takes a sip of her white wine and looks at me with reproach.

'Oh and a sort of extra surrogate son.' I tell her about Gabriel. And as an afterthought and to bulk the numbers out a bit – the young girl Emily.

'You don't want any more bloody sons, darling,' says Caroline. 'You want lovers. One would do, to start with.'

'I'm not sure I do,' I say nervously.

'You've wrapped yourself up with those kids for so long, you've forgotten.'

Caroline sweeps on. 'Of course I adore them too – you know I do – but you've got to let go now. Shall we try the internet dating again?'

'Don't you dare.'

I have never fully forgiven Caroline for the night in Finchley when she filled in an unsolicited and completely fictitious profile on my behalf while I was cooking the spaghetti, then chatted up likely suitors and agreed, as if she were me, to meet someone called Quentin, who looked amazing but who turned out to be passionate about military aircraft and visiting battlefields and who I couldn't shake off for months.

She tried to make it my fault for getting dinner together so late, saying her judgement was impaired after too much Soave on an empty stomach, and that we should do it properly, but I have told her in no uncertain terms: Never Again.

'I'll come down for the weekend and we'll find him together,' she declares now. 'I've got to see your gorgeous new house, anyway. I've found this sublime cushion shop in Kensington. I'll get you something stunning for a house-warming present when you've told me the colour schemes.'

'There's nothing gorgeous about any of it at the moment. You'll have a fit.'

Caroline's own flat is immaculately tasteful – all fresh gloss, with a throw here, a perfectly placed pot there and designer floorboards.

I look at her now, in her beautifully cut shift dress and

glass beads, highlighted hair smooth against her flawless skin, lipstick the exact shade of wine red to bring out the green of her eyes, and was lost in admiration.

I could wear that exact combination of clothes and make-up and would still look as if I'd thrown it together while running for a bus. If Caroline put on anything in my wardrobe, she'd be straight off the catwalk. But she's funny and kind and generous and hugely supportive – sometimes too much so, a la Quentin. We have nothing in common, really, except I was once married to her brother – but she's become just about my best friend ever.

'Lucky I love you,' I say.

'Love you too, darling. That's why I want you to have a wonderful man.'

'I can't play the games. I've forgotten what to say. It's difficult to get up the confidence when you're my age ...'

Caroline flicks a manicured finger in the air and a stylish young man appears at her elbow. 'Could you please bring my friend another glass of wine – and one for me too – she's delirious and making no sense.'

'I've got to go back to work ...'

Caroline narrows her eyes. 'May I remind you I am a year older than you and have no intention of ever giving up my sex life, however many times I need a fresh start!'

'Ah yes – how are they all?'

Caroline sighs. 'I had to end it with James – he started getting maudlin and talking about leaving his wife – Rick flies in and services

me when he has a long enough stopover and Laurence is

still Laurence.' Caroline gives a small secretive smile, as if she can't decide whether this is a good or a bad thing.

'You are incorrigible,' I tell her as I always do. 'And you look amazing.'

'It's all the endorphins, darling. And lots of botox. You, on the other hand, are naturally gorgeous but not making enough of your assets.' She looks at me critically. 'You have the most wonderful eyes, beautiful skin and great breasts. Really darling – men should be falling at your feet. Come to stay and we'll give you a revamp!'

I shake my head. 'I'm too busy. I'm behind with work, the kids are coming down and my mother hasn't been well. I need to see her more.' I can't face saying anything else.

'Rob okay?' I ask, wanting to change the subject. 'Tilly saw him last week but she hasn't said much.' I have a sudden image of my ex-husband stalking about switching off lights and think fondly of my new home, where I can have two radios on at once without anyone turning purple.

'Still a boring old sod,' says Caroline cheerfully. 'We'll find you someone more exciting next time.'

She presses a lipstick on me as we leave. And a new mascara that will give me an instant false-lash look without clogging.

'Kiss my nephews and niece,' she instructs, 'and keep your eyes peeled for opportunity. You can have fun now – unfettered by offspring! I'll visit soon,' she adds, 'and assess the situation.'

She kisses me on both cheeks and then hugs me. 'In the meantime darling, at least do your roots ...'

Chapter 9

Tilly was at full volume. Standing in the doorway of what had until now been Ben's bedroom, she tried once more to prise her brother out.

'You'll only turn it into a total slob den again and I've got more stuff than you!' She swung around and addressed me. 'Tell him, Mum. If he sleeps in the small room it will be easier to air.'

'Ben's still got stuff in here,' I said mildly. 'Those drawers are full of sweatshirts'

'Well, he can take them all back with him,' Tilly rustled a black bin bag. 'He's already said he's going back on Thursday for this gig thing. I'm staying much longer.'

'Are you?' I asked her in surprise.

'Danni really is mad. Even her mum says she's got to see someone. It's intolerable,' Tilly added dramatically. 'I can't live there.'

'What about your job?'

Tilly waved a hand as if the latter was a minor detail.

'She's only saying that,' Ben looked at me, 'so she can have this room. She'll go back for the hot social life she's always on about.' He lay back and stretched out his limbs. 'Mmmm a lovely double bed ...' Ben grinned. Tilly threw a trainer at his head.

'You can sleep in Oliver and Sam's till they get here.'

'No, he can't,' I said at once. 'That's ready for them. Don't mess it up.'

'How come Golden Boy gets all the special treatment?' said Tilly. 'Flowers, candles ...'

'I was trying to make it nice for Sam,' I told her. 'Since they haven't got a proper bedroom.'

I'd bought a sofa bed and new blinds for the funny old conservatory-type sunroom that led off the dining room, determined there would be room for all my offspring to stay. I even had a blow-up double mattress stowed away in a cupboard in case they brought strays. I had been moved to tears by the tale of one of Ben's friends whose mother and new boyfriend had turned his bedroom into a home gym the moment the poor lad went to university and who now had to camp out with friends during the holidays.

'My children will have a home with me for as long as they need one,' I had declared to Caroline, who had not been as traumatised by this story as I was.

'My friend Liz actually pays her teenagers to go away with their father,' she told me. Just so she can have an empty house. 'The minute they get pads of their own, she'll be changing the locks!'

This had made me cry more – and Ben hadn't even left yet. Caroline had bought me another cocktail and insisted I went to have my eyebrows threaded. 'Your lot will still be hanging around you in their thirties,' she'd said. 'And see? It takes five years off you!'

But how wrong she was. All three of them now had bedrooms elsewhere.

'On future visits, you could take turns to be down there,' I told Ben and Tilly now.

'Don't mind. I really don't care where I sleep,' said Ben.

Tilly pounced. 'Get your arse in that spare room, then!'

'But it's more convenient to stay where I am now ...'

I left them bickering and went downstairs, just happy to have them back. I poured a small glass of red and put two onions on the chopping board. I would make Tilly's favourite pasta tonight and do shepherd's pie tomorrow for Ben. I'd make a vegetarian lasagne for Sam at the same time. Or perhaps we could all have fish? Sam ate a lot of that – it was just meat she didn't like. On the other hand, Oliver wasn't over-keen on seafood – he preferred chicken ...

As I crushed garlic and tore basil leaves, I heard Ben come downstairs. Soon the sound of his guitar floated through from the sitting room. I stood in the doorway watching him leaning back, eyes closed, fingers moving over the strings. 'Want a beer?'

'Yeah, great,'

'Have you given in?'

'I rubbed my feet on the pillows. She doesn't want to sleep there now.'

'Ugh! Ben! How old are you?'

'I'm joking, Mum'

'He's not – he really did. He's such an animal.'

Tilly flounced past me into the kitchen and cut off a piece of Parmesan. 'Can I have some wine, Mum?'

I leaned up and kissed her. 'Of course.' I poured a can of cold lager into a tall glass. 'Give this to Ben and then you can tell me about Danni.'

I kept my face serious as my daughter gave me the full lowdown on her flatmate's bursts of hysteria, but as I sliced and stirred I wanted to beam. I'd forgotten how good this made me feel. Tomorrow Sam and Oliver would make it complete. I could hear Ben singing a James Blunt song in the background, as Tilly wagged her empty glass at me. 'I mean, I did use the last of the hair gel but you'd think I'd stolen money from her handbag the way she carried on.'

'Why don't you buy her some more?' I suggested. 'Make her an Easter basket of nice products and say sorry?'

Tilly got off the stool, refilled both our glasses and picked at the cooked pasta. 'Because she uses my stuff all the time and I don't go mental and I haven't got any money.'

I took a sip of the Valpolicella she'd put in my hand. 'Sometimes it's worth being the first to climb down.' I tried to remember what my balance had been at the cash point earlier. 'I expect I can help you.'

'I'm broke too, Mum,' Ben stuck his head over Tilly's shoulder and gave me a wide grin. 'I need money for Easter baskets and shampoo too or all the guys in my flat will cry as well.'

'Fuck off, Ben,' said Tilly. 'Loser.'

I didn't go to the pub with them. I cleared up and made coffee and lay on the sofa, full of rigatoni and contentment.

Caroline was off to a glittering awards ceremony tonight, one of the many invites she got in her job as PR director for a cosmetics company. She'd be drinking champagne, in a fabulous frock and killer heels, looking a million dollars. She'd despair of me sitting here in my pyjama bottoms, waiting for my grown-up kids to come in and raid the fridge again. Instead of putting my energies into getting a man.

But I couldn't imagine a partner sitting here. It might be nice to share things. But relationships were fraught with complications. Was the sex worth it? I couldn't really remember ...

Caroline, on her regime of organic, botanical, libido-boosting synthetic hormone injections – 'like having a shot of testosterone, darling, without the facial hair' – boasted an insatiable appetite and Jinni had said she kept a list of willing participants because she needed it at least once every couple of months or she got cranky. I hadn't had any for years.

My mother shared a bed with Gerald if they went away but had implied it was for warmth and to save a single supplement, and that even with my father 'that side of things' had dwindled quite early on. What, she had enquired, while vigorously scrubbing an already-pristine milk pan, was wrong with a nice cup of tea and a biscuit?

I suddenly had a bleak feeling in the pit of my stomach.

Suppose this was as good as it was going to get? The kids would come home less and less – Ben would finish university and live permanently elsewhere – there would just be me stuck in small market town, a slightly batty old lady with not many friends ...

'You're 47, not 80!' I heard Caroline's voice as clearly as if she were in the room. I gave myself a shake and took a swallow of coffee.

If it didn't work out I could move back to London. I frowned. It would have to be somewhere bloody small.

These cheering thoughts – I was now visualising a bedsit in a dodgy tower block miles from the tube, having been made redundant because I couldn't think up gripping Facebook posts – were brought to an abrupt halt by my mobile ringing. Fran sounded furious and close to tears.

'I have had ENOUGH. Jonathan isn't supporting me AT ALL. The kids are a nightmare. Bella is so indulged and he lets her speak to me however she likes ...'

I shifted into a more comfortable position with another cushion under my knees and made soothing grunts.

Jonathan had done nothing since coming home except sit and watch TV with his two older children, leaving Fran to deal entirely with the other four AND cook dinner. He had eventually bathed the twins but only because Fran had told him to, and Silas only grunted and Bella was far too used to getting her own way. Fran was phoning because she damn well *was* going to have an evening out with me next week and Jonathan could bloody well get back early and babysit.

'That would be really great,' I said. 'But I'm sorry you're having a hard time.'

'I suppose he feels he has to make the most of his time with Bella and Silas,' I went on cautiously. 'Could Bella help you with the twins?' I added, inspired. 'Teenage girls some-times like looking after little children. You could ask her to–'

Fran let out a long, exasperated sigh. 'Oh she'll jig them about for five minutes, then she gets bored. More interested in getting back on her phone. Oh bloody hell now Freya's calling. Jonathan!' her voice resounded shrilly against my head, making my eardrum vibrate. 'Could you please attend to your OTHER daughter ...'

I winced as I said goodbye. Fran took no prisoners once she'd wound herself up.

I lit the white jasmine candle my neighbour Paula had given me when I left Finchley and lay back again, suddenly relishing my own peace and waiting for the perfume to drift towards me.

There was someone on Radio Four talking about keeping a gratitude diary to promote inner peace and enhance happiness. Each night you had to write down three good things that had happened that day. I ticked them off. I didn't miss the train and nobody near me was eating burgers. I had a nice time with Caroline. Two of my children were home and the room smelled lovely ...

The programme rumbled on. I realised I'd been dozing when I heard them talking outside the door and fumbling with the key. They came in on a waft of beer and a scent I'd not had clinging to the carpets since Ben departed. Tilly was rolling her eyes while looking enviously at the white paper bundle in his arms.

'He's got chips,' she told me unnecessarily, 'AND a kebab!'

Within an hour of being in the house, Oliver was rolling his eyes too. 'You two,' he told his younger siblings, 'regress to

12-year-olds when you're back with Mum. Make him do it,' he told me, as I pulled Ben's jeans out of the machine.

'She runs round you too.' Tilly, sitting at the small table in the now- crowded kitchen, did not look up from her make-up mirror. 'So don't get all bloody superior.'

Ben, standing by the kettle, his mouth bulging with toast, threw open his hands in a gesture of helplessness.

Oliver, leaning his tall frame against the doorway, met my eyes and shook his head. 'Sam and I are going down the town. Do we need anything?'

'You can collect the turkey for me,' I said, reaching for my purse. 'I've got everything else.' I glanced at Ben, who was refilling the toaster. 'Though, possibly another loaf of bread. Or two.'

I watched my eldest son and his girlfriend as they went down the path. Oliver did seem so adult compared to the other two and yet he was only eighteen months older than Tilly. Maybe it was Sam, who always seemed so grounded, who had made him grow up.

I liked Sam. She was calm and smiley, much quieter than my daughter, and far more sensible. I sometimes worried that she couldn't get a word in edgeways with Tilly carrying on, but she didn't seem to mind. She was very girl-next-door with her pale skin and shiny brown hair and though she didn't always say much, had an infectious giggle once she'd relaxed.

Even Tilly, who was usually disparaging about any woman who, as she put it, was 'stupid enough to fancy one of my brothers' was fond of her.

Sam took Oliver's hand as they turned out of the gate and

he leant down and kissed the side of her forehead. I watched, touched, but felt a sudden pang – half longing, half loss – that I couldn't quite explain.

Ben came up behind me as I closed the door and put a hand on my shoulder. 'So, Mumsie,' he said in a comic child's voice, and giving me a squeeze. 'Where are the Easter eggs?'

Chapter 10

I'd eat two, Tilly at least three, Ben six, Oliver five, maybe, Sam probably wouldn't really need any as there was topping on her fish pie, but perhaps she'd have one ...

Twenty well-roasted potato chunks should be enough but somehow didn't look it. Ben, clearly depleted from the endless re-runs of *Top Gear*, and Tilly, in need of sustenance after an exhausting morning using all the hot water, were already 'starving'. And I could never shake off the notion that someone else might turn up. And, indeed, I'd just grabbed two more Maris Pipers and started chopping when the prophetic ringing of the doorbell brought forth another potential spud-muncher.

Gabriel, ushered through to the kitchen by my daughter and proffering a rather manic-looking chocolate rabbit, gave me an apologetic smile. 'You said to pop in and meet Ben but ... but I can see you're busy ...'

'It's fine,' said Tilly decisively. She jerked her head towards the tray of uncooked chipolatas. 'We won't be eating for hours yet.' She sighed and looked at Gabriel curiously. 'What would you want to meet Ben for?'

'Shall we invite him to eat with us?' I asked Tilly, when she reappeared to get beers. 'I feel sorry for him on his own.'

'I'd feel sorry for him being with us lot!' She swung open the fridge door. 'Have you got any crisps?'

I listened to them laughing in the other room as I stirred flour into meat juices a couple of hours later. I could hear Gabriel doing his Malcolm impression, Oliver's deep chuckle, Sam giggling. I heard Jinni's name mentioned and had a twinge of conscience about her too.

I put an extra plate in the bottom of the oven, announced the plan to the assortment of bodies sprawled across sofas and issued instructions.

'Ben – get the vegetables on the table will you? Oliver can you open another bottle of wine, darling. And get another chair out of the conservatory. Tilly, lay another place?'

My daughter began to gather up empties nudging her brother into action with her foot as she did so. 'She might say no.'

'She might say yes and then she won't feel welcome if we're scrabbling about looking for cutlery ...'

'I'll do it!' Gabriel sprang to his feet. 'Show me where it is ...'

I left Tilly solicitously leading Gabriel in the direction of the dining room and ran over the road.

Jinni opened the door wearing a paint-splattered man's striped shirt over a long orange skirt, looking surprised. 'I thought you'd be up to your armpits in kids.'

'I am – and I wondered if you'd like to be too. I've roasted a turkey and thought you might like to join us ...'

'Oh!' Jinni looked simultaneously pleased and disappointed. 'I've just eaten cheese on toast.'

'Come over anyway? Glass of wine and pudding?'

'But I could probably manage a little bit ...' Jinni grinned. 'I need a quick shower. Start without me.'

'I'll leave the door on the latch.'

'This is wonderful,' Gabriel gave me a beaming smile. 'Haven't had turkey since last Thanksgiving and then it wasn't anything like this.'

He waved a hand at the now decimated bird, and the array of half-empty dishes and tureens.

I smiled back, flattered. 'You'd better not say that in front of your mother,' I said, attempting modesty, although I had to admit it had all come out rather well. 'I'm sure hers was wonderful.'

'It was my grandmother who cooked it,' said Gabriel. 'She was over from the States. She said later it was the jetlag, but really it was the gins ... she makes a dry Martini that takes your head off. It's all gin. She brought her own cocktail onions.'

'Ah a Gibson! Good woman!' Jinni appeared in the doorway with a bottle of Rioja in one hand and a port in the other. She put them on the pine chest and headed for the empty chair, gazing at the table with relish.

'Look at those potatoes! Haven't had a roastie for months ...'

For someone who wasn't sure if she was hungry, Jinni tucked in with gusto. 'Marvellous,' she said, spooning cauliflower cheese onto her plate. 'Love this stuff and can never be arsed to make it ...'

'Mum's is the best,' said Tilly. 'Grab some sausages before Ben eats them all.'

'And what's this?' Jinni was peering at the earthenware oven dish next to Sam.

'Fish pie.' Sam held it out, smiling. 'Do have some. I can't possibly eat it all. It is delicious, though,' she said, looking at me. 'It's got all sorts of things in it.'

Jinni ladled a small helping on to the side of her plate and took a forkful. 'Mmm. I love fish pie too. Especially with mussels. You kept that quiet, girlfriend – didn't know you were one mean cook.'

'Oh, not really.' I murmured, suddenly embarrassed by all this praise. 'It's very easy ...'

'Mum says you're doing wonderful things to your place ...' said Oliver, helpfully jumping in. 'It looks huge.'

'Yeah, there's lots to do.' Jinni turned back to me. 'That reminds me. Guess who I saw driving past as I came over the road? Had the fucking cheek to wave!'

'Who?' said Tilly.

'Local wanker.'

'I saw him at the station,' I said. 'He was all friendly.'

'Huh!'

For a moment Jinni looked poised to launch into another Ingrid-fuelled diatribe, but then she picked up her glass and smiled.

'You must come over before you go back.' Jinni took a large swig of wine. 'I'll make you all gins.' She grinned at Gabriel. 'I can give your gran a run for her money ...'

By the time I'd got the chocolate tart on the table, Jinni and Gabriel were almost family.

'I think I might come,' Jinni was saying, as Gabriel was extolling the virtues of the open mic night to Oliver and Ben. 'I like a bit of live music – especially when it's a free-for-all.' She'd opened the bottle of port and was pouring generous measures. 'There's always someone convinced they're the next Susan Boyle, bringing out the neighbourhood cats.'

'It's usually Tilly,' said Ben, as Tilly stuck a finger up at him. He threw back his head and let out a high-pitched falsetto. '*I know him so well ...*'

He nudged me. 'Do you remember, Mum? Longest night of my life.'

'It wasn't that bad, you saddo.' Tilly turned to Jinni. 'It was a charity show when I was at drama school – we had to do songs from the musicals and I was with this ghastly girl who could only sing in one key.'

'But at least she could sing in one ...' said Ben.

Tilly made another rude gesture.

'When I was at Guildford, we had to choose a song at the beginning of term and then that was what we worked on every week for ever,' Jinni told her. 'I ended up with 'Bright Eyes'. I didn't like it, never could sing it and the singing teacher hated me. Put me off for years.'

'Sadly that didn't happen to Tilly ...' Ben got up and waved his empty pint pot at Oliver. 'Want another beer?'

'Hey, we could do a duet on Tuesday,' said Jinni, clearly enthused now by several glasses of red. 'Let's get some words. Got an iPad or something?'

Ben shuddered. 'Noooooo.'

When Oliver and Sam started yawning and announced they were going to bed early, I shooed the others into the front room. They got very little privacy, both sharing with others in small flats, where there always seemed to be extra bodies staying.

'Shall I make coffee?' I said, standing up as the couple disappeared into the adjoining conservatory, closing the blinds behind them.

Tilly began gathering dishes. 'You'd better,' she said. 'Ben's got that simple look on his face.'

She was looking a bit flushed herself. 'Leave the rest,' I said, as she dumped a pile of plates perilously close to the edge of the kitchen work surface. 'Look after our guests ...'

But Jinni and Gabriel appeared completely at home as I handed round mugs and Jinni poured more port into our glasses and returned to perch cross-legged in my largest chair. Ben was sprawled back on the sofa, guitar across his chest. Tess sat on the floor, legs out in front of her. Gabriel jumped up from his seat and took the last mug from me. 'Let me help you with the washing up.'

I smiled at him. 'The dishwasher can do that.'

Jinni grinned round at my own offspring. 'Or isn't that what kids are for?'

'In theory,' I smiled back. I did seem to have fallen back into my role of chief cook and bottle-washer with indecent speed, but they were only here briefly ...

I sat down next to Ben and poked him.

'Come on then – give us a song ...'

Ben sang a selection he knew I liked – from David Gray,

Snow Patrol and Ben Howard – and strummed along as Jinni and Tilly did songs from *Evita* – Jinni had a good voice, strong and clear, and Tilly stayed in tune pretty well behind her. Gabriel shyly demurred from singing – 'I'm not that good, not compared with Ben' – but promised to give us a tune on Tuesday in the pub. He looked at me.

'You're coming, aren't you, Tess?'

'I've got a long day at work, some important meetings.' I felt a twinge of angst as I said it. I had some plans to finish before then. Gabriel made a show of looking disappointed and I thought how polite he was to include me. Ben and Tilly wouldn't give a stuff if I pitched up or not.

I stood up. 'More coffee?'

But Jinni was yawning and Gabriel immediately got to his feet too.

'It's been a really great evening,' he said, kissing my cheek and looking at me with real appreciation in his eyes before turning to Tilly too.

'Such a pleasure,' I said, as she hugged him.

Jinni threw her arms around me. 'Fabulous,' she said. 'My turn soon.'

They walked down the path together. 'They're nice,' said Tilly, as I closed the door. 'Jinni's not that mad after all.'

'Apart from wanting to sing with you,' put in Ben behind us. 'Gabe's a good guy.'

I beamed at them both. 'It felt like we'd known them for years ...'

'I'm going to bed,' Tilly picked up her magazine. She prodded her brother as she went past. 'Don't make any disgusting noises.'

Ben made a face at her. 'Like you don't!'

As I put the chain on across the front door, I looked down at the wall that ran towards the start of the stairs, where the footwear had now multiplied. Oliver's loafers lay next to Ben's trainers, alongside a pair of boots belonging to Tilly, accompanied by some heels, socks, flip-flops and a neatly aligned pair of slippers that were probably Sam's.

Smiling, I remembered the permanent mass of shoes that used to form an unruly mound in the hallway in Finchley.

I recalled Rob coming in one night and tripping over a stray sneaker in the middle of the rug. Pictured him glaring at the heap beneath the hall mirror which had spilled off the shoe rack and spread halfway to the stairs, and the way he had flown into an unexpected rage, turning on me in fury, blaming my slap-dash attitude, poor parenting, lack of disciplinarianism and general hopelessness, for the lack of order in the house.

'They leave them there, because YOU let them,' he had shrieked, and I'd been so startled by his red face and shaking lips I'd choked on a strange bubble of hysterical laughter.

'They're only shoes,' I'd managed to say, while Ben and Tilly scuttled from hall to coat cupboard and Oliver, aged 16, had stood tall and looked Rob in the eye, and said: 'it's not Mum's fault, it's ours'.'

'Sorry', Rob had said grudgingly later. 'Bad day.'

'It doesn't matter,' I'd replied. Because it didn't by then. A decade earlier I'd have been anxious, tearful, mortified by his anger and my failings. Now, I was gloriously unbothered, probably trying to remember what was still in the tumble dryer and whether the cat had been wormed.

This evening, divorced and independent, in my own home, with no one to answer to, I kicked off the battered old mules I used for forays into the garden and added them to the pile.

Then I switched off the rest of the lights and went upstairs in the dark.

There would be no nightmares tonight.

There was a row of footwear down there that wasn't mine.

Chapter 11

I woke abruptly and sat bolt upright, heart banging.
The illuminated numbers on my radio alarm showed
5.32. I remembered my children were all here and everything
was lovely and slumped back against the pillows in relief.

Then I heard it again. Someone was throwing up.

I got out of bed, wrapped my robe around me and followed
the sound of retching to the downstairs loo off the utility
room, expecting to see Ben suffering the consequences of more
beers than I'd realised or the 2 a.m. munchies and a dodgy
take-away.

But it was Oliver standing anxiously in the doorway.
Beyond him I could see Sam kneeling on the tiles, head over
the bowl. Beside her on the floor was a towel and a bottle of
Dettox.

'She's really ill,' said Oliver. 'Both ends,' he mouthed.

'Oh, sweetie.' Sam gave another gut-wrenching retch,
although she clearly had nothing left to bring up.

'She's freezing.' I said, feeling the cold skin on her arms.
'Get something to put round her.

'Sorry,' Sam gasped. And heaved again.

'She said she was hot,' said Oliver behind me. 'She was sweating earlier.'

I felt her clammy forehead. 'There's a cardigan on the chair in my bedroom.'

I wrapped the garment around Sam's heaving shoulders and stroked her hair.

'Get her some water,' I told Oliver as Sam suddenly stiffened and scrambled to her feet. 'I need to go to the loo,' she said urgently, pushing me out. 'Not again ...'

I went back into the kitchen and put the kettle on. Oliver looked worried. 'Have you got anything we can give her?'

'I don't think so. I had a massive clear-out when I moved. There's only pain-killers.' I looked out of the front window. There were lights on in the rectory. 'I'll go and ask Jinni.'

She opened the door immediately, wearing a long towelling dressing gown and looking pale without her usual dramatic eye make-up.

'You're early!' she said. 'Did you get one too?'

'What?'

Jinni picked up a folded piece of paper from the small table in her hall and handed it to me. It was the article from the newspaper – with the large photo of her and the small unfortunate one of me. Someone had drawn a thick circle around her face and written in black marker pen: FUCK OFF BACK WHERE YOU CAME FROM THEN.

'Christ,' I said. 'No, I didn't.'

'I thought I heard something just after I'd gone upstairs last night,' Jinni said. 'Found it on the mat this morning.'

'I'm sorry, but I've come over because–'

'But it could have been there all evening, cos I usually come in round the side. I expect he did it after he'd seen me going over to you ...'

'You don't really think–'

'Him or his mad mother. I'll give them fuck off ...'

I looked at her set face and decided this was not a time to debate it. I told her about Sam.

'Ah!' Jinni looked rueful. 'I had the squits earlier too.'

'Oh my God,' I said, as the suspicion I'd been trying to banish took root. 'It must have been my food. But you had turkey, and Sam had her own pie and the only stuff we all ate was the veg and surely that wouldn't give you food poisoning. I'm okay and so is Oliver, and Tilly and Ben are all quiet. Cauliflower cheese?' I said, worried. 'Can that make you ill?'

Jinni shook her head. 'I wouldn't think so, but ...' she pulled another face. 'I'm sorry to say it, but remember I had some of the fish pie too ...'

'Oh bloody hell.' I clapped a hand to my mouth. 'Suppose I've given you both salmonella or E. coli. Oh Christ, Jinni, I'm so sorry.'

My own gut had gone into an anxious spasm.

Jinni led the way into her kitchen. 'Don't worry about me. I feel fine now. I've got a stomach of iron.'

She looked at me as she filled the kettle. 'But I only had a little bit.'

'Did it taste funny? Sam was probably too polite to say.'

'No, it was fantastic. How bad is she?'

'She seems to have stopped throwing up, but she's still got diarrhoea and looks terrible. Perhaps I should get a doctor.'

'I wouldn't panic just yet. I've got some marvellous stuff somewhere ...'

Jinni was rooting in a cupboard next to the range. 'Was given it in Mexico when I made the mistake of having the double-chilli devil burger and had to go on a bus for three hours.'

She produced a small brown bottle and thrust it at me. 'Do you want tea?'

'I'd better not stay.' I peered at the faded label. 'This is a bit out of date,' I said dubiously. 'Do you think it's okay?'

Jinni snorted. 'Course it is. They put use-by dates on bloody washing-up liquid these days. Get a couple of spoonfuls down her neck and she'll be sorted in no time.'

But Oliver shared my misgivings. 'I think we should get some proper medicine,' he said, when I got back with Jinni's potion. 'We don't know what this is. It might make her worse.'

Sam had progressed to lying on the sofa bed, under a mound of duvet, but was still a horrible shade of grey and looked as though she could be ill again any moment.

'I'll go down to the chemist and speak to the pharmacist,' I told him. Keep giving her water, if she can manage it.'

As I hurried along the road, head down against a biting wind, I ran through my ingredients. The white fish for the pie had been frozen cod – there'd be nothing wrong with that. The same with the prawns. I'd got the seafood cocktail – full of mussels and squid – from a small deli I loved in Soho. Maybe it was that. But the shop was spotless – I'd been using it for years.

And I'd put it in the office fridge, together with the ham

and cheese, as soon as I got back from lunch with Caroline. But then it had been in my hessian bag on the tube and all the way home on the train. Perhaps it had got too warm. Guiltily, I remembered how thrilled I'd been to see Ben already there when I got back. I'd made tea – we'd sat talking. Now I thought about it, I hadn't put the shopping away for ages. It had sat there in the bag, in the warm house, bacteria multiplying away merrily. Oh bloody hell, how long had it been? Sam chucking up for England was all my fault ...

The pharmacy was shut. The notice on the door said it opened at 10 a.m. on a Sunday – would that be the same for Easter Monday? It was only 8.30 a.m. I remembered another smaller, old-fashioned-looking chemist at the far end of the High Street. I wished I'd thought of Google before I left home.

I walked on, past the unlit post office and the shuttered butchers, glancing up at the offices of the *Northstone News*, wondering if Gabriel was in there. He'd said he had to work today. He might know about emergency help.

The small bow-windowed chemist was closed too. I peered in at a display of lavender bath products and body brushes and could see no sign of life. A cardboard dial on the door showed they'd next be open at nine on Tuesday.

Fuck it. Gabriel's mobile number was at home on the card he'd given me but not in my phone. As I hesitated outside the locked offices, a booming voice behind me called out in greeting.

'If you'd turned up earlier, we could have had breakfast,' said Malcolm, looking me up and down. He jerked his head in the direction from which I'd just come. 'The Northstone

Café and Grill. Also known as Stan's Greasy Spoon. Best bacon in town.'

I gave an involuntary shudder, shaking off thoughts of sick bags and gently rotting mussels. Malcolm looked disappointed. 'Most important meal of the day,' he said. 'What are you doing here?'

I explained I was needing help. He snorted. 'I wouldn't ask Useless what time it was, let alone for medical advice.' He laughed loudly while I frowned.

'Don't call him that,' I said. 'He's a lovely boy.'

'If you say so.' Malcolm pointed down the road. 'You'll get what you need in the Mini Mart,' he said. 'They've been open since seven.'

He clapped me on the shoulder as I thanked him. 'Remind me not to come for dinner.'

I smiled. 'I wasn't going to ask you,' I told him.

'That's where you're going wrong,' he said, tapping out numbers on a keypad next to the office door. 'I am excellent company.'

He probably would be an amusing guest, I thought, as I stood at the till in the little general store and paid for the Imodium. If I ever dared cook for anyone again. But I wished he wouldn't be so horrible about Gabriel. I'd be most upset if Ben had a boss like that – it must be very sapping to a young man's confidence. I might point that out next time I ran into the caustic Malcolm. Ask him if he could remember how *he* felt when *he* was starting out.

When I got home, Tilly was in the kitchen, wearing my dressing gown and making toast. 'Ben's still in his pit,' she said. 'Ollie's in the shower and Sam's been sick again. She's gone back to bed. Oh and the loo's not flushing very well.'

Terrific.

'I feel okay,' she added, as she unscrewed the lid of the peanut butter. 'And Ben was trying to get me to cook him sausages, so he hasn't got it either. He's got some bloody hope,' she finished, balancing toast and coffee in one hand and picking up her phone and the newspaper with the other.

'Your phone's ringing,' she called a few minutes later from the sofa. 'Don't recognise the number–'

Go away!

It was Gabriel, thanking me for a lovely time and wondering if there was anything he could do since he'd heard from Malcolm that someone was ill. I resisted asking him to come and stick his arm round my downstairs u-bend – I had poured half a bottle of bleach down there and emptied the cistern several times, but the water level was still higher than it should be, which was all we bloody needed – and told him everything was under control. I was about to tell him about Jinni getting the note when Tilly interrupted.

'Ask him what time he's getting to the open mic tomorrow.'

'Tilly wants to speak to you,' I said, handing the phone over. It wasn't my story anyway. It was up to Jinni. And I had enough to worry about. I could hear my daughter chortling as I went back into the kitchen, where Oliver was now standing by the kettle. 'She's asleep,' he said. 'I think I might try to get some too – we've been up most of the night.'

I gave him a hug. 'Good idea. Do you want some breakfast first?' Oliver blanched. 'I don't think I could.'

Ben had no such reservations. I left him frying and went into the dining room with my laptop. I'd had an email from Paul stressing about the meeting tomorrow, double-checking I was fully prepared as he didn't seem to have the plans for the office layouts in his dropbox and wasn't sure why not.

'For the very simple reason I haven't finished them yet,' I said out loud, on a wave of guilt. Millbury & Miles – retro department stores with traditional values – were our newest client and, as Paul reminded us daily, set to spend a small fortune with RG Quality Office Fittings, for the twenty-odd new outlets they were planning to open in the next two years, as long as we got this one right.

I pulled up the floor plans on my screen. I needed to get them uploaded sharpish before Paul – not one to let a small matter like a Bank Holiday get in the way – progressed to phoning.

I spent the rest of the day slotting desks and swivel chairs into place while still allowing room to swing a cat or open a filing cabinet as Oliver and Sam dozed in the conservatory and Tilly did her nails in front of the TV, keeping up a running criticism of Ben's choices of entertainment.

'You're going to have to get double-glazing,' she said, appearing in the doorway as I popped the last set of drawers into place. 'Can you hear that wind? It's Baltic out there. And half of it is coming in.'

'Stuff a tissue in the keyhole,' I said vaguely. 'Whoops, there's Paul.'

'Just sending to you now,' I sang gaily into my mobile. 'Sorry – been a busy weekend. I've got the kids here and ...'

I waved Tilly away as I chattered on, trying to imply I'd finished the project days ago but simply omitted to upload it, and attempting a soothing tone while Paul told me for the sixteenth time how crucial it was that I was fully on top of every last room-divide eventuality and could talk the clients through positioning of the workstations vis-à-vis staff comfort and optimum efficiency.

'They're arriving at 9.30 a.m. I've asked Ruby to get everyone assembled in the boardroom by nine,' he finished.

'See you, then,' I said cheerily, thinking I'd better get an even earlier train than planned. 'Give my love to Barbara.' I could imagine his wife rolling her eyes in the background as he rehearsed his powerpoint presentation yet again, and she said, as she always did, 'Don't be so boring, Paul.'

Tilly was making gestures at me to hurry up.

'You really need to get an iPhone,' she said, picking up my ancient Nokia, as soon as I'd ended the call. 'We can have a family WhatsApp group, and you'll be able to do Twitter and Facebook. You haven't even got your emails on here.'

'I don't want my emails on there. It's bad enough getting them on my laptop.' I could already feel a small rash developing at the mention of Twitter. 'Keep up the tweets!' Paul had said as he rang off, as if it were that simple. Who wanted to hear about our state-of-the-art beverages points late on a bank holiday? And what could I say about them even if they did?

'Could you look at the Facebook page I'm supposed to be in charge of, if I make supper?' I asked Tilly hopefully.

'What are we eating?'

'Turkey sandwiches?'

My daughter jerked a finger in the direction of the front room. 'You'll be lucky. Bloody Ben stuffed it all at lunchtime.'

I made cheese omelettes and salad and got some French bread out of the freezer. Oliver ate, but Sam, still looking pale and exhausted, said she couldn't face a thing.

'I'm so sorry if it was the fish,' I told her. Sam shook her head looking as if she might throw up on the spot. 'I expect it's just a bug,' she said weakly.

'No, it was the mussels, for sure,' said Tilly authoritatively. 'Mum says Jinni was bad too.'

'I think I'll go and lie down again ...' Sam took the peppermint tea I'd made as a peace offering and retreated.

'We're going to have to stay here another day,' said Oliver. 'I'm going to phone her in sick tomorrow and tell my lot I won't be in either.'

'Stay as long as you like. I'm going early.' I looked at Ben and Tilly. 'There's stuff in the freezer, but you'll need to get more milk.'

'Ben can,' said Tilly, 'We need cereal as well.'

'Sort it out between you,' I said, still feeling awful that I'd poisoned a potential daughter-in-law, but quietly pleased my kids would be around a bit longer.

As I went up to bed to the reassuring sound of the TV and the murmur of my offspring's voices, I looked across at the dark shapes of the trees swaying against the rectory, feeling a pang of guilt at not having paid more attention to the nasty note Jinni had received.

I didn't want to think about stealthy figures creeping through the black night when I was alone again, which would be soon. But Ben and Tilly would be here till at least Thursday.

That was good. Who cared about the electricity bill? Or – as I tripped over a damp mound in the dark bathroom and crashed into the radiator – the wet towels.

Chapter 12

Icame out of a deep dream about Jinni being trapped up a chimney and Malcolm instructing Gabriel to rescue her, while Tilly told me the whole town had toxic shock from my glazed carrots – to find the alarm in full, penetrating beeping mode and the time showing as 5.01 a.m.

As I sighed and stretched, every fibre of my body screaming to stay in my warm bed instead of getting up in the cold, I realised there was something strange about the room. It wasn't dark enough.

An odd light was bouncing off the walls and ceiling. Sitting up, I gazed out of the side window at the end of my bed across to the cottage roof next door and suddenly I was wide awake.

We'd had snow!

I'd heard something vague on the weather forecast but hadn't thought it meant Northstone. I pulled my robe on and went to look properly. The front windows revealed a white driveway, my car was a white mound, the road beyond covered in a white carpet. The coated branches of the trees showed a fall of at least two or three inches.

In bloody April, for God's sake.

I ran downstairs, boosted the heating, checked the loo – which was still making a gurgling noise and taking a long time to drop to the right level – and put on the kettle as I jiggled my cold feet up and down on the kitchen tiles, wondering where my slippers were and gazing out at the whiteness of the back garden.

I made a jasmine tea – glad I didn't like milk because there was none at all now – scribbled a note for Tilly telling her to ask Jinni for the number of a plumber, and hurried back upstairs, throwing myself in the shower while trying to think of what to wear that would be warm and still look half-respectable for the meeting ahead. Nobody stirred in the rest of the house as I pulled on thick coloured tights and put my leather ankle boots in a shoulder bag.

Then I collected up laptop and papers, put on gloves and wrapped a pashmina around me over my thick wool jacket, stuck my feet in my wellies and sent up a short prayer that the bad weather wouldn't mean delays.

There were no lights on at Jinni's as I made my way tentatively down the drive. The snow was even thicker than it had looked now I was picking my way through it. I turned out of the gate and, heaving the bag onto the other shoulder, began to plod down the road in the direction of the station.

It was freezing but rather beautiful – the undisturbed snow stretching away from me for as far as I could see, glittering in the streetlights. A fox appeared from a driveway and stood stock, still staring at me for a moment, then ran across in front of me, leaving a trail of footprints in the soft white powder. I wound my wrap more tightly around my neck, hoping the small coffee kiosk might be open when I reached the station. I was already feeling the need for caffeine. Not to mention, now I came to think about it, toast.

I hadn't left this early since I'd moved. But this was a three-line whip. I needed to be in the office by 8.30 a.m., to grab a coffee or three and get my notes in order. The 6.48 a.m. would get me into St Pancras at 7.36, which left plenty of time to get the tube to Liverpool Street and walk the ten minutes from there to the office and showroom. I should do it by 8.15 a.m. if I shook a leg.

Keeping up a brisk pace wasn't easy. I crunched onwards, stumbling slightly as a drift obscured the line between pavement and gutter and exchanging rueful looks with a newspaper delivery boy, who was heaving at a gate banked by snow on either side.

Eventually, face glowing, I turned the last corner and saw the lights of the station ahead of me against the leaden grey sky. This road had been gritted and the remaining snow was a wet dirty sludge. There were cars parked outside and a taxi came down from the station past me as I trudged up the small slope, relieved to see what appeared to be business as usual.

But as I walked onto the platform and almost collided with a ruddy-faced man in an overcoat, remonstrating with a long-suffering-looking rail employee, it was evident things were not running so smoothly after all.

'This doesn't happen in Canada!' he was saying loudly. 'It

doesn't happen in Germany. Only this country grinds to a halt the moment we get any weather.'

The ticket collector was a picture of studied politeness. 'Yes, I'm sorry about that, sir, unfortunately I do not control the weather myself, or choose when the trains are able to run ...'

A woman in a long red coat standing a few feet away from them met my eyes despairingly. I looked up at the electronic board above her head. It was blank. 'Is the 6.48 going?' I asked her anxiously.

As I spoke, the display flickered and returned. 'London St Pancras CANCELLED'. My heart sank to my wellingtons.

'Oh bloody hell,' I said to the woman. 'I really need to get there.'

The ticket collector turned to us. 'There might be one in an hour.' The woman shrugged and moved off along the platform, where knots of people stood about resignedly.

'Nothing going to London before that?' I wouldn't make the start of the meeting if I had to wait that long

The ticket collector shook his head. 'Doesn't look like it.' He flicked a gaze at the bloke with the briefcase, who was still glowering, 'and absolutely nothing I can do about it either.'

'No, of course not.' I thought of Paul and the new clients and his voice when he heard I wouldn't be there to explain the intricate strategies at work in the placing of the communal photocopier to the right of the recycling point and not opposite the coffee machine. His blood pressure would be off the scale.

'Unless you get the next one to St Alban's and change onto the Charing Cross ...'

I had to stand all the way, but by the time I hurried into the tube at Embankment I had a fighting chance of reaching the office before the clients. I'd sent Paul a text warning him I'd been delayed, but had no response. I imagined him pacing, on his umpteenth coffee, his poor, long-suffering secretary, Ruby, assuring him for the third time, that yes the iced water was in place and the biscuits were nicely arranged near the teacups.

It was raining at Liverpool Street and I dodged a sea of black umbrellas, as, head down, I hurried along the wet pavements.

'He's in a right flap,' Ruby looked me up and down as I ran up the stairs beside the showroom and burst through the doors at 9.22, hair plastered to my head, pulling off my damp jacket and pashmina.

'No trains,' I panted. 'Snow where I am.' I shot past her towards the loo. 'Tell him I'm here now?'

My eye make-up was smudged and my nose was red. I held my head under the hand dryer in an effort to fluff up my locks before applying another generous dollop of lipstick. I now looked manic.

'You are an absolute star,' I told Ruby, who held out a mug of black coffee as I emerged. 'Are they here yet?'

'Just arrived.' She put a sheet of paper in my other hand. 'Paul's latest staff briefing. Usual bollocks.'

I slid into the last chair nearest the door in the meeting room just as Paul was effecting the introductions between clients and 'the team'.

'Sorry,' I mouthed, as his eyes met mine.

He glared.

Presentation over, I spent the afternoon in a slump over the computer desk in the tiny corner I was allocated when in for the day. Nikki was away this week – her mother had broken a hip – so I missed out on our usual gossip. But the clients had smiled as they left and once Paul had done his yogic breathing, he had stopped by to tell me he was pleased.

'They're very keen for you to start work on Croydon,' he said. 'And they've now acquired premises in Dover.'

'Are they working their way through the alphabet?' I enquired. 'It was Basildon last time they were here.'

Paul looked pained. 'Let's not question their methods,' he said. 'Think of the turnover.' He brightened as he paused to consider it.

'And you get off,' he added kindly. 'If the weather is bad your end.'

I gathered up my folder of papers. I'd make the 17.11 if I left for the tube right now.

Jules, one of the sales managers, came thundering down the stairs behind me. 'Hope you get home okay,' she said. 'Baz just called and told me to get moving, there's a load more snow on the way and all the trains beyond Ashford are taking forever. It's been on the news.'

'Hope you do too, then,' I said. Jules and Baz were also living their dream, doing up a cottage near Wye in Kent, with half an acre, dogs, chickens and a wood-burning stove. The pictures looked gorgeous, but a couple of winters ago she'd been snowed in for three days and Paul had been in meltdown. Jules blew me a kiss and ran on past me. 'April!' she called, as she disappeared into the wet street.

April. It had been like this when I was pregnant with Oliver. We'd been staying with my parents in Faversham and the kids next door had built a huge snowman in the street. 'More chance of snow at Easter than Christmas,' my mother had declared, random statistics being her speciality, which Rob and my father, in those pre-internet days, had disputed with her for some time.

You didn't get arguments like you used to, I reflected as I turned, already wet and cold, into Liverpool Street station. When my father was alive, he and my mother would spend many happy hours wrangling over who starred in a particular film, the name of the major river in Cambodia or which news broadcaster was married to the children's author my mother had been to school with.

Encyclopaedias and atlases would come down from the shelf, friends and family consulted and it would still frequently not be settled until a trip to the library had taken place the next day.

Or, on one memorable occasion, my mother had phoned the BBC and worked her way through several layers of personnel until she got a definitive answer.

Would their marriage have lasted so long, I wondered, if there'd been Google?

I had to phone Alice, I reminded myself guiltily as I stood squashed into a corner in the tube, damp bodies pressing in all around me. I'd had another long email demanding a summit meeting on Skype to decide what was To Be Done. I had no excuse now Easter was over.

The tube reached Moorgate and more people piled in. I was glad I no longer had to do this every day. I wanted to be home on my sofa.

I walked into St Pancras and the crowd of commuters looking up at information boards peppered with delays. There appeared to be nothing moving in my direction at all.

Shit.

M&S was a bunfight, the new Italian coffee place heaving. I joined the queue for Pret a Manger that stretched across the concourse, spotting the red-faced man who'd been creating on the station this morning standing a few yards away talking to—

'Tess!' Ingrid's son David bounded towards me, putting his hands on my shoulders and kissing me on both cheeks. As I spluttered in surprise, he grasped my arm. 'There you are!' He shone a huge smile on me and propelled me away from the line of people. 'Let's get that drink.'

As I scrabbled among other people's legs for the bags that had been at my feet, he waved expansively at red-face. 'See you later, Frank!'

'The train could be hours,' he said in a low voice. 'And Christ, he's boring.'

He picked up the carrier with my boots sticking out. 'You came prepared, then? It's not just snow now. There's some sort of security alert – or more likely a body on the track – so we may as well amuse ourselves. Come on!'

Too taken aback to do anything else, I scuttled obediently

after him as he strode off ahead of me through the throngs, swinging my wellies as he wove his way around the bodies and up the escalator. He headed for Searcys Champagne Bar. 'I'm celebrating!' he said over his shoulder. 'Shall we have a bottle?'

Chapter 13

There was a crowd at the bar but David dived into it and emerged holding a stool. 'Here!' he said positioning it in a tiny free spot by the entrance. 'Sit there!'

He went back into the throng and returned with an ice bucket and two glasses. His suit jacket and tie were as crisp and magazine spread-ish, as if he'd just got dressed, his trousers sharply creased. I felt bedraggled and frumpy. My make-up had long disappeared. My hair, never good in the rain, was a frizzed disaster.

He was smiling at me as if I were gorgeous. Frank must be terminally tedious indeed. 'Did you have trouble this morning?' he asked, as he deposited the bucket on a ledge, lifted the white cloth and began to pour.

I told him the story. 'I saw that chap Frank on the station. He wasn't very happy.'

'He's always complaining about something.'

He handed me a glass and chinked his against it, leaning casually against the partition between bar and the rest of the station. 'I was delighted to see you standing there. I was afraid I'd be stuck with him till we got home.'

He sipped his champagne. 'Instead – what a treat.'

I smiled back awkwardly. 'What are we drinking to?'

'I got the new project I really wanted.'

'Well, congratulations. You're an architect, aren't you?'

He nodded, still smiling. He really was very good looking, I thought, as he began to tell me about the development near London City Airport. A Chinese consortium had bought a swathe of land and David's company had got the contract to design the centrepiece office block.

There were only four of them in the business – they had a tiny office in Holborn – but their client list was prestigious.

'My partner, Jason, is Eton and Oxford. All our first clients were called Bunny or Barrington-Babbington-Smythe and wanted us to give the Knightsbridge basement excavation a post-modern twist as a pleasant change from the country pile.' He laughed.

'But this is the most fantastic opportunity,' he went on, voice animated. 'It's the first time I've really been able to bring my own vision to a building. Usually one is so confined by the clients' needs and the existing structure. But an entirely new build – they've seen the artist's impressions and they're going with one of my ideas – I'm very excited.'

He looked it. His face was alight.

I drank some more as he talked about his plans, involving mirrored glass and steel and reflections from the river. 'It won't be quite the size of the Shard but it will be a prominent part of the skyline.'

He'd been working on the proposals for months, he told me, fighting off all kinds of competition and spearheading the project himself – this deal wasn't from one of Jason's establishment cronies. 'Though one did tip us the wink the Chinese were buying, long before it was public knowledge.'

The champagne had perked me up. As David talked on, about vertical villages, the high price of land and the need for every last square metre to be utilised to maximum efficiency and I nodded – familiar with these factors in my own work – I began to feel quite pleased the trains were delayed.

He gave me another huge smile. 'It's so nice to have someone to talk to about it on the way home.'

I laughed self-consciously. 'I don't talk about work very often either,' I said. 'The positioning of hot-drinks stations and how many drawers are required per employee isn't very gripping.'

'I'm interested!' He was looking as if he really was.

'Tell me more,' he continued. 'My mother said you'd moved from here. Fed up with the smoke?'

By the time we'd finished our second glass, I'd given him a potted history of my illustrious career, the move from Finchley in order to buy somewhere bigger than a rabbit hutch, and had progressed, without being prompted in any way, to the achievements of my children.

'And so it will be a great job one day,' I was saying, 'but Oliver's not earning very much while he's still training. And Sam's absolutely lovely but she works in a nursery and doesn't get paid very well either. Still they're getting a little flat together soon. Oliver says it's tiny and it's right out, but they can just about afford the rent and when he's qualified–'

'He'll do really well,' said David, clearly hoping to bring

my monologue to a merciful end. 'My friend Robin – Rob
– is a chartered surveyor. Makes a fortune.'

'My ex-husband is one too,' I gabbled. 'And he's Rob too
– but it's short for Robert, so it's not the same one. I trust!'
I added, wondering wildly if Rob had been making secret
millions I knew nothing about, while subtly changing his
name as a cover ...

David laughed. 'Not a chance. Robin is a great chap, but
he's v short, weighs eighteen stone and has a huge repertoire
of filthy jokes. I can't imagine you married to anyone like
that.'

'I have got a sense of humour,' I said primly, wondering
what sort of man he thought I *would* be married to.

'But I expect you go for the tall, dashingly handsome,
debonair types,' David said, still sounding amused.

Like you?

'And I expect they've been queuing around the block since
you became single again ...'

'Well, er no, not really–'

'Or have you already met someone new?'

I shook my head, feeling a small flustered thrill as he looked
pleased at my reply.

'So what brought you to Northstone?' I enquired, remembering one of Jinni's more scathing comments about the
dodginess of a 40-year-old living in the same town as his
mum.

'Investment opportunity. I'd been wanting to do a barn
conversion and the perfect one came up.'

I nodded. Fair enough. Anyway, mothers and sons being

close wasn't always such a bad thing. I thought fondly of my own boys and wondered if Tilly would really stay on a few more days. Although, from the way she'd welcomed Gabriel, I guessed I wasn't the main attraction.

'Does your new house need a lot of work?' David asked.

'It does!' I said, picturing the faded kitchen and dubious window frames. 'I'm still trying to decide how to do it.'

He was still looking so fascinated and the champagne was skipping round my veins so merrily that I found myself sharing my dream of a stunning set of 'before and after' photos and going back to my first love. 'I studied interior design and I had a little business sourcing the soft furnishings, mirrors and bits and bobs for private homes with occasional work for a development company setting up the show flats, but once I was on my own I had to earn regular money. I'd like to go back to something more creative—'

'I might consult you myself!' David shone another mega smile on me. 'And there are stacks of newcomers to Northstone, all giving their properties a make-over. I'll introduce you to a few people. Have you got a card? What sort of look do you go for?'

He poured me another glass of champagne. 'You'd better drink the rest – I've got the car the other end.' He pulled his phone from his pocket. 'Let's check what's happening with the trains.'

'I like the contrast of old and new,' I said, as he was tapping away. 'Futuristic lighting against exposed brick, say. Contemporary interiors with beams. Like the warehouses down at the docks, in fact. I love what Jinni is doing to the old rectory,' I added boldly, thinking I'd strike while the iron was agreeable. 'I love that mix of modern comforts while maintaining original features. I added. 'Perfect for a boutique hotel.'

'I agree,' David said. 'Ah – there's one in twenty minutes now.'

Do you?' I asked, astonished. 'I thought you wanted it yourself – to pull down and build flats.'

'I did look at it, yes,' he said, calmly, draining the last drops from his glass. 'I wouldn't have pulled anything down but restored the façade where necessary, as Jinni has done, and divided it into four.'

'Oh. How's that so different from what Jinni is planning, then? Four new flats would have still brought more cars and more people like me moving down from London, and whatever else it is Ingrid is upset about ...'

'Absolutely.' David remained unruffled. 'But as I tell my mother regularly, you can't hold up change! Since the new high-speed rail link, Northstone has become a seriously viable place to live while working in the city – at a fraction of the property prices – as you know! So, of course, yes, that will push up the prices in Northstone and the locals won't be able to buy in the same way as they once could. Sad for them, but that's how it is. Young people in London haven't a hope in hell of getting their own places anymore, so it's all moving outwards.'

I took another mouthful from my own glass as he made a sweeping gesture. 'Look at the sort of places getting trendy now. Peckham and Kensal Rise and Hackney Wick. Who'd have thought it? Gradually more and more places along the train route that were once dead will become golden postcodes. It happened to Whitstable a long time ago. Now it's going on in Margate–'

'Yes, my mother lives there.'

'I looked at a project there when I didn't get the rectory, but I didn't have the time to manage it properly from this distance.'

'Were you upset to lose Jinni's place?'

'It's the way it goes. I wasn't prepared to pay what she did. Good luck to her.'

There was something in his tone now that wasn't entirely convincing.

'I thought you were pretty fed up about it,' I said lightly.

'Who told you that? Jinni?'

'Someone's put a tree-preservation order on a tree she needs cut down. She thinks it was you or Ingrid.'

'Not me. And my mother hasn't mentioned it.'

'I wonder who it was, then.'

David glanced at me and shrugged. 'There's a whole group of tree-huggers in Northstone. You know the little park up by the tennis courts? All those new trees are theirs. They protest like mad if anything's chopped down. I expect one of them got wind of it.'

I looked at his well-chiselled profile. Was he lying through his teeth or was Jinni barking up the wrong tree – ha ha – by suspecting him?

'You know Jinni had a window broken?'

'Yes, I saw it in the paper. You were quoted as the Newbie

of Northstone. Outraged and Horrified.' He sounded amused. 'Nice photo, though.'

'Well, Jinni thought it might be something to do with one of you,' I said, throwing caution out with another mouthful of champagne, 'after all the petitions and complaints.'

David looked disparaging. 'My mother has strong ideals. And can be a pain in the backside. She's not a common criminal.'

'That's what I thought,' I agreed hastily. 'Well, not that she's a pain, of course. I mean, told Jinni I couldn't imagine–'

'And it would be a mistake to assume I always agree with her,' he went on coolly. 'That first day I met you is a case in point. I was dissuading her from taking accusations to the paper that would have made her look absurd.'

'But Ingrid does seem a little obsessed with what Jinni's up to,' I persisted. 'Jinni says she walks past the rectory every day. And I must say,' I added, apologetically, 'I do see her in our road a lot.'

'I expect you do!' David's tone had a note of scorn. 'She lives a quarter of a mile away in a straight line from it and it's her shortest route to the shops!'

'Oh.' Now I felt silly. 'I'm sorry. I just feel a bit concerned for Jinni,' I said awkwardly. 'She lives on her own and she was upset. And since then–'

'Probably kids,' said David. 'There's a few little sods who live on the estate behind the station. They like breaking things. And Jinni's tough, don't you worry.'

'She's had a note pushed through the door too.'

'Well, she does have a habit of upsetting people. She made

a totally unnecessary fuss about an extension on the house behind her–'

'–it was going to block out her light.'

'That, I'm afraid, is sheer fantasy.' David had long stopped smiling. 'I did the plans myself. Mark is a friend of mine. Jinni was being bloody awkward. Did she tell you she also tried to sabotage what I was doing to my barn by getting the tree lot onto ME?' He looked annoyed.

'Er, no, she didn't. It's something I'm still getting used to,' I said, trying to lighten the mood now. 'The way you all know each other. It's a long time since I've lived in a small town. Everyone's very friendly, though, aren't they? In the shops and places,' I finished lamely.

David didn't reply. He jabbed at a couple of buttons on his phone and put it back in his pocket.

'Not that I know many people yet,' I continued brightly, feeling anxious about his change of mood. 'Though I've met Malcolm, the editor of the paper, a few times. He's a character, isn't he? Do you know him?'

'Not really. We exchange the odd word.'

'I'm sorry,' I said in a rush. 'I shouldn't have said anything about what Jinni thinks. It's nothing to do with me and I'm feeling bad now I've spoiled your good spirits, especially as–' I stopped. He'd been friendly, bought me champagne.

David reached out and put his hand on mine for a brief moment. A jolt went through me. 'You haven't at all! I've had a delightful time.'

As we left the bar and headed back towards the platforms, he took the conversation smoothly back to my office-planning skills. Trying to ignore the unfamiliar sensation of walking alongside a man – he was so close we were almost touching – I wittered back, telling him about our latest project for Millbury & Miles and how it was lucky I liked jigsaw puzzles because sometimes that's exactly what it felt like ...

He sat opposite me on the train, leaning forward so our knees were only inches apart. 'So how long have you been divorced?' he said, when we were zipping through the darkening countryside.

'Rob moved out when Oliver was 17. But we agreed I'd stay in the house till they were all grown up. So we've only recently completed all the legal stuff.'

'So you're still friends?'

'I never see him, really. We email sometimes about the kids, but he wouldn't be my first choice to go to the cinema with.'

David laughed. 'Has he met someone else now?'

'Oh yes, he was living with someone very quickly.' I gave a wry smile. 'I think she was waiting in the wings.'

'Sounds like my father,' said David. 'My mother likes to think she kicked him out, but he remarried within days of the divorce coming through, so I think he was the one who really engineered it. She's pretty bitter ...'

'What about you?' I asked lightly. 'Are you in a – er – relationship?'

'No. There was someone on and off, but we split up.'

He talked till we got to Northstone, telling me a funny story about a divorcing couple in Holland Park who wanted the house redesigned into two halves – exactly the same. 'Neither could bear the other one to have so much as an extra cupboard!' David laughed. 'When his kitchen was in danger of being a metre longer than hers, all hell broke loose. We eventually persuaded them to share the sauna and gym in the basement – a friend worked out a rota so they wouldn't bump into each other.'

'How the other half live!' I said, remembering the early years after we separated, when Rob would waltz through the front door whenever he felt like it and was puce with outrage when I eventually changed the locks.

David insisted on giving me a lift. I followed him across the small parking area and down some steps, into a narrow road beyond. Snow still clung to the hedges, but had turned to grey slush on the pavements. He stopped by a low-slung black Porsche. As I sank into one of leather seats, I thought how much Ben would envy me.

Within minutes the snow began again. As David pulled up outside my house, it was falling thickly in big soft flakes. I watched them dissolve as they landed on the wet road. 'Might not settle,' I said.

We looked at each other for a moment. His expression was searching and I gave an embarrassed smirk. Then sneezed.

'Sorry!' I said, fishing for a tissue. 'Thank you so much.'

'It has been a pleasure,' he replied.

I opened the door and started to get out.

'Your boots!' He sprang out too and went round to the back of the car. He held them out and I took them, not sure now whether to shake his hand – which would be slightly difficult with a bag in one of mine and the footwear taking up the other – or kiss him in a friendly fashion.

As I stood there dithering, two things happened. He took the lead by putting a hand on my shoulder, kissing my cheek gently but with definite sensuous intent, just to the side of my mouth, saying something about seeing me soon, and my front door opened.

Ben, Tilly and Jinni came down the path, all three stopping to look comically amazed.

I flushed, feeling oddly caught out, and spoke firmly.

'This is my daughter, Tilly, and my son Ben,' I said, nodding towards Tilly's open mouth. 'This is David,' I told them. 'He kindly gave me a lift back from the station.'

'Hi there!' said David in jolly tones to my children, and 'Hello, Jinni,' more soberly to my neighbour, who replied in clipped tones and continued to stare at me as if I'd pitched up with a serial killer.

David walked back round to the driver's side of the car and addressed me across the roof. 'Bye, Tess, I'll be in touch. Nice to meet you, Tilly and Ben.'

Within seconds he was gone.

'How did that happen?' Jinni was still rooted to the spot, looking aghast.

'I met him at St Pancras,' I said. 'The train was delayed.' I shivered as snowflakes swirled around me in the wind. 'What are you three doing?'

Tilly, my newest scarf wrapped around her neck, rolled her eyes. 'The open mic night – we've told you about a hundred times. You coming?'

'Absolutely not. I'm going to have a bath and something to eat. You enjoy.'

Jinni was looking at me curiously. 'What did you talk about? Did he go on about me?'

I was saved answering by my son interrupting. 'I'm going–'

Tilly nudged Jinni. 'Yeah, come on, Mum can tell you when we get back. Gabe's waiting for us ...'

Jinni hesitated before following. 'I'll catch you later.'

'Have a good time.'

I went gingerly up the still-icy path. I was too knackered to be debriefed. As I put my key in the lock, I wondered if Oliver would feel like clearing the path for me – it would be treacherous when the others came back in the dark – and whether Sam was better. They were supposed to be going back tomorrow. If there were trains ...

All was quiet as I stepped through the door into the front room. Three large empty pizza boxes were heaped up on a side table with beer cans and an orange-juice carton. On the floor in front of the sofa were a couple of wine glasses and some scrunched-up kitchen roll.

'Thanks for clearing up!' I said, as Oliver walked through from the kitchen.

'Sorry,' Oliver shook his head. 'I did tell them, but Tilly said she'd do it later – Gabriel had to go ahead as he's helping and they wanted to catch him up.' He walked past me and picked up the boxes. 'Sam and I had pasta.'

'Is she okay now?' I went into the kitchen to put the kettle on. Dirty plates and pizza crusts were piled on the work surface, together with an almost-empty bottle of Rioja and several unwashed mugs.

I opened the dishwasher.

'Still got a bit of a bad stomach, but yeah.' Oliver crossed to the recycling sack. 'She's in your en suite having a bath at the moment – hope that's okay. Ben was in the shower room and she fancied a bit of a soak–'

'That's fine,' I sang, to stifle my groan. I went to the timer panel and boosted the hot water. I sloshed the rest of the Rioja into a glass and rummaged in the cupboard for my teabags. 'I'll have one after.'

Oliver began to drop cups onto the top rack of the dishwasher. 'She didn't bring a robe and all her stuff's in the wash. Do you think you could–'

'Of course,' I took a gulp of wine. 'I'll sort her some things out.' I walked past him towards the loo.

'It's still not working properly,' he said.

'Did Tilly get the name of someone?'

'I don't know.'

I peered at the water level and sighed. 'I hope it's not blocked.'

Oliver laughed. 'Do you remember when Ben–'

'I don't want to think about it!'

By the time Sam was back on the sofa with Oliver, dressed in a pair of my pyjamas, looking tired but a normal colour at last, I'd had two cups of jasmine tea and a second glass of wine, and was ready to sleep on my feet.

As I ran the bath, chucking what looked like much-depleted ylang ylang bath essence (Tilly had clearly been in here too) into the not-quite-hot-enough water, I hoped Jinni wouldn't really come back with them tonight. I wanted a plumber but I didn't feel like dissecting everything David had said.

Lying back, I stretched out my limbs and thought again about Ingrid's son. His development today from Smug Bastard to chatty drinking companion. His animation talking about his work, his interest in mine, the funny feeling I'd got when he touched me. And his evident dislike of Jinni and hers of him.

Perhaps feelings ran high in a small town and issues became personal in a way that wouldn't happen in the city. Even in suburban Finchley I hadn't known that many people who lived nearby – Paula next door and a few friends I'd made through the kids' schools. There'd been that hoo-hah with the bloke the other side whose dog wouldn't stop barking – Rob had been very un-amused about that one – but when the flats were built up the road we simply moaned for a day or two about the noise of the drilling and then put up with the extra cars taking all the parking. There were no petitions or storming of newspaper offices.

I'd scribbled my mobile number on one of my work cards. As I tried unsuccessfully to turn the hot tap back on with my big toe I hoped he would call. It felt strange and would probably be awkward with Jinni hating his guts – but Caroline would be proud of me.

As I thought again about his lips so close to mine, the jolt I got this time was unmistakable.

I fancied him.

Chapter 14

'Gabriel wanted to see you last night!' My daughter flounced into the kitchen. 'He came back specially.'

I sighed, keeping my eyes fixed on my laptop screen and the current battle to fit twenty-four desks into a space better suited to sixteen, while I waited for the dishwasher to finish.

'I'm sure he had a perfectly good time with you two.' The banging of kitchen-cupboard doors had gone on for some time, accompanied by occasional bursts of raucous laughter and the faint strains of the guitar. I prayed the walls were thick enough to have saved Meg and Jim next door from a rendition.

'And do you think,' I added, teeth pleasantly gritted, 'when you've brought people home, that you could clear up afterwards?'

'Sorry!' Tilly was still in a nightie and oversized sweatshirt. 'Ben made one of his monster sandwiches. You know what he's like.'

I raised my eyebrows. 'It looked like more than one and there were all the mugs left here too.' I jerked my head at the machine gurgling away. 'That's nearly done. You can empty it.'

'Okay. Don't be such a grump.'

'Did you get the name of a plumber?'

'I forgot.'

'For God's sake, Tilly. Go and see Jinni now.'

Tilly sighed too, as if I'd asked her to walk barefoot to Aberdeen.

'Why can't you text her?'

'I'm supposed to be at work!

'I'm not dressed.'

'Well, get bloody dressed, then. With all of us here, we can't have one toilet not functioning. I can't do everything–'

'I'll make coffee.'

'Thank you!'

The doorbell rang as she was pushing down the plunger on the cafetière. 'That'll be Jinni now. She said she wants full details.' Tilly was getting a third cup from the shelf. 'She can't stand that bloke who drove you home. Says you shouldn't trust him an inch.'

'I've got to get this done–'

'Are you seeing him again, then?' Tilly demanded.

I glanced at my phone, thinking about the text I'd got this morning. 'It was a lift not a hot date. Open the door!'

Jinni looked stricken. 'Oh my God, Tess, I'm so sorry. I never thought they would do this to you!'

I looked at her bewildered as she pointed outside. We went onto the front path and looked back at my house. Dark spray paint had been squirted in crazed squiggles all across the peeling white bricks. On the blank expanse between the two downstairs windows, someone had spelled out in wobbly writing: *NO MORE DFLS*. Above the door two caricature eyes had been drawn with staring eyeballs and cartoon eyelashes. I felt sick to my core.

'He is such a fucking bastard!' Jinni's voice rose in fury and distress. 'Going for me is one thing, but you too? What the fuck is he playing at?'

'Who?' Tilly was also looking horror-struck.

I was shaking my head. 'No really–' But there was no stopping her. 'This is all part of his horrible game. Look at the way he kissed you! That was all for my benefit. To show me he'd got you on side.'

'Jinni, no. He was fine with me – really friendly. He's sent me an invite this morning to a gallery opening. He–'

'Believe me!' Jinni said. 'He knows we're friends. That's why he put the note through the door. I bet he couldn't believe his luck when he got the chance to trap you in his car. He went on about the rectory, didn't he, and why it's so terrible what I'm–'

'No, he didn't,' I interrupted her. 'He agreed with me when I said I loved what you were doing and said he didn't always agree with his mother.'

'Hurrumph,' Jinni gave a huge, disparaging snort. 'He thinks he's so clever. That was all an act for you. He's trying to drive me out – waiting to buy it cheap when I give in. So he and his pervy mate can build a housing estate.'

I looked at her uneasily. This really was paranoia. David had nothing to do with this, but my heart was still pounding. Who *would* do it?

'Don't you see?' Jinni's voice rose further. 'It's for me – it's what I see when I look out of my window. Those eyes – they're to say he's watching me ... He knows I've put in another objection ...'

My stomach was a solid ball of anxiety. 'But he's got another huge project on the go and he seemed very excited about that – I don't think he cares about–'

'Oh no?' Jinni looked back at me stonily. 'Come and see this, then.' She swung on her heel and marched off. I followed her over the road, flinching in the cold wind that Jinni, dressed in a t-shirt and a torn pair of men's overalls appeared not to notice. She strode over the gravel, to the right of her front door, and led me around the back of the rectory.

'Look!'

She waved an arm at the wooden lean-to on the back of her kitchen – a somewhat rickety-looking affair, filled with plant pots and bits of wood and an old rusting, barbecue. One window was broken, but what made me gasp was splashed over the remaining panes. Huge quantities of red gloss paint had been thrown all over the walls and glass and up onto the low roof. Sticky, congealed drips hung from the guttering like blood in a gruesome horror film and spread in pools at our feet. The empty can lay discarded on its side in the largest of them.

'Christ,' I said.

Jinni folded her arms. 'Too much of a coincidence?'

I looked at her uncomfortably. 'Do you really think–?

'I really do.' Jinni walked the few yards to her back door and stepped over some broken concrete to open it. 'I suppose I'm going to have to keep this locked from now on.'

I realised I was trembling. 'I just can't imagine him, in the dark and cold, wading through the snow and chucking paint all over the place.' I insisted, picturing David's immaculately creased trousers. 'He said he was tired, he'd been up since 4 a.m.'

Jinni gave a dismissive wave of her hand. 'He wouldn't do it himself, would he? He'd have paid some kids. There are some right little scrotes, who'd smash anything up for a fiver.'

I hesitated, suddenly remembering that David had said something very similar – about the broken window being kids, about the ones who liked breaking things. But surely ...

'And you didn't hear anything?'

'Nope. The window was already broken. I knew nothing until I came down this morning.

She gave a harsh laugh. 'Irony is, I was going to pull it down anyway – all that's going to be patio. It was in a shit state and not worth rebuilding. So I don't give a flying fuck, actually, but what are they going to do next?'

For the first time, she looked afraid, and I was too. It wasn't David – I was certain of that – but who was it?

I sat down opposite her at the big table. 'What about that other woman, who had her tyres slashed? That wouldn't be David.'

Jinni ignored this. 'Gabe's on his way round, though what's the point in that if the old git of an editor won't run anything. I want them named and shamed.'

'We must call the police.'

'What can they do? I told them about the window and nothing happened. If there's no witnesses ...' Jinni shrugged and then exploded. 'Bloody hell – I can do without this. I've got that tree thing going on as well. The council stiff is coming tomorrow! Ah!' She slapped her hand down hard on the wood. 'That's another reason he's done it now – he probably knows when the appointment is and is showing me he does.' She took another swig. 'And I need to get it taken out so I can get the flagstones laid.' She gave another barking laugh. 'In the absence of getting laid myself!'

The doorbell rang and she got up, still talking as she crossed her large hallway. 'I was keeping my eye out for some talent last night in the pub, but it was all a bit thin of the ground.'

I heard her open the front door. 'Except for you, of course, my gorgeous boy. What a dark horse you turned out to be!'

She came back into the room with Gabriel and an older, rather crumpled-looking bloke, with a camera slung round his neck. 'Gabriel was the star of the evening,' she declared to me. 'Refused to sing but played like an angel.'

'I can't sing, that's why.' Gabriel crossed the room and hugged me. 'Tess, I've just seen your house. Are you okay?'

'We'll get it repainted,' said Jinni firmly. 'Did you want to keep it white or–'

'I had wondered about a deep grey–' I still felt sick.

'Classy!' said Jinni approvingly. 'We'll jump in the car and get the gear as soon as they're done here.'

Gabriel turned to Jinni. 'Do you want to show me the damage? Pete's got another job to go to.'

We all trooped back outside, where Pete attempted to position Jinni to the left of the most badly coated window.

'If you can point at the paint and look upset–' he directed.

Jinni shook her head. 'I'm not doing another one of those,' she said briskly. 'Just take the building.'

Pete looked at Gabriel, askance. 'He'll want the human angle,' he said flatly.

'I'm not upset, anyway,' added Jinni. 'I'm bloody furious.'

Gabriel scribbled something in his notebook.

'Well, shake your fist, then,' said Pete.

'Balls,' said Jinni rudely and walked back into the house.

'Would you be prepared to be photographed in front of your house, Tess?' Gabriel asked me hopefully.

'No thank you,' I told him.

I went in after Jinni as Pete began snapping the paint stains with bad grace. Gabriel joined us a few minutes later. He listened patiently as Jinni launched into a long diatribe about Ingrid and David, including her theory that David was deliberately targeting me to gain inside information on her restoration plans so he could sabotage them.

'But he didn't actually ask anything,' I put in. 'I think he was just trying to pass the time till the train came.'

Jinni shook her head at Gabriel. 'She doesn't know him like I do.' She swung round towards me. 'Why else is he asking to see you again?'

'It might be a work thing,' I said evenly, telling myself she'd had a shock and I should make allowances.

Gabriel, generous as always, leapt in. 'I'm sure lots of chaps would want to see Tess for a second time,' he said gallantly.

'I didn't mean it like that.' Jinni gave me a rueful smile. 'Sorry.' She turned back to Gabriel. 'I wouldn't trust him as far as I could spit.'

The house was the quietest it had been for days. I laid sausages in a hot baking tin and broke eggs into a bowl, grateful for the low murmur of Radio Four instead of the constant blare of daytime TV.

Oliver and Sam had gone back to London, and Tilly and Ben had been drafted into an impromptu working party by Jinni. Gabriel too had reappeared early afternoon saying he'd come to help me clean up – apparently with Malcolm's blessing.

We'd blotted out the worst of the graffiti with some new grey paint and I had been round one of the window frames in a deep navy blue, just to see if it would work. It would take a few more sessions, but I could see the end result would be stylish and at least those horrible eyes had been obliterated. I wanted to believe Jinni that they'd been pointed at her not me. She was quite volatile – perhaps David was right and she'd upset other people too ...

I was also trying to convince myself that the water level in the downstairs loo wasn't higher than ever – Aaron, the plumber Jinni had suggested, had been on answerphone when I'd called – while knocking up a toad-in-the-hole for when they all returned. Jinni had last been seen issuing sledge hammers and instructing the workers to smash her outhouse to the ground while imagining it was 'David's fucking face'.

She'd taken it for granted I was going to turn down his invitation, but I wanted to go, despite their silly feud. He'd introduce me to people who wanted interior design and might have work for me himself. Perhaps I should have told Jinni that in no uncertain terms, but I was afraid she'd explode all over again.

I looked at the clock as I whisked up the batter. I needed to call my mother, text Nikki, who sounded at her wits' end trying to sort home help for her own aged parents, and get back to Caroline to say yes I'd love to see her at the weekend. I smiled at the thought of *her* reaction when I told her I'd got a sort of date.

My mother didn't answer – I guessed she was probably glued to *Eggheads*, an evening ritual in which she frequently knew more answers than the contestants – so I left a message, bunged the tin in the oven, poured a glass of red and read the latest missive from my sister while I waited for *The Archers*.

Right now, I thought, as the theme tune started, and – praise the heavens – nobody talked over it, being on my own felt soothing. Was that because I knew they were coming back?

They came back filthy. Tilly, paint-spotted, with brick dust in her hair, disappeared upstairs ahead of Ben to shower, telling me Gabriel had gone home to clean up and Jinni would be over when she'd changed.

'She was hitting it like a mad thing,' Ben told me, leaning in the doorway equally grimy. 'She's bloody strong, Jinni. I wouldn't fancy taking her on!' He grinned. 'She's like that bouncer back at the Badger's Hole.'

'Hardly!' I said, recalling the less-than-salubrious East Finchley pub and the squat, muscle-bound woman on the door, to whom Ben and his friends would never dare offer fake ID after one of them was unceremoniously lifted off his feet and put up against the wall.

I looked him up and down. 'Get your hands off the paint-work and put those jeans in the machine. They look like they could bring something down on their own!'

The air was filled with the scent of shower gel – most of it mine – as we sat down at the table.

Gabriel, in another sparkling white t-shirt beneath an open hoodie, opened the wine he'd brought with him. 'I wanted to get you flowers,' he said, as he came in, 'but there was only the garage open and they looked a bit droopy.'

'It's very kind of you to keep feeding me,' he added formally, as he poured.

'Mum likes it,' said Tilly. She picked up the dish of spinach and handed it to him. 'And she makes masses because of Ben.'

'My sister being such a delicate little eater,' Ben said, nodding at Tilly's heaped plate.

'Demolition leaves you starving,' Jinni was spooning potatoes onto her plate. 'But very good for the biceps.'

'I've got to get toned up again,' said Tilly, flexing hers.

'Again?' Ben echoed with a grin.

Tilly ignored him. 'Is there a gym here?'

'I don't know,' I said.

'There's a sort of fitness centre place off the High Street,' said Jinni, but it's not very big. Most people go into Bridgeford. They've got a big pool there too.'

'I'll check it out tomorrow when Ben's gone.'

'Haven't you got to get back?' I asked my daughter.

She shrugged. 'Can we get one of those swivel things you

stand on? They're only twenty quid and they tone up your waist really quickly if you go on it every day.'

'Aren't work expecting you?'

'Sunday. In theory.'

Before I could ask anything further, she'd turned to Gabriel and was asking about his plans for the weekend. I met Jinni's eyes. She winked.

'He's good,' she mouthed, adding more loudly: 'They were all fantastic. Knocked seven shades out of that shit add-on. I must order a skip.'

I watched my daughter and Gabriel chatting. How would she pay the rent if she didn't go back to the diner? She'd been here nearly a week already; Sunday would make it ten days. She'd told me originally she was just taking the Easter weekend off ...

'Are you okay, Tess?' Gabriel was smiling at me across the table. 'You look worried. Try not to be. I'm sure–'

'Oh no, I mean yes. I'm okay,' I said. 'Just thinking.' I smiled back brightly. I had assured my offspring that whatever over-zealous protester – or bored teenager – had made their feelings clear on our paintwork it would be nothing personal and a one-off and I didn't want to start any conversation that would make anyone else anxious again. Especially me. 'Have some more gravy–'

Gabriel insisted on helping me clear up and was still sitting at the small kitchen table telling me about the trials of working for Malcolm, and the endless rounds of council meetings and fund-raisers, when my two appeared poised for the pub.

'I've just remembered,' said Tilly. 'Granny called this

morning when you were over the road. She sounded a bit strange.'

'How could you tell?' Ben grinned.

'Well, she was talking about you, for a start, about how you should go and play on the cruise ships because the bloke on her boat was out of tune and then she started going on about Mo and she said you were going to visit her, Mum, and she needed to know what time you're arriving so she can get the beds ready.'

I sighed. 'No, she's going to come and stay here.'

Tilly shrugged. 'Well, you'd better call her back, then. She thinks you and Ben are going next weekend.'

'Are you coming?' Gabriel asked me politely, repeating the question to Jinni, who was also putting her boots on.

'Not for me,' Jinni clapped him on the shoulder. 'I'm going home to train a shotgun out of the window and then hit the sack. I want to carry on clearing that rubble in the morning.'

'Don't get yourself arrested,' I said. 'You know what the police said. You call them if you hear anything.' She enveloped me in a hug. 'Thanks for the nosh – it was great.' She gave Ben a friendly punch. 'And you look after yourself.' She grinned at Tilly. 'See you tomorrow, probably.'

'Are you sure you wouldn't like a drink?' Gabriel kissed me on both cheeks as Jinni swung out of the front door and disappeared into the dusk and Tilly jiggled keys impatiently on the doorstep. Ben was already in the street.

'Had enough.' I drained the last drops of my red wine as I waved them off. 'And I need to make some phone calls. But thanks for asking,' I called, noting the palpable relief on my daughter's face. 'Another time ...'

I felt uneasy all over again when they'd gone. The thought of someone out there who could be totally unstable wasn't a nice one. I'd be here on my own again soon.

I sat on the sofa with my laptop and sent a holding message to my sister and read one from Malcolm.

He hoped I had recovered from the upset of what had happened and that the 'idiot boy' had been of some use. Since I would clearly be in need of comfort food and he was starved of intelligent conversation he was suggesting lunch on Friday.

I nodded as I hit reply. Malcolm would have a view on what sort of person might have done this and would agree it couldn't possibly be David.

And he'd make me laugh. Which, right now, felt like a bonus.

Chapter 15

Tilly wasted no time in stripping Ben's bed and emptying the contents of the drawers into two bin bags.

'I'm not carrying all that,' he said, finding them on top of the rucksack he'd already packed to bursting.

'You don't have to,' I told him. 'I'll put them away in the other room.' I frowned at Tilly. 'Take them back upstairs, please. And we'll have a chat when I get back from the station.'

I surveyed Ben's luggage. 'But have you got everything you need?'

Ben swung his guitar case over one shoulder. 'I'm not emigrating.'

'I'm glad to hear it.'

I fixed my smile as we pulled out of the drive. I loved all my children equally – I didn't know why Ben's departure gave me the biggest wrench. Perhaps it was being the youngest or maybe because he'd been the last to go. 'Have you got enough money?' I asked him, determined not to press him for when he'd be back.

He grinned. 'I've never got enough money – but yeah I'm

okay. Kerry has got us another gig in that pub in Streatham. That'll be fifty quid. And all our beer.'

'I must come to see you play together sometime.'

'Yeah. Gabe wants to come too – you could come with him.'

'I'm quite sure Gabriel doesn't want to turn up with your mum.'

'He thinks you're cool.'

I smiled to myself as I turned towards the station. 'Cool,' wasn't a word my own children would ever use about me. Even Oliver, who was the one who most appreciated that I might just have hopes and dreams that extended beyond getting dinner to the table and the washing on, had looked slightly unwell when Jinni had joked about the two of us going out on the pull.

'I expect his mum really misses him,' I said lightly. 'Don't forget if you get stuck ...'

'... You'll always pay my train fare to come home ...'

Ben gave me a brief hug and jumped out of the car, opening the back door and retrieving his bags and guitar before I could even undo my seat belt.

'Thanks, Mum, love yer.'

With a raised hand, he was gone, instrument against his back, headphones already plugged in. I watched the back of his coat disappear through the double doors.

'Well, it's not very nice, is it?' Tilly looked thoroughly wounded. 'You come home after seeing Ben off, looking like someone's died, but when I say I'm staying on, you get all funny about it.'

'I'm trying to be realistic,' I said. 'I love you being here and of course it's your home whenever you want it to be, but you've got a job and a flat. You can't just abandon them.'

'I can get a job here. The Fox are looking for staff.' Tilly's mouth hardened. 'And Danni can find someone else to share the flat.'

'But you're responsible till she does,' I pointed out, looking in despair at the clock and filling the kettle. 'And what about Ella? How's she going to feel if you up sticks and move out – you said she finds Danni difficult too.'

Tilly gave an exaggerated sigh. 'I also said she's never there. She spends literally every night at Jamie's. She'll be moving in with him when the tenancy agreement needs renewing. And I'm not staying after that, either.' Tilly glared at me. 'It's really awful, Mum.'

I picked up two mugs from the draining board and took a deep breath. 'It might all be different when you get back. And anyway the diner are surely expecting you.' I turned to look her in the eyes. 'I don't know how you've managed to have all this time off already. Isn't Easter a busy time?'

Till was unabashed. 'I told them we had food poisoning,' she said. 'They don't want me there with E. coli.'

'Tilly! What did you say that for? Nobody's got E. coli.'

'You said you hoped you hadn't given it to Sam.'

'I didn't mean it literally. You've got to earn money. How are you going to pay the rent? And everything else?'

'It's all under control.'

I put a hand on her arm. 'Is this about Gabriel?'

Tilly gave me a withering look. 'No.'

'Because it's no time on the train ... You can still be friends.'

Tilly scowled. 'It's nothing to do with him. I just can't stand my flatmate.'

'But what about your career?' I asked, inspired. 'What about being on hand for auditions?'

My daughter looked despondent now. 'There aren't any auditions and if there are, I never get them. I'm too tall or too fat or I haven't got the right hair.'

'You are not fat,' I put in automatically, as Tilly swept on.

'I haven't got an agent, so I'll never get anywhere. I spend hours trawling through the jobs on *Spotlight* and I know I haven't got a hope of getting any of them. I may as well give up and work in a pub here.'

'Your chance will come,' I said, as I always did. 'And a pub won't pay much. No tips like you get in the diner.'

'Who cares. If I'm not going to be an actress, I don't need money.'

I looked at my daughter. I knew once she got into one of these negative moods, everything would be shot down. I also knew she'd bounce back, because she always did.

'Why don't you stay for the weekend then?' I said reasonably. 'Caroline's coming on Saturday – she might have some ideas. And then go back on Monday. To sort things out!' I continued, as my daughter's mouth opened. 'You at least need to tell Danni you're not staying on when this tenancy ends, don't you? And you shouldn't mess work about. You might need a reference!'

'Okay,' Tilly said, mollified. 'I'm supposed to be seeing Daddy on Tuesday anyway. I'll go but I'll probably give my notice in because I hate that diner almost as much as I hate living with Danni.'

'Right, well, there's a plan, then,' I agreed, hoping Rob might have a fatherly chat. He was big on work ethic and would be none too impressed with his daughter walking out on a job without another one to go to.

I delivered a beam and my cheeriest tones.

'Could you strip the spare bed too? For your aunt. If I don't do some work, I won't have a job either.'

'Oh!' Tilly put a hand to her mouth as she suddenly remembered. 'Paul called.'

I bet he did.

Chapter 16

'TILLY!!!'

I stomped up the stairs and rapped hard on her bedroom door. I could hear music playing on the other side and then my daughter's voice, still croaky with sleep. 'What?'

Tilly was lying back, half-propped on several pillows. My laptop was open on the duvet, spewing out a stream of manic monologue from Radio One. She appeared to be simultaneously watching something else entirely on her phone, underscored with the sort of tuneless, thumping music I hated. Her eyes remained glued to the small screen. 'What d'you want?'

At the sight of her still comfortably ensconced in bed, I felt my irritation soar. Fearing for my boss's heart rate, I'd worked late into the evening to catch up with the preliminary plans for the Croydon office and got up horribly early this morning, only to find a double-flagged, high-priority email from Paul chucking me an urgent health and safety issue from a previous job to solve double quick too. Cross-eyed from staring at diagrams of dividing screens and fire escapes, I'd almost deleted the next email that pinged into my inbox as junk.

'Why?' I demanded, 'have I got a confirmation from Amazon that a deluxe body-shaping swivel board is being delivered tomorrow?'

'I ordered it earlier,' Tilly was still intent on her phone.

'And did you pay for it?'

'No, you know I didn't, I–'

'Put it on my credit card without asking! That's really out of order, Tilly.'

'I didn't do anything with your card. I used one-click.' My daughter had adopted a bored tone.

'And who pays for that? The fairies? It's the same thing – it's buying something on my account–'

'You said we could. We talked about it the other night.'

'No, we didn't. You said you wanted one. I didn't say anything.'

'I got it for us to share. You said you needed to get fit too.' Tilly finally looked up at me, as if she couldn't fathom what the fuss was about. 'It was only thirty quid.'

'Thirty-four pounds and ninety-nine pence. And I didn't, and even if I did, that's not the point.'

'It was reduced from much more than that.'

I shook my head. 'You're in no position to say "only", however much it was. I'm working my butt off here, while you're lying in bed letting me keep you. I've got all sorts of stuff to get done in the next few days so I can make a site visit next week before Granny comes to stay.'

'I'm not stopping you.'

Tilly had clicked off her phone and thrown it down, as if I were an unwelcome interruption to her packed schedule.

I took a deep breath. 'Well you are, actually, because I'm having to stand here and have this conversation when I'm very busy. What are you doing with my laptop anyway?'

'YOU wanted me to look at your stupid Facebook page, if you remember?'

'And did you do anything to it?'

Tilly sat up. 'What can I do? Obviously, you need to upload some before-and-after photos. Or a video tour. I've told you that. If you'd get a proper phone like I also keep telling you to, you could take a picture of the office space when you go on your *site visit* ...' She intoned the last words as if it were an unlikely concept. 'And then take another one when all your furniture is in there. And put it on Instagram too.'

I pushed down the twist of anxiety that spiralled up whenever I thought about learning how to do all this. I'd contributed nothing but three short posts about new clients since I'd been made an admin. I'd have to enlist Nikki's help when she was back at work – she was much more au fait with social media than I was. Why the hell Paul hadn't asked her instead was beyond me.

In the meantime, I wasn't letting Tilly off. 'I need you to do other things to help. You still haven't stripped the bed for Caroline and the kitchen was a mess again this morning and I've got God-knows-what to do before I meet Malcolm at one. I've got to pick up some shopping and try to get my fringe cut somewhere–'

Tilly pushed back the covers, swung her legs round and stood up. 'I thought you were "*busy*", she said, voice laced with sarcasm. 'What you mean is you're going out to lunch and having your hair done.'

I glared at her, feeling my temper rise further. 'I'm going to buy food for YOU to eat! After I've earned the money to pay for it!'

I stamped back downstairs, more rattled than when I'd gone up there. There was no doubt my productivity dipped badly when the kids were around, while at the same time they generated a whole lot more to do. I needed some quiet stretches of time in which to focus.

I sat back at the computer, fuming that Tilly had managed to wind me up. I should put off lunch with Malcolm, entertaining as he'd be, because I didn't have time, and from a waistline point of view had spent too many hours on my arse in front of this screen and was already eating out later. I'd been pretending to myself I might cancel David, but I knew I wouldn't. Saying no and cancelling things being no more my forte than tough parenting.

While I was dithering, Malcolm sent an email saying 'see you 12.45 p.m.', which made me feel bad – if I was the best he could come up with as a source of intelligent discourse, he was clearly desperate for company – so I plumped for a postprandial coffee instead.

A walk would do me good. We did need food and my hair was rapidly moving beyond shaggy chic to bag lady. I could see Caroline's perfectly waxed eyebrows shooting heavenwards from here.

I tried to phone, but the woman I spoke to, who I recognised as Grace on reception, told me grudgingly that Malcolm was already on a call and didn't offer to take a message. So I bashed out a reply, citing deadlines and over-anxious superiors, suggesting I join him at 1.45 p.m., having allowed him sufficient time to get through pudding. Half an hour later I received a response in his customary effusive style.

'**13.30**.'

Grace displayed no more enthusiasm in person than she'd shown on the phone. I gave her my most charming smile. 'I don't suppose you could recommend a hairdresser, could you?' I asked, indicating my unkempt locks. She appraised them deadpan.

'There's Cut Above the Rest,' she said, with a small sniff. 'Three doors down, when you've finished with his lordship.'

I beamed again. 'Thank you so much, Grace. Malcolm said you were an expert on all things Northstone.'

She remained impassive. 'Wonder what he's after.'

I entered Rosie's at precisely 1.30 p.m. to find Malcolm sitting at a bare table. He looked me up and down shrewdly, indicated the blackboard of specials, featuring damson crumble, and then held out a menu. 'I waited,' he said proudly. 'I thought you'd want one once you got here.'

I smiled at him with sudden affection. He was right. Once again I was suddenly ravenous. While he had the crumble with cream, I ordered a slice of banoffee pie.

'Delicious,' I told him. 'Thank you.'

Malcolm looked mournful. 'That twit of a boy was telling me what a fine toad-in-the-hole you serve up.'

I pulled a stern face. 'If you mean Gabriel, he seems far

from a twit to me. My son tells me he's an accomplished musician too.'

'I doubt that.'

I ignored this. 'I'll invite you next time.'

Malcolm immediately brightened. 'I like traditional English fare. Did you know the most popular dish in the UK is now chicken tikka masala – whatever that is. One of my girls brought in Thai – I didn't like that either.'

I laughed. 'What did you have today?'

'Lamb cutlets.'

'Not fish as it's Friday?'

'I'll have that tonight.'

I looked at him as he launched into a speech extolling the various virtues of lard versus oil when deep-frying chips, and giving me the inside info on which fish shops to patronise and avoid. He was incorrigible but I couldn't help being amused. 'Tony's was the best one by far, but he let us all down and retired. Wanted to spend time with his grandchildren!' Malcolm shook his head in disbelief.

'What do you think about the vandalism?' I asked, when we'd got our coffee.

Malcolm looked thoughtful. 'Difficult to know if someone really cares that much or simply wants to appear to care,' he said.

I frowned. 'Do you mean Ingrid?'

'I told you before, Ingrid isn't that stupid.'

'It's the third time something's happened to Jinni and she says the graffiti on my house was directed at her too. I insisted we phoned the police.'

'They probably think she's done it herself.'

'That's ridiculous. Why on earth would she?'

Malcolm shrugged. 'People do strange things. One woman brought a different death threat into the office every week. Floods of tears, the lot. My mate on the job told me it turned out she'd written all of them.'

'How weird. But this is nothing like that. Jinni's furious. And she's got this obsession about it being something to do with Ingrid's son David. I mean it clearly isn't. I was talking to him about it and he's really not–'

Malcolm looked at me keenly. 'Like him, do you?'

Embarrassed, I felt myself flush slightly. 'I don't really know him.'

Malcolm said nothing, just raised his brows.

'He gave me a lift back from the station when we had the snow and we had a bit of a chat but–'

Something about the way Malcolm was watching me made me feel compelled to confess all.

'–and now he's invited me to a gallery opening and dinner.'

Malcolm gave a wolfish grin. 'I know.'

It seemed Gabriel had dropped this nugget of information when reporting back on the goings-on. The young man was concerned for my wellbeing, Malcolm told me wryly, having learned from Jinni that David was Bad News.

'And do you think he is?' I asked him.

'Don't know enough about him,' said Malcolm seriously. 'I met him at some do or other when he first moved here and he seemed civilised enough. Bought an old barn outside town and converted it. Energy-saving, environmentally friendly – all that kind of thing,' Malcolm's expression suggested this wasn't something to particularly recommend it.

'I've heard rumours about sharp practice,' he went on, looking at me intently. 'Don't know whether you feel that affects his potential as boyfriend material – but then again, you women like a bad boy, don't you–' While I was spluttering my protest he went smoothly on.

'He fell out with the tree-lovers because he chopped down a bay tree that was going to undermine his swimming pool, and then got back in with them again by donating two dozen saplings to their Help a Bee, Plant a Tree campaign. I thought bees were more interested in flowers, but what do I know?'

'You seem to know an awful lot!' I said, remembering David had claimed it was Jinni who had set the tree people on him. Perhaps he *had* retaliated by slapping a preservation order back on her ...

Malcolm added more sugar to his coffee. 'It's my job to be informed. Just as well I am for all the use some of my reporters are – I send them out to get me stories and I learn more from Grace than any of them. And she doesn't leave reception all day!' He stirred. 'Where's he taking you?'

'I don't know.'

As I said it, I suddenly wished I wasn't going. I had no idea what sort of evening it would be, or what to wear. Maybe I should take a leaf out of Tilly's book and go down with something catching.

'He's got a few bob. Another of your champagne socialists, no doubt. Have you met Lucia yet?'

'No.'

153

'Hangs out with Ingrid. Will pin you up against the wall and tell you earnestly about how terrible it is people are moving in and making it all twee and pricing the locals out of the housing market. Remind you about the deprivation on the old council estate and the problems faced by the farming community. First one carrying the banner when Ingrid leads the march.'

Malcolm paused to crunch on the small almond biscuit balanced on his saucer.

'And where does she hail from? Back end of Islington, where she made a fortune buying up ex-council properties and making them chi-chi. Now she brings her chums down every weekend and they're all looking about at the dear little cottages with all that potential ... but that's all right because they are HER friends and all the improvements will be reclaimed-that and sustainable-this and have a solar panel on top of the second bathroom. PAH.'

Malcolm pushed his chair back and rose to his feet.

'It's been delightful to see you, my dear.' He nodded across to the waitress, who was polishing glasses behind the small bar counter and had clearly been enjoying the diatribe. 'On my tab, Jenny?'

As I got up too, he leant over and took one of my hands in both of his and gave it a squeeze. 'Don't worry,' he said.

He lifted an arm to wave as he disappeared through the door, delivering his last words over his shoulder, with an endearing grin. 'I'll hold you to that toad.'

They'd just that minute had a cancellation, so Christophe was free to do my hair, I was told in Cut Above the Rest. 'I've got time to do a colour, if you want one,' he said, wincing at my re-growth. 'Warm it up a bit?'

I looked at my watch. It would be one less thing to worry about. I could concentrate my full fretting on my choice of clothes. Paul was unlikely to phone for a second time today and if he did discover I wasn't at the end of the landline I'd tell him I was knocking off early and working tomorrow morning. Which I would do, before Caroline arrived.

I nodded.

As Christophe applied the russet-gold he'd chosen for me – which he assured me would bring out the hazel-green of my eyes – and extolled the benefits of a few blonde highlights to set off my shortened fringe, I wondered if I was making a mistake.

David had sent a text as I'd left Rosie's, telling me he would pick me up at 6.30 p.m. It would still be light and Jinni might easily look out of her window. She'd be furious with me for going.

I'd mentioned it to Tilly as a vague possibility and she'd wrinkled her nose. 'Why are you even thinking of it?' she'd asked.

Because, I might have said, I haven't been out for an evening with a man for a long time (not since the unfortunate Quentin). And I want to do something unpredictable, slightly dangerous, exciting ...

I imagined my daughter's face if I tried to express that. I thought of Jinni's scorn. If it was such an appealing prospect, why did I feel so anxious?

I could suggest to David I met him outside the pub – or

the corner shop? Did one do that? Though, suppose Jinni saw me get in the car there? Then it really would look as if I were sneaking around ...

By the time Christophe had washed off my colour and begun snipping, I was in a lather of indecision and felt like a teenager.

Which was what decided me. If it had been one of my own teenagers my advice would have been firm. Be completely honest!

As Christophe was wielding the dryer, I was resolved. I would pop over to Jinni's as soon as I got back and explain I intended to give David a full interrogation and wouldn't mention that the more I thought about him, the more I was focusing on his crinkly eyes and the peculiar jolt I'd got when he touched me. Especially as it had probably only been a rush of blood to the head. There'd been a full moon a day later and Jules at work said that always made her slightly peculiar.

'That's better, isn't it?' Christophe gave my hair a last spray and produced a mirror with a flourish.

It was indeed a vast improvement. While I had been quietly stressing he had given my messy locks a sleek new shape. The fresh colour had left my hair a rich conkerish brown with a reddish tinge to it and the subtle blonde highlights did work as well as he'd said they would.

Now I just had to get the slap on and find something to wear.

It was too late to do the shopping, but I stopped at the florist on the way home and bought an armful of spring flowers for the house and some tulips for Jinni. I'd say they were to cheer her up after the paint incident. Not a peace offering.

I lay the wrapped packages on the doorstep of my house as I fumbled for my key, but before I could fish it from my handbag, the door swung open.

'Where have you been?' Tilly looked me up and down crossly. 'Auntie Caroline's here!'

Chapter 17

'Sorry, darling! Didn't you get my message?' Caroline, beautifully tanned and blonder than ever, looked as if she'd flown in from somewhere exotic, rather than come in a cab from the station.

I shook my head, looking at my phone, which was showing two missed calls. 'I didn't hear it. I've been in the hairdresser's.'

'Yes, you look marvellous.' Caroline stood back and gave me the full once-over. 'Love that colour.' She hugged me again.

'My evening do was going to be painfully dull so I thought I'd get down here early and have a really relaxed weekend and a proper catch-up. You don't mind, do you? You weren't going out? I did get hold of Tilly and she thought it would be fine.' She beamed at her niece.

'Of course, it's lovely. I'm not doing anything.'

'Did you tell that creep where to go?' Tilly asked. 'I thought if you were out, then I could take Auntie C to The Fox.'

'What creep?' Caroline's head whipped round. 'Tell me all.'

'Let's have a drink.' I led Caroline into the kitchen and put the flowers in the sink, shoving the door to with the back of my foot as I went. 'Frascati?'

Caroline settled herself on a stool as I poured two glasses.

'Fabulous house, darling,' she said, raising her goblet towards me. 'SO much potential. And gorgeous to see you. Now – who is this man?'

By the time I'd finished the tale, Caroline was on her second glass of wine and had it all sorted. No amount of protesting would shift her and she'd clearly taken her opportunity to get Tilly on side because I returned from the loo to find my daughter was also adamant I was going on what was now being referred to as my 'date' with 'that creep'.

'Keep an open mind. Then you and I will go to this bar of yours and discuss your glittering future,' Caroline told Tilly, 'after I've given David a proper appraisal.'

'He'll be here in half an hour,' I said, looking at the clock in panic. 'And I'm not ready, I've not told Jinni and I'm going to be embarrassed with you two staring out of the window.'

'Nonsense.' Caroline pulled out a gold compact and applied a little more lip gloss. 'You get changed and Tilly and I will take the flowers over to Jinni when you've left and explain the situation. She'll be fine when we tell her you are only after the truth.' She grinned at me and then took a delicate sip of her drink. 'We'll let him in.'

I looked at her in despair. 'I was going to wait outside.'

Caroline shook her head. 'I don't think so – looks far too keen. And it's starting to rain.'

Even if it wasn't, she was clearly determined to get a look at my dinner companion, and with another despairing glance at Tilly, who smirked, I went upstairs, threw myself in the shower, to deal with the cold sweat I'd come out in, going through various contortions to avoid getting my hair wet while I mentally went through the contents of my wardrobe.

There were work suits for meetings and jeans and sweat-shirts and tracksuit bottoms and half a dozen summer dresses designed for a hot day in July. All I could think of that was vaguely suitable for a Friday night dinner with someone I didn't know, on a drizzly night in April, was a bottle-green, long-sleeved dress, which was quite fitted and looked good on a slim day, and a lacy red dress that could only be worn on a slim day or the zip wouldn't do up. I had a black cock-tail dress that was too formal, a black wool dress that might be too hot if the gallery was warm and a silvery dress that was too flimsy if the restaurant happened to be cold. And was a bit dressy.

Better to be underdressed than over, I reminded myself, wondering if black jeans and a silk shirt was the way forward.

Caroline appeared in the doorway and surveyed the hangers. 'The green,' she said decisively. 'Fabulous with that hair.' She rooted in the bottom of the cupboard. 'With these boots. I didn't know you had these, darling – very classy.'

'Got them in the sale.'

'Get your face on.'

I grabbed a tube of tinted moisturiser while she ferreted in my closets to familiarise herself with any other bargains.

We both stopped when the doorbell rang.

'I'll go.' She was already through the door. 'Don't rush.'

'Do me up first.'

I breathed in hard but the zip slid easily into place. At least the dress wouldn't split when I sat down. I struggled into my boots as I heard Caroline running lightly down the stairs.

Moments later, as I feverishly applied lipstick, I heard her voice, then Tilly's, then David's deeper one. I heard Caroline say I wouldn't be long and would he like a drink and then I couldn't make out the rest.

My heart was thumping. I thought of Malcolm squeezing my hands and telling me not to worry and found myself half wishing I was going for fish and chips with him instead! I'd feel a prune if this 'date' was a disaster.

But Tilly was smiling when I came downstairs and Caroline gave me a wink.

David was wearing the same aftershave he'd had on before and a rather nice shirt. He kissed me on both cheeks and stood back. 'You look lovely,' he said.

I suddenly felt about 14, standing there with all three of them looking at me, my daughter now openly grinning and Caroline giving me a surreptitious thumbs-up behind David's back.

'Shall we go?' I said awkwardly. David took a last mouthful from his glass and nodded. He turned to Caroline and Tilly. 'Seriously, come along too. Marta will be thrilled to see you. More the merrier and all that.'

I felt my heart sink. Caroline raised her eyebrows at me and I saw she was holding a piece of paper on which I could see a neatly drawn map. 'Ten minutes' walk at most,' David added.

'Lovely!' I cried brightly, hissing at Tilly as I passed her. 'Flowers for Jinni!'

'Jinni!' he said disparagingly, as he opened the car door for me. 'She's got a very vivid imagination.'

'What do you mean?' I asked, seizing my chance. 'The night you dropped me home someone threw red paint all over her outhouse.'

David frowned. 'I hope you're not suggesting the two events are linked?'

'No, of course not.'

'Good, because her neighbour, my friend Mark, says she's been making more of her hysterical allegations.'

'It's happened to me too.' I told him about the graffiti.

'Oh Christ, Tess,' he leant over the gear stick and touched my shoulder. 'That's appalling.'

'She thinks it was to get at her,' I said, watching him. 'And I suppose you and Ingrid are the only ones she can think of who don't like her.'

David looked sceptical. 'I imagine plenty of people find her an acquired taste,' he said acidly. 'And, for the record, I did like her when I first met her. Before I realised she was totally unbalanced.'

He started the engine as I looked nervously across the road.

'I think I got the inspection committee on side anyway,' he said, in a lighter voice, as we pulled away.

I laughed awkwardly. 'Caroline arrived early.'

'So she said. You could have cancelled. I wouldn't have minded.'

I glanced sideways at him. After being given the third degree by my ex-sister-in-law, he'd have probably been lightheaded with relief.

'Tilly was telling me she's an actress.'

'Really?' I couldn't keep the surprise from my voice. I'd only stayed upstairs long enough to smudge my mascara a couple of times and put some perfume on. I'd thought Tilly was all doom and gloom about her acting career. Still, 'what do you do?' is everyone's opening gambit and Tilly probably thought serving hamburgers on the Edgware Road wasn't quite the career profile David was used to.

'I know how tough it is,' he went on. 'I've got a friend in the business. I'm going to put her in touch with him. He might have something.'

'Oh. Gosh. Thank you. That's very kind of you.'

'Not at all.'

The gallery was at the end of a narrow road off the High Street. It was a large industrial-looking building that had been a body-work repair centre till the owner went to prison for VAT fraud, David told me as he parked nearby. Inside, clumps of expensively clad women stood about holding champagne glasses, heels tapping on the scrubbed wooden floor.

David did a lot of kissing, introducing me to an array of attractive females in their thirties and forties who had enviable handbags and designer-stubbled blokes in tow.

'Tess is an interior designer,' he told Marta, the striking-looking gallery owner, who wore a lot of statement jewellery and a red bow in her hair.

'How marvellous,' she said. 'Leonie's in total despair with her new place. 'I'll find you on Instagram'.

'Well, I'm not quite—' I began as David put an arm around

my waist and propelled me towards the next group, where he hugged a chiselled young man in crushed velvet.

'Kit this is Tess.' The young man kissed my hand. 'He and Nathaniel are newcomers too – they've bought a converted chapel down by the old cinema?'

'Bitten off rather more than we can chew–' Kit said, rolling his eyes as we were joined by an older, larger man in a jacket and tie, who shook his head affectionately.

'It's all coming along beautifully,' he said. 'Kit is a drama queen. You'd love it – you must come and see. You might be able to give us a few ideas ...'

'Well I–' I began again as David moved me on to meet Fiona and Tara and Sebastian and Tarquin and a chap called Steve who had made a fortune in the music business and was opening a recording studio a couple of miles up the road and used to hang out with Led Zeppelin.

'You'll have to get some cards done,' said David, who had taken my hand to lead me over to the next group.

'I will,' I said emboldened by my second glass of champagne and beginning to quite enjoy the vision of myself as a designer again. Not to mention David's attention. I saw the way the women greeted him and looked at me with a mixture of curiosity and envy. His fingers felt warm and smooth curled in mine. I suddenly wondered what it would feel like to have his whole body around me ...

'There you are!' A cross-looking woman with very dark, shiny haircut in a sharp geometrical style that came down in long points on one side and was cropped on the other, came towards us in a short black dress and high heels. I looked in awe at her long tanned legs and sinewy arms – she must spend hours in the gym. 'Jake's looking for you,' she said to David, her eyes only flicking to me for a nano-second. 'He's in a foul mood because the council have turned down the revised plans as well.'

David let go of my hand and swore quietly. 'Where is he? Tess, I'm sorry, I won't be a minute–'

'No problem.'

The woman followed him.

I began to move along the white walls, looking at the paintings – mostly colourful abstracts – and the occasional object on the floor or a plinth.

Across the room Pete the photographer was snapping what looked like a lawnmower engine surrounded by barbed wire. I looked about for Gabriel, but was surprised to see Malcolm with a napkin in his hand, peering at the fire extinguisher.

'Is this real or an exhibit?' he asked as I approached him. 'I only came for the canapés,' he continued. 'And they're very disappointing.'

He nodded across the room to where a waitress was proffering tiny green mounds of something from a slate platter. 'I like mini Yorkshire puddings with beef and horseradish,' he said. 'Or sausages.'

He shook his head. 'Aubergine mousse drizzled with beetroot oil – pah! As soon as you see "drizzled" on a menu, you know it's going to be a silly sliver of something unpronounceable with a side order of shaved Appalachian goat's foot.'

I laughed.

'Look!' He nudged me in the direction of a man with a

ponytail, who was gazing at a huge canvas beneath the skylight. 'What's he expecting to see? All that stepping back and sighing. It's a red square on a blue background! No amount of stroking his chin is going to change that!'

'Shhh,' I said, giggling, as the ponytail swung towards us. But Malcolm had only just got started.

'And why don't they put the name of the picture under the bloody picture? Why are they stuck in little clusters three feet away? Is it a Guess the Picture from the Caption game? I suppose it would liven things up a bit. Trying to decide if a green squiggle and a blue squiggle is Woods in Winter or the Village Postman'?

Malcolm looked into his empty glass and then at mine. 'Shall I try to find you another drink? If they'd bring out those little cones of fish and chips it would be something.'

I swallowed the last mouthful of champagne and handed him the empty flute.

'Won't be long – have you seen all that nonsense in there?' He jerked his head towards a side room, where more objects were arranged on various stands. 'Who buys that junk? Do you know anyone who'd pay four hundred quid for a lump of purple driftwood?'

I walked slowly around the exhibits, finding a sea-worn plank with 'I Wood' carved into it coloured in violet and a dustbin painted in candy-pink stripes filled with shells.

'I think it's four hundred for the pair,' I said when Malcolm returned. He snorted.

'Used to be a lovely little boozer up the road. Had a pinball machine. Now even that's a "gallery shop": Ale and Arty, would you believe. Last time I walked past they were selling old kitchen chairs. The sort your mum had. They'd painted all the legs black, apart from one which was yellow and they wanted two hundred and twenty-five quid for it!'

He handed me a glass of champagne and looked balefully at his own orange juice. 'Next time round, I won't bother teaching kiddie journalists how to spell "accommodation". I'm going to live above some shabby little grot shop, come up with a silly name like Clapham Junkshun, and flog rubbish to the gullible.'

'That's got a certain beauty,' I said, pointing to a structure of silvery twisted metal around a blue glass ball.

Malcolm looked at it blankly. 'I suppose you approved of Miss Emin's filthy bedsheets,' he said.

I smiled. 'I did find that bed quite mesmerising.'

As Malcolm's face twisted in revulsion David came up behind me, throwing an arm around my shoulders and holding a hand out to Malcolm.

'Enjoying the exhibits?'

'No,' said Malcolm.

'Caroline and Tilly are here,' David said to me. He was already moving me towards the other room.

'I'll see you in a bit,' I said to Malcolm over my shoulder. 'Nice to talk to you,' I added, feeling awkward that he'd fetched me a drink and now I was being whisked away.

Caroline, who had changed into a turquoise fitted dress and a pair of heels, had discovered Kit and Nathanial and was most of the way down her glass of fizz. 'Isn't this all gorgeous?' she said as we joined her and Tilly and Malcolm ambled towards a waitress with a tray.

'He's not bad either,' she murmured as David ushered over more arrivals to meet us.

The gallery filled up fast and I gave up trying to look at the art through all the jostling bodies. I was getting hot and needed some water. 'I'm just going out for some air,' I shouted in David's ear, as I tried to wriggle my way back towards the entrance, but he grabbed my arm and pulled in the other direction. 'This way.'

He was holding my hand again as he led me thought the knots of people to a door at the far end. It opened into a walled courtyard with benches and an old metal fire escape running up one side, the steps dotted with coloured pots and what looked like a summer jasmine curling around the handrail. A large modern sculpture of two bodies entwined sat in the middle of the flagstones. 'That's lovely,' I said, realising that I too was stroking my chin in the manner of ponytail earlier, and trying to think of something slightly more profound with which to sum up my findings.

'It's a Tristram Walters,' said David, as if this should mean something, so I nodded and stroked a bit more, hastily stopping as I felt a bristle under my thumb. Christ, how had that grown without me spotting it before? I poked it with my finger. It was clearly a monster.

David sat on a bench and gestured for me to join him. 'A bit more peaceful out here,' he said, looking at me. 'Yes, lovely,' I said again, hoping the last golden rays from the setting sun, which were streaking the mellow bricks, weren't also illuminating my whisker.

I felt in my bag, wondering if I had a pair of tweezers

with which I could give it a surreptitious tug when David wasn't looking. Instead I felt my phone vibrating. I glanced at the screen as I cut it off before it could ring. It was the second missed call from Fran. Another weekend meltdown about Jeremy's kids, no doubt. I pulled out a bottle of water and took a mouthful. David was still talking about the sculpture.

'Which contemporary artists are you into?' he asked.

I suddenly couldn't think of any. Then I remembered Malcolm and suppressed a giggle.

'I like Tracey Emin's blue sketches,' I volunteered, 'but I wasn't so sure about the tampon in a glass case.' Was this polite party chat? Caroline wouldn't think so.

But David was smiling at me. I kept my eyes fixed back on his to make sure they did not drop to my chin, where I could feel the hair waving in the light breeze. 'She does seem to have rather a preoccupation with bodily fluids,' he said.

He was still looking at me. 'Shall we go to dinner soon?' he asked, moving, it seemed, a fraction closer.

'Okay!' I squeaked, my hand scrabbling further and closing around a pair of nail scissors. Perhaps I could chop the facial growth back, in the ladies.

My phone started ringing again. I dropped the scissors and grabbed it, suddenly fearful it was one of the kids this time, with a crisis unfolding.

'Or would you rather stay a bit longer ...?'

I shook my head, glancing down at my handset. It was Fran again. I frowned.

'I'm sorry,' I said. 'I think perhaps my friend ...'

'You'd better see what she wants.' He sat back from me, his tone bright and brisk. 'I'll say some goodbyes ...'

I had the phone to my ear as he disappeared back through the door into the crowd beyond. I could hear the panic in Fran's voice.

'Please, Tess, I need you to help me. Can you come right now?'

Chapter 18

'So we need a taxi number,' I instructed Tilly, who I'd found talking to Gabriel beside a broken mirror with '*The next seven years of your life*' painted across it in black and white. I shuddered.

'So where's Jonathan?' she said, clearly annoyed at being interrupted.

'I've no idea,' I snapped. 'I just know Fran is there on her own with the children and she needs to get Georgia to A&E. Theo and Freya are in bed, she doesn't want to take Jac and I'm over the limit.' I stopped for breath and looked at Gabriel.

'Hold on ...' he pulled a phone from his pocket and began tapping the screen.

'What are you doing here?' Malcolm loomed up behind him. 'Is there a problem?' he went on, seeing my face. He looked at Gabriel too. 'What have you done now?'

'This is so kind of you,' I said again as Malcolm drove up the high street with me, Caroline and Tilly on board.

'Just don't ask me to hold any of them,' he replied, indicating to turn left and accelerating down the hill.

'Mum can do that.' Tilly was still grumbling about being dragged away. 'I don't know why I have to be here as well.'

'Because if the others wake up I might need help. And it wouldn't hurt you to do something for someone else for a change!'

My daughter gave an exaggerated sigh. 'Why are you in such a foul mood? Pissed off your date got cut short?'

As I turned, I saw Caroline give her a sharp nudge. David had shrugged good-naturedly and disappeared back into the throng, saying we would do it another time. I pushed down the pangs of disappointment as we

reached the outskirts of town and turned into the long, curved road of detached houses where Fran lived.

She was on the line again, her anxiety palpable in my ear. 'We're nearly there.' I cried, as Malcolm swung around the final bend. 'Oh God – are you giving her fluids?'

Fran looked whiter than the baby. She'd left the front door open and we followed the screams to the kitchen, where she was standing at the sink, in a vomit-stained sweatshirt, mopping at Georgia in her arms while rocking Jac, strapped into a child seat, scarlet-faced and howling, backwards and forwards with her foot. Georgia hadn't stopped throwing up and wouldn't take anything to drink. 'And now look at her–' Fran's voice rose. 'She's all floppy.'

'She's probably exhausted,' I said.

'One of the boys in Freya's class had meningitis,' Fran stared at me red-eyed, her voice rising further over Jac's wails.

'It won't be that,' I said, with more authority than I felt, 'but you're right to get her checked out.'

Fran nodded, looking around her wildly, 'I don't know what I've done with my keys.'

'You can't drive,' said Caroline, glancing at Malcolm, who was standing in the doorway looking appalled. 'You need to see to her.'

I'll take you,' he said from the doorway. Caroline nodded. 'Shall I come too?' she said.

'Absolutely.' said Malcolm meaningfully.

Fran looked at me. 'I'm sorry, Tess, I didn't know who else to ask – everyone's got children, ... Jonathan ...' Her voice shook. 'Where is he?'

Fran looked past me into the hall. 'Oh darling ...'

Theo stomped into the room in pyjamas. 'I want a drink,' he announced, surveying us all. 'Why is everybody here?'

'Auntie Tess is going to look after you,' Fran said. 'While I take Georgia to the doctor.' She looked at me bleakly. 'Jonathan's in Oxford with his kids. I needed a weekend off. I told him he had to take them to a hotel ...'

'Have you phoned?'

'He's not answering.'

She'd stopped rocking Jac and was rummaging in a quilted bag. 'I'm sorry,' she said again. 'I think Jac needs changing. There's nappies in their bedroom. I'd better take this one with me ...'

Caroline picked up the bag. 'Let's go,' she said firmly.

Fran followed her, Georgia pale and clammy in her arms. I peered at the tiny girl anxiously. Was it imagination or did she look a bit blue? Should we be calling an ambulance instead?

Caroline, as if reading my mind, said: 'How far is it?'

'Twelve miles,' said Malcolm. Fran looked panicked.

'Won't take long at this time of night.' Caroline was brisk. 'Better to start getting there ...' she murmured to me as she shepherded Fran in front of her. 'I'll call you.'

At the sight of his mother disappearing, Jac's shrieks reached new heights. He sobbed hysterically, thrashing about in the chair, that was now rocking unaided. I grabbed it and fumbled at the plastic buckles while Tilly looked on aghast.

'I want a DRINK,' said Theo urgently. 'And I'm hungry.'

An unmistakable aroma rose from Jac as I lifted him out of the seat. Tilly wrinkled her nose.

'Can you get Theo something?' I said to her. 'And us too. See if you can find some coffee?' I carried Jac upstairs, suddenly post-alcohol weary. He was still crying. The noise drilled through my head as I opened various doors. It was a long time since I'd been up here.

It was a long time since I'd changed a nappy too. Keeping Jac still while trying to work out which way round the Pampers went and keeping his foot out of the shitty baby wipes, had brought me out in a light sweat by the time I heard footsteps coming along the landing.

'Ugh gross.' Tilly surveyed the scene on the bathroom rug. 'He's had five biscuits and says he's still hungry.'

I pictured Fran's face. That was probably Theo's ration for the entire month. 'Look for some cereal.'

Jac was still wailing and evidently required sustenance too. I tried to remember what babies of his age had. No doubt there'd be pots of something suitably puréed and organically sound somewhere. Or was he on toast and Marmite by now?

As I gathered him up, finally fragrant, Freya appeared in the doorway in her nightie, a soft orange duck clutched to her chest, eyes huge. 'Where's Mummy?' she said in alarm.

After assuring her of her mother's imminent return, I quizzed the 5-year-old on her sibling's nutritional needs and enlisted her to locate the necessary.

Downstairs Freya clapped a hand to her mouth. 'Theo's not allowed hot chocolate,' she said, scandalised. 'He gets silly.'

This, it transpired, involved the 3-year-old running in high-speed circles around the living room swinging a Power Rangers figure above his head with accompanying battle sounds, until he was puce.

'Next time he gets water,' I growled to Tilly when I had finally got him back to bed and was slumped on the sofa in exhaustion.

'Next time,' she said, 'you're on your own.'

'We had to help. Imagine all four of them in the waiting room ...'

I looked at Jac, who, after a quite staggering amount of various milk and baby snacks, was out cold on a floor cushion, having resisted all attempts to get him upstairs. I'd thrown a blanket over him and was leaving him there – he looked unconscious, but I knew the moment I lowered him into his cot he would open one beady eye and scream the place down.

'Ugghh.' Tilly was slumped opposite me. 'How does Fran stand it?'

'I had three of you. I remember when Oliver was about

the same age as Georgia and he started fitting. Dad and I were terrified – I've never known him drive so fast – he went through a red light!'

Tilly looked suitably stunned.

'It turned out to be some sort of virus, I think.'

'Can't you remember?'

'And then when Ben fell off the bed – he was younger still. I cried all the way to the hospital ...'

'He's still not forgiven you for that. Says that's why he's got that great big bent bit in his nose.'

'He gets that from your father.'

'And then when you were two and I dropped the iron ...'

Tilly sat up, appalled. 'You're not going to look after my children!'

'You're not going to have any just yet, I hope.' I retorted. 'I'm not in any hurry to be a grandmother.'

'Don't worry – I'll probably never meet anyone permanent anyway,' Tilly said huffily.

'Of course you will! One day you'll find just the right person. And when you do, you'll settle down and have a lovely family.'

'Auntie C never has.'

'She likes her independence,' I said, not adding that Caroline's idea of the right man was one that came in threes.

'She's too old now anyway,' Tilly said dismissively.

'Don't let her hear you say that!'

I'd had a text from Caroline saying they'd got there and Georgia was being seen, but heard nothing since. It was nearly 2 a.m. Tilly was yawning and my eyes were heavy. I closed

them for what felt like a second and woke with a start to the
sounds of voices in the hall and Jac yelling.

'Oh my God. Has he been crying all this time?' Fran was
in the doorway taking in the sight of her son screaming on
the floor, Tilly sprawled across one sofa and me rubbing my
aching neck on the other. I hastily turned over the cushion
I'd been drooling on.

'He's been out for hours.' I croaked. 'He just that moment
woke up. Is she okay?'

I nodded towards Georgia, who was asleep over Fran's
shoulder.

'Ear infection. She's got antibiotics.'

She lowered Georgia into my lap and scooped up Jac, whose
wails subsided in gratitude that it wasn't me.

Georgia's eyes snapped open and she screeched in horror.

Fran retrieved her. 'I'll just put them to bed ...'

'Let's get out,' said Caroline in a low voice, as a duet of wails
reverberated up the stairs. 'Malcolm's waiting in the car and if
she starts on about Jonathan again, we'll be here till dawn.'

I prodded Tilly awake and began to put my boots back on.
By the time Fran returned we were assembled in the hall.

'They are asleep!' she announced.

'Fantastic,' I said. 'We'll be off, then.'

Fran put her arms around me. 'Thank you. Thank you to
all of you. Thank Malcolm again. Oh and you, Caroline. I'm
so—'

Caroline began to open the front door. 'You're very welcome.'

'I can't believe bloody Jonathan. Of all the times not to be
here ...'

'But I thought *you–*' I began, as Caroline frowned.

'Not that he's ever here, these days. And when he is, he's on his laptop.'

'I suppose he is working hard ...' I said, trying to be the voice of reason.

'He leaves too early to help with breakfast and he's home after they're in bed–'

'... to pay for everything.'

Caroline gave a tiny warning shake of her head.

Fran tossed hers. 'Yes, his money pays for it all! And, as he keeps reminding me, we have a big mortgage. But I still feel–'

Behind Fran's head, Caroline was sweeping her hand across her throat to indicate I should bring the conversation to a rapid close.

'He has got two families to support,' I finished lamely.

Fran's eyes widened. 'No, he hasn't! He's got ONE family and two children from his first marriage.'

Caroline looked at me in despair as Tilly rolled her eyes.

'I'm sorry,' I said hastily. 'Insensitively put. I meant he has maintenance payments as well. We must go now ...'

'But sometimes it feels like it! He was on the phone to Susie for hours about Bella's bloody parents' evening. Very friendly!'

'Oh come on,' I patted her arm. Caroline now had the door wide open and was stepping outside, waving at Malcolm's car beyond. 'He finds Susie a right pain. You know that. He was probably just trying to keep the peace.'

'You need to tell him how you feel,' I said, it being the only cliché I could think of as I edged after Caroline, knowing that

I, in my divorced and perennially single state, was hardly qualified to dispense relationship advice.

'Don't you think I've tried?' Fran's voice rose further.

I could feel Tilly's fingers digging into my back. 'Why don't you get some sleep?' I said desperately, 'and we'll talk about it tomorrow?'

Fran burst into tears.

Chapter 19

I felt like crying too.

Jinni had seen my lights on at 4 a.m. and called to see if I needed help. 'I knew your mother was with you so I thought I'd better check,' she'd said. Now, twelve hours later, gratefully allowing her to bring the wine hour forward considerably, it occurred to me to ask how.

'Did you see us arrive?' I enquired, pretty sure Jinni's car had not been in her drive the day I'd brought Mum back.

Jinni shook her head and looked around her. 'Where is she now?'

'Asleep. She's always restless at night. Twice I've woken up and found her standing in my room. She usually has a lie-down in the afternoon.'

There was a short, awkward silence. I'd seen nothing of Jinni since the gallery opening and Caroline had said very little about how Jinni had reacted, simply passing on thanks for the flowers.

Since then, my usually garrulous neighbour had been conspicuous by her absence, so I guessed the news that I'd been consorting with the enemy hadn't gone down well.

'David told me,' she said, as I twisted the cork from a bottle of red. I stared at her. 'Really?'

Jinni's expression was inscrutable. 'He sent me a text,' she said. 'Said you'd turned down the irresistible offer of his company because your mother was staying and would I like to meet him instead.'

'I didn't know he had your number ...' I said faintly, a stab of something unexpectedly painful going through me at the thought of David inviting Jinni out.

'Oh, he's got it from ages ago,' said Jinni dismissively. 'Before I found out what a wanker he is.'

'I expect he wants to improve relations with you,' I said, 'I told him I didn't want my having the odd drink with him to spoil *our* friendship.' As I said it, I felt my voice wobble. 'He said he'd make an effort.'

Jinni looked cynical. 'No, he wants to talk me out of objecting to his mate's outrageous planning application, and thinks getting you on side is the way forward,' she said flatly. 'Because he's a grade-A arsehole.' She chinked her glass against mine. 'But we won't let it affect us,' she said bracingly, giving my arm a brief, hard squeeze. 'Even though I think you're mad to have anything to do with him.'

'He's been helpful introducing me to people. You know I wanted to get back into what I used to do – buying up furniture and accessories and customising them for clients? Seems there could be a market for that around here.'

I told her about Malcolm and the chair with three yellow legs. Jinni laughed. 'Yes, there's lots of 'em with more money than sense.'

181

'And he's giving me some freelance work styling a show flat,' I went on, embarrassed to admit how much I'd begun to like him. 'He says I can put some bits of my own in it with price tags.'

On the phone, he was funny and interesting. I'd decided his Smug Bastard persona was just the front he put on when he didn't know someone very well and he was a perfectly nice bloke. An attractive one ...

'And you know – he hasn't done anything to me ...' I remembered his eyes on mine and suddenly wished he would. Feeling myself blush, I jumped up and opened a cupboard door.

'Well, make sure he pays you,' said Jinni. 'I'd get the money up front. And Tess, really – I'd keep it business-like!'

I tipped peanuts into a bowl, wondering if Jinni had also given Caroline the full catalogue of David's evil ways.

Apart the comment that he was good-looking, my friend hadn't been as pushy about the possibilities as I'd expected, changing the subject almost immediately from my announcement we'd be meeting again soon, to the possibility of grey floorboards in the downstairs loo, and then going straight out to buy me a large blue and white pot that was rather fetching, from the new arty shop by the library.

So what did you say, anyway?' I asked Jinni lightly. 'You know, when he called?'

'I told him to fuck off!' She lifted her glass. 'Cheers!'

The first time my mother appeared in my room, I screamed. I'd been dreaming – one of my more disturbing flights of fancy in which sinister strangers creep about the house and my legs have collapsed beneath me so there is no escape – when I woke suddenly to find her standing by the window.

My mother was calm; I wasn't even sure if she was properly awake. She explained without panic that we needed to save the children and get them on the boat.

'You've had a dream, Mum,' I said, my heart still pounding as I switched on lights.

She shook herself and gave a small laugh. 'Yes, that's probably it,' she agreed. Then went to the bathroom and back to bed.

I'd got used to it now. She woke me up most mornings between four and five to tell me something strange had happened.

Once she said Alice was arriving at three, and another time it was Tilly's wedding day. Always she needed to know when we were leaving. We're not going anywhere, I'd tell her, and that seemed to make it all right again. Neither of us mentioned it the next day.

But every time I came down in the mornings, leaving her asleep upstairs, and saw her shoes in the hall, neatly lined up with mine, my insides twisted with sorrow. Once she would have been the first in the kitchen, putting away plates, polishing the taps, scouting around for something she could reorganise or clean.

Now she hovered in doorways like a child, waiting for me to suggest a walk into town or a cup of tea. She went to the newsagent's a couple of times and came back with shopping for me and she wandered around the garden. But she didn't attack the weeds out there or tell me what I should plant in the borders. As the days went by, she said less and grew sadder. It was the first time I had ever seen her sit in a chair and just … sit.

I didn't like to leave her.

Jinni was brilliant, dropping in, chatting to my mother and cheering me along, but it was still exhausting. I'd had to cancel meetings and was behind on work, and though I'd been secretly relieved to have good reason to tell Fran I couldn't babysit while she and Jonathan 'talked things through', I couldn't arrange to meet David either. I felt bad but I was thankful that Gerald was coming to get her at the end of the week. He'd told me he'd stay with her all the time when they got back – 'it's what he's been after for years,' said Mo drily – or she could go to him.

'Will he be able to cope?' asked Jinni.

'I have no idea,' I told her.

I was trying not to think about the future. It frightened me.

I'd now told the kids and was trying to keep Alice informed. She wanted me to phone – complaining about the lack of detail in my emails, but my mother became tearful if we talked about what was wrong with her, and I couldn't supply my sister with the forensic description she'd want, with our mother in earshot.

Or talk to David the way I'd like to. He arrived, out of the blue, on Thursday, around six, wearing a loose Ralph Lauren sweater and smelling delicious. He had a smile on his face and a box under one arm.

I opened the door expecting it to be Aaron the plumber. My heart leapt.

'I got you this.' He held it out. 'Something to do in the evenings, while you're stuck in.' It was a thousand-piece jigsaw of a collection of works by Picasso. 'You can always frame it later,' he said.

'I will. It's wonderful,' I told him, touched. 'Thank you.' I hesitated, not sure whether to kiss him. He put a hand on my shoulder. 'Are you okay?' he asked.

'Have you got time for a coffee?'

My mother appeared in the kitchen doorway as I was filling the machine. 'This is David, a friend of mine, Mum.'

'How lovely to meet you.' She held out her hand. She'd just put on more lipstick and combed her hair. Her perfume wafted towards me. At that moment she looked as she'd always done – immaculate, from the short grey waves on her head to her neat shiny shoes, clothes pressed, pearls swinging, rings a little large now on her bony fingers but nails clean and filed. I shuddered inwardly at the descriptions I'd read about lack of personal hygiene and loss of interest. I prayed David wouldn't mention her having been unwell.

But he'd sprung up from the small table and was shaking her hand, saying how delighted he was too. I tried to smile my gratitude, realising how disloyal I would feel if I told him about the ravages going on behind the gracious façade.

'I'll go and read my book,' she told me, although we both knew she'd been looking at the same chapter since she got here, unable to concentrate on the story and needing to constantly go back over what she'd read the day before. And yet she'd supplied two answers about the genus of plants when I'd been doing the quick crossword and we'd had a long discussion the night before about a holiday to Cornwall when Alice was seven and fell off a rock.

'I'll bring you a coffee,' I called. Then I looked at the clock. 'Would you rather have wine?' I asked David. 'Or a gin and tonic?'

He shook his head. 'I'm going to eat with *my* mother,' he said, ruefully. 'Better not start before her ...'

He sat back down as I got cups from the cupboard. 'How busy are you?' he asked, suddenly brisk. 'I was going to email you the brief we talked about ...'

I watched him as he spoke, his eyes alight with enthusiasm. He'd been working at home that day, he told me, and was going to come round after lunch, but somehow he'd got so involved, the whole afternoon had disappeared ...

I sighed. 'I always seem to be trying to catch up,' I said. The interrupted nights and my mother's restless wanderings about the house during the day meant the only time I was free from distraction was when she went for her afternoon nap and, by that time, I felt like lying down myself.

'But I'll be on my own again by the weekend,' I went on. 'My mother's going back tomorrow.'

'She's obviously much better?' He asked in a low voice, eyes fixed on mine.

I looked away. 'She's got to have some more tests,' I said. 'We're not quite sure what it is yet.'

He didn't ask any more and stood up as soon as he'd drunk his coffee.

'Let me know when you're free for a drink,' he said, kissing me lightly. For a moment I was silent, the feel of his lips sending that shock through me again.

'Oh, er, yes,' I stumbled, feeling my face blushing. 'That will be nice.'

He was already walking through to the front room. My mother had disappeared. I followed him, embarrassed at my awkwardness, but he was out of the front door while I was still wishing I'd kissed him back. I attempted to galvanise my scrambled emotions into some sort of poise. 'That would be *lovely*,' I said with emphasis, feeling daft as the words burst out of my mouth, much more loudly than they were meant to.

He lifted a hand to wave back over his shoulder, not even properly looking around but striding towards his car.

Perhaps next time we met, I should explain that save the unfortunate Quentin, I'd not had any sort of romantic liaison for over seven years and was rather out of practice. Or would I just sound off-puttingly desperate?

It was only as he drove away, and I was left staring at the overflowing skip parked on the gravel before my neighbour's grey stone frontage, that it struck me he'd said nothing about texting Jinni.

Chapter 20

Riiiiiiiinnnnnggggggg!
I woke abruptly and scrabbled on the bedside table for my phone, knocking my book to the floor and sending half a glass of water plunging after it.

The ringing stopped and I peered blearily at the screen. What was Tilly doing phoning so early? I frowned as I sat up yawning and stared at the clock. It was 8.42 a.m. I'd meant to get up at seven, to get an hour or two's work done before my mother appeared, though now I felt so fuggy I was sorely tempted to drop straight off again.

I'd just stretched and closed my eyes to consider this, when another thought crashed in.

She hadn't woken me up.

My eyes snapped back open. I hadn't heard her wander about or go to the loo and she certainly hadn't made her usual nocturnal visit to tell me we must get packing.

I pulled on my dressing gown, pushing down the twinges of panic as I walked across the silent landing to what I still thought of as Ben's room, listened for a moment and then tapped on the wood.

'You okay, Mum?'

'Don't be stupid,' I told myself sternly, as the silence continued, and I stood hovering fearfully outside the door. 'Mum!' I said again, pushing it open.

The bed was empty. The covers pushed back in a rumpled heap and the pillows squashed and indented. Her slippers were next to the bedside table and yesterday's clothes were piled on the chair. The old robe of mine she'd been using was still hanging on the back of the door.

I ran downstairs, hoping to find her in the kitchen, having risen early, as in the old days, making tea. Perhaps the whole dementia thing had been a bad dream and she'd be bustling about, scouring the hob or polishing the teapot, nothing wrong with her at all.

Except that in the old days, the bed would have been straightened to within an inch of its life and the pillows relentlessly plumped. And the house had that gaping feel again that told me nobody else was in it.

It took only moments to check all the rooms and the downstairs loo. Her coat had gone and her shoes. But her handbag was still on the end of the sofa. Shit.

I tried to tell myself she'd simply gone for a walk or popped down to the newsagent to get some milk – taking a few coins – but it didn't feel right. I walked from room to room. I didn't want to go out in case she came back and couldn't get in. I phoned Jinni to ask if she'd seen my mother leaving the house. She hadn't. I ran back upstairs and got dressed.

Jinni was banging on the door a few minutes later, wearing

her boiler suit, hair scraped up on top of her head, hands with even more lumps out of them than usual.

'You go and look where you think she might be,' she said. 'I'll stay here and get the coffee on.'

I hugged her. 'Thank you.'

Richard in the newsagent's hadn't seen my mother. Neither had the woman in the florist's. She'd mentioned wanting to go to the hairdresser's, so I went in there too. Then I crossed the market square and carried on along the High Street, going up one side and down the other, looking through the windows of the small shops, entering the larger ones. She wasn't in the post office, she wasn't in the Co-op. My eyes scanned the pavements and flitted up the side streets, hoping for a glimpse of a small, brisk figure or the back of a green coat, but there was no sign of her anywhere.

I had come to the end of the main street, where the shops gave way to rows of terraced houses, a recreation ground and the community centre. The sun came out briefly from behind the grey clouds, and there was cherry blossom clinging to the damp grass outside the church, but there was also a sharp wind and it still felt colder than usual for late spring.

I wasn't sure which clothes my mother had on, but she must be chilled by now. I was already wishing I'd put on a proper coat instead of my thin wool jacket. Perhaps Alice had been right when she'd tried to insist my mother carried the phone my sister had bought her. The last time I'd seen it, the handset was on a shelf in her kitchen in Margate. Still in its box.

My mother wasn't known for her religious beliefs but I peered through the dark wooden doors of the church anyway. A couple of women were doing things with flowers, so I asked if they'd seen a short elderly woman with grey hair and possibly a strange light in her eye. They hadn't.

One of them smiled sympathetically – I was clearly looking more than usually wild-eyed myself. 'Would you like me to call the vicar?' she asked.

'There's no need, but thank you,' I backed out again, wondering what she had in mind. Would the good reverend have given me some words of solace or sent out a search party?

She wasn't on the roundabout or swings – she wasn't at the mother- and-toddlers group in the village hall. As I hurried back down the High Street, I realised the hopelessness of the task. Northstone wasn't huge but big enough for the odds of my happening on her by chance to be slim. Suppose she'd been run over. Or arrested. Without her bag, she didn't have any ID and even if she did, it wouldn't connect her with me.

I slowed down as I got to *Northstone News*, wondering if it was worth asking Gabriel to keep an eye open if he was around town. He'd sent me a sweet email and I'd been meaning to reply.

Grace jerked her head at the staircase as I approached. 'He's up there,' she said, before I could speak.

'Gabriel?' I enquired.

'Him as well,' she agreed flatly, eyes already back on her keyboard.

I went up to the office where Gabriel was studying his screen. He jumped up, looking touchingly thrilled. 'Tess!' He gave me a wide smile, flashing his beautiful American-style white teeth and hugged me as if I were his long-lost auntie from the other side of the world. 'I've missed you,' he said. 'How are things?'

I told him that as far as I knew Ben was doing fine at university, Oliver was busy, Sam was recovered, and Tilly, after a pep talk from her aunt, had gone back to her job and flat.

Gabriel grinned. 'I know – we've been talking on Facebook. She's not too happy with her flatmate, is she?'

So that would explain the call this morning. 'I don't know, to be honest,' I said, 'we've not yet spoken this week. I need to phone her back–' I remembered she hadn't left a message, which was unusual.

'But anyway, that's everyone else,' Gabriel was saying. 'How are *you?*'

He looked so concerned I almost got a lump in my throat. My children wouldn't think to ask. 'You look a little stressed, if you don't mind my saying,' Gabriel was saying. 'Is there anything wrong?'

'My mother's, um–' I stopped. 'Gone missing' sounded rather dramatic about an adult in broad daylight, but what else did you say about a parent with questionable judgement who was now at large? 'She's staying with me,' I explained, 'and she went out early and hasn't come back and–' I paused again. 'She's been having a few memory problems,' I said awkwardly, 'and I'm just worried that ...' I swallowed hard.

Gabriel's look of concern deepened. 'Do you want to let the police know? Would you like me to call the hospital, just in case?'

'In case of what, Mr Galahad?' Malcolm's voice boomed out behind me. 'What calamity are you saving us all from now?'

Gabriel reddened but his voice was even. 'Tess's mum has wandered off somewhere and she might need help.'

'Get Tess a coffee and a biscuit, then,' said Malcolm, as if this were the obvious solution. 'Or despatch one of your adoring females. Use the proper stuff. And make the calls.' He turned and looked at me searchingly. Then put a hand on my shoulder. 'Come and sit in my office. I'll get Grace on it.'

The coffee was good and as I sat cradling the cup, eating my second shortbread finger, I felt emotional as I thought how lucky I was to be living in a small town. This wouldn't happen in London – the local paper editor organising his staff to help me and setting a network in motion, making me feel so cared for and reassured.

Malcolm had asked for my mother's full name and description and made a rapid-fire call to reception, instructing Grace to put the word around.

'It's like the bush telegraph down there,' he told me. 'The tom toms will beat out around the teashops and nail bars of Northstone and your mother will be returned!' He laughed wryly. 'If it were my mother, I'd be thanking my lucky stars and changing the locks.'

'How old's she?' I asked, surprised. I hadn't imagined Malcolm with parents.

'Ninety bloody six. Spent all my inheritance on nursing home fees years ago and steadfastly refuses to die.'

'And is she still – compos mentis?' I asked, amused.

'Runs the place with a rod of iron. God help those poor little girls if they're late with her gin.'

'How often do you see her?' I was now fascinated. Malcolm was already bored.

'First Saturday of every month. Duty visit at Christmas. Let's talk about your mother instead.' He took a mouthful from his own cup. 'If we have to talk about relatives at all.'

Gabriel put his head around the door. 'I've reported it to the police and given them your mobile number – told them she was vulnerable – and I've called the hospital. Nobody's been brought in of that description.'

He looked at me kindly. 'Try not to worry. I'm sure she'll turn up. Perhaps she's just shopping–'

'Yes, thank you!' Malcolm interrupted. 'Now see what you can do about finding some news to fill my paper.'

'There's been two more break-ins up near the recreation ground.'

'Good,' said Malcolm encouragingly.

'Both of them,' Gabriel inserted a small pause during which Malcolm narrowed his eyes, 'in houses belonging to DFLs.'

Malcolm raised his eyebrows. 'And your point is?'

'Well, that they're still being targeted.'

'Or,' said Malcolm, with exaggerated patience, 'it could just be that those who've moved here from the smoke are the ones with the flash cars outside, and the freshly painted front doors, and that says to Johnny Burglar – here's a flat screen TV and a few laptops for the picking!'

'Yes, but–'

'And aren't they semis up there?'

'Yes, but I—'

'Statistically, semis are twice as likely to be burgled as any other category of housing. Figures released last month.' Malcolm paused too, clearly pleased with himself. 'Though why they haven't got alarms, Lord only knows.'

'One of them did but the owners were away and the neighbours thought it was faulty.' Gabriel spoke quickly, finally managing to get a sentence out.

'Excellent! You can run me off a nice little piece on how there's no community spirit anymore and we're all afflicted by apathy. Burglary on the increase. A spate of them right here in Northstone and you could be next. Frighten the buggers.' He looked at Gabriel over the top of his reading glasses and snorted. 'Even you can manage that.'

'You're really not very nice to him,' I said, when Gabriel had gone.

'He'll be glad of it one day,' replied Malcolm tersely. He looked at his watch. 'It's nearly half-past eleven – if you want to hang on for an hour or so, I'll buy you a restorative lunch.'

'Oh God,' I jumped up guiltily. 'I had no idea. I've left Jinni at home holding the fort in case my mother turns back up.' I put my coffee cup down and grabbed my jacket.

'You've been so lovely,' I said. 'Thank you so much for all your help.'

As he stood up too, I leaned forward and kissed his cheek. He cleared his throat, looking both pleased and startled. 'Think everything of it,' he said gruffly.

I smiled. 'I'll email soon with a date for toad-in-the-hole.'

Malcolm visibly brightened. 'Food of the Gods.'

'Unless you'd prefer slow-cooked pork shoulder,' I suggested, 'or lamb hotpot. Or I do a mean beef cooked in Guinness?'

For a moment Malcolm appeared to be lost in reverie. Then he beamed at me, his voice newly animated. 'Can you do steak and kidney pud?'

I thanked Grace profusely on the way out. She looked at me strangely. Maybe she wasn't used to anyone showing appreciation – perhaps Malcolm barked at her in the same manner as he addressed Gabriel.

I felt a real affection for him as I thought about his kindness this morning. Underneath that crusty exterior there beat a soft heart. I felt guilty I hadn't stopped to thank Gabriel once more but had simply waved and blown him a kiss as I'd rushed from the room.

My guilt increased as I raced home. For a moment or two there, chatting to Malcolm, I had forgotten my mother rudderless in deepest Northstone, possibly confused and unable to remember the way home. I calculated she'd now been gone for a minimum of three hours and probably a lot longer than that.

I sent Jinni a text as I stopped by the pub to catch my breath – telling her I'd be home in five minutes. My heart beat faster as I strode on, knowing Gerald would be arriving soon to collect my mother and I'd have to tell him I hadn't got a clue where she was.

But Gerald was there already, sitting at my kitchen table, in his usual tweedy jacket and tie, drinking tea and appearing engrossed in Jinni's account of insulating her extensive lofts. He stood up when I appeared gasping in the doorway, eyes questioning under his shock of silver hair. I shook my head as Gerald came forward to embrace me, nodding with his familiar air of stoicism.

'Oh dear,' he said.

'Your boss phoned,' put in Jinni. 'I told him to give you a break cos there was a crisis.'

When we'd packed Jinni off to finish her attic manoeuvres – promising to call her when there was news – and I'd made Gerald more tea and a cheese and pickle sandwich, I sat down opposite him and looked into his solid, capable face and saw how weary he looked around the eyes. 'How long have you known?' I asked.

He gazed back, sadly. 'I think it was a little while before she did,' he said. 'I knew something wasn't right when she kept seeing things.'

It had begun with the dawn awakenings and squirrels on top of the wardrobe.

'She's always been a one for her dreams,' he told me. 'And I said: you're imagining it, Flora.' He shook his head. 'But then she kept saying odd things and she was forgetting all sorts. And you know your mum usually. Mind like a steel trap.' He gave a little chuckle and then looked serious again. 'Didn't want to go to the doctor, didn't want Mo to know–' He shook his head again. 'But Mo's no fool either – she'd started helping with the housework by then.'

We looked at each other, both knowing the significance of my mother accepting any sort of assistance with the cleaning.

'Why didn't you tell me?'

'She made us promise. And we were managing. So we were

waiting for you to visit. I was trying to persuade her to talk to the doctor – in case there were tablets that could help – when she had that turn and went to hospital. Then they found it.'

Gerald gave a deep sigh. 'Poor Flora.'

Fear gripped me. 'I wonder how it's going to–'

'I've told her, we'll just get on with it.' Gerald interrupted me firmly. 'I told her a long time ago I'd always look after her if she'd let me and I meant it.'

'That's so good of you.' I got up and refilled the kettle, so he wouldn't see me cry.

'I told her I'd still marry her tomorrow.'

I flicked the switch, swallowed and sat down again. 'What did she say?'

'Told me not to be so soft.'

I laughed, then saw the pain in his eyes. I leant across the table and squeezed his arm. 'She's very lucky to have you,' I said.

He shook his head, seeming unable to speak. 'I never thought it would happen to her,' he said eventually. 'And I don't know how she's going to bear it.'

An hour ticked by. A policewoman called my mobile, wanting to know what my mother was wearing and sounding faintly disapproving when I said I didn't know.

I'd done another search of the bedroom and could only establish that she didn't have yesterday's clothes on but I wasn't sure what else she'd brought with her. It was quite a big case. I said I didn't think she had any money with her and – since

I'd found it in the bathroom – she wasn't wearing a watch. The policewoman rang off.

Gabriel called to see if we'd found her and if there was anything he could do to help. And Malcolm sent an email to say he was looking forward to sampling my cooking, adding: 'PS hope you got your missing person back.'

Gerald shifted restlessly at my kitchen table rustling the newspaper. 'She's not done this one before,' he said, for the third time. 'I think I'll take another drive around.'

'Don't you get lost too,' I told him. 'We don't want to send a search party for the search party.'

I was twitchy too. I snapped the lid of my laptop shut and went into the garden, breathing in the sharp air and crouching down to peer into the murky depths of my pond.

This was going to be one of my summer projects. Now it was clogged with leaves and slimy fronds of rotting lily. Any tadpoles from the single pile of spawn I'd spotted at the end of February were keeping themselves well-hidden. I scooped some leaves out with my hands – the water was freezing – and jumped as what looked like a large woodlouse straggled wetly across my palm.

'Ugh!' I threw the leaves and bug onto one of the weed-choked flower beds, and then jumped up as the unmistakable sound of the bell chimed faintly from beyond the open back door.

I ran inside, wiping my grimy fingers on my jeans, and shot through the kitchen and across the sitting room.

'Hold on, I'm here,' I cried, tugging the solid wooden door open, my heart beginning to pound as a split-second film reel of possibilities flitted across my imagination. Gerald back already? My mother calmly returned, wondering what all the fuss was about, a solemn uniformed duo, bracing themselves to break the bad news and then make tea. They always came in pairs when there'd been a fatality. I gasped as I registered there were indeed two figures on my doorstep.

'OH!'

One was my daughter with a wheelie case, looking less than pleased at the delay in being admitted and the sight of my shocked face.

The other was shorter and squatter. Good God!

'Hello, Tess, I hope this is okay,' he said uncertainly, looking from me to Tilly.

'Of course, it is.' Tilly stepped into the house and fixed me with a defiantly bright smile.

'You don't mind Daddy coming to stay, do you?'

Chapter 21

'What the hell are you doing?' I hissed at Tilly in the kitchen, as she got cups from the cupboard and started putting biscuits on a plate.

'I thought it would be nice for him to see Granny,' my daughter said, not looking at me, 'and I wanted to see her too.'

I glared at her. The last bit I believed – Tilly had always loved her grandmother. But Rob and his mother-in-law had regarded each other with tolerance at best – my mother viewing Rob as rather stolid and dull, and he finding her exhausting. I didn't know what my daughter was playing at but my ex-husband, looking a bit rounder and redder but every bit as annoying, was about as welcome as head lice.

'Well, she's not here,' I snarled. 'I woke up this morning and she'd disappeared!'

Tilly turned her head now and frowned. 'What?'

I let Gerald tell her. He'd returned to report no sightings, with the suggestion that we phoned Mo in case my mother had been in touch with her.

When Mo had repeated everything she'd said last time, I left Tilly listening wide-eyed to Gerald's account of my mother forgetting the word for acrylics after the art appreciation cruise, and Rob sitting on the sofa reading my *Guardian* with a pained expression, went upstairs, shut myself in my bathroom and breathed deeply.

I wanted Rob out and my mother back. It was hard to analyse my mass of conflicting feelings – an unreasonable rage at her for wandering off, a huge dollop of guilt for sleeping through it, fear at where she might be now and an over-whelming sadness and pity – but they were whipped up together with outraged disbelief that my daughter would pitch up with her bloody father in tow, today of all days. For fuck's sake! I felt nauseous from too much caffeine and eating only biscuits. Where the bloody hell was she?

I must have been flushing the loo when the doorbell rang the next time. I heard the voices from the landing, Tilly saying: 'Oh, Granny, you're not even dressed' and ran downstairs to find my mother standing in the middle of the sitting room with her coat and what looked like a man's jumper over her nightie.

She looked up and straight into my eyes. 'Oh, Tess,' she said, upset. 'Don't be cross with me.'

It was only as I hugged her that I saw who else was in the room, just inside the door, casually elegant in a green waxed jacket and boots, an embroidered purple scarf thrown loosely around her neck, looking very country woman about town.

'She's fine,' Ingrid said calmly. 'No harm done.'

'I am so grateful,' I told her, when my mother had gone to have a bath, and I was making yet more coffee and rather missing the subversive influence of Jinni, who would surely have pointed me in the direction of a large brandy instead. 'And Mum is too. As well as very embarrassed.'

It had taken some time to piece the story together, but it appeared my mother had woken early, convinced she had to get a plane urgently and, still in a dreamlike state, had gone into the town and got on a bus and travelled some considerable distance through the countryside and into another town before she realised she didn't know where she was.

So she'd got off the bus and gone to a café and bought a cup of tea – she'd 'packed' by putting bus pass, comb, lipstick and four pound coins into her pocket – and then got on another bus and off that and into another coffee shop where she'd sat reading their paper for a very long time, wondering what to do until the nice owner had asked her if she was okay.

My mother had not wanted to say she was lost and couldn't recall my phone number, so had simply asked where the bus stop to Northstone was, and another customer had shown her where to go and instructed the driver to tell her when she was there. 'I think they thought I was mad but harmless,' she said.

She'd eventually got back to the town, by which time she was hungry, so she went in a third tea place. When she undid her coat to see if there was any more money in the inside pocket they noticed she only had a nightie on. Someone asked her where she lived and she told them she was staying with me, who none of them had ever heard of, and couldn't remember the address.

They gave her a coffee on the house and were about to call the police, but when Ingrid – who had heard in the delicatessen I had a mother who'd scarpered – met her friend Marion in the street and got wind of a stray old lady tucking into a free teacake in her nightwear, she got there just in time to say she knew where I lived and would take care of it.

'Just lucky I happened along at the right time,' Ingrid said now, taking the cup from me and adding a tiny dash of milk, 'and had the car with me for a change.'

'It was very kind,' I said again. 'I'll thank the people in the coffee shop. Where did the jumper come from?'

'It's an old one I had in the boot,' said Ingrid. 'It belonged to David, I think.' I was silent for a moment, reminded of the back of his head going away from me. But Ingrid went on. 'She must have walked a long way, and got quite cold. But she strikes me as quite tough!'

I smiled. 'She is.'

'What precisely is her condition?'

I explained what I knew, and she nodded. 'You need to find out exactly,' she said, 'and then look after yourself. It's exhausting dealing with anything that affects mental health.' Her voice dropped. 'And it can be frightening too.'

I gazed at her and she looked steadily back.

'Do you?' I began awkwardly. 'Do you have someone in your family?'

'David's father was quite unstable. It wasn't easy when David was growing up. It's what's made him so successful now, though,' she went on. 'He became very driven. Work always comes first with David.'

'Oh!' I looked into my coffee cup and nodded at hers. 'Do you want a brandy in there?' I asked her.

Ingrid gave me a sudden smile and her face changed completely. It instantly reminded me of the way David lit up. She was still very attractive, with her good skin and lively eyes and she must once have been really beautiful. 'I don't suppose you've got a whisky?'

Rob appeared in the doorway as I was tipping us both generous measures, following my hand with a look I remembered well.

'I thought we'd go out to dinner,' he said heavily. 'Is there somewhere you particularly like? I'll make a booking ...'

I frowned, irritated. 'I don't know. I can't think at the moment – ask Tilly.'

Ingrid looked at him. 'There's a new French place – La Reine – opened behind the Co-op,' she said coolly. 'People say it's good.'

She turned to me. 'Did you enjoy the gallery opening?' she asked. Her expression was unreadable, but something in her tone made me wonder if she disapproved of David taking me out.

'Yes, it was lovely,' I said smiling.

Ingrid didn't smile back. 'Not really my sort of thing.'

When Rob had retreated back into the other room, and I'd distributed mugs, signalling to Tilly to leave us in peace, I sat on a stool, enjoying the glow as the alcohol hit the back of my throat.

'What a day,' I said to Ingrid, trying to fill the silence. She nodded.

'I'll wash the jumper and get it back to you,' I said.

'There's no need. As I said, it lives in the car.'

'I'm sorry we were interrupted just then,' I tried. 'I had no idea Rob was turning up today.'

Ingrid looked back at me, eyebrows raised. 'I've never clapped eyes on my ex-husband since the day he left.'

Lucky old Ingrid! I'd forgotten the all-pervading nature of Rob's presence. I'd reluctantly made up the sofa bed in the conservatory and he'd disappeared to survey it but I could feel his vibes from here.

I'd refused to go out. My mother was exhausted and it was obvious she needed to stay another night. Gerald went off to buy a toothbrush and I found him a t-shirt of Ben's and some jogging bottoms.

'I'll do spaghetti,' I told Tilly crossly. 'You can lay the table and then get back in here and tell me what's really going on. And why the hell you didn't ask me!'

'I did try to phone,' said Tilly, pulling forks out of the drawer.

'You didn't leave a message.' I countered. 'Because you knew damn well I'd say no.'

'And I just sort of mentioned it to Daddy, and he sort of jumped at it.' She busied herself clanking spoons. 'I don't think he wanted to spend the whole weekend in the hotel ...'

'Hotel?' Before I could grill her, the doorbell rang and she shot away.

'Hey!' She sounded jubilant. 'Fancy going to the Fox?'

Gabriel came through to the kitchen and hugged me. 'Am

so glad your mum's safe,' he said. 'Grace told us Ingrid had brought her home.'

'Oh God, I'm sorry – I should've let you know, it's been all go–'

'No worries. What happened?'

By the time I'd told the tale, Tilly had her jacket and shoes on. 'What about food?' I said, as she swung her handbag over her shoulder.

'I'll get something out.'

'Are you able to come for a drink later?' Gabriel looked at me sympathetically. 'I expect you can do with one after all that.'

'She's got Granny here – and my father!'

'A veritable houseful,' I said, pulling a face to Gabriel to indicate it had not been my doing.

Tilly had an arm through his. 'See you later!'

I was going to have serious words with my daughter, I fumed. Dumping her father on me and now waltzing off and leaving me stuck with him. Why wasn't she working? I was going to tell Rob in no uncertain terms that he needed to have a stern word with her about responsibility. If she'd chucked that job in and expected me to bail her out, she could think again.

But Rob got to me first. After we'd had supper, during which, I had to grudgingly admit, he was charming to my mother and kept up a stream of chat with Gerald about the implications of EU fishing rights in a post-Brexit world, which sounded exceptionally tedious but in which Gerald appeared enthralled, and I had cleared up and said good night to my mother (who was still apologising), and Gerald (who now looked as if he could sleep for three days), my ex-husband poured us both another glass of the red wine he had at least had the decency to go out and buy and announced he had something to say.

I sat down on the sofa opposite him, noticing he had commandeered the big chair and was sitting in it as if he owned the place, and wondered what was coming.

'We have to talk about Tilly,' he said importantly.

'I know,' I said shortly. 'She's not happy in her flat and wants to give up her job. I was hoping you'd speak to her.' I took a mouthful of wine. 'This is good. I like Fleurie.'

Rob looked at me as if I were a child who'd interrupted the teacher. 'Did you also know I've just paid off her credit card again?'

Again?

'Er no,' I said. 'I didn't know that.' I waited. Rob breathed heavily and flared both nostrils in the way he always did when about to express his disapproval. I felt a giggle rise inside me and shoved it down hard, arranging my features into a display of equal censure. 'But she always has had champagne tastes and beer money ...'

'It's not funny,' said Rob tightly. 'She's got to learn to budget and live within her means.'

'Yes, she has. I've told her that too. I'm not laughing at the debt, I'm not really. I just ...' I stopped, knowing Rob would not share my hilarity at the workings of his nasal passages. 'I feel slightly hysterical from the shock,' I offered. 'How much was it?'

'Three thousand pounds.'

I felt my jaw plummet. 'Three grand?' I squawked, my horror genuine now. 'What had she spent all that on?'

Rob raised his eyebrows. 'Living, she said. It was two last time.'

'But how could she? Especially for a second time. Didn't you make her promise? Cut up her card? She can't just be allowed to–'

Rob glared. 'Of course I did!'

'Well, she obviously didn't take much notice!' I shook my head in frustration. 'Because she knows you'll bail her out. Like you did when she was at drama school. I keep telling her she needs to go to work. She took far too much time off over Easter and then I suppose she couldn't pay the rent. I really thought YOU'D be the one to come down on her like a ton of bricks. You can't just keep–'

'Don't blame me!' Rob's voice rose. 'This isn't my fault, Tessa.'

I recognised the tone. 'Are you saying it's mine?'

Rob gave a martyred sigh. 'You do rather favour the boys–'

'What?' I swallowed another large mouthful of wine and tried not to spit it all over him. 'How can you say that? I treat them all exactly the same.'

Rob gave an infuriating, patronising smile and took another sip from his own glass. 'The problems arising from being the middle child is a well-documented phenomenon,' he intoned, while I slumped back and gawped. 'She feels she's never had as much attention or praise as her brothers.'

'Did she say that?' My annoyance deepened. Tilly had

always been able to wind Rob around her little finger, but this was pure manipulation.

'Not in so many words, but it's clear where the root of the trouble lies–'

'It's not "trouble",' I snapped back. 'Lots of young people on low incomes run up credit card debt trying to pay the bills. I'm not happy about it, but don't you tell me–'

'She feels she's failed,' Rob persisted. 'She wants to be an actress and instead she's serving up chips.' His face showed he didn't think much of it either. 'And you spend a lot of time saying how proud you are of Oliver and she feels–

'I'm proud of ALL of them,' I said hotly. 'And Oliver does work hard. Remember when he was a Christmas postman? He was up at–'

'And Ben upsets her with his personal comments.'

'Oh Rob, for God's sake.' I sloshed some more wine into my glass, grinding my teeth. 'She and Ben have always wound each other up. She has plenty to say to him too.'

'And–' noting his pointed expression, I leant over and gave Rob a refill too – 'they are *adults* ...'

Rob looked sceptical. Clearly Tilly had been laying it on with a trowel.

'And I don't think my sister helps, with her endless beauty advice ...' my one-time husband continued stuffily. 'She increases our daughter's inferiority complex.'

'What?' I was almost choking now. 'Caroline adores Tilly and she gives us all beauty tips. Tilly looked pretty pleased to me with the handfuls of freebies Caroline brought down ...'

'The fact is she feels in everybody's shadow. She's not academic like Oliver, or musical like Ben and let's face it, she was always a bit gawky, wasn't she? She was the tallest in her class.'

'So what?'

Rob looked at me once more as if I were particularly thick. 'That's difficult for a girl. You take it for granted – being pretty and small-boned. She told me she feels she lumbers about like an elephant next to you and Caroline. We should be trying to boost her self-esteem.'

I was stunned into silence, not knowing which was more startling. Rob's unlikely transformation into an expert on the female psyche or him paying me the first compliment I could remember in twenty-five years. Pretty and small-boned? I gave my thigh a surreptitious pinch, both to see if it had miraculously become lean and honed, and to check I wasn't dreaming.

He was still talking. Holding forth about how loving and caring Tilly was and how all he wanted was to see her settled and that he was convinced her overspending was a cry for help.

'Or it could be,' I put in, still needled by the way all my daughter's apparent, hitherto unchartered, areas of dysfunction were being laid at my door, 'simply the result of taking too much time off and having no cash.'

As I said it, I felt a small stab of remorse. Perhaps it had been horrible for Tilly to be in a flat with someone she no longer got on with, doing a job that wasn't at all what she wanted. Perhaps I hadn't listened enough, or shown enough understanding. Been too caught up with moving and work, and new friends and Fran and my mother, and that fucking Facebook page ...

'And she's been so supportive to me ...' Rob was saying.

I snapped back to the issue in front of me. 'What *are* you doing here? Tilly said something about a hotel–'

Rob drank some wine without meeting my eyes. 'It's nothing. Only for a few days ...'

'Has Fiona thrown you out?'

Now he shot me a look of irritation. 'We've agreed to have a short time apart.'

'Oh?' I raised my eyebrows.

'She's been in charge of a difficult project at work and there've been problems with the neighbours. We were going to be moving and then the offer on the house fell through. She's upset, that's all.'

There was a small silence. 'The stress has affected our relationship,' he finished stiffly.

I nodded, struggling once more to keep a straight face. There was something surreal about sitting opposite Rob, here, in my own house, discussing his domestics.

'Well, I hope it can be resolved,' I said nicely.

'She thinks I'm controlling,' he added in a sudden confessional burst.

I pressed my lips together and attempted to fix my look of polite concern. From the little I had gleaned about my ex-husband's new partner, she sounded terrifyingly in charge herself. Tilly had reported that the house was like a show home, with everything speck-free and folded to precision. Fiona had an Excel spreadsheet for her shopping list, used towels in strict rotation and was a devotee of leaf shine. She and Rob had always seemed a match made in heaven.

Rob was looking pained. 'We had a rather regrettable row over some book cataloguing.' There was a tiny pause. 'She was tired,' he finished.

'Oh dear,' I said, having a sudden flashback to one of Rob's seminars on the correct way to stack a dishwasher, and feeling a small frisson of sympathy for Fiona.

'Got almost aggressive,' he said with forced jollity.

I nodded. 'So you'll be going back to the hotel tomorrow, then,' I said firmly.

'I think Tilly thought Sunday,' Rob said casually. 'I said I'd buy her an outfit for her interview and I thought we could both spend some time with her, boosting her confidence ...'

A pang went through me. 'I didn't know she had an interview.'

'I thought a friend of yours arranged it.'

It was fair enough, I thought, as I boiled the water for some calming herbal tea and Rob opened another bottle of wine. If Tilly had seen her father and he'd been helping her out financially, it was only natural he should hear her news first. I tried not to mind. But I couldn't help thinking it would have been nice if she'd sent me a short text – just to say the friend of David's with the theatre company wanted to meet her – even if it was Rob she went to with her overdraft.

But I wouldn't make a thing of it – I was not going to give Rob the satisfaction of seeing that Tilly had wound me up, as she was so adept at doing.

After all, perhaps she simply wanted to tell me in person – as it had indeed been my new friend who'd brought it about – here I reflected fondly on David's dark curls and crinkly eyes and thought how good it would be if he could meet me this Sunday, and with the wine sloshing about my veins and clearly lowering my inhibitions, I even allowed myself a small vision of him coming back for coffee in my-then empty-again house and kissing me for rather longer than the previous peck. Of my suggesting we made ourselves comfortable on the sofa and then him leaning towards me, and saying ...

'Have you thought about double glazing?' Rob was in the kitchen doorway, handing me another glass. 'You've got quite a draught coming in that front bay.'

Chapter 22

I also, it transpired, had a leaky tap in the downstairs loo as well as the flushing problem (Aaron still hadn't shown), dodgy-looking electrics in the conservatory, some rendering to be patched up on the external back wall and guttering that needed attention.

By the time I was preparing to wave off my mother the next morning, I was cursing myself for not being assertive. His voice was drilling through the slight headache I had, and my nerves rattled with exasperation.

It had been a long evening, with Rob increasingly repetitive and maudlin as he'd climbed his way down the red wine, alternating as his top choices of sparkling conversation between what I should to do my house with what had gone wrong with him and Fiona.

I had drunk too much myself, as my dry mouth and thumping head had reminded me this morning when I'd been woken at 4 a.m. by the sound of my mother wandering the landing and Gerald gently, and at some length, persuading her back to bed.

I looked at the thinning hair on the back of ex-husband's

head as he followed Gerald outside with the bags. How the hell had I been talked into him staying another night?

'He's only trying to be helpful,' said Tilly defensively, after his latest observation about the state of the paintwork. 'Don't be so horrible.'

I was saved answering by my mother coming down the stairs. 'I do hope I haven't left anything behind,' she said. 'I have to keep checking where my handbag is ...'

'I'll check your room, Granny.' My daughter bounded up the stairs and my mother looked at me sadly. 'I'm sorry for all the worry I've caused.'

'It's fine, Mum.' I gave her a bright smile. Gerald looked tired this morning. I hoped he'd manage.

Tilly reappeared. 'There's nothing there or in the bathroom.'

My mother smiled. 'Thank you, lovey. Now where's that man gone?'

'I'll tell him you're ready.' Tilly ran fingers through her unbrushed hair and went out of the front door.

'There's no need to come to this doctor's with me,' my mother said. 'Gerald will take me. You're too busy.'

'I want to support you,' I told her. *I need to know what we can expect and how soon* ... 'I want to hear what he has to say ...'

'Well, we'll see.' My mother looked anxiously around the room. 'We don't want to go mob-handed ...'

'Let me know when you get the date through.'

We stood awkwardly for a moment until the others came back in. 'David's over the road ...' said Tilly.

My solar plexus gave a jolt. 'Oh! Is he coming in?'

'Dunno. He's talking to Jinni. I waved but I didn't want to go over like this.' My daughter indicated the pyjama bottoms she was still wearing beneath one of Ben's sweatshirts and laughed. 'And she's probably having a go at him ...'

'We should get going.' My mother had her hand on Gerald's arm. We all trooped outside. David's empty car was still parked opposite. There was no sign of Jinni.

Eventually they were gone, amid a last minute flurry over imagined forgotten items and assertions from Gerald that he would look after her. I waved with relief and unease.

Then I hurried back into the house, not wanting to be seen staring at the empty vehicle, thinking pain-killers and strong coffee.

Was David in there with Jinni? She clearly hadn't been so quick to tell him to sling his hook this time ...

'Just what I need too!' said Rob, as I rinsed out the cafetière.

'Ask Tilly to get some more milk, then ...' I held up the last quarter inch in the bottom of the carton.

'Why don't you keep more in the freezer?' said Tilly, appearing in the doorway. 'Like you used to?'

'I do,' I said shortly. 'One of you got it out and didn't replace it.' I glared at her. 'I don't even drink the bloody stuff!'

Rob frowned. 'Go on, Tilly.'

She changed and went immediately, since Rob had asked, and came back some time later with biscuits and *Hello* maga-zine and the news that Jinni was going away for two days.

'She's got some voice-over work on Monday,' Tilly told me. 'Said the money was too good to turn down, but she's going to London today to see some friends.' Tilly grinned. 'Said she was on a promise. She wants us to keep an eye on the house. She'll be back Monday night.'

She poured herself a coffee, added milk and unwrapped the chocolate cookies. 'What time are we going, Dad?' she said, flicking open her magazine.

Rob had agreed to drive her to Angel Village, a designer outlet shopping centre twenty miles away and frankly I couldn't wait.

Rob looked at the clock. 'In thirteen minutes,' he said.

What sort of promise?

I walked into the front room, narrowly avoiding tripping over the waist-swivelling thing, and collected mugs. David's car had gone.

'I'm surprised she didn't come over and tell me herself,' I said, opening the dishwasher.

Tilly got another biscuit from the pack. 'She was in a rush ...'

Now I came to think about it, Jinni had only sent the briefest **'good'** by text when I'd let her know Ingrid had found my mother.

'We agreed 11.30 last night,' Rob added.

'And you expect her to remember that?' I jerked my head at Tilly, who was still munching. I was trying to be supportive but I still felt furious with her for producing her father and not bothering to tell me what was going on in her life, but as usual she had managed to dismiss my objections with a flick of her hand. She'd rolled in from her evening out, flushed and happy, assuring me she'd been just about to talk about her job opportunity but had been sidetracked by 'the crisis with Granny' and then Gabriel arriving.

Rob gave me a look. 'We really will go out to dinner tonight,' he said in jovial tones as he methodically patted his pockets for wallet and keys. 'You book somewhere nice.'

'Tilly can,' I said tersely. Rob had always had a habit of addressing me as if I were his secretary. Even if he didn't look at my legs in quite the same way.

'Ingrid says there's a new French place,' I told my daughter. 'Look it up on your phone while Dad's driving.'

She nodded. 'Gabriel could come with us?' she said hopefully. 'He said to send you his love and he'd see you soon.'

'Ask your father.'

Gabriel was delightful, but I'd rather the three of them went on their own. When Tilly and Rob had finally departed, somewhat over-schedule at 11.42, after Tilly had mislaid her phone, and Rob had stood by the front door twitching, I stomped through to the kitchen, where the breakfast things were still piled up on the counter, filled the dishwasher, kicked the washing machine and went upstairs to strip the spare bed.

David probably hadn't come in because he'd seen Gerald's car and thought I was busy ...

As my eyes flicked towards my laptop I wondered if he'd emailed me the spec for his job. I was keen to do the work – now I was feeding the five thousand and my house was falling down – and it would provide a good reason to get in touch.

But there were only the usual shopping offers, an anxious memo from Paul about a meeting on Tuesday and a missive from Caroline with the link to a potion that would magically thicken my eyelashes, of which she had procured me a sample.

David had promised to make an effort with Jinni – that's why Tilly had seen him brokering peace talks.

He could have put his head around the door …

I remembered him leaving after giving me the jigsaw, the way he'd waved a hand without glancing back. Perhaps the suggestion of a drink had been a nicety. Maybe when he'd copped another look at me in daylight (had I been wearing make-up? Unlikely), he'd rather changed his mind.

I was still dithering about whether to text him when the doorbell rang. I rushed to the mirror and tried to smooth my hair, grabbing at a lipstick and scrabbling in my handbag for my tube of tinted moisturiser or anything that would make me look less dishevelled and knackered.

As I rubbed a stray blob of make-up into my chin I recalled the optician telling me that over the age of 45 more than ninety per cent of people needed reading glasses. If I got up close enough, all my imperfections should blur before David's eyes. 'Coming!' I yelled, heart thumping, as the doorbell rang again.

'I was beginning to think you were out.' Malcolm thrust two huge carriers at me and gave me a keen look. 'Or are you about to be?'

'Er no, not right now.' I said looking at the bulging bags, which appeared to be full of vegetables. 'What are these?'

'Got called into the doctor's for a cholesterol test this time,' Malcolm's disgust was palpable. 'Nurse said I should be on the Mediterranean diet, whatever that's supposed to be. Made the mistake of mentioning it to Vera and she brought all this round.' He shook his head. 'I thought you could use it as you have all these relatives coming and going–' he looked around him as if he expected a herd of them to come stampeding down the stairs. 'Then we could go out to lunch?' Malcolm looked hopeful. I peered into the bags. I could see celery and tomatoes and avocados and a bag of baby leaf spinach.

'Is Vera your–?' I paused, remembering the wife who'd died and the wife who'd left him '–friend?'

'No,' said Malcolm emphatically. 'She just likes interfering.' He carried the bags through to the kitchen and dumped them on the work surface. 'What is one meant to do with this?' He pulled out an artichoke.

'They're quite nice braised,' I began. 'And there's a salad you can make with mint and–'

'Sounds deeply unappealing,' Malcolm interrupted. 'There's rather a good pub on the way to Bridgeford. Does an excellent chicken and bacon pie, shall we–?'

'We can make lunch from some of this,' I said, laying out asparagus and red peppers, suddenly cheered by the thought of a bit of jolly banter. 'It would be much better for you.' I pointed to a tin of sardines. 'Oily fish – full of omegas to protect your heart.'

'Don't you start!'

'We'll mash it up with a bit of crème fraîche and lemon juice. And have it with toast,' I added, as Malcolm looked doubtful. He brightened. 'And a big crunchy raw veg salad,' I added firmly. 'You can start chopping!'

I handed him an apron – suppressing a smile at the sight of his large frame in my cramped kitchen.

'This knife's blunt,' he said, halfway through slicing an onion.

'I know. They all are. I keep meaning to–'

'Where's your sharpener?'

'I think it's in a box of God-knows-what I haven't unpacked yet. In that cupboard. Mind the–'

I laughed as the handle came off in Malcolm's hand. 'The whole bloody kitchen is falling apart. I am planning a new one.'

'The place at the top of the High Street is well thought of. Eric's one of our advertisers – I can probably get you a discount. They do the usual free designs–'

'I've done one already. I used to plan kitchens for a living!' I smiled as Malcolm raised his eyebrows. 'What I could do with is a trade deal on the units and the name of a decent fitter.'

'Can't your friend David help with that?' There was a very slight edge to the word 'friend', which I decided to ignore. 'Don't know, not seen him lately,' I said lightly.

'I'll have a word with Eric and email you,' said Malcolm briskly.

I rummaged in the box and handed him the sharpening block.

'You seem so part of it all here – do you ever miss London?'

'Never. It's why I took the job here – I'd had enough of the noise and the traffic and all those bodies on the tube. I wanted some air and some green.'

He began to expertly whet my largest knife. 'And the doctor said I was killing myself'.

'Were you really drinking a lot?'

'An obscene amount. That's what it was like then.'

'So you don't feel guilty about being a DFL?'

'Certainly not.'

He gave a sudden shout of laughter. 'Do you ever read Marina O'Loughlin in the *Sunday Times*? Writes about a lot of poncey restaurants with a reduction of this and an infusion of that, but when I first came across her she was living in Whitstable. When the DFLs came under fire, she wrote a great rebuttal. Said if it wasn't for people like her buying up unwanted properties, then Whitstable would be 'just another downtrodden British seaside town that smelled of wee' – got all sorts of abuse for it.' He laughed heartily. 'Top woman!'

'Were you still married when you got first got here?' I enquired as I blended olive oil and vinegar for a dressing.

'Second one was here for a few weeks. Before she went back to town with Matilda, or whatever her name was. Terrifying creature. Had been some sort of boxing champion – badminton was the least of it.'

He was pulling other knives out of drawers and honing them too.

'What did your first wife die of?' I said, hesitantly as I took one of the freshly sharpened implements and began slicing through tomatoes. 'Oh, thank you – that's better.'

'She had a heart condition. It got her before she had time to divorce me.'

'Really?' I said casually – longing to know more but not wanting to appear as if I were interrogating him.

'We were too young to get married.' He pulled a wry face.

'The sad truth is I was drunk when I proposed. And she seemed so pleased I didn't have the heart to disappoint her in the morning.'

There was a brief moment when he looked almost sad. Then he

grinned at me. 'What was your excuse?'

By the time I was putting the last spoonful of sardine pâté – which Malcolm was eating with surprising enthusiasm – onto his plate and we were finishing off the salad – still viewed with some suspicion – and we'd swapped potted life histories, I really felt we were friends.

When he got up to leave, we'd had our second coffee and I was laughing at a story from his early days as a reporter when he was sent out to doorstep a suspected conman and got a bucket of water thrown over him.

'At least I hoped it was water – one really didn't want to dwell on what it smelled like–'

'Ugh!'

He was reaching for his jacket. 'Thank you for that unexpectedly palatable lunch,' he said. 'I shall buy you dinner next time in gratitude.'

He took one of my hands in both of his as we stood in the doorway. His eyes looked very blue and I almost found myself wishing he'd stay longer. He paused as if wondering whether to say something, then spoke briskly.

'Have a splendid evening, whatever you're doing.'

I pulled a face. 'It'll be a bundle of laughs, I'm sure. I'm out with the ex.'

Chapter 23

Ben once told me about a breathalyser gadget you attach to your computer. If it decides you're pissed, it doesn't let you online. So you can't shop, gamble, post naked photographs or send messages that are ill-advised.

I need one fitted to my phone.

I was not going to have any alcohol on Saturday night. By the time Rob and Tilly returned from their shopping trip – Tilly with several carrier bags and Rob a haunted expression – I really didn't want to go out at all. I'd had a small doze on the sofa after Malcolm had left and could now feel one of those evening hangovers setting in and knew what was needed was camomile tea, toast and Marmite and an early night.

Rob and Tilly, however, seemed set on an evening out with bells on – even if Gabriel had to be elsewhere. Both looked aghast when I said I was fragile.

'Still?' frowned my ex-husband. 'You didn't drink that much,' he added disapprovingly.

This meant I hadn't drunk as much as he – who has never admitted to a wine-induced after-effect in his entire life – had, and if he were okay, then so should I be.

Tilly, keen to show me her new shoes – vastly reduced in the sale – new jacket – twenty-five per cent less than she'd have paid in London – and new jeans, 'I did need some more, and while they were so cheap ...' was not remotely interested in my faint feelings of nausea and simply informed me the table was booked for 8 p.m. and I'd be fine once I'd had a cocktail.

'And we got this!' she said, holding up a funny little shrunken jumper in a rather alarming blue. Behind her Rob raised his eyebrows.

'Wonderful!' I cried. 'I'm so proud of you.'

Tilly looked startled. 'You see,' I went on meaningfully, pulling her into an embrace and scowling at my ex over her shoulder. 'That's what you've got that your brothers both lack. An eye for a bargain ...'

She shrugged away from me. 'You're being really weird, Mum. You definitely need a drink.'

The French restaurant was nice, a dry Martini immediately made me feel better, and for a while I felt myself brighten up. I even felt a certain limited benevolence towards Rob who, after all, was the father of my children and who, though it all seemed rather woolly now, like the sort of dream that goes round in circles before one wakes with indigestion, I had spent some twenty years of my life disappointing.

He was doing his best to be a good host, being solicitous to my needs, guffawing at his own jokes, and saying the right sort of things to Tilly about striving and effort and the best things being worth waiting for.

'It was very tiring for your mother, going back to work when she had three of you,' he informed her. 'But if she hadn't done it, then, she wouldn't be where she is now.'

Tilly had glazed over, more interested in the mayonnaise she was spooning onto her plate, but Rob was oblivious. 'She had a career plan,' he said, 'and she followed it.'

The way I remembered it, it was a case of having a large hole in the roof at the same time as we discovered the dry rot in the upstairs windows, and I wasn't aware I had a 'career' now, but I nodded. If Rob wanted Tilly to believe my scintillating years as a hastily trained kitchen planner for one his clients, had all been part of a grand scheme, then so be it.

We'd gloss over the fact that I'd just managed to escape kitchens and was building up a nice little business that was both creative and potentially lucrative when he announced he had to 'find himself' (aka spend six months shagging the girl on reception) and forced me into the joys of office fittings to keep three stroppy teenagers in lipstick and bacon.

'And we really needed the money,' I put in, to remind her that in our day there was no father with a cheque book roaring to the rescue.

Tilly gave us both a tolerant smile. 'These frites are amazing.'

All the food was good but as the evening wore on and Rob began to reminisce about family holidays when the children were small, I found myself zoning out and thinking about David. His eyes on my face, the way he'd slung his arm around my shoulders at the gallery, as if ...

I should have been more sparkling, made more jokes.

Apologised more for having to leave abruptly. But he'd said he wanted to do it again ...

I shook myself. This was mad. I didn't even like him when I first met him. Jinni said he dyed his eyebrows ...

But then Jinni said all sorts of things.

I recalled calling after him as he walked away and gave a small involuntary cringe. Rob's head shot forward.

'Are you cold?' I felt his hand clamp down on my knee under the table. I jerked it away, banging my shin on the table leg.

'I'm tired,' I said glaring.

'Let's have a port with the cheese.'

Was it something in the Northstone water? Jinni necked back port, now Rob was ordering me a large tawny. It was rich and warming and I felt myself relax again and my spirits rise a little. I would text David after all and suggest tomorrow evening ...

Rob was chortling over the time Oliver fell off the side of the jetty at Broadstairs and around us tables were clearing. 'It wasn't all bad, was it?' he said, when Tilly had gone to the loo. 'We did have some good times with the kids?' He leant out as if to take my hand. I ignored it.

'Of course. We just grew apart – as they say ...'

I didn't add: *particularly after you tried to get your leg over the woman down the road who was only in our house to buy a distressed set of drawers and a hand-painted watering can from ME* as I didn't think he knew I knew that and Tilly would kick off if I soured the evening.

I nodded at the waiter who'd been hovering. 'Can we get the bill?'

228

I walked behind them both on the way home, mentally composing a short, bright message. Jinni's house was in darkness.

While the kettle was boiling, I tapped it out. **'Hope you are having a good weekend. How about a drink tomorrow evening? Tess x'** And then, in a spirit of wild abandon, I added another **x** and pressed the button before I could change my mind.

I made lemon tea for me and Tilly and poured out the last remaining port from the bottle Jinni had brought, for Rob, who'd now got a taste for it. He was in the biggest chair again, Tilly was sprawled on the sofa. They were laughing at the way Rob used to shout at Ben for never shutting the garage when he got his bike out and the day he'd dragged him out of bed at 6 a.m. when the door had been banging all night in the wind. 'What a terrible father I was,' declared Rob happily, as my phone pinged.

I hurried back into the kitchen to retrieve it.

'Sorry. Away til Monday.'

Disappointment rolled over me. No suggestion of an alternative date. No kiss. Away until Monday. Like Jinni.

I fought paranoia and tears. Jinni didn't like David. David said she was mad. It was a coincidence, nothing more or less. But he could have sent a x ...

'Oh dear,' Rob was in the doorway. 'Is this my doing? Talking about the past?' He put a clumsy arm around my shoulders. 'You'll always be special to me, Tess.' His other hand was still holding his glass. He stretched out and put it down. Then tried to pull me to him. 'We were married for many terrific years and we have three wonderful children ...'

I shoved him off. 'It's not that—'

Now Tilly was also in the room. 'What's up, Mum?'

I sensed Rob mouthing something at her.

'Oh!' Tilly was pouring more hot water into her mug. 'A bit strong ...'

I assumed she was talking about the tea but gave a high-pitched, slightly hysterical, laugh to allay any fears.

'I'm just tired and over-emotional,' I cried, shaking my head wildly. 'It's all that port ...' My daughter and ex-husband were both looking at me quizzically. I saw Tilly's eyes travel to the phone in my hand.

'And the situation with Granny,' I improvised.

Tilly scooped out her teabag, nudging opening the cupboard that housed the bin with her foot. She looked back at me with raised eyebrows. 'If you're that upset,' she said wickedly, 'you could always get back together.'

Chapter 24

'My brother is such a plank,' Caroline laughed again. 'Trust him to think you were looking distraught over HIM!'

I gave a mock shudder. 'Can you imagine us remarried? I cooked breakfast on Sunday morning and he was practically following me round the kitchen, telling me how to do it.'

'Oh, he's always like that!' Caroline rolled her eyes. 'Last time he came to my place he said I'd cut the lemon for his gin in the wrong direction. I told him to just bloody drink it. Or choke.'

She stopped smiling and frowned. 'But why *were* you so upset?' She scrutinised me for a moment more. 'I thought there was something wrong when you got here. Are you really that keen on David?'

'No, not really. Well, sort of. I have been thinking ... And I suppose I was just feeling–'

Caroline put up a hand to stop me and got off her bar stool. 'Those people are leaving!'

She strode over to a booth in the corner and put her glass down. 'Sit there,' she commanded, then waved to a waitress.

'We need a bottle of the Macon,' she told her, 'and some water and olives, please.'

'I'm not sure I can drink that much,' I squeaked as the girl departed. 'I worked all through lunch.'

'And some of those breadsticks?' Caroline added, as the wine arrived. 'Now–' she poured two generous glasses and sat back and surveyed me. 'Tell me all of it.'

I recapped on the jigsaw visit and the agreement we'd have another drink and then my text and his less-than-expansive reply. I explained – haltingly, and with frequent sips at wine because I felt so silly – that I'd had a restless night and when I'd finally said goodbye to Tilly and Rob, I'd done a lot of therapeutic housework (here Caroline, with her long-serving Filipina cleaner, looked perplexed) and got the place straight again and then composed a business-like email, not mentioning meeting him, but thanking him again for the contact he'd given Tilly, and enquiring whether he still wanted me to look at his show flat, as I'd need to schedule it in, if so.

'And I didn't send it till Monday morning, so it would look as though it were simply part of my working day, and I didn't say anything about him going into Jinni's house so I wouldn't sound like a mad stalker!' I finished.

Caroline's eyebrows shot up. 'What's that?'

I took a gulp of wine now. And explained about Tilly seeing them. Adding that I'd waited all week, but David hadn't replied to me, and there was still no sign of life at Jinni's either ...

'I know I'm being stupid,' I finished, embarrassed. 'They don't even like each other ...'

I stopped, waiting for Caroline to agree that I'd been adding

two and two and making twenty-seven. Instead, she got a
Chanel lipstick out of her handbag, and a small shiny mirror
and carefully repainted her beautifully shaped lips and turned
her green eyes on me thoughtfully.

'I wasn't going to tell you until I'd seen how things
progressed,' she said. 'But you might not be imagining things
after all ...'

My stomach gave a horrible lurch as Caroline poured me
another drink. The night I'd gone out with David, she'd taken
the flowers over to Jinni as Tilly was still getting ready, and
ended up staying for a drink. 'Jinni seemed to want to talk
to me,' Caroline said, 'and I liked her. Although, my goodness,
the state of her hands. All that building work she does herself!'

'She needs to keep the costs down,' I said faintly, wondering
what was coming.

'And she seemed very fond of you ...'

Caroline took a small sip of her wine. 'But she was quite
disturbed about you going out with David. Said he was only
doing it to get at her.'

'She really *is* paranoid,' I put in. 'She thinks he and his
mother are plotting against her, but Ingrid protests against
everything – it's not personal – and he's only irritated because
Jinni's been objecting to –'

'Did he also tell you they'd slept together?'

I stared. 'I'm sorry,' she said, looking at my shocked face.
'Have a breadstick, darling.' She pushed them towards me.
My hands were trembling as I took one.

'I guessed they had some sort of history,' Caroline went
on. 'She was too agitated, going on about how he was a

narcissist who wasn't to be trusted and I should warn you off. She cared too much for it to be just a planning issue.'

'And she told you they had?' I laid the breadstick down on the table, uneaten. 'Why's she never said anything to me?'

'I asked her outright. I think she's embarrassed about it.'

'And they're still—?'

'She said not. Said it was over very quickly.' Caroline pulled a wry face. 'I think drink had been taken and Jinni was simply wanting a shag, to be honest, darling, but if he didn't hang around—'

Caroline reached across the table and laid a hand on my arm. 'This is why I worry. You're not like me, darling – you want romance and commitment.' Caroline looked as if she were talking about strange animal parts she wouldn't want to eat.

'In a way it doesn't matter what's going on with them. If he's the sort of personality I think he is, he'll break your heart.'

My mind was reeling. *I did like her when I first met her.* I'd believed him that they'd fallen out over planning applications. I'd believed both of them.

Caroline was still talking: 'It was all reasonable enough on one level. Jinni's after regular, uncomplicated sex and possibly some conversation over breakfast, not for them to stay all day. She's not looking for love or marriage or even the same time every week, but I expect her pride was a bit hurt if he didn't even stay for the coffee and toast.'

She picked up a breadstick and snapped it in half.

'It's nice if a chap makes a play of hardly being able to bear to part from you, even if he doesn't much care either. Jinni may say she thinks David is a smug, self-satisfied bastard, who she wouldn't cross the road to put out in a fire, but really she's worrying why he lost interest so quickly. Whether she isn't quite as good in the sack as she thought she was. Whether her bum is getting too big or her tits too saggy.'

'Did she tell you that?' I said, astonished.

'She didn't need to.' Caroline gave a small smile. 'We recognised each other.'

I looked back at her miserably. 'I feel such an idiot.'

'There's no reason to. How would you have known?'

'I wondered why you weren't encouraging me.' I felt suddenly annoyed. 'Why the hell didn't you tell me before?'

Caroline squeezed my arm again. 'I didn't see the point unless I had to. It was Jinni's story. I didn't want to make your friendship with her awkward. And you might have gone out with him just that once and never again.' Caroline looked at me appealingly, holding up her hands. 'I was hoping you wouldn't like him ...'

I was hoping too. My heart had been beating a little harder that morning as I'd walked onto Northstone station, in case he was waiting there. And despite feeling like a fool, a small part of me couldn't help it again this evening.

Even though the chances were that Sunday had gone so well with Jinni, they were making an entire week of it.

There was nobody I recognised on the platform. I leapt onto the train at 20.17 and found a seat at a table in the middle opposite a suited bloke hunched over his laptop. If David were here, he'd be down at the end.

Part of me wished I could see him, just to be sure. In case it had all been a mistake and really he was still gagging for me.

Yeah right.

David had gone to bed with Jinni. But he hadn't even got that far with me. He'd brought the jigsaw round and sounded keen by email before that. I must have looked pretty ghastly and been dreary that afternoon, while Jinni had appeared dramatic and alluring. She was always going to be a bigger catch than me, with her vibrant personality and exotic good looks. It was how it was.

The late spring evening had been warm in London but I felt cold. The bloke opposite kept sniffing. I hoped he'd get off before I felt compelled to hand him a tissue. I felt a bit sick and really tired. I shouldn't have let Caroline pour me so much wine when I hadn't eaten more than an apple and a flapjack all day. I could feel my eyes drooping.

My phone suddenly burst into life, making me jump. Sniffer's head came up abruptly too.

My daughter, as usual, was shouting over the noise of a bar. 'You know that Shane I met? I really liked him!'

I cupped my hand around the mouth end and tried to talk quietly. 'Oh good.'

'He might have some work for me.'

'Brilliant.'

'Beginning of June.'

'That's terrific.'

'You don't sound very pleased,' Tilly yelled.

'I'm on the train,' I muttered.

'WHAT???'

'I'M ON THE TRAIN.' I saw the couple on the other side of the aisle exchange glances and I squirmed. I dropped my voice again. 'I'll call you when I get home.'

I kept my head down and sent her a text. **'Fab news but not really hear as on train. Speak later. Xx'** As an afterthought I added: **'PS proud of you.'**

Thank you, Rob Freud-Jung-Bowlby-Proops, for your invaluable insight.

Tilly texted back an hour later as I was walking wearily down the road from the station in the fading light.

'Out now. Call tomorrow. Tell David he's awesome x'

Huh! She could have his email address and heap praise on him herself. I was delighted if David's intervention had brought Tilly the acting work she longed for.

But I wouldn't be seeing him again.

Chapter 25

I like living on my own!

In an effort to banish evil thoughts and fairytale notions, I had thrown myself into another cleaning frenzy and the house was now polished and shiny, fragrant and dust-free. I'd arranged the cushions Caroline had sent, bought flowers, hung a few more pictures and splashed out on another hideously expensive perfumed candle.

I did miss my children from time to time, but there was a certain appeal in the constant hot water, peace in which to work and coming home to rooms scented with the essence of fig and gardenia rather than late-night bacon and abandoned socks.

In addition to churning out plans round the clock, I'd been making the most of the light evenings and had cleared all sorts of stinky vegetation from the depths of the pond and started digging up the flowerbed that ran along the fence. Perhaps it was the physical activity that was helping me sleep better – my nightmares were rare now – and it was all serving to keep my mind off whatever was going on over the road.

Almost.

I knew Jinni was back because her windows were flung open and she was having a tree cut down. The sound of the electric saw sliced through the still afternoon and I could smell the sawdust and broken leaves hanging on the warm air as I walked down to the town. There was a truck parked on her gravel, the back filled with lopped-off branches. Clearly she had won the day over the preservation order!

She'd also sent me a text – **'am back see you soon thanks for keeping an eye'** – but she hadn't come the short distance over the road and knocked on the door.

I felt sad because I missed her, hurt she'd not been honest about why she was warning me off and a bit stupid and somewhat nauseous at the vision of her and David having unromantic, uncomplicated sex before he thoughtfully disappeared after breakfast.

I dragged my eyes away from the old rectory. I had other friends. Gabriel had sent me a chatty email asking how I was and Malcolm had sent one of his terse ones saying it must be time for another lunch. Fran was still threatening a night out; Nikki had theatre tickets for next week.

In the meantime, I'd organise the steak and kidney night, possibly inviting Gabriel along, especially if I did it on the weekend Ben was threatening to come home. Tilly had told me Gabriel was fed up that Malcolm still wasn't letting him do anything meaty, so maybe, away from the office, they could bond over the short crust (I was hoping Malcolm would show equal enthusiasm for a pie as for pudding; I always felt rather faint at the prospect of boiling suet).

I would say it was to thank them both for their kindness

and help when my mother had gone AWOL. Strictly speaking, I should invite Ingrid too, but she'd argue with Malcolm and I'd be embarrassed if the conversation turned to ...

I jumped as the phone rang. Tilly sounded buoyant. 'Shane called and I've got three days' work NEXT WEEK!'

'That's wonderful, what is it?'

'Something about bullying. I need school uniform.'

'What? Would it fit you?'

'Thank you, Mother!'

'I didn't mean it like that,' I said lamely, cursing myself for being insensitive, as Tilly rattled on.

The wonderful Shane, who had apparently gone to school with the equally sainted David (he had apparently referred to Tilly as 'striking', which had gone down extremely well) had a company doing what was known as Theatre in Education – TIE – and Tilly had been promised a part in the next production, which was touring schools after the May half-term. Now, however, one of the girls in the current play had got glandular fever and couldn't finish the last week of the run. Tilly had been sent the script and was to step in.

'As far as I can see, I just have to cry a lot,' she was saying, 'and tell one of the teacher's my life isn't worth living ... Anyway, they said they'll get the costume and I'll have to wear the same tie as the others, but actually, you know, the skirts and jumpers are navy blue so if I had my old stuff ... I haven't put on THAT much weight since I left school ...' She gave me a sharp look.

'Of course you haven't,' I said.

I'd wandered into the kitchen and turned the kettle on

while she was talking, but now found myself back at the front window looking at Jinni's place. Her front door was open.

I switched my attention back to my daughter. 'But aren't you quite old to play a school girl?'

'I told you! It's like that in TIE. Everyone's in their twenties. Well, Shane isn't. He's 41 ...'

I found I'd turned around again. The front door of the rectory had closed. As I gazed at the building, I saw the outline of what looked like Jinni cross an upstairs window. And behind her ...

It was over in a split second. It was a man, for sure, the right height probably. There was no car outside. But he'd probably left his car in a side road. Hoping I wouldn't notice him slide into the house. They wouldn't want to flaunt it in front of me, would they? Not when they couldn't stand the sight of each other.

My heart was pounding. My interest in David was over. What was I doing carrying out surveillance behind the curtains?

'Well?' My daughter was demanding in my ear. 'Do you think so, or not?'

I backed away from the window. 'Sorry, I ... Could you say that again, I didn't quite hear you, darling ...'

At the end of the line, there was a long growl of exasperation.

'Mum! You're not even listening!'

'I'm listening.'

Oliver was already waiting at a table under the awning

241

outside, when I hurried along the top concourse of St Pancras to the Betjeman Arms. He sounded uncharacteristically solemn when he called to arrange this and he looks very serious now.

Alarm runs through me although he's promised me neither of them are ill or have lost their jobs, or – I have now added this to the list of possible disasters in the light of the Tilly's credit card debacle – are deeply in debt.

It feels like a long time since I've seen him. It's probably my imagination but he already looks older. Oliver is taller and slighter than Ben, more studious-looking. He's always seemed more responsible than the other two but not as grave as this. I wonder anxiously if he's split up with Sam and hasn't wanted to tell me on the phone. And I will it not to be that. Sam is part of the family.

He hugs me and smiles, slightly self-consciously, it seems, as I sit down opposite him. We order beer and wine and water. He doesn't say anything else.

'Do you want to eat?' I ask him, as the waiter puts a menu down.

'Not yet. Maybe after.' His eyes slide away from mine. 'I want to talk to you first.'

My unease deepens. 'Go on,' I say.

My eldest son looks straight at me and appears to take a deep breath. 'Sam's pregnant,' he says. Adding slowly – as if I might not be familiar with this state of affairs, 'we're going to have a baby.'

In retrospect, I will realise I should have made the moment on St Pancras station memorable for my son. I should have shrieked. Or embraced him. Taken his hand and delivered some profound sentiments that expressed my unrivalled joy and pride. Not sat, mouth flapping like a goldfish, trying to paraphrase the mixed thoughts and emotions chasing across my mind, fuelled by the bewilderment in his eyes.

My lips open and shut a bit more as I try to form something congratulatory, bracing and maternal, which will demonstrate my unconditional love and unwavering support.

'Oh my God.'

'I know,' says Oliver. 'That's what I said.'

We order burgers to get us over the shock and while we are waiting for them, Oliver explains how, within mere days of missing a period – which she never, ever does – Sam had started feeling sick and so encouraged by her friend Gemma from the nursery, had taken a test, even though she knew she couldn't possibly be ... or thought she couldn't ...

'She phoned me at work. Just said to get home as early as I could,' Oliver tells me. 'She was looking so pale I was really scared. I thought she was going to say she had something terribly wrong with her.'

He swallows. 'I couldn't believe it. She hadn't even told me she thought she might be ...'

I nod in sympathy. 'Weren't you er ...?'

'Yes, she was on the pill, of course. The nurse at the doctor's said it happens.' Oliver looks uncomfortable. 'She asked if Sam had had sickness or diarrhoea in the last couple of months.'

I clap a hand to my mouth. 'Oh God,' I say again.

It is all the fault of my fish pie.

'I'm SO sorry. But,' I add hastily, 'it's lovely isn't it – a baby, imagine!'

I search his face for traces of joy, my insides wrenched with guilt. What had I been thinking of, dragging seafood home on the train?

Oliver shrugs ruefully. 'It's not very good timing, money-wise–'

I am ready with the platitudes for this one. 'Your grandmother always used to say that if everyone waited till they could afford a family, there'd be no babies born at all,' I tell him brightly and squeeze his arm. 'You've both got jobs and you'll be earning a lot more once you've finished your training and I'm sure Dad and I can help you. Sam's parents are always very generous, aren't they ...?'

I've never met them as Sam's father has some big job in Singapore, but I've spoken to her mother on the phone, who sounds very nice and I know they are comfortably off. Sam has some fabulous jewellery and they paid for the airline tickets and all sorts of trips when Oliver and Sam went out to visit.

He nods. 'Sam's already phoned them.' He gives his first small smile. 'They were pleased, apparently!'

'I am too,' I say immediately. 'It was just a surprise.' I grip his forearm even more tightly. 'Really, darling, I am thrilled to bits.'

I have a sudden picture of a tiny baby with a shock of dark hair, like Oliver himself when he was born.

'The thing is–' Oliver hesitates. 'We can't move into the

new flat now. We were about to sign, but we've had to let it go.'

'Oh.'

'We couldn't *really* afford it before, but we were going to economise and maybe get some evening jobs or something. But now, if Sam will be stopping work before the end of the year ... And we can't stay where we are. Sam's flatmate has already found someone new and everyone in mine got notice anyway. The landlord's selling.'

'Well maybe–' I want to tell him there'll be an answer – that now they are going to be parents there will be other options and assistance, but Oliver sweeps on.

'Sam's mum and dad have been great. They say we can live in their flat in Battersea. It sounds amazing – they bought it as an investment, but we can use it and just pay the running costs, they said. Until we can afford some rent.'

'Well, then, that's brilliant–'

'But it's got a tenant in it until the end of June. Sam's parents are over here in the first week of July and they say we'll sort it out then. In the meantime ...' Oliver stops, his eyes fixed on mine and suddenly he doesn't look older at all. I am already nodding as he asks.

'It will only be for a while, Mum, but can we come and live with you?'

Chapter 26

'It's only for a while.'

Tilly wasn't even asking but had phoned to tell me she'd got it all planned.

'Danni's mate wants to move in as soon as she can, and as I'm going to be away doing the schools run for at least four weeks, I may as well get out now. I'll be in digs weekdays anyway, so you'll only have to put up with me at weekends.'

'Are they paying you well?' I asked, hopefully.

'Not really,' my daughter said cheerfully. 'But it's what I want to do. I loved doing that bullying play and I cannot wait to finish at that bloody diner. I was there till one o'clock this morning. My feet are agony–'

'Well, make sure you leave on good terms,' I put in. 'In case you need to go back.'

'Thank you for your faith and positive attitude,' Tilly said huffily.

'You know I didn't mean–'

'And you won't make a fuss if Daddy brings me down, will you? I've got too much stuff for the train.'

'Where are you going to put it all? Oliver and Sam have got the spare room, of course–'

'And Ben might come in the car too as he's got no money again.'

Tilly sounded disapproving. I resisted the urge to point out that neither would she have if her father hadn't stepped in. And made a mental note to suggest that since Rob was so keen on all our children being treated equally, he might like to give a small hand-out to the boys too.

'So I thought I'd have the conservatory, if you've given them my room,' Tilly was saying, as if she were bestowing a major favour. 'And Ben can have the tiny one. He'll be going back on Monday.'

I shook my head. The double room had originally been Ben's if anyone's and I'd hardly be putting a pregnant Sam on a sofa bed.

'We've got Malcolm and Gabriel coming to eat on Sunday,' I said. 'I expect Gabriel told you.'

'Yeah – there's some amazing guitarist on at the Fox Saturday night, that's why Ben's coming.'

'Oh, not to see his poor old mum, then?'

Tilly laughed. 'That too – he'll have all his manky washing with him.'

'I expect you'll have yours too.'

'I will!' Tilly was shouting now as there was a fresh outburst of voices around her. 'I've got to go!'

'I'm making steak and kidney pie,' I shouted back. 'With pasta for Sam. You can have that too as you don't like kidney.'

There was more noise and her reply was lost.

'WHAT?'

'I said NO I CAN'T,' my daughter yelled just before we were cut off. 'I'M NOT DOING CARBS.'

I'd heard that one before, I thought, as I finished crimping the pastry round the edge of my largest pie dish and began to snip apart a mound of sausages. I'd decided to make a toad as well – Tilly could always hoik out the meat from the batter if she was still on her regime by this evening (never a given) – and do lots of vegetables. Then I'd thrown together a coq au vin too, mainly because I had half a bottle of wine left I didn't much like – it was one Rob bought – but was too parsimonious to pour down the sink. And I wanted to put on a good spread for Malcolm.

He had sounded almost rapturous about coming to eat, sending me quite long sentences by email and checking twice what time I wanted him to arrive.

A small, disloyal, part of me half-wished we'd be dining on our own. Not so long ago I'd have been over the moon to have all my children under my roof, but I'd sort of got used to the house tidy now. And quiet ... I couldn't remember the last time I'd had the place to myself.

As I was stirring, Sam appeared in the kitchen doorway, looking wan.

'You not feeling well again, sweetheart?' I said, as she rummaged in the cupboard and pulled out the peppermint tea. She gave me a weak smile. 'Not too bad.'

'I'll make you pasta with pesto and pine nuts, is that okay?'

'Yes, that's lovely. Rich in magnesium and iron,' she recited.

'Something that's actually good for you in pregnancy. I've got a great long list of foods that aren't!'

'It was only soft cheese and raw eggs when I was doing it,' I told her. 'That you had to avoid, I mean,' I added hastily. 'Not that were good.'

Sam had been very sweet about the fish pie, and had only shrugged philosophically when I'd apologised for turning her life upside down. 'It should have occurred to me I'd been sick,' was all she'd said, but I noticed she was now fully vegetarian and nobody was queuing up for my nutritional advice.

'You go and sit down,' I said now, as she poured boiling water onto her teabag. 'Take it easy while you can.'

I hoped the sickness would pass soon. Mine had disappeared altogether after a few weeks, I kept telling her optimistically, adding that then I'd felt fantastic, and keeping very quiet about my friend Marie from Oliver's toddler group who had thrown up every day for the full nine months.

Sam nodded and disappeared into the front room. I began to count out potatoes, making generous provisions for hungover sons – I'd heard Gabriel's and Ben's voices floating up the stairs at 1 a.m. followed by the smell of toast (my scented candle was in a cupboard for the foreseeable) and hadn't seen my youngest since – and a daughter whose concept of carbohydrates could be elastic. Glad I'd been firm about not letting her father hang about.

Rob had dropped her and Ben, three suitcases and a dozen half-filled bin-liners at the house the previous afternoon. He'd let me know that Fiona had relented and they were once again bonding over Farrow and Ball charts for the new property

Fiona liked. But it hadn't stopped him lingering hopefully or Tilly hissing in my ear about dinner.

'You like feeding people,' she'd said accusingly. 'You always say one more doesn't make any difference.'

Unless it's an ex-spouse with a penchant for breathing on you.

As I dumped the boys' empties in the recycling bin, I spotted Ingrid coming down the road.

'How's your mother?' she asked, softer and more sympathetic than usual. I told her about my detour to Margate after I'd been measuring in Dover. Now Gerald was there, the house looked more loved and homely again. 'She's finally seeing a consultant at the end of the month, I said, adding as I felt a rush of gratitude to Ingrid, and before I could stop myself: 'Would you like a coffee?'

'You look busy,' she said, surveying the trays and dishes lined up next to the hob. 'Got all the family here?' The usual sharp note had returned to her voice. I pulled china mugs from the cupboard and smiled at her.

'Yes, Oliver and Sam are staying with me for a while. Ben and Tilly arrived last night ...' I explained about my daughter's new job and how she too was going to be around for a bit. 'I don't know how she's managed to accumulate so much stuff. There wasn't a spare inch of space left in Rob's car–'

I stopped abruptly, hoping talk of my offspring wouldn't lead to Ingrid mentioning David ...

'He's back again, is he?' she said, tartly.

'Only long enough to remind me why we got divorced. Biscuit?'

As Ingrid shook her head, I moved quickly onto the garden and the work involved in getting it straight. Ingrid nodded. 'I'd like to see your pond ...'

We carried our cups outside. It was warm and the grass was long and springy beneath our feet. 'I've got a lawn-mower at last,' I told Ingrid, 'I'm hoping to persuade one of the boys ...'

'But the daisies are so pretty.' She bent over my pond, looking into the depths. 'Any frogs or newts?'

'There was frogspawn–'

'Mum!' Oliver was standing in the back doorway. 'Jinni's here.'

She was already stepping outside. I looked at her, startled, as Oliver reappeared, his tone more urgent: 'I think you need to look in the oven ...'

I sprinted past Jinni and got the pie out before the golden perfection of its crust could descend into charcoal, gave the potatoes a poke, the casserole a stir and added the batter to the now-sizzling sausages before racing back out into the garden, where Jinni and Ingrid stood facing each other two metres apart as if ready for a shoot-out.

Jinni swung around and gave me an exuberant hug. 'Hello, girlfriend! Long time no see. Sorry about that. I've had a wood burner installed!' She was smiling widely, dark hair tied up in a bright scarf, silver bracelets jangling. She indicated her dusty overalls. 'I've spent bloody hours stacking logs!' She turned to Ingrid. 'I had that tree chopped down,' she said, challenge in her voice. 'The bloke from the council agreed completely. Said I'd better get on with it before it rotted completely and fell on me!'

Ingrid shrugged. 'Oh, if it was diseased–'

Jinni gave a hard laugh. 'Don't you care anymore? That's not like you, Ingrid. You don't usually let a spot of reason put you off. Losing your edge?'

Ingrid shrugged again and gave one of her steely sweet smiles. 'I've got more pressing concerns with the new leisure centre. It's a monstrous building – it's going to ruin the view, the back elevation will be blocking out the light to a child's bedroom–' Jinni was already looking bored.

'No doubt they'll soon back off when they see you coming,' she said dryly.

Ingrid ignored her. 'So,' she went on smoothly, 'I have, as David would put it, bigger fish to fry.' There was a small pause while Ingrid looked at Jinni with an expression I couldn't read. 'And he doesn't want me to cause trouble for you.'

Jinni gave a sarcastic smile and adopted a sugary tone of her own: 'How generous of him.'

I looked from one to the other, confused, my heart beating harder at the mention of David. 'I'm sorry, I really need to get back in the kitchen,' I said uncomfortably. 'I've got cooking to do. Would either of you–'

'I must get on too.' Ingrid was brisk. 'Thank you, Tess.' I followed her through to the front door, leaving Jinni in the kitchen. Gabriel had arrived while we were outside and was perched on the arm of the sofa chatting to Oliver and Sam. He jumped up and hugged me. 'Tess! You're looking great.'

He rummaged in a rucksack at his feet and produced a box of chocolate mints. 'I brought you these.' He pointed to a carrier bag on the floor near Oliver. 'And there's some beers ...'

'That's really kind of you.' I gave him a kiss. 'You know Ingrid, don't you?'

As Ingrid was saying goodbye, Tilly sprinted down the stairs, wearing a new top and a lot of make-up. 'Gabe!'

Then the doorbell rang.

Malcolm strode towards me and pressed a bottle of red wine into my hand. 'It's a decent one,' he said. 'I've been wanting it to go to a good home.'

Ingrid, beside me, looked Malcolm up and down. 'Are you well?' she enquired.

'I'm still here.'

'I hope you're going to be reporting on the goings-on with that so-called community centre,' she said. 'The head of the company that's got the contract to build it is in the Masons with Dick Barford! Head of Planning,' she added, as Malcolm remained impassive.

'I know who he is,' he growled. 'Speak to him–' Malcolm jerked his head towards Gabriel. 'He's head of conspiracy theories.'

Gabriel flushed and Malcolm gave a loud guffaw. 'You can do one of your "investigations".'

'He's been very good, actually, as far as my problems go!' Jinni was now in the doorway behind us, putting special emphasis on the word 'problems' and flashing Ingrid a look. My heart sank.

But Malcolm appraised her keenly and then gave a grin. 'I don't think we've met,' he said. 'Although I've heard how camera-shy you are.'

'I hate those posed pictures,' Jinni said. 'Pointing at the damage with a long face.'

'Yes, they're terrible,' agreed Malcolm. 'But then Pete is a terrible photographer.'

'You should be a bit more loyal to your staff,' said Ingrid tartly.

'They've got jobs, haven't they?'

Ingrid shook her head as if he were worth no further effort and opened the front door. She nodded at me. 'Give my best wishes to your mother.'

'I was worried there for a moment,' said Malcolm, when she'd gone. 'Thought she was staying.'

'That's enough to put anyone off their food,' said Jinni. 'She's such a pain. Her and that tosser son.'

'Do you want to eat with us? Having Jinni here again in my house, humming with energy, made me want her company despite my wounded feelings. But she'd just been rude about David, so presumably she wasn't ...

'I can't!' Jinni pulled a face. 'I'd love to but –' She gave me a wink. 'Something just came up ...'

'Have fun,' said Malcolm.

'Are you in tomorrow?' Tilly asked. 'I've got a TIE job I want to tell you about.'

'Hey fab! Yep – come over.' Jinni turned back to me. 'We've got to catch up too. I don't where the time has gone.' She blew a kiss around the room. Then winked again. 'Well I do! Have a good one!'

She was gone and aromas from the kitchen were calling me. 'Where's Ben?' I asked Tilly.

'Still lying on his bed groaning,' she said, smiling at Gabriel. 'Was he really rotten last night?'

'He was okay,' said Gabriel tactfully.

'Well, tell him to come down now,' I instructed. 'And Oliver, could you do some drinks for Gabriel and Malcolm, please. 'Tilly, finish laying the table, darling? I got distracted when Ingrid came ...'

'I'll help you.' Gabriel sprang to his feet as usual. Malcolm looked cynical.

'He's a lovely boy,' I told him firmly, when they'd gone into the dining room. 'Always so considerate.'

'He could do with considering what makes a decent news story,' said Malcolm, but there was none of his usual rancour. 'I'm looking forward to this,' he went on. 'I haven't had steak and kidney for months.'

He looked almost moved when I brought in the serving dishes. 'You are truly an angel in human form,' he declared, unfolding his napkin. He surveyed the table. 'Toad in the hole too. My cup runneth over.'

Ben, who had brightened up since the food arrived, took the slab of batter and sausages Tilly passed him and began to pile potatoes onto his plate beside it. 'Next best thing to a full fry-up,' he said. 'I've been gagging for one all day.'

'You're vile,' said Tilly, looking at his plate disapprovingly and helping herself to broccoli spears, 'you'll be dead of a coronary by the time you're thirty.'

Ben, his mouth full, made a disparaging noise in his throat. 'You can talk,' he said good-naturedly, when he'd swallowed.

'Bet you're back on the cake and chips by tomorrow latest.'

I frowned. 'Stop it you two. Tilly, why don't you have some chicken with that?'

'Or would you like some of this pasta?' Sam offered her the bowl.

My daughter glared at her brother and shook her head at Sam. 'Can't. I need to lose weight before I start the new run. I'm doing high protein and veg only.'

'Till someone opens the biscuits ...' Ben said, and he and Oliver both laughed. Their sister scowled.

'You look great as you are,' Gabriel said gallantly, and suddenly she smiled, looking unusually bashful. I wondered how far their relationship had progressed. It would be nice if they got together. If my daughter could be happy and settled like Oliver and Sam ...

I watched as Oliver put a hand on Sam's arm. I felt fiercely protective of the teeny prawn-baby growing there across the table. I pictured tiny curling fingers and toes. We'd agreed to keep the news in the family for a few more weeks but I couldn't wait to start buying things.

'You all right, Mumsie?' Ben looked quizzically at me between munches. 'Your face has gone wonky.'

I jolted back to the present and looked around at the various plates.

'What can I pass you now, Malcolm?' I said, proffering more gravy

He shook his head. 'Not a thing. I am enjoying this wonderful pie.' He shook his head. 'A rarity indeed. A beauty who can cook!'

For once he seemed to be serious. Ben made a come-off-it-mate face as I felt myself flush at the compliment.

Malcolm did look surprisingly content. I gestured to Oliver to top up the wine, but Malcolm covered his glass. 'I'll just drink this one slowly. Not supposed to do it at all.' He pulled a face. 'That's the trouble with the medical profession. Anything remotely agreeable, they ban it.'

'Would you like some of this elderflower cordial?' Sam asked kindly.

Malcolm looked askance. 'It's not quite got that bad.'

Sam giggled. She had a bit more colour now. Although she wasn't eating much. Probably afraid my pesto was rancid and she'd end up with twins.

'Are you okay?' I mouthed at her.

She nodded. 'This is lovely, Tess.'

'Splendid!' Malcolm beamed around the table.

Ben was still talking about breakfast. 'I didn't want to risk dragging my poor body down the town and then finding there was nowhere open on a Sunday ...'

'Your instincts were half-right,' Malcolm told him. 'Stan's is closed on a Sunday – a situation I would be attempting to rectify if I lived in town and it affected me in the slightest – but the second-best breakfast in Northstone is available ...' They fell to discussing the attributes of the ideal greasy spoon, with Ben putting up a case for hash browns and 'non-flobby' eggs, Oliver for crispy bacon, and Gabriel chiming in about fresh orange juice and proper coffee. 'Don't start coming over all American,' growled Malcolm.

Tilly raised her eyebrows. 'He is half ...'

'Pah,' said Malcolm. 'It's got to be butter on the toast – I won't patronise a place that serves that margarine muck – and sausages with meat in them, not the sawdust sweepings from the floor.'

He turned to me. 'If you want a proper start to the day, I'll introduce you to the pleasures of Stan's one morning this week. I want to talk to you about writing something for me.'

'Me?' I squeaked. 'I can't ...'

'You can't be any worse than the twerp they sent me this week. English graduate! Could barely write his own name–'

'Work experience,' explained Gabriel. 'He was–'

'Going to be the next John Pilger – came over all concerned about "inequality",' Malcolm shook his head in disgust. 'If there wasn't inequality, there'd be bugger all news.'

'You can always supply the content and let Golden Boy here write it up for you,' he continued. 'We're going to start a series of debates on local issues with different people putting their point of view. You can be our newcomer. I might ask your neighbour too. Pit her against Ingrid. Might as well make some use of the annoying woman–'

I wasn't sure which one of them he was referring to as the irritant – Ingrid most likely – but decided, knowing Malcolm, it could be both. 'I don't know–' I began.

'We'll discuss it over double eggs. And mushrooms!' he added, with a gleam in his eye. 'They're important.'

He took another roast potato. 'Wednesday.'

The light was fading by the time we'd moved into the sitting room and I was offering around the mint thins. 'I don't think

258

I could,' said Malcolm, taking one. 'Superb lemon tart. I really shouldn't have had the ice-cream too—' he rubbed his stomach. 'But all absolutely magnificent, my dear.' He put his coffee cup down and stood up. 'Now, I must be off.'

He shook hands with Ben and Oliver, and gave Sam a crooked smile. 'You want to feed her more,' he told Oliver. 'She's looking a bit peaky.'

He rested his eyes on Gabriel. 'Do you need taking somewhere?' he said gruffly. Tilly was coming through from the kitchen; I saw her eyes flick towards him.

'No, I'll walk, thanks,' Gabriel gave an easy smile. 'It's a lovely evening.'

'Nice to see you again!' Tilly gave Malcolm a kiss and settled herself on the arm of the sofa next to Gabriel, leaving Malcolm looking comically surprised.

I followed him to the door. The air was soft and a new moon was hovering over the dark outlines of the trees framing the rectory. There was one small light on downstairs.

Malcolm stopped and faced me and seemed to hesitate. I gave him a hug and he clasped me back. 'You must come again soon,' I said, filled with affection for him and all of them, thinking how relaxed I was, and how good it felt, after all, to have friends and family around ....

'I'll see you for breakfast,' Malcolm replied.

'I'll look forward to it ...' I smiled at him thinking how much I really would.

And then over his shoulder I saw the car draw up, and my warm, happy feelings dried instantly into a hard lump below my ribcage.

I fixed my eyes back on Malcolm's and shut the door the moment he'd turned to wave from the drive. 'Could you put the blue wheelie on the pavement for me?' I asked Ben, hurriedly shutting the curtains.

'You all right, Mum?' Oliver was looking at me.

'I've just remembered it's bin day.'

I gathered up Malcolm's empty cup and my wine glass and went through to the kitchen.

I heard Ben complaining he had bare feet, Gabriel offering to go outside for him, Tilly telling her brother he was the laziest little gimp she'd ever known, Oliver saying something to Sam about getting to bed.

For a faint moment I had hoped.

But nobody had rung at my doorbell. There was no text on my phone.

It wasn't that I cared if Jinni and David were having a fling – they were probably well-suited. It was the way they were going about it. The manner in which David had abruptly dropped me even as a friend, or business colleague. It wasn't as if anything had happened between us.

And why did Jinni pretend? *That tosser son...*

I threw back the last mouthful of red wine from my glass and dumped the crockery down hard. It wasn't that I cared at all, but why treat me like an idiot?

Because you are one, I told myself bitterly. *You are a total tool.*

Chapter 27

I woke at half-past six, to the sound of footsteps thundering up and down the stairs and the dulcet tones of my daughter resounding from the landing. 'Will you get out of that fucking shower room!'

I staggered onto the landing. 'Tilly!'

My daughter was wearing a long t-shirt and a furious expression. 'I've just found out we've got a rehearsal today – I thought it was Wednesday. I've got to get the train with Oliver and Sam, and Ben – who's got fuck all to do apart from lie in bed all day – is clogging up the–'

'Go in my en suite.'

'I wanted a proper shower. Yours needs descaling.'

'Have a stand-up wash in the bath. Or just be quick!'

'He's a bloody liability.'

I sighed as Tilly flounced past me into my bedroom and I headed for the loo downstairs, grateful the previous owners had been firm believers in facilities, even if the bloody thing was still temperamental. Sam was in there so I put the kettle on.

'You okay, Mum?' Oliver looked as tired as I felt. 'Sorry if we woke you.'

'It wasn't you.' I yawned. I'd had a restless night waking out of peculiar dreams every couple of hours, feeling hot and disturbed. I told myself it was the rich food and too many glasses of red, but I knew at least one of the dreams had been about David. I smiled wearily at Sam as she appeared in the kitchen, also looking washed-out but dressed for work.

'Sorry,' she said.

'No problem.' The loo was making that gurgling noise again.

'Mum, we've got to go!' Oliver's voice came through the door as I was washing my hands. 'Tell Tilly we can't wait – she'll have to get the next one ...'

'Okay!'

I heard feet hammering down the stairs. 'I'm nearly ready!'

'We're going to start walking!'

I could hear Tilly swearing, then more hammering. This time on the front door.

'ANSWER IT IN CASE IT'S THE PLUMBER,' I screeched, as the swirling water in front of me rose almost to the top of the bowl.

I emerged as Tilly, hair still damp, had got there. Jinni burst in as Oliver and Sam hurried out. She also looked as if she'd just got up. Her hair was a wild tangle around her make-up-less face.

'Oh my God, Tess, I don't fucking believe it!' Jinni shook her head wildly at me as Tilly shoved her feet into trainers, still doing up buttons on her shirt.

'Mum, have you got a fiver so I can get a coffee. I'll pay you back tonight.'

'I don't know. I need cash too.' I looked at Jinni, thinking how little I cared. A row with David? Another leaflet from Ingrid through the door?

'Fuckers.' Jinni was pacing back and forth across the floor.

'Can I look?' Tilly was holding up my purse.

'What about your ticket?'

'I'll put it on my card.' Tilly waved a note at me. 'Give it to you later.'

She shot out of the door, calling to Jinni she'd see her soon.

'Now what?' I said shortly, tired of everyone's dramas and just wanting to get under the shower myself.

'Look at the front of your house! All over the new paint. It's going to be an absolute bastard to clean off.'

My heart thumped. I followed her numbly outside and looked back at my house. A sticky yellowy-brown porridgey substance was splattered high across the dark grey bricks and had already set in hard streaks down the front door. Blobs clung to the downstairs window, where nobody had yet opened the curtains. My kids had clearly all rushed down the path without a backward glance.

'Flour and eggs,' said Jinni grimly.

I felt sick. 'Who would do this to me?'

Jinni snorted. 'Well, I wonder! And so soon after I see Ingrid here!'

I stared back, mind whirring. 'No—'

'Well, it's a bit strange, don't you think? This should happen so soon after I wound her up about the tree? I expect she went straight home and told that wanker David and he sent one of his lackeys round. I know YOU think he's wonderful but I told you–'

What? 'Hang on a minute, why the fuck would they do it to MY house because YOU wound them up?' I said furiously. 'And don't treat me like a bloody cretin. I know you and he are–'

'What?' Jinni's eyes were hard.

'Seeing each other.'

'Are you mad? Whatever gave you that idea?'

'His car outside your house? Tilly said you were talking to him. And then last night–'

Jinni was looking at me as if I were crazed. 'He said he was going to see you,' she interrupted. 'He said we should make a bit more of an effort to get on. As you and he were "friends" now. I knew he was only smarming around me because his tosser mate's just put in the next set of plans for over the back. So I told him to sling his hook. We talked for about two minutes! I had a train to catch!' She stared at me some more. 'Why, what did you think?'

'Well, he didn't come to see me, and then his car was still there, and he wasn't in it, and you said you were going away for the weekend–'

'Not with him!' Jinni frowned. 'Are you kidding?'

'His car was still there for quite a while ...'

'He was probably casing the joint, once he'd seen me go.'

'No, you were still there, you spoke to Tilly–'

Jinni shook her head impatiently. 'Well, perhaps he'd gone to see someone else, then. The dark-haired bird – I don't know where she lives–'

'Who?'

'One of the many females he hangs out with – youngish – in her thirties. I've seen her with Ingrid. He gets around, Tess!'

I stared back at her, feeling sicker than ever. I had no right to feel jealous – nothing had happened between us yet I'd allowed myself to imagine ...

'You can't seriously think–' She shook her head again. 'I can't stand him! This is some sort of joke, right?'

'No,' I said, embarrassed. I sounded paranoid now too. 'I just thought – because you said to Tilly you were on a promise ...'

Jinni's face still said I was unhinged.

'Caroline told me! I said hotly. 'You know, that you and David–'

'Oh,' Jinni said flatly. 'That was nice of her.' There was a silence. Then she took a deep breath and looked directly at me. 'Yes, we screwed,' she said. 'A long time ago, when I first moved here. We were both drunk and it was a mistake. So, we've not done it again. Nor would I.'

She took a step towards me. 'You do believe me, don't you?'

I nodded dumbly, my solar plexus still in a tight ball at the thought of the dark girl in her thirties. I'd asked him. He said there was no one ...

'I'm sorry I didn't tell you before, but really – I can barely remember it.' Jinni paused. 'I've not seen him or heard from him since that weekend you're talking about.'

'Neither have I.'

I told her about the abrupt text turning down a drink and

how he'd been away when she was. 'Caroline wouldn't have told me otherwise.'

'I went to stay with friends from drama school and a load of us went out to dinner,' Jinni explained. 'Including a one-time boyfriend who'd just split up with his wife.' She pulled a face. 'And now I've seen him again, I can understand why.' She laughed. And then I did this interminable voice-over, which I told Tilly about. Which ended up going into a third day ...' She stopped. 'David didn't come into it.'

'And then I thought I saw a man at your window,' I said dully.

'Ah.' Jinni suddenly grinned. 'That would have been Craig. My friendly tree-feller. His wife has left him too. But in this case, her loss is my gain. Not much of a conversationalist but lots of stamina. It's why I've been somewhat, preoccupied, you might say ...' She grinned a bit more. 'Sorry about that. I probably won't see him much now he's finished the job, because he's moving away when they've sold the house. But he filled a gap, as it were.' She laughed. 'I was getting a bit desperate.'

She was abruptly straight-faced again. 'So no, I have not been up to anything with David. He's pretty disturbed if he comes telling me you're *friends*, when he's already dumped you!' She snorted. 'Look, Tess – he doesn't hang around anyone for very long–'

I winced. 'Well, there was nothing to dump, really. We'd only seen each other a couple of times – as friends ...'

'With friends like that ...'

'He didn't do this.' I looked back at my facade. A fragment

of eggshell clung to the curved bricks around the door. As I said it, I pictured David's car drawing up across the road as I'd said goodbye to Malcolm.

Jinni was still in full flow about calling Gabriel and the possibilities for revenge. 'We'll see how the wanker likes it when there's an omelette all over his Porsche.'

My mobile vibrated in my dressing pocket. I pulled it out and looked at the screen. My stomach turned over.

'I've got to have a shower,' I said. 'I'm supposed to be working.'

She nodded. 'I'll get some wire brushes and help you clean this off before it gets any harder.'

Back inside, I stared at the text message again in disbelief. **'Hello Gorgeous. When we going to have that drink? X'**

Chapter 28

'**B**astard!'

I wasn't going to send it but it was cathartic to let the rage rattle down my fingers. How bloody dare he!

Have the gall to bugger off for the weekend when we were supposed to be having a drink.

Ignore my email.

Make me behave like a complete prat by lurking outside Jinni's house and not coming to see me.

And then – most heinous of all – fraternise with a woman in her thirties when I was 47!

'**Smug, supercilious, eyebrow-dyer**' I added therapeutically, while my mind was racing. Why hadn't I told Jinni he'd been outside last night? And why was he there, unless Jinni was right and he really was the phantom egg-thrower. I jabbed at the buttons in frustration. None of it made sense.

Oh shit! I had hit *send*.

I looked at the small screen in horror.

Suppose he forwarded it to all his friends? And it went viral? Suppose he told Shane from the theatre, who then told my daughter, who would then think I was mad? Making a mental note to keep a running check on my paranoid tendencies in case I needed some sort of behavioural therapy, I threw the phone down. It rang immediately.

Agggghhhh. Too late it struck me I should have ignored the call and pretended my mobile had been stolen by a lunatic. David's tones were deep and smooth.

'Oh dear, I seem to have upset you. Please don't be annoyed, Tess. I was going to call in but–'

'You weren't out buying flour were you?'

'What?' His voice was immediately sharp.

'I saw you pull up outside last night.'

'I was going to pop in.'

'But you didn't, did you?'

'You had your arms around someone else.'

'Don't be ridiculous.' I mustered as much scorn as I could manage. 'I was saying goodbye to a friend.'

'Well, I didn't want to disturb you.' David said coolly. 'I was only passing anyway.'

'You seem to do that a lot!'

'What are you talking about?'

'This morning there's eggs and crap all over my house.'

'You don't think I did it?' He sounded incredulous.

'No, of course not. But Jinni does! Things always seem to happen when you or Ingrid have been around.' I felt immediately guilty. Ingrid had been kind to my mother and to me. I felt my voice break. 'I'm sorry. I'm just upset.'

'My mother wouldn't dream of damaging anything,' said David icily.

'No, I know she wouldn't. I–'

'Are you going to be at home?'

'Yes. Why do you—'

But he'd already ended the call.

When the bell rang, I flung the door open, half afraid, half thrilled.

'Hello!' I said loudly.

'Oh, Tess,' Gabriel stepped straight in and gave me a hug. Over his shoulder Pete, camera slung over his shoulder, was surveying the front of my house.

Gabriel scanned my face anxiously. 'Are you okay?'

'It's a bloody pain but I'll get some hot water in a minute ...' I glanced at the clock, hoping he wouldn't stay long.

'I'll do that, when we've got some pictures,' Gabriel said immediately. 'So you didn't see anyone?'

'I'd gone to bed, hadn't I? I went before you left ...'

'I thought maybe out of the window – someone running away?'

'No, nothing, I didn't even realise till Jinni–' I stopped, still sick at the thought.

'I don't want photos in the paper.' I said. 'It's horrible being targeted like this–'

Gabriel shook his head, looking concerned. 'It's a campaign against incomers and development. It's not personal.'

'That's not the way Jinni sees it.'

'I'll talk to her. Did she see anything?' I shook my head. He put out a hand and took mine. 'Please don't be upset. I will come straight back and help you clean it off.'

'Don't you have to be at work?'

I certainly did. Jinni and Gabriel were already outside with buckets and brushes when I emerged from the shower, grateful but anxious, wondering how to squash in an extra hot beverages point and a photocopier above the store in Dover.

I stepped over Tilly's damp towel, hurrying as I heard the landline ringing below, knowing it would be Paul gearing up for a coronary. As I reached the top of the stairs I jumped as a door opened behind me.

'Jesus, Ben!' I clutched at my chest as my son stood sleepily on the landing, in boxers and t-shirt. 'I'd forgotten you were here.'

Ben gave me a lop-sided smile. 'That's nice – overlooking your favourite offspring.'

'No university?'

'I've got a reading week.'

'Oh!'

He opened the shower-room door. 'So I thought I'd hang out here. The other guys have gone home.'

'Lovely!'

I averted my eyes from the crockery piled up in the kitchen and took my laptop into the dining room.

As soon as I sat down the phone rang again. 'Sorreeee!' I screeched. 'My hand was literally on it as it stopped.'

'Hmmm,' said my sister disapprovingly. 'At least you're there now. We need to talk about mother,' she swept on. 'I know your answer to everything is to stick your head in the sand, but we should be thinking one step ahead ...'

I felt the familiar rage and frustration rise in my throat as

Alice, safely ensconced behind her desk in Boston, began to outline my duties.

'Hang on!' I interrupted, when it became clear she wasn't going to draw breath any time soon. 'She's nowhere near needing a care home and I really cannot have this conversation now. I've got work to do and–' I added, as the doorbell rang and someone began to knock at the same time '–I've got a crisis to deal with.'

'It's open!' I yelled over my shoulder.

'Do you have to shout in my ear?' my sister snapped.

'Yes, I do,' I shrieked. 'I'm waiting for the plumber so he can fix the loo before it starts flooding the whole of downstairs and someone's pelted the front of my house – which I'd only just had painted to cover the fucking graffiti–' I heard my voice break again '–with eggs!'

'Heavens,' she said. 'You've only been there five minutes. Made enemies already?'

'I don't see how I can have,' I said to Malcolm, as I blinked back tears from the sense of childlike impotence and injustice my sister never fails to inspire.

'I don't know anybody.'

'Well, you do,' he said calmly. 'But why any of them would want to do this, we're not yet sure.' He patted me reassuringly on the arm. 'But I shall make it my business to find out!' he went on. 'And if you like, I shall attempt to cheer you by cooking my famous prune and sausage casserole.' He pulled my shopping list towards him and wrote on the bottom of it. 'There's the postcode. I expect you've got one of those sat-nav things, nobody can use a simple map any more. House is called Sunny Dove. If you end up in a ditch you've gone too far.'

'Sunny Dove?' I smiled for the first time.

'Previous owners were a pair of simpletons.' Malcolm grinned too. Then looked into my face and said seriously: 'It's unpleasant, but try not to worry. It's going to stop. I'll have a word with one of our advertisers and organise some home surveillance kit. Don't tell anyone it's going up. I'll explain later – come round about seven?'

'Oh I don't know – I've got all the kids here and–'

As if on cue, Ben bounced into the room. 'No bacon!'

'Well, buy some,' I told him irritably. 'And get some mince. I was going to make a chilli to go with everything that's left over from yesterday but maybe I won't be here–' I looked at Malcolm. Ben looked forlorn. 'I was going to eat the toad now.'

'I'll write you a list ...'

'Very fine toad,' said Malcolm looking wistfully towards my kitchen, where Ben was now clattering.

'And you can finish clearing up!' I yelled.

'We've done rather a fine job of it, actually!' Jinni came in through the front door in red dungarees, swinging a bucket. 'When Gabe's finished up the ladder, you'll be like new.'

I hugged her. 'That's so good of you. Let me make you coffee. Do you want something to eat?' Jinni shook her head. 'Got to get back to swilling my own place out. I'll pop back later.'

Gabriel appeared moments after she'd gone. He had wet

marks down his usually pristine t-shirt and looked rather flushed. 'It's all off'.

'Time you were, then!' said Malcolm immediately. 'Go back to the office and get this dastardly deed written up and then get along to that chap with the giant pork pie.' He turned to me. 'Ten kilos of prime shoulder in there, allegedly. He's going to raffle it off for some unfortunates somewhere.'

'It's to raise money to fund a sensory farm experience for disabled children,' Gabriel explained. 'Somewhere safe where they can milk cows and feed pigs.'

Malcolm gave a guffaw. 'Funded by a load of blokes down the pub eating a couple of them.'

I gave him a look. 'That sounds like a very good cause,' I said to Gabriel. 'Can't you have a coffee first?'

'No,' said Malcolm. 'Hop it.'

'Why are you so hard on him?' I said when Gabriel had kissed me and left. 'I'd be really proud to have a son like that.'

'Hmmm.'

'Do you want a coffee yourself?'

'I thought you'd never ask.'

Chapter 29

When the bell rang, I thought it was Ben with no key as usual. I was laughing as I walked across the room – Malcolm had been sharing his views on the bloke with a ponytail and pink trousers who had just opened an emporium near the post office.

'How do they make any money?' he was saying as I pulled open the door. 'They're closed half the time. I suppose Tabatha or Hugo need time off for Pilates and to sit in a coffee shop braying about how hip they are.'

The rush of adrenalin that jolted through me at the sight of David made my heart thump. The laughter stuck in my throat and came out as a sort of yelp.

Malcolm immediately stood up.

'I'll be off, then,' he said. 'My chap will be in touch with you later. Don't forget what I said–' Had I imagined it or had he just shot David a hard look? 'Keep it quiet.'

Did he suspect David too? Surely not.

Malcolm gave my shoulder a squeeze and walked out – grunting a greeting at David as he passed.

David was also serious. 'I've got something for you.'

He picked up the large cardboard box at his feet, came in and put it on the sofa. 'CCTV. It streams straight onto an iPhone, or iPad if you've got one. Or there's a monitor in the box. Twenty-four-hour surveillance at your fingertips.'

He was wearing casual cotton trousers with loafers and an open-necked shirt. His black hair looked shinier than ever and his features ever more chiselled. A waft of his signature musky aftershave caught at my nostrils.

I suddenly understood why Jinni had fallen on her tree man and the gleam in her eye when she'd joked about him knowing how to handle a chopper. I felt my mouth twitch inappropriately and David looked at me hard.

'You'll be able to see who's really doing this. I'm used to Jinni's irrational rantings but I didn't expect you to think—'

'I don't!' I said. 'But look at it from her point of view. We know it's all coincidence but you were out there last night, you'd just dropped me off when the paint and graffiti happened and you and she do like to make trouble for each other, don't you? Trees and things?'

Now you no longer go to bed together … I added silently.

'I'd park right outside, wouldn't I?'

'Well, why *were* you there?' I demanded, noting he hadn't denied the tree business this time. 'Why suddenly when you've been ignoring me?' I stopped. It sounded as if I cared.

'I haven't been ignoring you, I've been busy.' He shrugged. 'I didn't know you were that bothered. You rushed off from the gallery. You put off seeing me again, and said your mother was ill and then I dropped in with that puzzle and your mother was fine and you didn't seem very enthusiastic about arranging anything else–'

'I was. I just–'

He put up a hand to silence me. 'I *thought* you weren't very keen and then I heard about your mother and I was going to try again. I'd bought you some flowers.'

I raised my eyebrows.

'The first time I came, there were a couple of men outside putting things in a car so I had a word with Jinni – asked her if we could put this stupid feud behind us and be a bit more civil. I told her I liked you.'

My heart jumped. He gave a tight smile. 'And she told me where to go, of course. For the second time. I'd texted her before.

And then I walked down the road for a coffee with my mother, thinking I'd come back later when your visitors had gone. And she mentioned your ex-husband, which since you'd told me you never see him, seemed a bit odd–'

'I don't ever see him. Tilly brought him!'

'–and it seemed from her description he was probably the younger chap outside your house and had stayed all night, which seemed even stranger, so I'm afraid I rather assumed–'

'Tilly had a problem and Rob was helping her and Tilly said–'

'You don't have to explain. It's none of my business.'

'I didn't want him here!'

David nodded. 'I've spoken again to my mother since.'

'Why didn't you just ask me?' I said.

'I don't know. I was keyed up about a site meeting with the

277

Chinese clients, so I went the office on Sunday and stayed over so I'd be there early.' He gave me a proper smile for the first time. 'Just in case it snowed again! Thought I'd see you when I got back ...' There was another pause.

'But you didn't,' I said

'Sorry.'

'And you didn't reply to my email about the work. The visuals you wanted?'

'I didn't get it.'

I looked at him doubtfully.

He raised his eyebrows. 'Are you saying I'm a liar as well as an egg-thrower?'

'I'll forward it again.'

'That doesn't answer my question.'

I shrugged. 'Perhaps it's in your spam.'

'I'd still like you to do some plans for me.' His tone was formal and I felt awkward. He poked a foot at the box still lying on the floor. 'There are instructions in there. And Jinni's a very capable woman – I'm sure she'll help you.'

'You just had it lying about, did you?

'I have a friend with a security business.'

'You have a lot of useful friends.' I stopped. One of them had given my daughter a job.'

'I'm sorry,' I said ashamed. 'Tilly is so grateful to you. She's rehearsing with Shane today.'

David nodded.

'I'm very appreciative too,' I added stiffly.

'Let me know when you've caught the culprit, if there is one, and we'll go out and celebrate.'

I frowned. 'What do you mean – if there is one? *Someone's* been chucking eggs about.'

David looked deliberately across the road at the rectory. 'Someone – probably unbalanced – who wants it to look like me!'

I shook my head. 'You're not seriously suggesting Jinni would do this. What have I done?'

David raised his eyebrows. 'Who knows?'

'I do. We're good friends.' There was a small silence. 'So what happened to my flowers?'

'I gave them to my mother.' He stopped. 'What are you thinking?' he asked.

'I was wondering if you really dyed your eyebrows ...'

He gave a shout of laughter. 'What is this?'

'Jinni said ...' I stifled a giggle.

He shook his head. 'Always bloody Jinni ...'

He took a step towards me, placing his hands lightly on my shoulders.

I realised I was trembling. Heat flooded through me as he continued to gaze at me.

'No, I don't. I am naturally dark, like my father. I have an uncle in his eighties who still hasn't gone grey. Next question?'

'Why didn't you tell me you'd been to bed with Jinni?'

He stepped back, dropping his hands to his sides, and throwing his head back to stare at the ceiling. Then he looked back at me.

'Because I imagine she regrets it as much as I do. Because, as a general rule, I don't go around listing women I have been intimate with – and because–' Here there was a pause. 'I didn't want it to ruin anything with you.' He raised those dark eyebrows. 'Okay?'

I looked back. *Not really*. I wanted to know why he regretted it, when Jinni was so attractive, and why she was so very angry with him now.

'She does seem very determined to sabotage anything we might have started.'

A peculiar pain went through my middle. *Was that no longer an option?*

'I'd rather know ...' I said. I took a deep breath. 'I'd like to know all about you.'

I'd taken a step forward without thinking and he leant out and took my face in his hands.

'I would like that too ...'

I wanted to pull him to me, kiss him passionately and very probably fall onto the sofa with him in a tangle of limbs. But I made myself ask:

'Are you having a relationship at the moment?'

He frowned as if it were a strange question. 'No!'

I leant forward.

And then suddenly he was kissing me back, and I had my arms around him, my whole body pressed into his. Something deep inside me flared into life and delicious sensations shot through to my fingertips.

'Mmmm.' He gave a low appreciative sigh and I could hear my own breaths coming hard as his hands stroked my shoulders and sides and I ran my fingers up his chest, feeling the smooth fabric of his shirt, brushing the buttons ...

'I want–' he murmured, and I, feeling the heat pulsing

between us as I melted into him again, kissed him even more fiercely. I wanted too ...

I felt him pull away from me even before I'd registered the sound of the door opening. Ben stood just inside the room, eyes wide, a carrier bag in one hand, the other held up as if to stop traffic.

'Oh. Whoah. Sorry!' He stared at us, startled for a moment, and then bolted with remarkable speed across the room and out of the other door down the short hall to the kitchen. I heard another door firmly shut.

I felt the flush rise up my face till my cheeks were burning. 'Oh God!' I gasped as David's face broke into a smile.

'Oh dear,' he echoed.

My heart was now pounding. I stared back at him, embarrassed. 'I'm so sorry!'

'I'm not!' He put his arms back round me and I leant my forehead against his chest, breathing deeply. Then I straightened and moved away from him again, anxious Ben might return or somebody else might appear through the still-open front door. I tried to laugh. 'The one time Ben actually remembers his key ...'

My body was still jangling. I heard a faint chink of plates from the closed kitchen.

'Come round at the weekend,' David was saying. 'Saturday evening. Let's really–'

I was nodding but I needed David to go while I got my head around it all. 'Um,' I edged away from him further. 'I have to–'

Then I froze. Over his shoulder I saw the top of a head.

'OH!' Jinni stopped on the doormat and folded her arms, doing nothing to disguise her disapproval. She shot David a poisonous look and then addressed me. 'Thanks for the text and your kind offer to come and eat,' she said, deliberately. 'But I'm already doing something. A last hurrah,' she added meaningfully. She flicked David another killer glance. 'I'm rather looking forward to it.'

'David, has um–' My voice was high and strange. 'Brought some CCTV kit.' I was still shaking, and I saw that Jinni had noticed. 'We can set it up to–'

I trailed off at the look of pure scorn on her face. 'How very clever of him.'

David looked back at her with dislike. Then put a hand on my shoulder and kissed me on the cheek. 'I'll look for that email,' he said in professional tones. 'And be in touch.'

Jinni gave a snort. 'I know your game,' she said. 'And soon, everyone else will too.'

He turned to Jinni. 'I hope you find out who has been doing this to you and Tess. But until you do, I suggest you are very careful not to make any more public accusations. You may not be fully conversant with the law on what constitutes libel, but I am. And if you damage my reputation, I can, and will, sue!'

'I'll text,' he murmured, turning briefly back to me before he strode past Jinni out through the door.

'Prick!' she said loudly to his retreating back.

'He's got nothing to do with it,' I said, reeling from his abrupt departure.

Jinni looked at me as though I'd claimed to believe in

the tooth fairy. 'We won't catch anyone on that, believe me.'

'Well, shall we set it up and try?'

She shrugged. 'If you like. But not now. Craig's coming round. He moves on Thursday so I won't see him after that.' She didn't look bothered about this. She gave a small smile. 'Must make the most of it while I can–'

She was straight-faced again. 'So you ARE still seeing the wanker ...'

'He suddenly sent me a text.'

'He's obviously nuts. A criminal psychologist would have a field day with him. He trashes your house and then pops up here for a swagger. Like a murderer sending anonymous letters to the police to brag about it.'

'Hardly!'

Jinni looked at me hard. 'Gabriel went over to see Jim and Meg next door? They said there was "a sort of sports car" there when Jim put the bins out last night. Now – who do we know with one of those?'

Something stopped me telling her he'd been hoping to see me. I knew she'd think me an idiot for believing him.

I echoed the point he'd made. 'Surely he wouldn't be stupid enough to park right outside?'

'That's what he wants you to think.' Jinni shook her head pityingly. 'He's playing you like a fiddle.'

I wished somebody was. David had woken up bits of me I'd thought had shrivelled up years ago, and now I couldn't switch them off. I'd achieved nothing all afternoon, except for a brief foray into the kitchen – where Ben had said nothing but given me a quirky grin – to start a chilli and put the rest of the casserole in the oven.

'I'm going to have a bath.' I told Ben now, with as much dignity as I could muster. I jerked my head at the pot simmering on the hob. 'Keep an eye on that, will you?'

'Sure,' he wandered in front of me, picking up his guitar from the corner of the sitting room and settling himself along the length of the sofa. I breathed deeply as I reached the landing, trying to feel soothed by the sound of the chords.

As I pulled off my clothes, I heard Oliver and Sam come in, the murmur of voices and a sudden burst of laughter. I wondered if Ben had told them what he'd seen.

I blushed at the memory, felt a thrill rocket through me and then blushed again. I poured in some more ever-tranquil bath elixir – another freebie from Caroline – and lowered myself into the hot scented water, feeling deeply unsettled.

Jinni was obsessed. It wasn't David, but who *would* want to target us? Jinni was only converting her place into a B&B – not building six skyscrapers. All I'd done was move here. I felt a small anxious knot form in my stomach at the vision of someone creeping about in the dark with a dozen free-range.

I'd get Ben to help me install the camera. In the meantime it was David's dark curls I saw. The memory of his hands on my shoulders, his lips, his dark grey eyes looking so intensely into mine ...

I felt my muscles slowly relax and my mind unwind as I drifted off into a delicious fantasy in which Ben didn't burst in and Jinni was too busy with her tree man to pitch up, and

David lowered me gently onto the sofa and I not so gently began to tug at his clothes ...

'MUM!' Tilly's voice screeched from the landing. 'That chilli's sticking–'

I leapt out of the bath, scattering water across the tiles. Grabbing my towelling robe I strode across my bedroom, leaving a trail of splodgy wet footprints on the carpet.

I met Tilly in the doorway. 'I asked Ben to watch it,' I snapped.

'Oh well, you know what he's like–'

'You were there, too! Is it beyond the wit of any of you to UN-stick the bloody chilli? To give it a stir? Perhaps if it isn't too much trouble to turn a dial or boil some water, you could even make a supreme effort and make some rice?' I tightened the cord on my dressing gown and stamped past her. Do I have to do fucking EVERYTHING?'

My daughter's eyebrows had shot sky high. 'I have turned it down,' she said, startled. 'I just thought I'd tell you it's ready–'

'It's not ready. It should have been made hours ago. But it will have to do.' I began to stomp my way down the stairs, nerve ends jangling. 'So lay the table,' I shouted back over my shoulder, 'start that rice and tell Sam there's a quiche in the fridge. And if Ben and Oliver can possibly prise themselves from the sofa, one of them can make a salad.'

'Okay, okay,' Tilly came scuttling down behind me. 'What's up with you?'

I saw Oliver's head come up in surprise as I came to an abrupt stop at the bottom of the stairs, narrowly avoiding tripping over a trainer and causing Tilly to almost career into me.

'Nothing!' I yelled, as I surveyed the jumble of footwear inside the front door. I kicked at the nearest flip-flop. 'I just wish you lot would get a grip occasionally and clear up these BLOODY SHOES ...'

Chapter 30

Two days later, the bloody shoes were still in an almost-neat line.

Oliver had convened a crisis meeting entitled Mother in Meltdown and I'd arrived home after the others the previous evening, having had to manage a small crisis myself over an order of storage units, to find not only was there an M&S macaroni cheese and garlic bread in the oven, but that someone had hoovered!

'We'll do more,' he said. 'Tilly can cook tomorrow.'

'I can't. I'm rehearsing,' she said airily. 'And staying over at Danni's after.'

'OH – are you all friendly again now? I asked in surprise.

'She's got a boyfriend,' Tilly explained. 'He's a complete dry lunch but at least she's stopped bursting into tears and screaming at everyone.'

'Perhaps you should try it,' said Ben.

I shot him a sideways look to check who he was addressing, but he was smirking at his sister. She pulled a face. 'You are SO fucking hilarious ...'

Ben appeared not to have shared the trauma of discovering

his mother clasping a strange man to her bosom with his siblings, or at least not with Tilly, who would have tied me to a chair and got the torch out. It was possible he'd told Oliver, who was being terribly grown up about it and assuming I was awash with middle-aged hormones and would recover if he galvanised the household into doing the washing-up.

I'd not seen Jinni since our encounter with David, but he had sent several texts. Saying how great it was to see me and he was looking forward to Saturday. I was invited to arrive at seven and he would order in some amazing Thai food. He'd also sent directions. I wondered if he was expecting me to stay the night. Should I put an overnight bag in the boot? Or go in a taxi as we were bound to drink? Would the bag then look a bit obvious? Was it best to stick a toothbrush in my handbag and borrow his deodorant?

Every time I considered these burning issues, my stomach flipped over. I couldn't tell if it was excitement or terror.

Right now, I was running late for breakfast with Malcolm. I'd not heard from him, either, since I'd turned down his offer of sausage casserole and let him know I'd already been given some CCTV, save one of his usual clipped emails instructing me to meet him outside the office at 8 a.m.

It was already five past.

I'd stayed in bed till I'd heard various doors finish slamming, both to avoid clogging up the kitchen and because Tilly was in my en suite again. By the time the house was quiet and I was dressed, it had turned into 7.45 and I was still unpacking the dishwasher.

I sent Malcolm a brief missive to say I was on my way and rushed out of the door. The sun was already pouring down onto my front garden and I stopped by the gateway to pick a head of lavender and crush it between my fingers. Breathing in the scent, I made my way rapidly along the road, reminding myself I to call my mother. Tilly had apparently spoken to her before I got home the night before but had failed to tell me till 11 p.m. She said Granny had asked her three times what her job was and had forgotten who Sam was, altogether.

I rounded the corner into the High Street and hurried down towards Northstone News. It was 8.21 a.m. There was no sign of Malcolm and the front door was still locked. I peered through the glass panel and saw Grace sitting at the reception desk. I rapped on the window.

Grace looked up, face stony, made an exaggerated gesture of looking at the clock on the wall behind her and then got slowly to her feet. She came over to the door as if weighted down by concrete and stretched up to slide a bolt across.

'Yes?'

'Good morning, Grace. I'm here to meet Malcolm.'

She folded her lips inwards. 'Rather you than me.'

I attempted a wide smile. 'Shall I go up?'

'He's in a right mood.'

Emily was at her desk in the corner and one older woman was standing at a filing cabinet, but apart from that the upstairs office was empty. I went into Malcolm's room at the far end to find him sitting in his large swivel chair, staring at a pile of newspapers in front of him. He didn't look up.

'I'm sorry I'm late,' I said.

Malcolm grunted.

'But I'm here now,' I went on cheerily, concluding that my holding up the commencement of his first meal of the day had not gone down well. 'And ready to go. Looking forward to it.'

Malcolm looked irritable. He stood up and walked to the doorway. 'Emily!' He bellowed across the open-plan office. 'Any chance of making us coffee?'

He returned to his seat and indicated I should sit opposite.

'The other one would start bleating on about stereotypes in the workplace,' he said with disgust.

'Are we not going to Sid's?' I asked, as he continued to look morosely at the pages on his desk.

'Not yet ...'

I looked at the clock. I had a feeling Paul might phone soon after nine. 'Is there a problem?'

'There certainly is.' He started to push the newspaper across the desk when something caught his attention in the outer office and he walked past me to the door, raising his arm and beckoning.

Gabriel appeared in the doorway and smiled at me in greeting.

'What are you doing here?' Malcolm barked.

Gabriel looked uncertain. 'Well, I was going to write up the—'

'I meant,' said Malcolm, with slow menace, 'what have you come here for at all? I thought you worked for the *Daily News* ...'

Gabriel frowned. 'I don't know what you mean—'

'Don't you?' Malcolm turned the paper around so we could both see it. He jabbed a finger at the headline at the top of the page above a few inches of print and what appeared to be a picture of my front door. I leant forward to see: 'Protestors target Northstone Newbies as property prices soar.'

'See that?' He looked straight at me, then at Gabriel. 'Where did they get that story from, then? It doesn't come out in our paper until Friday.'

Gabriel started to speak, then stopped as Malcolm brought the flat of his hand crashing down on the newsprint again, making us both jump. 'And this? Graffiti sprayed at the station?'

Malcolm leant across his desk and swung his computer screen round. *The Daily News* website showed a picture of a train pulling into Northstone.

'I didn't even know about that! And apparently it happened yesterday!!' He carried on thumping. 'Rebels paint the town red? What sort of a caption is that?'

He glared at Gabriel. 'You tipped off a national over your own paper, you sneaky little git, and they couldn't even come up with a decent headline.'

He shook his head, looking for a moment genuinely bereft.

'It was eggs and flour, dammit!' he exploded. He looked back at me. 'How could they miss that? It's sheer incompetence. I saw it straight away. "DFLs take a battering!"'

I gave an involuntary snort of laughter, which I tried to strangle as I saw the alarm on Gabriel's face.

Malcolm swung around to him, in fresh fury. 'That should have been bloody obvious, even to a simpleton like you.'

'I didn't,' began Gabriel.

'YOU DID!' roared Malcolm, making me jump again. 'Don't take me for a fool, boy!' He took a step towards Gabriel, who had gone slightly pale. 'You gave them this story and don't you dare try to deny it.'

Gabriel flicked an anxious glance at me. 'I mean I had nothing to do with the headline.'

Malcolm looked at him witheringly and I saw Gabriel shrink. 'Of course you didn't. Nobody would ask you, would they? You can't do anything. You're just a brainless, ill-educated, inane, gibbering TWERP.'

'Malcolm!' I was shocked into response. 'Really, stop now, that's nasty ...'

Malcolm threw me a look of pity. 'You can be Mother Teresa if you want to, but there's no room in this office for disloyal idlers. Clear your desk, you little bastard ...'

'Malcolm!' I shrieked again, seeing Gabriel now looked stricken. 'That's enough!'

Malcolm slammed shut the paper, folded it up, tucked it beneath his arm and strode towards the door. 'If you still want breakfast, I'm going now,' he said without looking at me, and disappeared across the open-plan office.

I put a hand on Gabriel's arm. He was standing very still. 'He can't just sack you,' I said quietly. 'There are laws and regulations. He'll have to give you a warning – I'll talk to him.'

Gabriel gazed back at me, shaken. 'It wasn't meant to happen like that,' he said. 'I was pitching a feature to them as Malcolm wasn't interested any more – about the effects of the high-speed on the community, the rising house prices and the backlash against the DFLs and newcomers benefiting at the expense of the locals.' He took a big breath. 'The editor of the Sunday magazine liked it but he said I didn't have enough. He said they'd need concrete evidence it was a concerted campaign. He said so far it sounded like a dispute with neighbours.'

Gabriel stopped and breathed again. 'So I told them about the eggs and that someone had sprayed an anti-DFL slogan at the station – I was just trying to stay in touch – to show I was gathering the proof. I never thought it would be run as a news story ...' Gabriel stopped and looked miserable. 'They probably don't want the feature now and I've lost my job.'

I gave his arm a squeeze. 'I'm sure Malcolm will calm down,' I said. 'I'll go and find him,' I added, as Emily appeared, also looking traumatised, with two mugs. 'You two have them,' I told her. 'And try not to panic,' I finished as Gabriel sank into a chair outside Malcolm's office. I left Emily hovering over him solicitously and went back downstairs to reception, where Grace was on the phone.

I waved a hand in farewell before I realised I didn't know where I was going. I waited until the receiver had been crashed back into place.

'Oh Grace, where is Stan's?' I asked nicely.

She frowned. 'Opposite Nat West.' There was a pause while she scrutinised me. 'You religious?'

I frowned too. 'Not particularly.'

'Hmm.' She went back to her keyboard, leaving me blinking.

Was she suggesting I needed help from The Above to deal with Malcolm?

'Thanks,' I said, as I pushed at the door. She didn't answer.

I found Malcolm already in front of a coffee and a plate of toast.

'I didn't know if you were coming or were too busy molly-coddling that idiot boy,' he said, by way of greeting. 'I'm having the power plate – what do you want?'

I looked at the board. If I missed a call from Paul I'd have to pretend I'd been opening the door to the postman, who then collapsed and needed mouth-to-mouth. 'Erm, just eggs on toast would be great. Scrambled, perhaps.'

Malcolm rapped out the order to a small thin man in a striped apron and then looked into his cup in disgust.

'It's not going to taste the same now,' he said crossly. 'Do you want a job as a reporter? At least you're half-way intelligent.'

'You're not really going to sack him, are you?'

'I certainly am. Ungrateful little twerp. All the training I've given him. And he goes to someone else. When was he going to tell me about the graffiti? We could at least have got it up on the website first.'

'They could have found out about it on Twitter anyway,' I offered.

'Don't make excuses. He gave them the details.'

Malcolm crunched down hard on a piece of toast. 'No sense of loyalty,' he growled between munches. 'The little bastard wants to remember who pays his wages. He won't get a job with the *Daily News*. A, because he's an idiot and B, because they've just laid off six people and even real reporters can't get work.'

He took a mouthful of coffee. 'Do you know how much they gave him?'

I shook my head. 'I don't think he got anything.'

'Pah!' Malcolm pushed his cup aside as a huge plate was brought to the table crammed with sausages, bacon, eggs, mushrooms and tomatoes. Malcolm prodded at it with a fork. 'Then he's even more stupid than I thought he was,' he said. 'Where's the black pudding?'

By the time Malcolm had worked his way through what was probably the government's recommended cholesterol allowance for the next three months and had a second cup of coffee, he was almost benign again.

'In the normal way,' he told me,' I'd have demanded half the money and given him a few baby shows to visit and that would have been the end of it.'

'Isn't that a bit hypocritical?' I asked, shocked. Malcolm shrugged. 'It's how it worked in my day.'

'When I tipped the *Sun* off an Arsenal striker was going to Man City, and the manager was resigning as a result, my local editor chased me down the street threatening to punch my lights out. Made me give him ALL the dosh. But he took me out and got me slaughtered on it when he'd calmed down.' He gave a guffaw. 'All a learning curve.'

I shook my head in disbelief. 'If you've done it yourself, you should be a bit more understanding. Gabriel didn't intend them to print anything yet – he was just trying to sell them the feature you weren't interested in, so he'd have some cuttings.'

Malcolm rolled his eyes. 'The boy needs to get a grip on the real world. You can't run a story on hysteria and hearsay. How were your eggs?'

'Pretty good. And brilliant toast. Just too much ...'

Malcolm inspected my plate. I pushed it towards him. 'Try.'

He leant out and took a forkful. 'Not bad at all. Never usually eat scrambled egg out, because my own is so bloody good.' He used my knife to get the last vestiges onto his fork.

'My kids say mine is the business too,' I told him.

He looked at me intently. 'What's your secret?'

'Lots of butter, a good splash of milk and cook it slowly ...'

'Exactly!' Malcolm thumped the table in triumph. 'Michael Winner was an odious man but he knew about food. Apart from scrambled eggs. He said he could do them in a few seconds. Proper scrambled eggs take half an hour.'

'I wouldn't go that far–' I began, but Malcolm had a zealous light in his eye, and was in full flow about foaming butter and the right sort of wooden spoon.

'I just mix it all together first, tip it in and keep stirring,' I offered.

Malcolm looked appalled. 'You need to try mine,' he said firmly. He stood up. 'We will arrange it. Now I must go back and see if that boy's stopped snivelling.'

He put a twenty-pound note on the table, gestured to the small man I assumed was Stan and picked up his newspaper. Then he looked at me hard. 'So your boyfriend's supplied cameras, has he?'

'He's not–'

'Let my man do his installation. I've got a feeling about this. Trust me?'

I nodded. Realising how much I did.

'Do you think–?' I began, but Malcolm was already heading for the door.

'Didn't you want to talk to me about some article?' I called after him.

'Too late now,' he said over his shoulder. 'Save it for the next lot of eggs.'

Chapter 31

B en was frying three of them when I got home.
'I've just finished the bread,' he said helpfully. 'Where's that bread-maker you used to have? That was good, when you used to make it every night.'

'In a box somewhere.' I poured boiling water on a lemon teabag. 'Nobody phoned from the office, did they?'

'I've still got to finish some coursework on acoustics and recording techniques.' Ben looked suddenly woebegone. 'I think I'm doing the wrong course, Mum.' My heart sank. The landline extension in the dining room rang. I thought about my computer sitting there and the pile of files. 'I've got to answer that,' I said.

Paul, who wouldn't win prizes for précis at the best of times, was in expansive mood. The clients were pleased with the new office layout in Croydon and my boss was buoyant because he was going out to tender for the contract to furnish the new headquarters of an apparently massive insurance company I'd never heard of.

It was all hands to the pump, he told me happily, and he was convening a team briefing at 10 a.m. on Friday. He'd email me the spec. Could I possibly do some initial space plans incorporating a visual walk-through?

Of course I could, I told him, equally brightly. As long as I didn't sleep …

By the time I'd put the phone down, taken some deep breaths and reassured myself it was all perfectly achievable as long as I started now and got in a proper day tomorrow, Ben had repaired to the sofa and was eating the last of his fry-up with Jeremy Clarkson.

'Do you want to tell me about it?' I asked. He shook his head. 'Talk later,' he said, eyes not moving from the screen.

I went back into the dining room, feeling the fluttering in the pit of my stomach I always got when one of my children had a problem.

I hauled my desktop computer, with its wide screen, from its corner onto the table, recalling wryly my original plan to kit out a proper office in the smallest bedroom or conservatory, with a sofa bed for occasional use. Right now, I couldn't get through the door of either. Ben's extraordinary talent for covering every inch of flooring with discarded clothes was being nurtured in one and Tilly's entire life was stacked in the other.

While I waited for the larger machine to boot up, I looked at Paul's email on my laptop. There were hours of work here that somehow had to be done by tomorrow, but I couldn't complain because we both knew there were other quiet weeks when he wouldn't comment as I jogged along at a relaxed pace, drawing up two days' worth of plans over a leisurely five. If I had to work till two in the morning I would – it was our unspoken deal and I hadn't let him down yet. Although, as I pulled up a blank template, I did wonder why the team meeting couldn't just as easily be Monday morning instead ...

I wondered afresh as I heard the doorbell ring at lunchtime, and Ben's voice announcing: 'through there'. Trying not to groan, I pressed save, glanced at the clock and smiled as kindly as I could as Gabriel appeared in the doorway, looking drained.

No, Malcolm hadn't sacked him, he confirmed. In fact Malcolm had told him that perhaps there was a story after all, and that if Gabriel thought he was so clever he should do a proper investigative piece and if he did it properly 'highly unlikely as that is' – Gabriel took off Malcolm's gruff tones – Malcolm would give him a by-line and make a splash of it online.

I smiled. 'It's all bluster with him,' I said. Clearly the breakfast had put a whole new complexion on things. 'He cares about you, really.'

Gabriel looked doubtful.

'And you can't let him down now he's given you a second chance,' I added firmly. 'Now he's getting this equipment put in, you might catch the culprit red-handed. Perhaps we could use the other set on Jinni's house.' I told him about David bringing the CCTV too.

Gabriel was immediately agog. 'When's it going to be installed?' he asked eagerly. 'So are you saying it's high enough quality to really see whoever's doing it?'

'So David says!'

Gabriel nodded. 'I think it's some sort of group. Like the

kind who used to burn Welsh cottages back in the eighties. I've read a lot about that and–'

'I hope not!' I interrupted, alarmed. 'I know it's a nuisance for locals with all the new development and house prices soaring but–'

'At least you can sell up one day and make a fortune,' put in Ben. 'When you're *really* old and have to retire.' He grinned, his earlier angst apparently forgotten.

'I rather like it here, as it happens,' I said, the memory of David's hands stroking my shoulders giving me a delicious frisson. 'But I'm disturbed about this–'

'When's the camera going up?' Gabriel asked again.

'I'm waiting for a call, but I'm in London Friday, so it will probably be after the weekend now – unless you boys want to go over and help Jinni set the other kit up ... But not now!' I added hastily, remembering Jinni's plans. 'She's busy.' I began to pour coffee. 'Let's sort it on Saturday. Nothing will happen that quickly, will it? These other incidents have been spaced out ...'

Gabriel looked thoughtful. 'But they do seem to upping the ante now. And the spray paint at the station ...'

'Jinni will probably say David is behind that too, to put us off his trail–'

Gabriel shook his head. 'I really like Jinni but she's a bit over the top about this one. He might be fed up with her objections but not to that extent. It doesn't make sense.'

I handed him a mug. No it didn't. I still wondered whether I'd heard the full story. Was it simply hurt pride as Caroline had suggested? Was Jinni jealous that he and I–'

'And he'd hardly offer CCTV ...' Gabriel was saying.

'Jinni thinks that's a double bluff,' I told him. 'Says we won't catch anyone on it.'

'We should still put it up and see,' said Ben. 'Send Jinni a text and see if she does want us to go over.'

'I've got to get back.' Gabriel looked at his watch. 'I've got to keep Genghis happy – he'll go mad if I'm late.'

He got up. 'So Saturday, then?' he said to Ben. 'I'll come round first thing.'

'Not too first.' Ben lightly punched his arm. 'Fox tomorrow night?'

'Maybe – if we go late. Think I've got to cover some charity fashion show first.' He pulled a face. 'I'm getting all the best jobs ...'

'Might be some talent ...' Ben laughed. 'Every cloud, mate. A late one would be good ...'

I listened to them bantering as they went through to the front door. Ben seemed in perfectly good spirits now so I'd ask him about his course later. He'd come to me if it was that bad, I reasoned, torn between maternal duty and anxiety about work. I wondered if Gabriel had told his mother about his problems.

'Is his family being supportive?' I asked, when Ben poked his head around the door to tell me he was finally going down the town and had I got cash for the bread. Ben shrugged. 'He's 24, Mum.'

'Doesn't mean he doesn't need someone to talk to!' I retorted. 'That's why he's coming round here, isn't it? I'm a sort of surrogate. Which I'm very happy to be but–' I felt another pang of guilt. 'Ben, I do want to hear about your difficulties with your course, darling. Even if I can't be much help.'

He looked gloomy. 'I don't even know if I want to be at uni at all. I wish I'd had a gap year now, and gone travelling and busked.'

My mind whirred. What about his student loan if he just threw it all in now? Could he go back later? 'Have you discussed this with your brother?'

Ben shook his head. 'Ollie's got his own problems, hasn't he?'

Another bolt of alarm went through me. 'Has he?'

Ben gave me an odd look.

'He was worried about money and where to live, but that's all sorted now. Sam's parents will be back soon, and Dad and I will try to help too—' I stopped, silenced by Ben's expression. 'Is there something else?'

Ben shrugged uncomfortably. 'I dunno. I just get the feeling he's a bit—'

'A bit what?'

He shrugged again. 'What else d'you want me to buy?'

When it was clear I wasn't going to force any more out of him, I gave him twenty pounds and a short list and turned back to my computer and the very long list of measurements.

But my brain kept sliding away to Malcolm and Gabriel's showdown and Ben's discontent, and the hint at new worries for Oliver, and if I was honest with myself, the thought of David's crinkly eyes and dark (apparently un-dyed) brows and what might happen on Saturday …

I made more coffee, bracing myself for the fact that I'd be coming out in blotches any time soon, and tried to get back to the job in hand. I'd just got rid of a cold-caller wanting to sell me a funeral plan and was absorbed in a new set of drawings when I heard the front door open.

I stood up, disconcerted by Ben remembering his key for the second time in three days, only to see Oliver appear.

'I told you, Mum,' he said tightly. 'We've had the first midwife appointment this afternoon.

'Is everything okay?' I scanned his face for bad news.

'It's all fine. It was just to take the details.' Oliver looked as if he had a funeral planned himself. 'We get a scan next time,' he said flatly. 'And then we hear the baby's heartbeat.'

'That's lovely! Where's Sam?' My own heart was beating a little harder. I wasn't used to this Oliver.

'In the loo,' he said. 'She's not feeling well.'

Sam came into the room moments later, looking pale. She smiled weakly. 'I feel really sick,' she said. 'I'm going to lie down.'

'You do that.' I looked at my son, who also looked nauseous. 'Both of you go up. I'll make tea. Peppermint?'

'I can do it.' Oliver's voice was sharp.

'What's the matter?' I asked him in the kitchen as we stood waiting for the kettle to boil. 'Do you want to talk about it?'

'Not really.'

Chapter 32

I tried to get back into Personal Storage Units and grapple with the six versus eight drawers conundrum, but I felt knotted inside. I'd never seen Oliver so closed and distant.

When Ben eventually reappeared with half of what I'd asked him to get, I wasn't much further forward. I'd had an email from Malcolm – an unusually expansive missive for him – talking about my going for brunch at the weekend and including a link to an interview with a chef who claimed an electric whisk should be employed in pursuit of the perfect scrambled eggs, but not mentioning the debacle with Gabriel at all.

And a fraught-sounding one from Paul enquiring how things were going. (*Very slowly, since you ask ...*) Oliver and Sam were both still upstairs.

After a small internal wrestle during which respect for privacy and personal space pitted itself against motherly responsibility and the latter bulldozed its way through, I tapped on the bedroom door. 'Are you happy with an avocado salad?' I called to Sam.

She opened the door in her dressing gown, looking wan.

Oliver lay, still in jeans and t-shirt on the top of the duvet. He appeared to be engrossed in his phone.

'I'm so sorry, Tess,' she said. 'I should be cooking tonight ...'

'It's no problem,' I told her, adding brightly: 'Is everything okay?'

'Oh yes.' Her face lit up. 'Kerry the midwife was lovely and she said she'd just had another girl in who'd got pregnant being sick. She'd had the norovirus and couldn't understand why she wasn't getting any better. By the time she went to the doctor she was three months ...' As Sam chatted on, telling me about blood tests and the date for the first scan, I stole a look past her at my son. He was still intent on his screen, tapping at buttons, showing no interest in the conversation.

'I'll doing a chicken Caesar for us,' I said, when Sam had paused for breath. 'And there's a quiche.'

'Great,' he said, without enthusiasm.

I went back downstairs, unsettled. Had I traumatised him shrieking about the shoes? I heard Ben's voice when I'd expressed concern for Gabriel. *He's 24, Mum.* So would Oliver be in a few months' time and after that he'd be a father ... But I still couldn't bear his face shut towards mine.

As I fried croutons in olive oil and shaved off slivers of Parmesan, Ben came to lean in the doorway. 'Have we got any beers left?' he asked hopefully.

I shook my head. 'But you could open a bottle of wine.' I forced a smile. 'I think I could do with one.'

I looked at the back of his head as he wielded the corkscrew. 'Have you started your essay yet?' I asked, knowing he hadn't. He sighed. 'Nope. Need to though – it's twenty per cent of my first year.' He groaned. 'And then I've got to do stuff for the exams ...'

I looked at him in alarm. 'When are they?'

'Next week.'

'I didn't even know he had exams,' I told Oliver, when Ben was back in front of the TV and my eldest had carried a pile of plates into the kitchen after dinner. 'This year is galloping past. Did you know he's thinking of changing his course? Or leaving altogether?'

My eldest son did not look up from the dishwasher. 'He's just freaking out at all the revision he hasn't done,' he said. 'He's only got two – and one of them is a multiple choice. The rest is practical.' Oliver straightened up and reached for a bundle of cutlery. 'He always wants to change course when he has to do any work.' He looked at me and smiled for the first time that evening. 'Remember how many times he wanted to leave school when he was doing his A levels?'

I smiled back and nodded.

'He's bad at sticking at things,' Oliver said. 'He can't deal with commitment.' He was abruptly straight-faced again. For a moment he looked as he had done in the bar on St Pancras Station when he'd told me about the baby.

I stretched clingfilm over the remaining salad. 'He's only young,' I said, struck by the edge to Oliver's voice. I hesitated for a moment. 'Is that what's worrying you?'

Oliver came back when Ben was in front of the TV and Sam had gone to have a bath. I'd booted up the computer again, but felt too washed out and shaken to concentrate on the plans.

'I'm sorry I shouted.' he said.

'It's okay.' I saved the document in front of me and tried to smile. 'It is indeed my bloody fault. I should have got the mussels – if that's what the midwife thinks it probably was – in the fridge quicker or not brought them home on the train at all. I am entirely responsible for Sam getting food-poisoning and I am truly sorry, but I know that in the end when you have a beautiful son or daughter and I have a very special grandchild it will all be meant to be ...' I trailed off, a huge lump in my throat.

Oliver looked at me. 'You don't have to pretend. I know you don't want it either. You told Tilly you didn't want to be a grandmother when you were looking after Fran's kids.'

'No I didn't!' I said hotly, cursing my daughter's lack of thought. 'I said I wasn't expecting *her* to have any children YET.'

Oliver continued to gaze at me – his face sceptical.

'I'm not one of those mothers who would put the pressure on. You know I'm thrilled. I just wasn't expecting it,' I finished lamely. *You don't seem old enough*, I added silently. Even though he was exactly the age I was, when I had him ...

'No, well, it's taking some getting used to,' Oliver said awkwardly. He crossed to the pine cupboard with the bottles on top. 'Can I have some of this port?'

I watched as he poured himself a hefty measure. I'd noticed at dinner he'd drunk most of the wine we'd opened. I'd been trying to sip slowly so I could still get some work done, but after Oliver's outburst I'd refilled my glass too.

'I understand, darling. I can remember being pregnant with you,' I offered, swallowing hard. 'I would wake up sometimes at four in the morning, and worry. Even though I wanted you so much,' I added hastily.

'It's natural,' I went on, warming to my theme. 'It's the thought of the responsibility. Knowing you've got to look after this little person for the next twenty years. I smiled at him. 'Or probably a lot longer.'

Oliver gave a weak smile back.

'But I promise you won't mind a bit because when the baby is actually here – a real, tiny person, then you simply feel–' I stopped, as Oliver shook his head miserably.

'And I expect Sam feels like this too, sometimes. Have you talked to her about it?'

Oliver shook his head again. 'It wouldn't be fair. She's not feeling well and she's worried about how we're going to afford everything. And when we first found out, and I suggested, just once, that maybe–'

He stopped. 'I didn't really mean it but I thought we should at least discuss options.'

I nodded. 'You were thinking it through.'

'She got really upset. Said she could never get rid of my baby. She was hurt I even mentioned it. I can't express doubts now.'

'She may be having them herself. As I said, even though I'd planned it, I used to–'

'Mum!' Oliver's voice stopped me in my tracks. 'It's not the baby.'

The theme tune from *Family Guy* floated through from

the front room and moments later I heard Ben give a shout of laughter. I got up and pushed the dining-room door closed.

'What is it, then?'

Oliver was studying his glass, turning it round and round in front of him. 'It's Sam,' he said with difficulty. 'I don't know now if we're meant to be together or we just have to be ...'

I took a mouthful of my own drink. I'd expected money or lack of parenting skills.

'I mean I love Sam, of course,' Oliver was saying. 'I still love her but it's kind of changed. It's not ...' He stopped and looked embarrassed. 'And if we're going to have a baby, then we're going to have to be together for ever. I couldn't leave her for years, could I? What sort of bastard would that make me?' Oliver looked anguished.

'But you don't want to leave her. Do you?' I asked in a low voice. 'You were going to live together, you told me how good it was, you'd made plans.'

Oliver didn't reply. He drank some port.

'You were so happy–'

Oliver shook his head.

'You're just panicking,' I said. 'You were going to get the flat and–'

'Everything's changed,' he said in a rush. 'It's–

He was abruptly silent again as the landline rang. 'Hold on a minute,' I said. 'I'll tell Paul I'll ring him back.'

But it was Tilly demanding to know why I hadn't answered my mobile and in full flow about rehearsals and the run starting and a possible flat share in Tooting with the gay cousin of Shane, who was 'adorable'.

Oliver started to get up, but I flapped my hand at him to stay, while I waited for my daughter to draw breath. Tilly had realised she would be much happier sharing with a man because although Danni was calmer and had asked Tilly to consider staying on, it would only be a matter of time before she went bonkers again.

Oliver topped up his glass and sat back down, looking morose. 'Tell me in a minute,' I mouthed.

'So I'm going to stay there for ten days and then after the run, I'll probably be moving in with Matthew,' Tilly was saying, 'so I'll just be back weekends till then.'

'Okay, well whatever–'

'It really doesn't matter,' Oliver said in a low voice.

'IT DOES,' I mouthed back. Tilly was still talking. 'Tilly, that's all lovely but I'm having a chat with Oliver–'

'Oh!' Tilly did not sound pleased.

Across the table, Oliver shook his head crossly and stood up again.

'And it's important,' I said firmly, flapping my hand again and ignoring Oliver's black look. 'So can I call you back, darling?'

'No, I'm going out,' Tilly was sounding bored now. 'If you're okay with all that, I'll see you Friday night.'

'It's fine!' I trilled, ringing off and leaping across the room to grab Oliver's arm. 'Darling, please talk to me.'

'It's nothing.'

'What's changed? Apart from being pregnant and having

311

to move in here,' I added, realising it was a stupid question, because everything had. 'You'll have your own place when Sam's parents get back and—'

Oliver had his face turned away from me. I sat down and after a moment he did too, taking another big mouthful from the tumbler in his hand. He was slightly flushed.

'I suppose we've been together nearly three years now,' he said slowly, eyes still averted. 'And it's not going to be the same as in the beginning ...'

'No,' I took quite a large swallow of wine myself, sensing I had to get whatever I said, absolutely right. 'Relationships do change ...'

'She feels sick a lot of the time and she's very tired ...'

'It won't always be like that ...' I said, reflecting that actually, yes, that was my life for what felt like a decade when the three of mine were all under six and I was constantly knackered. 'She'll start to feel better soon and—'

'But people still stay together, don't they? Even though—'

I tried to think how to summarise tactfully, showing motherly insight that would not make him sink into a pool of embarrassment.

'Of course,' I began. 'One can't realistically expect to keep up the level of romance and passion one feels at the very beginning, but gradually that is replaced with something deeper, warmer ...' I stopped.

Oliver raised a wry eyebrow. 'Is that what happened with you and Dad?'

'Yes!' I said firmly. 'We had many happy years together,' I went on, my determination to be positive making me declare this rather loudly. 'And even though we wanted different things eventually that doesn't mean–'

Oliver was looking at me now, expectantly. I had to be reassuring.

'–I wouldn't change a moment of it. We have three amazing children and your father and I were only agreeing the other day,' I paraphrased, 'that we were so glad we'd married and it was all so worthwhile.'

Oliver gave a small nod and I ploughed on.

'It's all quite usual you start off hardly being able to keep your hands off each other and then–' I hesitated as Oliver winced, clearly uncomfortable with this level of sharing from his mother. 'Then things settle down.'

Had I been unable to control myself in the face of Rob's animal magnetism? There was that incident in the bus shelter, but we'd both been drinking ... Did he ever turn me on the way David had the other day? Maybe I'd been drinking too much now – my glass was empty.

'Sam's a lovely girl,' I went on, 'and she makes you very happy. You told me she was your best friend.'

'Yes, she is.'

'Imagine how you'd feel if you went upstairs now and she said she was leaving you?'

Oliver nodded. 'Devastated. I know.'

'It will all be okay. I know it will.'

Oliver shrugged. Then gave a small, resigned smile back. 'It's going to have to be, isn't it?'

'Talk to her,' I urged. 'Ask her how she's feeling about it all ...'

The dining-room door swung open and Ben waved an iPad

at us, grinning widely. 'Hey bruv, you've got to see this clip on YouTube. It is sick!'

Oliver swilled down the last of his drink, put the glass on the table and got up. 'I'm there.'

There he still was when I gave up and went upstairs. The wine had made me foggy and tired and I'd decided the best thing I could do was set the alarm for dawn. If I had a clear run tomorrow, I'd get everything finished.

Sam was on the sofa with the boys, wearing pyjamas. I was relieved to see her leaning comfortably against Oliver, who was holding her hand. Both turned to smile at me. Ben waved the remote control but kept his eyes fixed on the screen. 'Night, Mumsie!'

As I sat on the edge of the bed, weary to my bones, my mobile beeped twice.

I grabbed it, hoping it was David. It wasn't.

Caroline wanted to know if I had time for a drink before I caught the train on Friday. Gabriel was thanking me for my support. Scrolling down, I found a text from Gerald I'd missed earlier, asking if I'd be in time for lunch on Monday. I looked at it guiltily. With all that was going on, I'd barely given my mother's appointment a thought.

My fingers hovered over the keys. 'Never text a man drunk, unless you're already at the stage where you can summon him for sex,' Caroline had advised. I put the phone down and went through to the bathroom. Roll on Saturday.

A shame we weren't at the summoning stage right now …

Chapter 33

'But you will be soon?' said Caroline.

She was perched on a stool at the champagne bar in St Pancras, looking impossibly stylish in a cream linen dress with ruby-red bag and heels that perfectly matched her lipstick.

I felt sallow and crumpled. The make-up I'd blearily applied on the early train this morning had long gone and my own linen – in the form of a pair of wide-legged blue trousers – looked as if someone had been chewing it.

As Caroline crossed one smooth golden leg over another and grasped the ice-filled bucket, I was glad that at least I was afforded limb cover. Epilation was high on my to-do list.

I'd tried to protest that I was feeling too tired, looking too tatty and rendered incapable of intelligent speech after a sixteen-hour stint getting the plans ready and a morning team meeting that had lasted all day, but Caroline had still ordered a full bottle.

'It will perk you up,' she'd said. She was now filling my glass. 'You said you've nothing on tonight.'

'Tilly's coming.'

'I bet she goes straight to the pub.'

I took a mouthful of the deliciously cold bubbles. Caroline was right. I could feel my spirits lifting already. 'Probably.'

'So tomorrow's the night.' Caroline was back on the subject of David. 'I suppose that's sensible. Get him into bed and sort it out one way or another.'

'I can't just–'

'Of course you can. Get your hair done–'

'And my legs waxed–'

'Obviously. Oh, and try this.' Caroline pulled a tiny pot out of her glossy bag. 'It is fabulous.' She unscrewed the lid and held out a pale pink cream for me to see. 'Smells divine but wait till you put it on your face.' She produced a small gold mirror too and handed both to me. 'GG Glow mousse. Just about to be launched. Reacts with your skin's ph to provide the perfect individual colour and coverage just for you.'

She tilted her face on one side for my inspection. 'I've got it on but it will look different on you.' I surveyed Caroline's flawless complexion and sighed.

'I'm sure it will.'

Actually, I had to admit, the fluffy potion was nothing short of miraculous. By the time I'd smoothed it over my nose and cheeks and Caroline had whipped out a palette of eye colour, which she expertly dabbed into my sockets, I looked quite restored. 'Now this,' she instructed, thrusting a huge mascara wand at me and ignoring the curious looks of the businessmen behind us. 'Two coats.'

She dropped all the make-up, including the bit-too-shocking pink lipstick I was now sporting, into my bag. 'I've got shed-loads of it, darling. You look amazing!' She topped up our glasses again. 'He won't be able to resist you.'

I peered into the mirror again and admitted I had scrubbed up quite well.

'Text him on the train, while you're feeling gorgeous,' she urged. 'Start razzing him up.' She fished a miniature phial of perfume from her bottomless clutch and dabbed some on my wrists. 'This is new too. Isn't it heavenly?'

By the time I'd hugged her goodbye and made my way to the Northstone train I was feeling mildly glamorous and pleasantly sloshed and dreaming David might appear in my carriage, also smelling heavenly, and be so bowled over by my make-over he immediately suggested a romantic dinner (I was quite hungry now too) before whisking me home to his no-doubt super-cool house and massive, crisp-sheeted and firm-mattressed bed in his thrillingly masculine sleeping chamber.

Somewhere during this reverie I did start dreaming – some-what bizarrely – of Malcolm bringing me poached eggs in bed because there was no milk to scramble them with – and woke up abruptly with my neck bent sideways, to find the train at a standstill somewhere between stations and my mobile ringing.

I looked around hastily, afraid I'd been snoring, but the carriage was empty save a young man with a rucksack who was also asleep.

I looked at the time and the darkening foliage on the steep banks outside the window, and concluded I must be just outside the town. I felt exhausted, my earlier buoyancy gone.

Tilly hadn't left a message but I imagined she was calling to tell me she was out with Ben and Gabriel. Perhaps, I thought hopefully, Oliver would go too, or he and Sam would already be in bed.

If the train didn't move soon, everyone would be.

Ten minutes later there was an announcement from a weary-sounding bloke apologising for signal problems and the train rumbled forwards and crawled into Northstone.

The young man opened his eyes and stumbled onto the platform. As I followed, I saw a group of people getting out of the end carriage. I heard someone call out goodnight. Then they separated out and two of them, walking close together, began to come towards me.

I jumped back on the train.

A uniformed figure was coming down the row towards me, eyebrows raised. 'You all right there?'

'Er – yes, sorry. I thought I'd dropped something.' I made a show of examining the empty seats. The ticket collector leant down and looked under the table. 'Can't see anything, love. But we get all sorts left. At least one iPad a week. You'd think they'd look after one of those, wouldn't you? More money than sense. My two are the same ...'

I did some nodding and thanking and a bit more pointless checking and when I couldn't find any reason to stay another moment, stepped cautiously back onto the platform. It was empty, apart from a girl wheeling a bicycle towards the exit.

I breathed a sigh of relief. It couldn't have been David. Just someone tall who looked like him.

I tried to analyse my panic. It wasn't just because the reflection in the train window had told me the make-up was well past its best – or that my hair was flattened one side from where I'd been slumped in the corner.

The thought of sending him a bold, encouraging text now the champagne had worn off, seemed far too brazen for a Friday night. Even a conversation on the platform, with others about, would feel awkward. But I'd be seeing him tomorrow ...

As I walked up the path to my house, hugging this thought, I saw the curtains were half-drawn. A figure I didn't immediately recognise crossed in front of the light in the middle. It didn't look like either of the boys. And was too stocky to be Gabriel. The front door opened as soon as I put my key in the lock. 'I phoned you!' said Tilly. 'I was worried when you were so late.'

'Drink with Caroline.' I kissed her before she stepped back and I saw who else was in the room. 'Oh for God's sake,' I said, gracelessly. 'What are *you* doing here?'

'Mum!' Tilly shot me a furious look 'You said it was fine!'

'Hello,' said Rob, getting up from the chair. 'You look nice.'

'I didn't take that bit in,' I told Tilly crossly, as I kicked off my shoes, reeling at the shock of my ex dishing out his second compliment in as many months, bringing the grand total to more than he'd managed in twenty years.

'Dad's helping me take my stuff back. I knew you weren't listening,' she said, martyred. 'Too busy with Oliver.' She shot her father a knowing look.

'Don't start that, Tilly,' I said sharply. 'We were right in the middle of a conversation that was important.'

'Is everything all right?' Rob asked weightily.

'Yes fine. Where are the boys and Sam?'

'Oliver and Ben have gone to the pub, and Sam's upstairs skyping her mum. I was going, but Gabriel's got to work late so I thought I'd keep Dad company till you got back.' Tilly made it sound as though she were doing me a favour.

'I'm going to get changed. Perhaps, Tilly,' I said tightly, 'you could bring me up a jasmine tea?'

'What exactly are you playing at?' I exploded, when she arrived in my bedroom proffering a cup and a defiant expression. 'He's got a bloody overnight bag in the hall. Where exactly is he going to sleep?'

'In my bed in the conservatory,' she said, as if it were obvious. 'I can sleep with you, can't I? It's only for one night. I did tell you he was going to drive me back tomorrow.'

'I'm quite sure you didn't tell me you wanted him to stay here first.' I glowered at her. 'Why couldn't he come in the morning?'

'Fiona's being stressy. She's all wound up about the move. So I just thought—' Tilly gave an exaggerated shrug, as if there were nothing odd in the arrangement.

I frowned. 'And how does she feel about him staying with his ex-wife?'

'I think she's glad to get him out of the way so she can carry on with her labelling.' Tilly raised innocent brows, 'You're no threat are you, after all this time?'

'No, of course not but—'

'Fiona can be a pain in the arse but she's still really attractive and she's got a fantastic body.'

The implications were clear. I glanced at my reflection in

the full-length mirror as I started to pull the clothes from my ordinary, slightly squidgy body to put on some pyjama bottoms. Knowing Rob, he'd not told her anyway. He'd probably fabricated some visiting client or business club knees-up. I knew his techniques of old.

'Anyway,' Tilly was now lying on her stomach across my bed. 'There's no need to be so nasty. Dad's being helpful. He's doing a shift on the surveillance screen till Ben gets back. We couldn't get the alert sound to work on the iPad, though. I think it's all right on Jinni's computer ...'

'What?'

Having decided my brain cells had imploded from lack of nutrition, Tilly made cheesy Marmite toast while she filled me in on the day's events and Rob provided pompous interjections to explain the technology.

Jinni, forgetting I'd be in London, had come over early this morning in an excitable state to report she'd definitely seen someone skulking around her wheelie bins in the early hours of the morning when she went to the loo but had frightened the figure off by throwing open her front door, shrieking and hurling a dustpan at it.

Ben, after recovering from being awake before nine, had seized upon this as an opportunity to delay his revision and had spent the rest of the day setting up the CCTV from the box David had left. Some sort of wireless webcam was now installed above her front door with infra-red light so it could capture images even in the dark, with a second beam homing in on our driveway, and was sending pictures to her computer and to his iPad.

Ben had also been on hand to pass things while her electrician installed a powerful security light outside her back door and had his business card in case I wanted one.

Jinni claimed the person who had run away was the right height and build to be David (Tilly, loyally, doubted this) but if not, had almost certainly been paid by him, but she was determined to capture the culprit whoever it was. An alarm would sound at her end when anyone broke the beam trained on her front gravel, and she then intended to utilise the broom handle she was keeping just inside the front door, along with an aerosol spray, to beat him into submission.

'I really don't think that's wise,'

I said. 'She should phone the police.'

'When Ben gets back he's going to have another go at making the alarm come through here. It's supposed to make a noise and send an email when it detects something. He thinks it might work on your laptop. Then we can leave it on loud and if things get hairy we'll be able to phone the police too!'

'Is this completely necessary?' I asked wearily, my visions of a long, stress-free night of catching up on my sleep, shattered not only by the prospect of my daughter shifting about beside me but an ear-splitting beep going off every time a fox decided to nip across Jinni's garden.

Tilly rolled her eyes. 'Ben said you were the one who wanted it set up! He and Gabe were going to do it, but it's sorted now.' She frowned. 'I've not heard back from him. Ben said he had to go to a fashion show?'

I yawned. 'Yes, Malcolm is keeping him to the grindstone.'

I was now on the sofa with my second cup of tea. Rob was settled in the chair with a red wine, grating on my nerves with regular bulletins from the screen of the iPad, on which I could only see some wavy things that looked like bits of plant. 'Why don't you tell us when something *has* happened, not when it hasn't?' I said waspishly, earning another glare from my daughter.

I was just announcing I was going to bed, to see if I could get in an hour before Tilly came clumping up to join me, when the front door burst open and my sons spilled into the room, clutching take-aways.

'Mumsie!' Ben cried jubilantly. 'You're back!'

'And you're pissed,' said Tilly.

Ben grinned at her, kissed me and went over to hug his father. 'We've had a pint or two, haven't we, bruv?' he said, looking at Oliver, who also seemed pretty relaxed.

'Sam okay?' he asked Tilly. His sister nodded. 'She said to tell you she was going to read ...'

'So,' Ben was perched on the arm of Rob's chair, eating a chip. 'I've got to get this email alert set up ...'

'Couldn't you do it in the morning?' I asked. 'And perhaps get a plate?' He was now hauling a kebab out of the box, scattering shreds of lettuce onto the carpet.

'We've got to be ready,' Ben said loudly. 'Ollie and I are going to get him, aren't we, bruv?'

I sighed and got up. 'I doubt anyone will come back tonight if Jinni was throwing things at them last time. And if you do see anything, you call 999. You don't want to be arrested yourselves for causing an affray. Suppose he–'

Oliver walked past me to the kitchen. 'Don't worry, Mum. It's all cool.'

Rob straightened up and pointed to himself in a gesture that conveyed he was there and would be supervising proceedings, so after making a small gesture back – in the direction of his wine glass – I gave up.

'I'll leave you to make sure your father's got all he needs,' I said, with sweet menace, to Tilly, still seething at the prospect of her kicking me half the night.

'If one of us blocks off his exit,' I heard Ben say, 'the other one can jump him.'

'Suppose he climbs over the back?' Even Oliver was joining in now.

I shook my head as I climbed the stairs. Perhaps I'd been wrong to foist my Enid Blytons on them. As if to confirm it, I heard the word 'dog'. Then the low murmur of Rob's voice and Tilly laughing.

My legs ached with tiredness as I burrowed under the duvet, having put a pillow around my ears. It had been after midnight by the time I'd checked everything for the meeting, and I'd been up before six.

I yawned deeply and rubbed my eyes. I still had Caroline's mascara on.

Chapter 34

I woke with a jolt just after 1 a.m. Tilly hadn't come to bed. Outside I could hear a wild whooping, like a war cry.

Stumbling to the window, wobbly with fatigue, I looked across the road to where dark figures were moving about outside Jinni's. I could see torchlight. As I heard another triumphant cry, I realised it was Ben over there making all the racket.

I grabbed my dressing gown and hurried downstairs. The front door was open. As I stepped out onto the path, Tilly came running towards me.

'Come on,' she panted at me. 'They've seen someone.'

'Have you phoned the police?'

'Jinni says we'll catch him first ...'

'I expect he's miles away by now, with all that noise.'

'I know – Ben's a moron.'

'Where's your father?'

'He went to bed. Jinni wants you. Come ON ...'

'I'd better get dressed.'

'What for?'

With Tilly almost shoving me through the front door, I put flip-flops on, tied my dressing gown tighter and allowed her to lead me across the dark road to the rectory. As we crunched our way over the gravel, Jinni opened the front door, in an orange kimono. 'This way,' she said in a stage whisper. 'Tilly, help me close the gates.'

While I waited in the unlit hallway, she and Tilly dragged the big iron gates shut and secured them with what looked like a bicycle padlock.

'That'll sort the bastard,' Jinni said with satisfaction, as she came back in.

Confused, I followed her into the kitchen, where Oliver and Ben were standing near the open back door. 'What's actually happened?' I yawned. 'Can I make some tea?'

Jinni flicked a switch on the kettle. 'He's out there,' she said, nodding towards the back garden.

Jinni, it transpired, had already gone to bed when my three, still sitting up drinking, had spotted movement on the iPad screen. Ben and Oliver, clearly invigorated by another round of beers, had charged over there, only to see a hooded figure running around the side of the building. They'd given chase, but whoever it was had disappeared. But they knew he was still there because there'd been no sounds of anyone trying to scramble over a wall and they'd now got a row of wheelie bins blocking the exit back round to the front.

'And we've been watching the whole time,' said Ben.

'He must be bloody uncomfortable,' said Tilly. 'Lying in all those bushes.'

'There's loads of nettles down the end there, too,' Jinni added. 'And rubble and all sorts. Serves him right. Hope the rats get him.'

'Have you got rats?' I asked, nervously.

'Who knows,' said Jinni. 'But they like undergrowth, don't they?'

'They say there's one within twenty metres of every house,' said Tilly.

'One and a half million in the sewers,' put in Oliver.

I shuddered. 'Can you stop it? Who else wants tea?'

Everyone ignored me. 'Right, this is the plan,' said Jinni. 'We're going to make a big deal of waving the torch about and then shutting the door and turning all the lights out, as if we think we've lost him. Then we sit here in the dark and wait. When he thinks we've all gone, he'll come out and then we'll pounce ...'

As my offspring all nodded, I looked with disbelief at their shining faces. I really was in the middle of a *Famous Five* novel. 'Are you absolutely sure there's anyone there?' I asked. 'Who actually saw the hooded figure?'

'Ben,' said Oliver, at the same time as Ben said: 'I did', and the first seed of doubt appeared in Tilly's eyes.

'It wasn't someone delivering pizza leaflets?'

'What? At one in the morning?' Jinni raised her eyebrows.

'If they're students, doing a holiday job ...' I shrugged.

'There was nothing through the door.'

'Perhaps you scared him off before he could leave it.'

All four looked at me as if I were ruining everything.

'I'll make tea,' I said.

As I dropped a Darjeeling teabag into a mug, Jinni's voice rang in from the garden. 'There's no one here. You boys go home. Tell your mum I'll call her in the morning ...'

'Okay, sure.' Ben was playing along.

'I'm knackered,' Jinni was telling him. 'I'm going to hit the sack.'

'Okay,' Ben was now sounding rather staged. 'We'll be off, then.'

They came in and Jinni made a fuss of jiggling the key in the lock as she turned it. Then she turned off the last remaining light, leaving just a small glow coming in from a lamp in the hallway.

She went through to the hall and we heard her open the front door. 'See you! Thanks for your help!' we heard her bellow, before the front door was slammed shut.

'That should have carried,' she said in a low voice as she returned. 'Now stay glued. Thank God it's a clear night.'

She and Ben and Oliver took up position on three wooden chairs a couple of feet back from the dark glass. I sat at the table in the gloom with my tea. Tilly sat opposite. She drummed her fingers on the wood and yawned. 'I hope he comes out soon – then we can give him a smacking and get to bed.'

'You won't!' I frowned at her. 'You mustn't do anything illegal. Do you hear that Ben? Oliver?' I added, thinking of Rob's face if his sons were carted off by the long arm of the law. So much for him keeping an eye on proceedings! Both boys grunted.

'The police take a dim view of vigilantes,' I continued. 'I think we should phone now and let them take over.'

'Take over what?' said Jinni. 'They're hardly going to come rushing round because we say we think there might be someone in the hedge–'

'I think they will,' I protested. 'If you say you're a single woman on your own and you're frightened ...'

Jinni looked cynical. 'They didn't do a lot last time. Said to call if it happened again. Much better to phone them when we've made a citizen's arrest.' I gave up. My phone was still next to my bed.

'We must keep really still,' said Jinni. 'Though I could do with some coffee. Not to mention a small port ...'

Half an hour later I could feel my eyelids drooping. I'd long finished my tea and was ready to go back to sleep. 'I think I'll slide quietly out of the front,' I said. 'I really am knackered. Whoever you might have seen has long gone.'

'You can't get out,' said Jinni, in a low voice, still staring through the glass. 'Do you want to lie down on my– LOOK!'

She grabbed Oliver's arm. 'See!' she hissed. 'Something moving over there!' All three leant forward. Tilly leapt up from her seat and crouched down beside Ben.

'He's crawling ...'

Despite myself, I joined them at the window and peered out. 'Keep back,' whispered Oliver. 'Is it someone or the bushes are blowing about?'

'That's a body.' Ben was adamant. 'Come on!'

'I'll open the door,' Jinni was saying. 'Then we charge ...'

'Suppose he's armed?' My voice came out in a squeak.

Tilly threw me a disparagingly look. 'He might have some eggs in his pocket.'

I leant forward as far as I dared and looked into the darkness, I could make out shrubs and trees and then I saw it too – a black shape moving slowly along the edge of the grass, keeping back against the bushes. We all seemed to be holding our breath. As we watched, the shape straightened up and a figure could clearly be seen creeping along past an old shed at the bottom of Jinni's garden. I was shot through with fear. 'Oh my God, what are we going to do?' I put a hand over my mouth as Jinni sprang into action.

Suddenly a beam of bright light fell across the garden and she had the back door open. Before I could move, Oliver and Ben were running across the grass towards the intruder with Tilly behind. I heard Jinni yell: 'Bastard!' as my sons threw themselves on the dark figure, bringing him flat down onto the ground and Jinni swung a flashlight over the three of them. Someone shrieked – it was probably me – and Tilly chucked herself down on the grass too, grabbing one of the jutting legs, holding onto it with both hands to prevent escape.

But the figure pinned to the floor wasn't struggling. He lay face down, the hood of his sweatshirt pulled up over his hair, and made no noise. 'Oh my God,' I squeaked again. 'Have you hurt him?'

'I hope so!' said Jinni, grimly. 'Let's have a look at you, you weasel ...'

Breathing heavily, Oliver and Ben sat back and rolled the man over.

A can of spray paint was pushed into the damp grass where he'd been lying. He winced as Jinni shone the torch into his face and we all gasped.

I heard Ben mutter: 'Oh mate,' as my daughter gave a screech of fury.

'You!' Tilly spluttered. 'You stupid–' She stopped, seeming

to struggle for the right words, while we all continued to gawp. 'You complete and utter TWAT!'

I stared at the blonde hair and pale face of the young man lying in front of me, his eyes wide with shock, as Tilly – totally uncharacteristically, and to everyone's astonishment – burst into tears.

Chapter 35

Ten hours later we were still in varying states of undress and misery.

'I don't believe it,' said Tilly, for the sixth time. She sat at the table in her nightie and pushed her hands through her hair. 'What was he thinking of?'

Ben, opening the freezer in his boxers and collecting several slices of bread, yawned. 'Stop going on. He was trying to get his story, like he told us.'

Tilly shook her head. 'Jinni's furious.'

'She'll calm down,' I told her. When the screaming had ended the night before, I had packed Gabriel off with my sons as escort, for his own safety, suggesting the matter was discussed today when we all felt more composed.

I had got the feeling that, irate as she was, Jinni's main source of outrage with Gabriel was disappointment that she could no longer blame David. 'Did he put you up to this?' she had demanded as Gabriel, looking broken, had tried to explain himself.

He was waiting at my gate when I finally crossed the road, Jinni having eventually agreed to go to bed after one more port for the shock. Tilly had already gone ahead and I imagined the boys, now they'd seen Gabriel off the premises and away from Jinni's threats to 'kill you, you little scrote', were indoors also.

'I was going to clean it off in the morning,' he'd said. 'Once I'd got the photo. I've always made it right again.'

I'd nodded, too tired to speak. 'Tell me tomorrow.'

'I'm sorry, Tess.'

He'd walked away under the streetlight and disappeared into the darkness. It took me hours to get to sleep.

'At least now we know what this was all about,' I said to Tilly. 'Not a nasty group. Or anything like that,' I added, thinking about the way I'd almost begun to doubt David. 'It was stupid but as he told us, he's been trying to repair the damage as he's gone along. He only threw paint over the outhouse because he'd heard Jinni say it was being pulled down …'

'I don't want to talk about it,' Tilly flounced to her feet. 'I'm going to have a shower.'

Ben pushed down the lever on the toaster. 'She's talked about nothing else.'

'And get your stuff together,' I called after her, irritated. 'Your father wanted to leave at eleven and I can't bloody wait!' Rob had been stalking up and down the front room, looking at his watch, since 10.29 and I was ready to swing for him.

Tilly stomped back towards me. 'You are so bitter and nasty!' Her eyes were narrow slits. 'What if Dad hears you?' I was just about to tell her I didn't give a toss and that if he ever pitched up on my doorstep again I'd disinherit her, when, bang on cue, Rob appeared from behind me.

'Your plumbing's in need of attention,' he announced.

I swung around, my annoyance ballooning into full fury. 'I KNOW the plumbing needs attention! I have been waiting for the plumber to come and give it some. When he is over his various crises that have involved floods and exploding boilers and his girlfriend crashing her car, all of which have conspired to prevent him getting to me on any of the sixteen occasions he's promised to!' I took a deep breath as Rob took a half-step back.

'I just hope,' I continued shrilly, turning to include my offspring in my wrath, 'that when he does eventually deign to turn up he doesn't charge more than ten quid because–'

'Oh no, I should think–'

'BECAUSE,' I yelled over ex-husband's interjection, 'that's all I have left after you lot have eaten your way through my entire salary and doubled the electricity bill!' As if to illustrate my point a blackened piece of toast sprang into the air, making me jump.

'That's not fair! You–' I saw Tilly's eyes flick towards her father for support.

'It certainly is!' I shouted across her. 'I do everything for all of you. You are spoiled and indulged and–'

Ben was looking at me wide-eyed, his hands out in front of him as if to ward off an approaching tsunami. 'Sorreeee', he mouthed, with a lop-sided smile.

'TOTALLY SELF-CENTRED!' I screeched.

'I'll go and buy a newspaper,' said Rob heavily. 'You'd better hurry up,' he added to Tilly. 'We're leaving when I get back.'

'I need to get dressed too,' I said to Ben, when Tilly had stormed upstairs. 'You can let him in.'

Ben nodded, his mouth full. 'Are you going to tell David?' he mumbled.

I glanced at my phone lying on the kitchen counter. It was a question I'd been asking myself since dawn. If I said we'd caught someone, he'd want to know who it was. Perhaps I'd just take the CCTV back and say Malcolm had provided some instead. Let Malcolm's chap install some for a week or two, then report nothing doing.

Ben swallowed. 'Gabe'll lose his job if his boss finds out,' he said. 'And he won't get another one. He told me last night. Said nobody will ever give him work again if they know what he did.'

'Well, of course not,' I replied sharply. 'What does he expect?'

Ben shrugged and slotted another slice into the toaster. 'I'm just saying ...'

'Gabriel can't expect us to lie for him,' I said.

'He doesn't.' Ben was rummaging among the pots in the cupboard and didn't look at me. 'But we don't have to be the ones to drop him in it, either.'

I stomped upstairs, still annoyed. I didn't want to drop anyone in it, but David had been falsely accused by Jinni, and was clearly harbouring return suspicions about her, and Gabriel was guilty of criminal damage. Even if he had cleaned up after himself. He was bloody lucky we hadn't called the police.

Jinni wouldn't want to admit to David she'd made a mistake. But he should at least be told he was in the clear ...

As I stood under the shower, letting the hot water hammer down on my back, I suddenly felt a deep weariness that went beyond lack of sleep. I wanted peace and quiet, some space in which to think clearly–

'MUM!' It was Ben's voice roaring from the bedroom beyond.

'Dad's only gone and told Malcolm!'

'What the fuck were you doing?' I demanded furiously, 'answering my phone in the first place?'

Rob looked peeved. 'It was ringing and ringing,' he said. 'I saw the caller was "Newspaper", so I thought it might be important. I was trying to be helpful,' he continued huffily. 'In case it was your work.'

'On a Saturday?' I said crossly. 'And since when have I worked for the press?'

I sighed loudly as Ben continued to look aghast. Not only had Rob decided to act as my receptionist, he'd explained where I was and given the full lowdown on why I'd had such a late night. I still wasn't washed.

Malcolm had asked a lot of questions.

'He's a journalist,' I snapped. 'You didn't have to answer them.'

'How was I to know?' Rob muttered back.

'Could you tell him Dad got it wrong?' put in Ben hopefully.

'I don't think so.' I turned back to my ex-husband and glared. 'What did he say anyway?'

'Said to tell you he'd make sure the boy never worked again.'

Oh Christ. I didn't know what had propelled Gabriel to do something so insane to impress Malcolm – but I was sure he was misguided rather than a criminal. 'Can you talk to your mum about it?' I'd asked as I'd sent him on his way. He'd shaken his head bleakly, looking utterly wretched.

I wished now I'd listened longer. Maybe it would have helped me to put in a word with Malcolm. The answerphone was on at the news office now and I'd never known his mobile number. We always emailed.

I remembered him writing down his postcode when he'd invited me to eat – had he written a phone number too?

I left Rob shouting at Tilly to get a move on and stamped to the kitchen to make coffee. How the bloody hell had I ended up in the middle of all this?

I was rifling through the various bits of paper piled up on the kitchen worktop when I felt a hand on my waist. I jumped. 'What?'

Then I felt a warm sensation on the back of my neck and realised Rob was breathing on me again.

I twisted around and narrowly avoided head-butting him. 'What are you *doing?*'

'Are you happy?' he asked.

What?

'Oh yes,' I said. 'Ecstatic.'

Rob sighed. 'I hope so,' he said. 'Despite your–' he paused, '–outburst.'

I gritted my teeth but he was still talking. 'I'm still very fond of you, you know that, don't you? And if ever–' He abruptly clasped me to him and transferred his hot breath to my ear. 'I would always be–'

I pushed him back against the freezer. 'I don't think so,' I said briskly. 'Enjoy the move with Fiona!'

Rob sidled forwards again. 'But I'll see you when the baby's born. And we're grandparents together–'

I frowned, not keen on his emphasis on the last word.

Not if I see you first.

Usually I'd fret about his liver, but when Ben announced his hangover had just kicked in and retired for a lie-down with his iPad and the last of my Paracetamol, I felt only relief.

I thought uncomfortably of the indecent haste with which I'd waved my daughter off too.

'I'll see you in three weeks,' she'd said grumpily through the open window, as Rob made a meal of adjusting his mirrors.

'Will you?' I'd heard the surprise in my voice, quickly trilling: 'how lovely!' and just stopping myself from adding: 'so soon?'

'It's your birthday, remember?' Tilly frowned. 'Won't you want to do a dinner?'

Not really, no, I thought as I picked up my phone and went into the garden. I had not given my impending anniversary a single thought and if I considered it now, spending the day horizontal with a glass of wine and a cheese sandwich sounded much more the ticket than hours in the kitchen.

I had three texts. I was surprised Rob hadn't thought to read them too and apprise me of the contents via bullet points.

I thought of his sweaty hand clamped over mine before he'd finally got into the car and shuddered.

The first was from Caroline. **'Fab to c u darling. Will phone when facialist gone. Got goss. Xxx'**

Another new man? I hoped I'd have some 'goss' myself later when I'd finally got round to David's. The second one was from him.

'Looking forward to having you for dinner…. X' which sent me into a small paroxysm of anticipation and further deliberations over what I might wear.

The third was another desperate-sounding one from Gabriel, saying he needed to speak to me urgently and could he come round? I sighed.

First I would have to see Malcolm.

Chapter 36

The sat nav took me to the outskirts of Northstone, out past a petrol station and the garden centre and left down a long country lane. The hedgerows were dotted with wild flowers in pinks and purples, the sun shone over the fields beyond. I saw rabbits beneath trees, cows munching, two walkers with rucksacks crossing a meadow towards a stile.

I envied them strolling across the springy grass, in the soft breeze, listening to the birds, heading for the woodlands in the distance. I wanted to wander with the warmth of someone else's hand in mine. (Not Rob's clammy one, obviously.) I was still suitably stunned by his assumption that I would consider, in my wildest dreams, falling back into his flaccid, liver-spotted arms.

I imagined David's well-toned triceps closing around me and enjoyed a small frisson at the thought of this evening as I rounded a final corner past the sign for Haverfordsham and saw the church spire and postcard-pretty cottages clustered around a tiny green.

I knew Malcolm lived in a village but I'd expected his abode to be functional and bachelor-like. The low whitewashed house around the corner at the far end of the main street, set back behind a hedge, was the loveliest of them all, its thatched roof and tangle of roses in the front garden like something straight from a selection box.

I looked for a name in case there was some mistake. The oak front door had no number but the words Sunny Dove in faded white paint were just visible along the top of the slightly rickety gate. I pushed it open and went up the path, suddenly anxious. But Malcolm had suggested brunch this weekend – he wouldn't mind my coming however angry he was with Gabriel. I picked up the big brass knocker and knocked.

The woman who opened the door – early sixties, blue-checked overall, severe grey hair – regarded me sternly. I stepped back.

'OH!' I said, stupidly. 'I was hoping to see Malcolm.' She continued to look at me impassively as my brain whirred. He'd never actually said he was single – had just implied it with tales of multiple divorces. I looked at the cloth in her hand and deciding she must be there cleaning.

'I'm Tess,' I offered, smiling at her. 'I'm a friend of his.'

'Another of his lost causes?' The woman sniffed. 'I should get in quick before he's given it all to the refugees.'

'Sorry?'

'I'm the housekeeper.' She had her arms folded now, as if determined to block my entrance before I made off with the silver. 'He's out the back with that bird of his.'

Had he got a girlfriend as well? Feeling like I'd stepped into an episode of *Downton Abbey*, I followed her down a narrow hallway through a large sunny room with antique furniture – I took in a beautiful chaise longue and carved writing desk – and out through a pair of French doors onto a breathtaking country garden of hollyhocks, more rambling roses, ornamental thistles, giant poppies, hibiscus and banks of flowering bushes I couldn't name.

A large, curved pale sculpture stood in the middle of the emerald lawn at the centre. Water tumbled down it into a shallow bowl, overflowing and glinting in the light as it disappeared below. I stopped, mesmerised.

Beside me Mrs Hughes-Bridges sighed. 'Shed,' she said.

She stepped across the grass to a weathered wooden hut half-hidden behind a mass of pale-mauve lavatera and put her head through the open door. 'Your friend is here,' she announced grandly. 'I'm going to finish the mirrors.'

I poked my head into the dim, warm interior. It smelled of earth and creosote. Malcolm was squatting down among watering cans and garden tools, apparently engrossed in some sheets of newsprint. He didn't look around. 'Can't fly yet,' he said over his shoulder.

I went further in and peered around him. A young blackbird was squeaking on the newspaper, beak straining open. I watched, entranced, as Malcolm proffered a lump of what looked like mashed fruit, touched by the delicate movement of the tiny tweezers in his large hands.

I crouched down too. 'No parents?'

'Don't seem to be and a cat will have him if I let him out.'

Malcolm straightened up. 'I thought you couldn't make it today?'

'Not for brunch no, but–'

'You've come about that despicable little twerp. He'll wish he'd stayed in America when I get hold of him.'

He walked outside, waited for me and closed the door gently behind him. 'Let me send Vera the Smearer packing and I'll make some tea.'

'So she's your housekeeper?' I enquired, smiling.

Malcolm snorted. 'She's supposed to come for three hours a week to dust and hoover but because she drives her own husband to distraction and he spends his life hiding from her in *his* shed she turns up here to plague me until I'm forced to hide in mine. Always got some little job to finish!'

'She's probably lonely,' I said.

'Never stops talking.'

I pointed to the sculpture. 'I didn't think you were into modern art.'

Malcolm looked at me with pity. 'It's a bird bath you daft mare.'

He left me sitting on a bench outside the French doors with the sun on my face and disappeared inside. I watched a bumble bee crawling along a buddleia flower and breathed deeply. Despite his words, he did not seem as enraged with Gabriel as I'd thought he would be. It would be hard to feel anger for long in a garden like this.

'Do you do it all yourself?' I asked, when Malcolm had returned with two china mugs and sat down beside me.

'Yes! There's an old boy in the village who thinks he does it. But he's bent double and can't see. Turns up, cuts what he thinks are deadheads off my prize dahlias, pokes about in a flowerbed for five minutes, I give him twenty quid and he goes home. Then I do the rest.' Malcolm suddenly chuckled. 'Can't stop him when he's that old. Did you want a biscuit?'

I shook my head, heartened by this display of employer care.

'Gabriel was so upset,' I said, 'He was shaking.'

'Because he was caught.'

'No it was more than that – he seemed ...' I trailed off, unable to find the words for the desperation in Gabriel's eyes. 'I wouldn't have told you.' I said. 'Rob shouldn't have either.'

'Have you taken him back?'

'I'd rather chew my own leg off. I was furious that he said anything.'

'I knew already.'

Malcolm leant back, the top of his arm touching mine. He felt warm and solid and for a strange moment I wanted to put my head on his shoulder. I turned to look at him. 'Did Jinni–?'

Malcolm was staring straight ahead up the garden. 'I suspected him as soon as he did it to you.'

'But why? He's become like family. He–'

It was the same question I'd asked Gabriel the night before, sick with hurt that he'd cause me distress after the affection we'd shown him. The question that had left him shaking his head hopelessly, repeating 'I'm sorry,' over and over.

'Don't you know?' Malcolm was still looking stonily ahead.

'To have something to write about – for you?'

'Not for me.'

'You can't just sack him.'

'I most certainly can.'

'If you'd seen him – he looked so defenceless – like he'd been stripped bare–'

'What do you want me to do? Get him counselling and give him promotion?'

'Just talk to him. See if you can find out–' I didn't really understand why I felt so upset for Gabriel, despite all he'd done, but my gut told me he wasn't a bad person. It didn't make sense.

'I should have sacked him last time.' Malcolm's voice was grim. 'Instead of listening to you. And the females in the office wailing because I was shouting at him on the day his mother had died or whatever it was.'

'What?' I sat bolt upright. 'His mother's died? Jesus, Malcolm, no wonder the poor boy's in a state. Why didn't he tell me?' I was almost shouting now. 'Why didn't YOU?'

'Not literally that day, you silly woman. It was ages ago – a year, two years.'

'That's not long. I had no idea – all those times I've said his mum must be proud of him. Oh my God.' I put my head in my hands, mortified. 'You can't sack him now, no wonder he's messed up. I've been a mother substitute and–' I stopped and glared. 'Why didn't you let me know?'

'Why would I? How did I know you didn't know already?'

I was on my feet, pacing in front of him in fury. 'You listened to me talking about her! I can't believe how selfish and unfeeling you are. And don't you dare call me a silly woman, you chauvinistic old–' I stopped, floundering for a word that would sum up my feelings of rage as Malcolm regarded me impassively, '–GIT!'

345

'My wives said I was a bastard,' he said calmly.

'I'm not fucking surprised!' He flinched and I felt a pang. It disappeared as he ploughed on.

'So your poor little wounded soldier lied and connived and created a whole fantasy world in which he could be the hero. He slashed tyres, broke windows–'

'No, he didn't. The tyres and the nasty letter he was looking into,' I said, 'they were real. But that gave him the idea. To carry it on. He said he'd heard about another town that got a new station and the house prices doubled and there was a lot of bad feeling against the city people who moved in, and he thought–'

'I'm going to shake him till his teeth rattle,' said Malcolm.

'It would make the feature for you,' I went on. 'And it would be something he could show.'

'So he started smashing windows, himself–'

'He didn't. Some boys did, by accident, on the way home from the pub. But he saw it and when Jinni thought it was a personal attack, he let her think that–'

'Idiot!'

'But he did get it repaired for her–'

'So his mate could get free advertising.'

'And he only did things he could put right again. He repainted my house–'

'Regular little Robin Hood. Shall we nominate him for the Nobel prize for community service?' Malcolm's face was set hard. 'That is the biggest load of bollocks I've heard for a long time. He did it because of you.'

'Don't be ridiculous!'

'And why did he try and get one final lot of damage in last night? Because YOU told him I was getting the CCTV put in. I knew you would. I told you not to tell anyone–'

'I didn't think you meant–'

Malcolm gave a grim smile. 'I knew I was right. Hack's nose. So I wound him up a bit – said we'd make a splash of it, told him the sort of profile I thought it was – that they'd return to Jinni's because she was so gobby about it–' Malcolm looked satisfied. 'And back he went. Like shooting fish in a bloody barrel.'

I stared at him in disbelief. 'That's horrible.'

'But accurate! If you hadn't disturbed him, he'd have had another go at you too.'

'Why?'

'Because then he could be Sir Galahad.' Malcolm put on a whiny voice 'Oh, Tess, let me help you clean all this nasty paint off.'

'OH Gabriel,' he pitched his voice even higher – 'you're such a lovely boy. Your mother must be so proud.'

'Stop it! That's disgusting. I feel terrible.'

'He wanted your attention,' Malcolm said in his normal voice. 'Because–'

'Because,' I said emotionally, 'he is clearly in a terrible state about losing his mother.' I thought about Ben – parentless in a strange town with nobody to talk to and felt the tears come into my eyes. 'What happened to her?'

'I've no idea.'

'Well, you should have,' I raged at him. 'You had a duty of care.'

'Pah.'

The sound of his contempt ignited me further. 'Stop being vile. He needs help and support!'

'No doubt he'll get plenty from the unemployment office.'

I picked up my handbag, almost knocking my mug over, and considering briefly throwing it at Malcolm's self-satisfied face.

'Your wives were right,' I said, choked. 'You are a bloody bastard.'

I sat in my car, heart thumping, overwhelmed by rage and sorrow. I'd thought Malcolm's brusque exterior masked an empathy and compassion he clearly didn't feel at all. Poor Gabriel was emotionally disturbed and needed help. I pulled my phone out, ready to ring him and then put it down again fearing I'd sound so upset myself I'd make it worse.

I wished I had someone to talk to. Jinni had been spitting rivets – I didn't know how long it would take her to come round – and Caroline had just sent a text to say she'd phone tomorrow because something had come up. This was accompanied by a smiley face. Fran would be knee deep in kids on a Saturday afternoon. Oliver and Sam had been going out to lunch with friends of hers and Ben would be out cold. Had Tilly known about Gabriel's mother? Surely she'd have told me.

As I sat, taking deep breaths, my eye fell on the text I'd had this morning. I scrolled through earlier ones for the postcode and then jabbed at the sat nav. He was only two miles away. Suddenly I wanted to see David's smiley, crinkly eyes, smell his delicious aftershave and feel his arms close around me. I started the engine, shaken by how upset the altercation with Malcolm had left me. I wanted a hug.

The sun beat down on my forearm as I gripped the wheel. As the narrow lane straightened out to an empty expanse of road ahead, I put my foot down and sped down into a dip and up an incline the other side and on round another bend until the small screen on my dashboard told me I was almost there.

I slowed down as I approached. Long Barn House was on its own at the end of a small turning, at the top of a sloping garden. I had never seen anything quite like it.

The original barn construction was still there, with mellow brick walls and massive beams, the small rose and grey roof tiles clearly original. But the huge steel-framed windows running the whole height of the building and a massive glass extension gave it a cutting-edge, almost futuristic, look. A flight of sharp concrete steps cut through the turf up to the thick glass and wood front door. Terraced flowerbeds on one side were filled with lavender bushes and a tall spiky blue flower I didn't recognise. It was enormous.

The black-metal barred gate stood open onto a large stone-paved area with a tall, industrial-looking steel floodlight to one side and David's Porsche parked beneath it.

All at once my heart was beating hard. I put the handbrake on and ran up the steps before I could change my mind.

He opened the door surprised. 'Tess!'

He was wearing black jeans and a loose, short-sleeved grey

349

open-necked polo shirt that brought out the colour of his eyes. His black hair was soft, as if it had just been washed. He looked delectable.

My mouth flapped open.

Over his shoulder, lolling in a doorway behind him, I recognised the woman with the shiny black hair from the gallery. She was wearing a short denim skirt, an extra button or two open on her top, her brown feet bare on the polished wood floor. Her gaze left me in no doubt I was an unwelcome intrusion.

As I stared back, she gave a small, tight smirk of greeting and threw David a look. His eyebrows were raised. Keeping his back to her, he gave me a small quirky smile as if we shared a secret and raised his eyebrows some more, as if her presence were entirely beyond his control. His eyes flicked to his watch. 'Sorry, I wasn't–'

I felt completely embarrassed. 'I've brought your stuff back!' I blurted out, praising the heavens I'd slung the box in the car while I was waiting for Rob and Tilly to sling their hooks.

I indicated the car below and turned and ran hot-faced back down the steps.

'Here it all is.' I heard him behind me, but didn't look round as I busied myself pulling open the rear door of the car and tugging at the box.

'Let me.'

I stood aside as he leant over and lifted it easily from the car. I could smell soap and something spicy. I wanted to touch him. He put the box on the low wall that edged the garden where the lawn swept upwards.

'So have you caught someone already?' He enquired, turning back to me. 'Did you manage to nail the real culprit?' He stressed the 'real' with another sardonic brow raise.

'Sort of,' I said. 'Er, no, not really. The newspaper got us some other equipment–'

'Tell me later,' he said, moving closer and putting his hand on my arm, making my skin tingle. 'I wasn't expecting Lucia to call by. I'll make sure she–'

'What an amazing-looking place,' I interrupted him.

'Thank you.' He hesitated. 'I'd invite you in but–'

'You're a bit busy in there?' I finished for him brightly. 'It's really no problem. I've got a lot on too. We can do it some other time–'

My heart was pounding. And then my phone rang. We both looked at it lying on the front seat of my car. 'I'll just–' I muttered, seeing his look of irritation as I reached for it, unable to break the habit of quickly checking who it was, in case something had happened to one of the kids ...

It was Gerald's name flashing up on the screen and alarm gripped me. I pressed answer.

'Your mum's gone off again.' For a moment he was hopeful. 'She hasn't come to you?'

'I'm sorry,' I mouthed at David, unable to break the apologising habit even if he did have another woman stashed up there. A woman who was now standing in the open doorway looking down at him. He walked away, putting the box on the bottom step and sitting next to it in the sunshine as I paced between our cars while Gerald explained.

My mother had been getting increasingly agitated about

her appointment, asking Gerald constantly what time it was and where she was meeting me, twice getting her coat and shoes on, despite his reassurances it wasn't until Monday (here I felt a wash of guilt for both forgetting and not replying to his text earlier).

This morning he'd gone to get the shopping and left her, apparently contentedly, listening to the radio in the garden and when he came back she'd gone. He'd been driving around Margate looking for her and had called her friends. But there was no sign of her and Mo thought she might have got confused again and got on a train to see me.

'Would she be able to do that?' I asked anxiously.

'Probably,' Gerald sounded equally worried. 'Her handbag has gone – she's got money. She's got your address in the back of her purse. I put all our numbers there. But I don't know whether she'll think to look.'

'I'm not there at the moment,' I told him. 'But Ben is – he'll phone me if she turns up.' As I said it, I realised Ben could be fast asleep or have rallied and headed down town for a fry-up. I knew Rob had given him some money before he left ...

'I'll go home now,' I said.

David got up as soon as I'd put the phone away. 'Is everything all right?'

'Family problem. I've got to go.'

He touched my arm again. 'But I'll see you this evening?'

I shook my head. 'I don't think I'll be able to.'

'Oh come on! Lucia will be going soon.' He smiled as it were all rather amusing. 'Is that why you ran away last night?

I didn't know she'd be on the train either.' He gave a short laugh. 'Look, we had a bit of an on-off thing and–' his hand was now curled around my wrist. 'Put it this way – she wants it to be "on" rather more than I do. He gave me one of his huge, disarming smiles. 'I would like *us* to –'

I got hurriedly into my car. 'I must go!'

'We'll finish this conversation later?' He was leaning down to look at me through the window as I started the engine. Frustration, disappointment, worry about my mother, the image of Lucia and the way she'd been looking at David, the way she was now leaning against the doorpost, very much at home, welled up inside me and for a moment I felt as though I was going to cry.

I looked at him as I pushed the gear stick into reverse, confusion, misery and humiliation making my voice hard.

'I really can't see the point.'

Chapter 37

Caroline was right. I wasn't like her, who found it exciting to have several men on the go, even if it meant sharing, or Jinni, who only wanted them for sex pre-breakfast.

My stomach churned as I drove slowly along the High Street, scanning the pavements and shop doorways, thinking about Gabriel damaging my house, my horrible row with Malcolm that I had no idea how to put right, the sight of Lucia pointing her cleavage at David. And where the hell my mother had got to this time.

I'd managed to rouse a foggy-sounding Ben, who'd heard nothing. If she'd got a train here and followed the signs to town she'd walk past the house. Would she recognise where she was then? From what I could gather from Gerald she had good days when she was almost her old self and hours when she seemed cut off from reality.

I stopped at the station before I went home but the ticket office was closed. I looked along the near-empty platform, at the group of teenagers standing around a bench and the young woman with the shopping bags, clearly just off a train from London, and recalled David's face that first time he met me, standing right here – the way he'd smiled, his hand holding mine …

First impressions were usually the right ones!

I turned and walked back to my car, stomach still in a knot, past the advertising billboard defaced with red spray paint courtesy of Gabriel's ambition.

DFLS GO HOME. Perhaps that's what I should do. Or move down to the sea, where I could keep an eye on my mother. And start all over again …

On the passenger seat, my phone was ringing. I grabbed it too late. As I started to call Ben back, a text pinged in. **'Granny found!'**

There was another text too. **'Sorry about that. Will call later. Hope your problem gets sorted x'**

Actually pal, you're my fucking problem!

I couldn't cope with this roller coaster of emotions, not to mention the sensations raging through my body whenever I thought of David's hand on my arm. It was too bloody exhausting.

As I turned into my driveway, I felt lonely and overwhelmed and I longed for the house to be empty. Ben hadn't answered when I rang back but I knew I'd have to phone Gerald, find out where my mother was and probably go back out to fetch her. When I wanted to hide away and forget.

I could hear the voices even before my key was in the lock. Sam was making the policewoman a cup of tea while Oliver sat on the sofa holding my mother's hand. She was wearing a bright dress and matching cardigan and wearing lipstick; her silver hair looked as if it had just been done.

But I could see the lost look in her eyes.

'I'm sorry, Tess,' she said sadly as I came in. She peered up at my face. 'Are you crying because of me?'

I shook my head. 'No Mum, not because of you.'

'I'm just tired,' I told Ben, in the kitchen, after Sam had hugged me and left the room. 'I need an early night.'

'Gerald's on his way,' Ben said. 'He says he'll be here by seven.'

Gerald looked exhausted. Heart sinking, I knew I couldn't expect him to drive home again. Especially when I found him in the garden, puffing on his inhaler. 'How is your angina?' I asked him guiltily. Caring for my mother was clearly taking its toll.

He attempted to sound hearty. 'Not usually a problem at all. Just a tricky day.' He smiled at me. 'We still have a laugh, you know. We manage.'

My mother had convinced herself her appointment was today and she had to get to me to go to it. By the time she was on the train to Northstone she'd 'come to' and realised her mistake but couldn't recall my address, although she thought she remembered the way.

The taxi driver, getting increasingly concerned about driving around in circles for a woman of possibly unsound mind – 'He thought I was batty' – my mother laughed round at the assembled company then exchanged a painful look with me – suggested they went to the police station. They looked in her purse.

'I did give him ten pounds,' she finished. 'He didn't want

to take it – he was a very nice man – but I said: I expect you've got a family and we all have to earn a living.'

Sam made omelettes and I watched my mother nodding and smiling as she listened to Oliver tell her about the baby. But when he momentarily turned away to pass salad across the table, I saw the light in her face go out. When I spoke there was a split second where she appeared bewildered.

I watched Gerald pat her hand and Oliver getting up to refill Sam's glass of water. Sam looked better. She was no longer pale and her skin was beginning to glow. 'Are you okay?' I mouthed. She smiled and nodded.

I took some deep breaths. I felt Ben watching me, so I beamed at him too. My children were healthy and doing things with their lives; I had friends and a home that would be lovely when I got double-glazing and the loo was fixed. On Monday we would see my mother's consultant in Canterbury and find out what could be done to help her. As she'd put it, she wasn't totally ga-ga yet – medication might keep her stable.

My sister Alice, who had been spot-welded to Google since the first announcement, had sent acres of information on many different types of brain degeneration and links to dozens of information sheets on drug therapies. She was now researching the benefits of a course of treatment with a clinical neuropsychologist. I was to phone her when I was back from the appointment and we were to make A Plan.

Things were not that bad. I only wanted to cry because I hadn't had enough sleep.

I left Oliver and Ben clearing up while I changed beds, intending to sleep in the conservatory and give Gerald and my mother mine. They both looked as if they needed a proper night's rest and I didn't know how comfortable the sofa bed was, although nobody had complained.

Tilly would have done for sure, I thought, as I pulled off the crumpled pillow cases and pushed her remaining strewn possessions into a pile in the corner.

It was warm in here, despite the blinds closed against the afternoon sun and I opened the two small windows at either end to let a breeze blow through, thinking about a long bath and the earliest possible night.

When I turned around Ben was leaning in the doorway. 'It's been an action-packed weekend, so far, hasn't it?' he said. 'Finding out your mate is the phantom paint-sprayer and having to track down the missing granny.'

'How much tracking did you do? You were in bed!'

He grinned back. Then stopped grinning. 'Would you be annoyed with me if I gave up uni and got a job in Portugal?'

I felt the last of my energy drain out through my feet. I flapped the duvet cover at him. 'Help me.'

I looked at his face as he was taking the corners. His hair had grown longer and gone lighter in the sun. He needed a shave. My heart twisted but he was nearly 19. He could go anywhere he wanted.

'Portugal?' I echoed. 'What are you going to do there?'

I was glad when the boys went off to the pub and happy to see Sam go with them – not just because it meant she was feeling better enough to venture forth for a fizzy water, but because I was talked-out.

'Tell me the rest tomorrow,' I said to Ben, hissing at Oliver to get the full story on the role of 'Maria', temporary barmaid at the Fox – here to learn the language but due to return home at the end of the summer, and mentioned twice as a friend full of useful info on Mediterranean relocation – in his brother's sudden desire to teach English in Lisbon.

Right now, as I stood beneath the shower along the landing, not wanting to disturb my mother and Gerald by running a bath in my en suite, I only wanted to get to bed.

I didn't even recognise the tapping on the door at first. I was in the kitchen, making camomile tea to take out to the conservatory, and thought it was a noise from the street. Then, as the sound became more persistent, I realised it was someone quietly but repeatedly rapping the knocker. I tied my dressing-gown cord and went through to the front, sighing. It wasn't like Jinni to be so restrained. Not more dramas, surely.

It was Gabriel. Looking pale and anxious. 'Tess, I'm sorry,' he said, taking in my attire. 'But I've got to talk to you.'

'Oh, Gabriel.'

'Please. It won't take long. I've got to tell you something.'

'Malcolm told me.'

'What?' Gabriel stared at me shocked. I watched him as the kettle boiled, sitting at my small kitchen table, his hands moving nervously, remembering the relaxed, smiley young man I'd first met at the quiz night. Now he looked anguished.

'Oh, Gabriel,' I said again, feeling desperate for him. 'Why didn't *you* tell me about your mum?'

'Oh.' He shook his head. 'I can't talk about it.'

'But that's what this is all about, isn't it? You were in a bad place and you–'

He leant towards me. 'I never did any lasting damage. I always put it right afterwards–'

'You keep saying that,' I interrupted. 'But the police wouldn't see it that way. It was still criminal damage.'

He nodded.

'Why did you do it to me?'

Gabriel looked at the table. Then past me to a corner of the kitchen.

'I wanted to show Malcolm I could do a meaty story. I was hoping more things would happen after those tyres were slashed and that woman got the poisonous letter and when they didn't ...'

'So who did do that?' I looked at him suspiciously. 'Are you sure that wasn't you too?'

Gabriel shook his head again. 'It was the husband's girl-friend. The wife called me later when she found out – she wanted me to expose her.' He sighed. 'Of course, I couldn't have done that.'

'But you did the spray paint and eggs. And the graffiti at the station.'

'I didn't do all of it,' Gabriel said quickly. 'There's been more added by someone else.'

'Maybe. But you started it.'

Gabriel looked down at his mug. 'I didn't want you to be worried it was just you.'

'Why did you do it to *me* at all? I thought we were friends ...'

Gabriel still didn't look at me.

'And how could you send that vile note to Jinni? She's your friend too—'

'I didn't!' Gabriel said immediately. 'I promise you, Tess. I wouldn't do something like that.'

'Really? What about her window? I defended you to Malcolm but I don't really see how those boys could have done it by mistake. And they didn't seem the type to do it deliberately—'

'They were messing about, and a couple of them took another one's trainer off and threw it over the hedge.' Again, he looked at me pleadingly. 'They panicked and ran away. I went and picked the shoe up and I was going to tell Jinni and then I suddenly thought—'

'And you just happened to be passing?'

Now Gabriel blushed. 'I was walking behind you,' he said. 'I was going to catch you up and talk to you, and then I saw Tilly come along. Well, I didn't know it was Tilly then, obviously ...'

'Malcolm's going to fire you.'

Gabriel nodded, eyes down. 'He phoned and said I was the most stupid, dim-witted and deluded reporter he'd ever had the misfortune to employ and he'd go into more detail on Monday.' Gabriel gave a feeble smile. 'I'll get my official sacking then.'

'Well, you can't really blame him,' I said, having gone over and over our awful argument and realising that Malcolm had a point about cracking down on fake news. I took a sip of tea. 'What will you do?'

'I don't know. I thought I wanted a big job in London and

361

I wanted to impress everyone with my by-lines. But now–' He stopped. 'Over the last few weeks–' he stopped again. 'I want to stay in Northstone.'

'You still haven't said why you did it to me?' There was a pause while Gabriel continued to stare at the table. 'I was worried, it scared me.'

'I was just trying to–' He looked at me now, fear and embarrassment on his face. 'Look, Tess, the thing is ... I've been wanting to tell you ... and I waited till you'd be on your own. Ben's been so great to me but–' His words were coming fast and jumbled now. 'And I couldn't come till I knew Tilly had gone. I know she's really angry with me–'

Suddenly the penny dropped. I leant across the table and patted his hand. 'Oh, Gabriel, it was just such a shock to her,' I explained. 'I know how much you like her, and she'll be okay, honestly. Tilly flies off the handle but then she calms down again. The reason she was so upset is because she does like you too. I'm sure she'll come round. Just give her time and then you–'

I stopped as Gabriel pulled his hands away from me and threw them up in gesture of frustration. 'No, Tess!' he burst out, emotionally. 'I do like Tilly, of course. She's a great friend, and she's funny and pretty.' He stared at me wide-eyed.

'But don't you see? The one I can't stop thinking about ... is you ...'

Chapter 38

'Respect!' Caroline gave another long peal of laughter. 'All these men to choose from. Goodness, darling, you're doing better than me!'

'Hardly,' I said morosely. 'David called right after Gabriel dropped his bombshell – I just let it ring.'

'Poor darling boy. And from what I recall, he's gorgeous. Could you really not–'

'NO!' I could feel my stress levels rising. 'Not least because my daughter clearly adores him. And I'm about to be 48. Gabriel is the same age as Oliver! How could I even contemplate–?'

'Well, quite easily, actually,' said Caroline smoothly. 'When I see young men of that age smiling at me I quite often think, well, yes please–'

'And I think – I bet your mother's proud of you,' I interrupted sharply, my insides twisting at the thought of Gabriel's poor mother, who, Gabriel had eventually and haltingly told me, had died suddenly from a brain tumour. 'So no, there's only David and he–'

'I was including Malcolm and my dickhead brother,'

Caroline laughed again, unfazed by my bad mood. 'Believe me, "are you happy?" is his idea of a major chat-up line. He's beginning to realise what he let slip through his hands now Fiona is kicking off big-time. That's what I was going to tell you.' I could hear her glee rippling down the phone line. 'Mind you, darling, you were always much too good for him. I was forever amazed you lasted as long as you did and managed to produce those adorable children. Are you sure you didn't get a sperm-donor? Or ravage the gardener?' She dissolved into more joyous giggles, clearly finding my tortured lack of love life entirely hilarious.

'It isn't funny!' I could feel myself growing hot and upset. 'Malcolm and I aren't speaking, I feel awful about Gabriel, Rob drives me insane and I've made a complete fool of myself over David.'

I swallowed hard. 'My children have all got issues, I'm behind on my work, and tomorrow I've got to go to Canterbury to find out exactly what's wrong with my mother. I don't know how we're going to cope if she gets any worse because Gerald has angina and the strain is–' I made a big snorting, gulping sound as I tried not to cry.

'And it's all very well for my sister Alice sitting over there on the other side of the Atlantic, issuing instructions, but if she sends me one more email telling me what to say to the consultant I shall scream ... And now!' I screeched, pulling the fridge door open with my free hand. 'Bloody Ben has finished all the bloody milk. Again! And I need to make Gerald a cup of tea ...' At which point I gave up all semblance of self-control, kicked the fridge door shut again and began to sob with frustration.

Caroline had stopped laughing. 'Darling–' I heard her say with concern, as Ben appeared in the kitchen doorway.

'What's happened?' he asked, startled.

I thrust an empty carton towards him. 'Get some fucking more!'

What indeed had happened, I wondered, as I shoved sheets in the washing machine. I was used to being a calm person, known for my serenity in the face of crisis, not a squawking, weeping harridan teetering on the edge of a breakdown because we'd run out of groceries.

'You're exhausted,' said Caroline, when she rang back to see if I had been carted off in a straitjacket. 'The excitement has been too much for you.'

'I do need sleep,' I said, ashamed of my earlier outburst. 'I woke up every hour last night.'

The sofa bed wasn't really uncomfortable but it felt different from my own bed and there'd been one noise after another – someone flushing a loo, cats or foxes fighting outside – culminating in Tilly's back-up travel alarm going off at 5 a.m.

By the time I'd located it from the bottom of the pile of stuff she'd left behind – stuffed into a cosmetics bag with a squashed tube of toothpaste and some dental floss – the dawn chorus was in full swing and there seemed little point in trying to doze off.

Especially since my mother was up before six, chinking cutlery as she bizarrely rearranged my kitchen.

It was with relief that I'd waved her off, Gerald assuring

me he wouldn't let her out of his sight till I met them in Canterbury the next day.

'And when are you at the office?' enquired Caroline.

'Thursday,' I said, wondering if I would ever again get a blissful day at home alone.

'Take a bag with you.' she instructed. 'You're coming to stay with me.'

I didn't want to. After the grimness of the hospital appointment and a hot day at work, with Paul in overdrive – the uber-clients were fair racing their way down the alphabet now and had acquired a site in Paddock Wood – I needed to collapse at home.

But Caroline had insisted and now we were spread out on her sumptuous sofa, in our pyjamas – mine striped cotton with a t-shirt top, hers ivory silk with trimmings – a glass of very cold champagne at my elbow, delicious-looking nibbles on the low table in front of us, I had to admit I felt more relaxed than I had for weeks.

'You needed a change of scene,' said Caroline firmly. 'And a rest from everyone hanging off you.'

'They're not really–' I protested, but she swept on.

'They are. You need a break.' She paused to take another sip from the crystal flute in her hand. 'I tried to book you a Kayla facial massage but she's over at the Dorchester doing Beyoncé. Oh, my God, the girl looks like an angel – a simply divine creature, cheekbones to die for – but fingers of iron. It's two Nurofen and a large Chablis as a bare minimum.'

I winced. 'It actually hurts?

'Agony, darling, but my God it works. Botox, fillers and a non-surgical lift rolled into one. Look at me!'

Caroline thrust her right cheek towards me. Her skin did look remarkably smooth and firm, but then it always did. 'She gets right inside the mouth and pushes your cheek muscles up from behind your teeth. Terrifying, but gets results. I'll buy you one for your birthday ...'

'Thank you,' I said doubtfully.

'You've got to keep as gorgeous as you possibly can. I got you here so I can sort out your sex life.'

'That's the least of my worries.'

'Oh darling, sorry. Tell me about your mother.'

'It's definitely not Alzheimer's.'

'Thank God.'

'But it doesn't sound too good ...'

I told her as briefly as I could. I'd been up till midnight writing it all down in an email for my sister, trying to pre-empt every question Alice could possibly ask and ending THIS IS ALL I KNOW, aware this wouldn't stop her demanding more.

'... there's deterioration in frontal lobes, she's going to see someone else – a specialist in that type of dementia. Or the type they think it is. Only a post-mortem will finally tell.' I was silent for a moment. Remembering the look on the consultant's face as he told me that. Compassion laced with a searching look – as if he wanted to be sure I understood the gravity of what we were looking at, as he pointed out the areas of damage on the brain scan.

'Drugs may help,' I went on briskly. 'The condition can cause hallucinations and her sort of waking dreams where she thinks she has to go somewhere – she's fairly text book so far – dipping in and out and appearing almost normal one minute and out of it the next, is all part of the pattern ...'

Caroline wriggled down the sofa and gave me a hug. 'I'm really sorry, darling.'

'Mum and Gerald seemed almost cheered by it,' I told her. 'Mum was relieved it "wasn't worse". Gerald was pinning hope on the idea of medication and the consultant saying it could be very slow.'

'Well, perhaps it will be.'

'Perhaps.'

We sat in silence for a moment, Caroline continuing to look at me with sympathy. I smiled at her and took another swig of champagne. 'Let's not talk about it,' I said, trying to push down the knot of fear in my stomach. 'Alice will be on the phone soon and, believe me, I'll be discussing it for hours ...'

'But it's someone to share the burden with.'

'I suppose.'

'Music!' cried Caroline, jumping up from the sofa and bounding across her stripped floorboards to the Bose in the corner. 'Wine, song and a few more breadsticks and then we'll go through your potential men!' She grinned as she returned to sit cross-legged beside me, propped against an embroidered cushion, the remote control in her hands.

'Paolo Nutini or Sam Smith?'

'Aren't they both a bit young for me?'

'Ha ha, you are hilarious, darling.'

The quip cost me another twenty minutes of explaining to Caroline why I couldn't, under any circumstances, have a fling with Gabriel. 'Quite aside from Tilly's feelings, can you imagine Ben's face? Even if I did find young men attractive, it would feel entirely immoral and wrong. He's grieving!'

I held out my glass for Caroline to refill it. 'I was still quite flattered. All these weeks I've been thinking he comes around because he misses his mum. Well, he does, of course,' I added quickly. 'But he said I was beautiful–'

'You are!'

'And Malcolm was right – in the end it was more about me than the story. He threw stuff at *my* house so he had an excuse to spend time with me–'

'And you didn't even notice the lust in his eyes.'

I frowned. 'I miss Malcolm,' I said sadly. He used to send me an email most days. Something short and grumpy but ... funny. I'd sort of got used to them ...'

'I found him very entertaining,' said Caroline. 'When we were waiting for Fran at the hospital. He was good to take us, wasn't he?'

I nodded reluctantly. 'But although intellectually I know he was probably right to, I still can't forgive him, emotionally, for the way he sacked Gabriel. It seems sort of – brutal,' I swallowed. I'd made it my business to catch Emily leaving the office one lunchtime once I'd calculated Malcolm would be safely stuffing in Rosie's and she'd confirmed Gabriel had not been back.

She didn't know where he'd gone and Malcolm had told them nothing. Gabriel hadn't answered her call. I'd thought

369

about pressing Grace for details but instead I texted Gabriel myself. He didn't reply to me either.

'Perhaps you should give Malcolm a call?' Caroline enquired, tipping the last few frothy drops into her glass and looking disappointedly at the empty bottle. 'If a man makes you laugh ...'

'No,' I shook my head. 'I do – did – like seeing him, but we're not–'

I remembered how kind and practical he'd been when my mother went missing. How amusing he'd been about his 'housekeeper', his caustic humour that had drawn me to him at the quiz night ...

'He's not my type is he? I finished lamely.

'Which is? Not that I trust your taste after marrying my brother ...

'Rob looked all right in his day ...'

'Not my sort, darling.

'Well, I should hope not.'

'Shall we have another?' Caroline sprang up again. 'I got given a case of this stuff so we might as well drink it.' She disappeared into her small but state-of-the-art kitchen, where I heard her opening the fridge door. 'So are you telling me you're still lusting after Dodgy David?' she called.

'No, I'm not! Well, yes, I suppose I suppose I do find him attractive but–' I stopped as Caroline returned with another bottle and a disbelieving expression.

'But he's obviously still involved with that Lucia.' I squirmed at the memory as I took the newly filled glass.

'Perhaps they have an open relationship or she turns a

blind eye.' Caroline offered. 'James always maintained his wife knew he had other women but she was prepared to pretend she didn't, as long as he paid the school fees and she got her quota of shoes.'

I shuddered. 'I'd hate to live like that.'

Caroline shrugged. 'I'd hate to be married at all.' She raised her glass at me. 'If you're that keen, you could ask him straight! David – do you want to shag me or not? And if so, what's the story with this other bint?'

I squirmed. 'I couldn't!'

'No! Quite right.' Caroline looked serious. 'He's not right for you, really darling. A bit too pleased with himself. I thought that as soon as I clapped eyes on him. He was flirting me while you were getting changed – he's that sort – it's a reflex action. I knew then he wasn't going to be any good long-term.'

'Come off it! You said "mmmm" at the gallery.'

Caroline looked surprised. 'I was talking about Malcolm.'

'What?'

'He's rather sexy,' Caroline mused. 'In a sort of lived-in, craggy, TV detective sort of way. And he obviously likes you too–'

'He says his ex-wives said he was a bastard.'

Caroline laughed. 'Maybe he's mellowed. At least he hasn't been performing with your neighbour. As far as we know! Now, did you let that poor boy down gently ...?'

The London sky grew dark and the lights from surrounding buildings shone through the open window from the street beyond as I related the conversation. The way I'd assured Gabriel of my fondness and concern for him and my total lack of romantic interest, explaining as gently as I could that he'd be much happier with someone of his own age ....

'I mean,' I said to Caroline now. 'At some point he'll want children.'

She rolled her eyes. 'And right now he's a young man full of testosterone.'

'I know, but ...' Caroline always made me feel so straight and old-fashioned. Was it so weird to want an ordinary, traditional relationship, where you did intend to spend the next twenty years together? Where you loved each other to the exclusion of anyone else? I had an image of Malcolm tenderly feeding that motherless blackbird. Suddenly I felt lonely and sad.

'Don't get maudlin, darling!' Caroline cried, sloshing more champagne into my glass and jumping off the sofa again. 'I love this!' She pointed the remote control across the room and pushed up the volume. 'I play it at the gym!'

She pulled me to my feet and began to dance, singing along loudly to Paolo Nutini's 'New Shoes', swaying her hips, her brightly painted toes bobbing up and down on the striped rug. After a moment, I joined her, the champagne hitting me as I jigged about.

Caroline was clapping her hands and twirling to the music. I grinned at her as she slid into step beside me and bumped her thigh against mine, the rhythm infecting me too. I found myself moving to the beat and as I shook my head and felt my hair swinging to the pulse of the melody I felt suddenly free and silly and young again. I grabbed my glass and took a big gulp of the champagne, laughing as the bubbles hit the back of my nose, wondering why I didn't have fun like this more often.

'This is good too!' Caroline cried, as the song came to an end. 'This whole playlist is good for dancing ... Yay!' She began to writhe faster to a Madonna number, throwing an arm around my shoulder so I had to move with her. I looked at her with affection as we danced together, giggling. Other ex-sisters-in-law might have faded away but Caroline and I had grown closer. She was a fantastic friend to me and she was right I should spend more time with her, having a good time ...

We were on our fourth number when I saw my phone flashing on the sofa. I stopped dancing and grabbed at it. Caroline turned the music down. 'Who is it?'

'Missed call from Tilly. And she hasn't left a message. I'll have to call her back.'

Caroline flopped down on the end of the sofa and looked at me despairingly. 'Darling, she's a grown woman. If it was that important she would have left one, wouldn't she. Or she'll call back.'

'Supposing she's found out about Gabriel's crush on me and is upset?'

'Why would she? He won't tell her, will he ...?'

'He said he once told Ben he fancied me and Ben thought he'd had too many beers and was joking!' I pulled a face. 'I think he had had too many beers, actually.'

'Well, he won't tell Tilly,' Caroline said with authority. 'And even if he does, it's hardly your fault you're a MILF, is it?' She gave me a grin. 'You see, you may say you don't care about having a sex life but subconsciously you are putting out all the chemical signals of the mating female and the men around you are being helplessly drawn ...'

I threw a cushion at her, blushing. 'Don't be daft–' I looked at the screen as my phone rang again. 'Oh, my God,' I yelped, holding it away from me. 'It's him!'

'Answer it!'

'I'm drunk!'

'Good! It will lower your inhibitions. You can tell him to sling his hook.'

I stared frozen as David's name continued to flash in front of me.

'Give it to me!' Caroline's hand shot out and whipped the phone from mine. I shrieked.

'Don't you dare!'

The ringing had stopped but Caroline had taken the phone to the other side of the room and was tapping on it. 'Caroline – do not!' I said desperately. 'It's not funny!'

'Remember the internet-dating,' I added.

Caroline squealed with laughter. 'Oh God, that was hilarious ...'

'PLEASE!'

Caroline reluctantly handed the phone back to me. 'I've told David to sod off and told Malcolm you're crazy about him. We'll see who answers first!'

She laughed again as my face collapsed in horror. 'Relax – I'm joking.'

'What *did* you say?'

'Nothing. I deleted it again,' she added, as I scrolled through to check.

'Promise me you won't text anybody. I'd be mortified.'

'Okay.'

'OR phone,' I said, suspecting that Caroline may have sent a number to herself. 'I mean it. I'm going to worry ...'

'I promise!'

Caroline looked stern. 'But you need to forget David and make it up with Malcolm. He's been a good friend to you and you said you were missing him.'

'I'll email him in the morning.'

But all I could think of when I opened my eyes in Caroline's spare bedroom was where she might keep the pain-killers. My head pounded, my mouth was parched. Caroline had left a note in the kitchen telling me she'd gone to work, to help myself to everything and stay again tonight.

I put the kettle on, filled a glass with water, rummaged in her bathroom cabinet for ibuprofen and tottered back to bed, already resolving to take her advice. I could work here on my laptop, Oliver and Sam would probably be happy to have the house to themselves, and frankly I wasn't sure I could make it to St Pancras.

I lay back on the pillows and stared at the ceiling, thinking about David and Malcolm and Gabriel and the evening before. David had left a voicemail message, which I'd found sometime later, saying he was off to Beijing the next day but hoped to see me when he got back. Could I give him a quick ring?

Caroline and I had spent some time debating whether this deserved a response, with me feeling slightly beholden as he'd been so good to Tilly and wondering perhaps whether it was work-related, and Caroline stating unequivocally that men with Aren't-You-Just-Longing-to-Shag-Me eyes were always a nightmare and he was clearly just excited by the chase and only keen again because I'd turned him down.

In the end we'd gone for the middle ground, with me typing out a therapeutic: **'Not if I see you first! Thought you said you weren't having a relationship, so what was Lucia doing with you twice in two days, you lying bastard?'** And then deleting it as sending anything at all would suggest I gave a fuck.

Now I sat up and reached for my laptop. And having sent a few reassuring words to Paul about my progress on the latest project, thought about what to say to Malcolm.

I felt a twinge of shame when I thought about calling him a bastard. But still filled with outrage at him not telling me that Gabriel had lost his mother. And while I could see his point professionally, as I'd said to Caroline the thought of poor Gabriel, alone and jobless with nobody to talk to brought out all my parental feelings and I couldn't help feeling that Malcolm could have shown just a bit more bloody compassion ...

But most of all I wanted to sit opposite him in Rosie's and get his daily caustic emails once more. I wanted us to be friends again.

I took a deep breath and typed.

'I'd like to talk to you. Shall we have lunch soon?'

The answer came through in minutes. Not exactly brimming with enthusiasm but not turning me down either.

'Thursday.'

Chapter 39

I felt a bit nervous as I went into reception.

I was planning a positive approach. I would go straight up to Malcolm and give him a firm hug and say I was really glad to see him.

And had been fondly imagining us apologising to each other and going in jaunty fashion for an apple crumble and had hoped Malcolm would know where Gabriel had gone and that after it had transpired that leaving Northstone had been the catalyst for some sort of silver lining to present itself, and he'd sent a postcard from wherever he was currently having a wonderful time, that Malcolm and I would both agree that all was well that ended well and life was too short to fall out. But as I pushed open the door I had a bad feeling in my stomach.

'Hello, Grace,' I said brightly, ignoring the woman's stony expression. 'I'm here to meet Malcolm – shall I go up?'

'Not if you know what's good for you.' Grace picked up a piece of paper and scanned it. 'He might miss his slot.'

'Sorry?' I looked at her blankly. 'We're having lunch.'

'Not now, you're not.' She looked at the paper again. 'He's working through it. Says he'll call you later.'

I frowned. There could be a nuclear missile warning and Malcolm wouldn't miss lunch and surely he'd have emailed me himself if he needed to change things.

'I'll just pop up briefly,' I told Grace firmly. 'Just to say hello.'

She shrugged. 'On your head.'

I went slowly up the stairs. I couldn't believe that Malcolm would abruptly cancel, though perhaps he'd decided he didn't want us to make up after all ... It was a bleak thought.

Upstairs there was no sign of Emily but a couple of other women I recognised were sat typing busily at their screens, one looked up briefly and nodded but made no attempt to speak to me. I remembered how friendly everyone had been when I first came up to these offices. Did they all know I'd rowed with Malcolm? Was I now persona non grata all round?

Malcolm's door was shut. Through the glass I could see him talking earnestly to a smooth-faced man in a dark-grey suit, who was listening with a fixed smile. His hands went up in protest, as if Malcolm had said something he didn't like the sound of and, at that moment, Malcolm leant forward and saw me. A look of alarm crossed his face.

My heart sank. He really didn't want to see me. I instinctively stepped back but Malcolm was now standing up and had placed both hands on the desk as he said something emphatic to the suit and then raised one hand and signalled in my direction without looking at me, in a way that could have meant 'wait there' or, equally, 'sod off'. I stepped back a bit more and dithered. I could hear the rise and fall of their voices – the conversation now sounded slightly heated – although I could only make out the odd word.

Then suddenly the door swung open and the suited man strode past me, and Malcolm appeared in the doorway and bellowed across the office. 'GLENIS!' One of the women sprang up and scuttled across the floor. Malcolm handed her a sheet of paper. 'Got him! Insert the figures – I'll be writing up the rest of his infantile posturing.'

Then he turned to me, his voice curt. 'Didn't you get the message?'

'Oh yes,' I said, tone as clipped as his. 'I've got the message all right.'

Malcolm rolled his eyes. 'Don't do that one. Is it urgent? Do you need to speak to me right now?'

He was looking at me intently. I opened my mouth, wanting to say that it could wait, that I was sorry we'd rowed and only wanted to make it up with him but was put off by his brusque manner. 'What happened to Gabriel?' I said instead.

Malcolm shook his head in disbelief. 'Now THAT I don't have time for!' he said, already turning away from me. 'Bastard that I am!'

'You said it!' I shot back.

As I walked away, I heard him say, 'Oh for heaven's sake. Don't be–' and then he gave a loud sigh, as if I were not worth bothering with, and went back into his office and slammed the door. As I looked back he had his head down and was typing furiously.

I blinked back tears as I went back down the stairs and out onto the street, glad Grace was on the phone and not able to say she told me so.

I'd felt disappointed, hurt and let down when David had

failed to be the knight in shining armour I'd built my fantasies around, but this was much worse.

I'd become attached to Malcolm as a real friend. But he wasn't the man I thought he was either ...

Chapter 40

Ode to Mum on the occasion of her 48th:
Happy Birthday Mumsie
Have a brilliant day
I'll buy you a pint when I get home …

Ben had drawn a smiley face, a beer, a glass of wine and what
I think was a plate of chips.

… But you might have to pay …

I smiled and put the card on the kitchen dresser with the
one from Tilly, and began to open the envelope Oliver and
Sam had left on the table with a box of chocolates.

They'd disappeared early to spend the weekend with Sam's
parents, who'd just flown in from Singapore, full of apologies
for leaving me alone. 'But Ben's back this evening,' Oliver had
reminded me. 'And no doubt Jinni will be over!'

I'd reassured them it didn't matter a jot and kept quiet
about the fact that Ben had said he'd probably only just make
last orders as he had his room in London to get cleaned out

and had to have a last drink with his housemates. And that Jinni's son, Dan, was arriving back today and Jinni would be collecting him from the airport.

I'd been equally bright with Tilly when she'd told me they were doing an extra performance for a youth club, and I'd told Caroline I was really looking forward to a quiet day on my own, when she'd explained about the charity fashion dinner.

The funny thing was, it was true. The prospect of a day pottering around an empty house, listening to the radio and doing a spot of gardening seemed heaven-sent. A few short months ago I was bereft not to have my children around me. Now I was a person happy to live alone.

Or rather I would be when Oliver and Sam had actually moved into her parents' apartment and Ben had finally made up his mind whether to go to Portugal. (I had gathered from Oliver that Maria, now officially Ben's girlfriend, was very attractive but quite volatile. Oliver privately thought the relationship sufficiently tempestuous to be over before Ben got around to raising the money for his plane ticket, a nugget of information, despite my new-found independence of spirit, I'd received with some relief.)

It was a good feeling and if it came with any small pangs of sadness or hollowness inside then I was ignoring them. I missed Gabriel popping in and felt sad he didn't feel he could be in touch with me. There was a big gap in my life where Malcolm had been, despite my disappointment with him. But by immersing myself in work and the garden, and practising the yoga breathing I'd learned from my first class in the original crumbling community centre the locals were still arguing about, I could achieve something that almost amounted to inner peace. Especially after a glass of rosé.

I'd seen and heard nothing of David and had no idea whether he was back from Beijing, but if he did pop up I wouldn't be sucked into any suggestions about meeting him. I will have a relationship when the time is right, I had told Caroline firmly and she, for once, had dropped the subject of dating apps and moved swiftly on to the latest in eyelash extensions.

She'd sent me a fabulous pair of ivory silk pyjamas, like the ones of hers I'd admired, and a hand-written voucher for a Kayla facial, reminding me to have a drink first in order to cope with the rigours of having my gums poked and my entire face lifted from within.

There was a card with a cartoon picture of two tipsy-looking women in high heels clutching glasses of champagne. 'Us soon, darling!' she'd written inside, followed by lots of kisses.

I smiled again. I still had the bottle she'd given me in the fridge. I'd crack that open later.

But right now it was Saturday, the sun was shining and I had no pressing office projects to catch up on that couldn't wait till Monday. Dressed in an old pair of shorts, I headed for the tangle of bushes and weeds at the far end of the newly cropped lawn.

By four o'clock I was ready to drop. Apart from a brief trip indoors for a cold drink and some cheese and, ever-mindful of Caroline's entreaties about free radicals, to slather on more sun lotion, I'd barely stopped except to read a nice text from

Nikki and send a stern one to Aaron the plumber, who continued to assure me cheerily and unconvincingly he'd be round 'later'.

Now I stretched out my aching back and looked with pleasure at the garden that had been so bedraggled and cheerless when I'd moved in and now had colourful shrubs and trimmed edges and borders of French marigolds and pansies. I was sweaty and scratched and there was mud up my arms but I felt content. I gathered up my tools and the bit of old carpet I'd been kneeling on, and headed for the bath.

I had just lowered myself into the steaming water when the doorbell rang.

'Bollocks!' I said aloud as I dripped my way back out again. The downstairs loo was pretty much unusable now and I was getting worried about the others – I wasn't going to let a plumber get away if he was finally here. I ran downstairs, a towelling robe wrapped hastily around my wet body. Jim from next door looked bemused.

'You got trouble with your lav, Duck?'

I gawped. Did the old man work for the elusive Aaron?

'Ours is bad too. Every two years it happens.' Jim shook his head. 'Can I have a look?'

He walked purposefully through my house and out of the back door, and stopped in front of a square manhole cover I'd never noticed, set into the paving stones. 'Under there's the culprit. Got a stick?'

I looked around the garden as if one might miraculously appear, while Jim explained the curious nature of the shared plumbing. An underground pipe the other side of Jim's side of the house had started to collapse and needed renewing and this caused a periodic build-up of debris below the cover we were looking at, which Jim and Angus – the previous owner of my house – had taken to clearing manually as required, since they'd been hanging on for the water board to come and replace the whole length of the waste-water channel since 2011.

'Like waiting for Christmas,' said Jim glumly.

I forbore to point out that unfortunately that particular stress-fuelled and costly delight came around a lot more frequently, and instead enquired what exactly I was required to do.

'I'd better put some clothes on,' I said, when Jim had finished outlining the procedure, which involved one of us holding the cover up while the other poked underneath it and sounded fairly high risk of my dressing gown flapping open.

Jim looked embarrassed. 'Might be best, Duck.'

Meg, he told me, when I had returned in my shorts and a clean t-shirt, had been nagging him all week as she was very hot on checking her own downstairs lav was fully functional and did not like the look of it last Friday. 'Not much gets past our Meg,' he said, producing a large screwdriver and prising up the edge of the metal cover.

'Pooh,' I said, as I peered down the hole where a gulley was clogged up with leafy brown sludge.

'Hold it, it's heavy,' Jim was leaning into the hole, jabbing at the sludge with a long spindly stick that, quite clearly, was not nearly robust enough to shift the blockage.

'What about a rake?' I offered.

'Have you got one handy?'

'No.'

Garden tools were on my list. My only spade had snapped a couple of weeks ago and I'd been working with trowels and hand forks ever since.

'Angus always did this bit,' Jim observed. 'He had rods,' he added helpfully.

My arms were aching. 'Let's put this down a minute,' I said, lowering the metal carefully onto the ground and going up the garden to the pile of foliage I'd dumped there earlier. I came back with two thick bendy branches from the buddleia I'd chopped back and pushed the largest one into the opening. I prodded the obstruction, moving it along several inches and seeing water trickle behind it. 'Got it,' I said jubilantly, digging the end of the stick underneath the gunge and attempting to flick the debris over the side of the gully.

The stick bent obligingly then sprang back shooting a spray up and over me. I watched a splatter of brown droplets land on my pale top and felt them rain across my face. My legs were dotted with dark splodges. Jim – showing remarkable agility for a man of his age – leapt back several metres while I shrieked.

'Oh fuck!' I yelled, looking at my spotted arms. 'It stinks!'

Jim nodded gravely from a distance. 'Raw sewage, Duck. Backs up here from all down the street.'

I was still honking from the thought, the smell still in my nostrils even after I'd scrubbed myself from head to foot and lathered my hair twice with a cocktail of my most highly perfumed unguents. 'Yuck,' I said aloud. 'Many bloody happy returns.'

'I hope you are having a magical day,' Jules from the office had posted on Facebook by the time I got downstairs to see how the washing machine was progressing with the boil cycle. *Thank you. I am covered in shit …*

But at least the loo was emptying at normal speed now. Having allowed me to be pebble-dashed with the entire neighbourhood's effluence, Jim had suddenly remembered some fast-acting, supersonic acid-based drain-clearing solution he had in his shed, that dissolved the rest of it in short order.

The phone rang in the middle of an experimental flush. My mother sounded better too. 'I'm sending you rose bushes,' she announced. 'But they won't get there till next week.'

'Thanks Mum,' I said, touched. 'Are you okay?'

I listened while she told me about her own garden and Mo's view on gladioli and something I didn't quite get the full thrust of about BBC licence fees. But I was heartened to hear she didn't sound any less comprehensible than she had ever done and probably a bit brighter.

When Gerald came on the phone he reported they'd had a very good week.

'She knew it was your birthday,' he said proudly. 'She woke me at five a.m. It was the first thing she said.'

It was daft to cry and I don't know why I did. But when I put the phone down I was overcome. I sat at the bottom of the stairs and wept silently into my hands, for her, for me, for Gerald, for the small achievements we'd now make ourselves celebrate as we tried to hang on.

I had a sharp memory of her, also in tears, on one of the rare occasions I'd ever seen her moved, when my father had died. 'Will you be okay?' said a kindly woman I didn't know, as she had kissed my mother goodbye. My mother had nodded. 'We will get on with it,' she'd said.

Adding to Alice and me, as we stood drying up when the last mourners had gone home and we were left to collect plates and sherry glasses and adjust to the suddenness of his going. 'What else can we do?'

What indeed? I asked myself, as I fell back on the sofa in my new pyjamas.

I was not going to worry about my mother or my son's exam results or the long-term career prospects of my daughter or the balance sheet of a young couple thrust into parenthood. I would not concern myself with my long list of necessary household repairs, failing strategies on social media or about shrivelling up into a partner-less old age ...

I eyed the swivel thingy in the corner which I hadn't used since Ben had videoed me and then put it on Snapchat, stretched one leg out in front of me and tried to tighten the muscles in my stomach. I could aspire to be one of those elastic old ladies like the one in my yoga class who must be eighty but could still get her knees around her neck.

Exercise, they had told me on *Woman's Hour*, was especially crucial in middle age ...

I opened the chocolates. The only energy I felt like expending right now was clicking on the film channel.

I'd only managed a nut twirl and a coffee cream when my

phone pinged with a text from Jinni inviting me to meet Dan and have a drink. I knew she was being kind – probably tipped off by Tilly I was on my own today – but I was quite sure she didn't really want visitors on her first night of having her son back from the other side of the world and I certainly couldn't be arsed to get dressed or do anything with my frizzy hair.

I sent her a brief reply, citing knackeredness from gardening and malodorous drainage crises and said I'd pop over tomorrow.

My mobile rang when I had my top off and was trying to reach behind my shoulders to put after-sun on my glowing back, while watching *Tootsie*.

'I could really do with some help,' Jinni said.

I sighed. 'Isn't Dan there?'

'He's popped out,' said Jinni.

Already? 'Well can't it wait till he gets back? I'm in the middle of moisturising and Dustin Hoffman's about to take his dress off …'

There was a silence as Jinni digested this. 'Not really,' she said. 'I'll come over and explain.'

Before I could answer she'd gone and I sighed some more. If she wanted me to hold a step-ladder while she brought down a ceiling, she'd just have to leave it till tomorrow.

'Hold on!' I called, as she rapped on the door and I struggled back into the top that now stuck to me.

Jinni looked stunning. Her dark hair was in loose shiny waves down her back and she was wearing a long red dress that looked amazing against her tan, with deep-red lipstick and nails. 'Gosh, you look glam,' I said.

She smiled. 'Are you okay?' she enquired, as she took in my damp hair and pyjamas. Her eyes rested on the open box of chocolates. 'Has something happened?'

'Just having a quiet night in. Relaxing,' I added, as Jinni didn't reply. 'It's my birthday,' I said awkwardly, as the silence continued.

'Is it?' Jinni looked pleased. 'Well then you MUST come over for a drink ... come on, get changed ...'

My heart sank. 'Jinni, really, that's sweet of you but I haven't had any time to myself for days. I just want to curl up and have a drink on my own. Or with you – here,' I continued hastily, thinking this sounded both lush-like and rejecting. I saw the way Jinni's face had fallen and rushed on. 'I've got a bottle of champagne in the fridge and I'll open some crisps–'

'No!' Jinni said loudly. 'Thank you,' she went on more quietly, as I looked at her startled. 'You enjoy it with the kids. Please, Tess, could you just come over for a few minutes – there's something I need to show you. I'd really appreciate it ...'

Grumpily I pushed my feet into flip-flops. I knew she'd keep on until I gave in.

'Do you want to put some proper clothes on?' she enquired as I dragged my body towards the door.

'I'll only be a moment,' I said firmly. 'The neighbours are used to me rushing about in my nightwear by now.' I knew I sounded churlish but it was ridiculous. What could possibly be so pressing?

Doubt set in as we crossed the road and by the time she had opened her front door, and pushed me in first, I was washed over with foreboding. I felt her hand on the small of my sticky back as she propelled me down her hall towards the closed kitchen door. It swung open. I gasped. They chorused.

'S-U-R-P-R-I-S-E!'

Chapter 41

'You could have insisted!' I said, taking a mouthful from the champagne glass someone had put in my hand and looking down at my pyjama bottoms.

Jinni laughed. 'I was beginning to worry I wouldn't prise you out of there at all ...'

'We'd have had to truss her up and blindfold her,' said Tilly. It was the grinning faces of my three children I'd seen first, crowded into the kitchen with Caroline and Sam and Fran, a tall, good-looking, deeply tanned young man I assumed was Dan, plus another couple of chaps I didn't know. And over to one side, standing with Emily and Grace – Malcolm. I felt a rush of pleasure and then looked at him embarrassed.

'Invited to bulk out the numbers,' he said drily. 'Can't have a surprise party with only six guests.'

It would have been less bloody awkward, I thought silently, wondering why Jinni had included him when I'd told her about our row. He didn't seem interested in pursuing the conversation and I didn't know what to say to make it better between us.

'Have you heard from Gabriel?' I asked Emily boldly. She nodded. 'Yes!' she said, happily. 'And so will you soon. He's–'

'Not the best topic of conversation in this house!' interrupted Malcolm, as Jinni swept back towards us with Caroline in tow.

I glared at him. 'He still exists!' I said, as Caroline directed me towards a kitchen stool and produced a bulging make-up bag. 'And I'd like to hear how he is–'

But Malcolm was steering Emily away from me and Jinni was topping up my glass. 'He's insufferable,' I said, wishing I could rewind to a time when he was making me laugh, and holding up my face obediently as Caroline, like the make-up girl on a film set, dabbed it with a sponge.

'Bark somewhat worse than bite, I would say. Keep still!' Caroline added, as she expertly applied blusher. 'While I transform you.'

'What for?'

'So you look as gorgeous as you should do on your birthday! Why are you so grumpy? As if I can't guess. Why don't you–?'

'I'm not, I'm very touched,' I cut across her hastily, before she could suggest I did a search on Tinder for a potential bunk-up or threw myself at Jinni's son. And it was true.

'I hope your parents don't mind your being here,' I told Sam, who was positively glowing.

She shook her head. 'Not at all. We had lunch with them and they're really looking forward to meeting you.' She put a hand on her abdomen. 'Dad bought me a Doppler.'

'A what?'

'You use it to hear the baby's heartbeat. We tried it and

could hear something, but I think it was my stomach rumbling.'
She giggled. 'But it will be nice when he's a bit bigger ...'

'Or she?'

'Yes, of course. Oliver keeps saying "him" but it will probably be a girl now ...'

I imagined a little boy clambering onto my lap or a small
girl standing on a chair in my kitchen, hands in a bowl of
flour, and suddenly felt proud.

When they asked where babies came from, it wouldn't be
about birds and bees. My first grandchild, I could tell him
or her, had all started with a rogue prawn ...

Oliver came over. He looked better too.

'You all right, Mum?'

'Absolutely!'

The champagne was zinging nicely around my bloodstream
now and I felt filled with love and gratitude to them all. I'd
hugged my kids, shaken hands with Dan – who had Jinni's
honking laugh and bright eyes – and also his friend Jake,
who'd travelled back with him and was keeping away from
Malcolm. As he drifted towards the food, I prepared to quiz
Emily on what she'd heard.

But before I could reach her there was a small tap on my
shoulder and oh, there he was, smiling nervously, holding out
a wrapped gift. 'Happy Birthday, Tess.'

'Oh, Gabriel!' I shrieked, then gave him a deliberately motherly embrace. 'Where did you come from? What's been
happening?' I glanced over at Malcolm, who had turned his
back on us and appeared to be studying a plate of pork pies.
'Are you okay?'

Gabriel nodded, looking overcome.

I wittered on to fill the silence. 'It's lovely to see you and I know Ben's missed having you around.' I nodded over to where my youngest, lager can in hand, was talking to Jake. 'I've not met Maria yet,' I added. 'What did you think of her?'

'Er – she's very pretty,' said Gabriel. 'Like Emily,' he added quickly, as the young girl joined us. She gazed at him adoringly as usual and then slipped her hand into his. To my consternation he squeezed her fingers back and smiled down at her. She leant her head against his shoulder.

I felt a pang of alarm. I'd noticed Tilly hadn't come over to greet Gabriel, but how would she feel if he was parading a new girl on his arm? I looked anxiously across to where she was talking to the chap I'd only heard was called Matt. I'd told Gabriel he needed someone of his own age, but I hadn't meant ...

'Oh!' I said, looking back at him. 'Are you two ...?' But Tilly had seen me watching her and was beckoning me over. 'I'll be back in a minute,' I said.

Tilly was wearing a short black dress I'd not seen before. 'Mum, this is Mattie.'

'Pleased to meet you.' I held my hand out to the spiky-haired young man, wondering what his connection was with Jinni. He was in his late twenties, beautifully dressed in a silk shirt and skinny chinos, sporting just the right amount of designer stubble, a pair of expensive-looking sunglasses jutting from his top pocket. My daughter was gazing at him, with much the same expression I'd seen on Emily.

'Are you local?' I asked politely.

Tilly shook her head as if I were very dim. 'Mum! Mattie's my new flatmate. He lives in Tooting. I told you!'

'OH!' The house share, with Matthew, the cousin of Shane. It was coming back to me. But ...

Tilly had her arm through his now. In fact, they had their arms right around each other. If I wasn't very much mistaken, his hand was right over my daughter's left buttock. 'Have you moved in yet, darling?' I asked faintly.

'Next week.' Tilly looked apologetically at Mattie, who was nuzzling her ear. 'She never listens ...'

'I did listen,' I hissed, when Mattie had been despatched by Tilly to refill our glasses. 'But you said he was–'

'I thought he was,' Tilly gave me a wicked grin. 'But he definitely isn't ...!'

I would like Mattie when I got to know him, she assured me, because he was in touch with his feminine side and not an unreconstructed yob like Ben, so could he stay the night, if he slept on the sofa?

I was distracted from answering by Jinni clapping her hands in the kitchen doorway.

'A late arrival!' She cried. 'And very special guest. Fresh from the airport in time for Tess's birthday celebrations ... I give you ...'

Everybody had stopped talking. I saw Caroline's eyes fixed on the door, alight with expectation. I squirmed inside. Surely Jinni hadn't relented to the point where she'd invited – *Oh please no – not in front of everyone* ...

But as Jinni stepped aside with a flourish, it was a woman with short brown hair and business-like expression who entered the room and looked me up and down. 'Good to see you've made an effort!' My sister dropped her handbag on the floor and hugged me hard. 'You look like a goldfish,' she said.

I hugged Alice back. I realised my hands were shaking.

'It's not that much of a shock, surely,' my sister was saying. 'I did tell you I'd be over soon ...'

I nodded dumbly as Tilly put a drink in her aunt's hand. 'We thought it would be a lovely surprise,' my daughter said accusingly. 'You were out when the call came ...'

'It is!'

'Oliver told me what they were planning, so I said I'd do my best.' Alice yawned. 'I won't be up late, though.'

'You'll have to sleep in my bed. I'll go back and change the sheets ...'

My sister put a hand up to silence me. 'I'll sleep in the old ones. Or anywhere! I was on a mud floor in Ecuador. Enjoy your birthday!'

I smiled at the familiar bossy tones. 'Have you really just got here? Did you get the train?' My sister was an intrepid traveller who could have back-packed here from the Outer Hebrides for all I knew.

'Flew in early this morning. Had a meeting in London with an agrologist who's over here from Chile – it was a one-off opportunity. The work he's doing is ground-breaking ...'

'A what?' said Caroline. 'She doesn't get any easier to follow.'

'It will be something to do with soil,' I explained. 'It's her speciality. She lectures all over the world now. She's the clever one.'

'But also quite dull,' Caroline whispered, as Alice instructed Oliver and Sam on the latest innovations in crop rotation. She herself was arresting in a short, fitted jade dress with matching jewelled mules, which had earned her appreciative looks from Dan and Jake. 'Are you enjoying yourself, darling?'

'Yes – yes I am,' I said firmly, stealing a sideways glance at Malcolm, who still wasn't looking at me. 'But I must speak to Gabriel.'

He and Emily seemed to have disappeared. I hoped Malcolm hadn't driven him out. The light was fading outside and Jinni had lit candles around the kitchen. Glasses and plates covered the table. Someone had set up an iPod and dock next to the range and Jack Johnson's mellow voice was coming through the speakers. The air coming in from the open back door was warm and Jinni was standing outside on the paving stones, where the outhouse had been, with a cigarette, blowing the smoke out in expert rings, which Fran was ostentatiously flapping away.

'Are you under duress?' I asked. Jinni shook her head. 'This is a treat ciggie not a stress one.'

'Terrible for the skin,' said Caroline, joining us. 'And you look so good ...'

'Just goes to show they can't be all bad, then.' Jinni grinned.

'It'll get you when you're older,' Fran gave a small cough.

'How are things?' I said, steering her away from Jinni, who was gesturing behind her back. 'We haven't spoken for ages. Is Jonathan with the kids?'

'Yep, I said I wouldn't stay long.' She took a mouthful of

what looked like fizzy water. 'We'll be able to have lunch again soon. I'm going back to work!'

'Gosh! But what about–'

'Only four days a week. We're getting an au pair.'

'Will she be able to–?'

'She's a mature student from Switzerland. Wants to come for a year. Done childcare. Not very attractive.' Fran looked pleased. 'Don't want Jonathan getting any ideas.'

'Well, that's great!', I said, looking around for Gabriel as Fran rattled on about the new job and how ironic it would be that we'd probably see more of each other when we could meet in London, than we did living in the same town ...

'When my mother was my age,' she said, 'I only ever remember her cooking and knitting. She wasn't knackered all the time like we are.'

'Probably didn't have your opportunities, either,' said Alice sternly, coming past us with a mug of something. She yawned.

'I might try knitting,' I said, thinking about the little heart-beat Sam would soon be able to hear for sure.

'Try sex instead, darling,' Caroline was behind us. 'Forty-eight is the new twenty-seven – you're supposed to be out there having a ball!'

Fran rolled her eyes. 'Chance would be a fine thing.' She emptied her glass. 'I'm going to say goodbye. The twins wake at five.'

'I think your sister is ready for bed too.' Jinni pointed through the window to where Alice was now sitting in a chair with her eyes closed. 'She could have stayed here,' she went on. 'But I've only got the one proper guestroom ready and–'

'I'm to be the very first customer,' Caroline smiled. 'Fabulous space, have you seen it?'

I saw Gabriel and Ben were back in the kitchen carrying bottles of beer. As I reached Gabriel's side, I heard Jinni's voice hard behind me: 'What's he doing here?'

I swung around, ready to defend the young man who'd found the courage to come back and face us, but Jinni was staring past me to the door to the hall. Where, standing next to my daughter, smiling at me over an enormous bouquet, was David.

I left Tilly, explaining he'd only popped in briefly and hustled David back into the hall. He held out the flowers. My hands were shaking again. There were orchids and stephanotis wound in among creamy roses, finished with greenery, tied with raffia, the sort of arrangement I adored. I brought it up to my face to play for time.

'Thank you,' I said primly. 'They're beautiful and they smell gorgeous too.'

'I would say "like you" but it would sound cheesy,' he said.

'It also wouldn't be true,' I said, catching sight of myself in the mirror and remembering I was wearing pyjamas. My hair, left to its own devices, looked decidedly unkempt and I was flushed from shock and booze. I didn't want anything to do with David, but vanity made me wish I'd not waved away Caroline's offer to do my face properly and had listened when she suggested I nip home for a dress. Was I even wearing deodorant?

'You look pretty good to me,' he said, hands on my waist,

stroking my sides through the thin fabric. 'All dressed for bed, I see ...'

'I wasn't expecting– it was a surprise,' I squeaked, my nerve ends leaping despite myself.

'Yes, Tilly told me ...'

'She shouldn't have done really, not with Jinni–'

'She only told me it was your birthday – I asked her what you were doing.' He took the flowers from me and laid them on Jinni's hall table. 'I was hoping to get here earlier and see you alone,' he went on, 'but I've only just got back from the airport ...' He pulled me closer to him and began to brush his lips gently across my cheek. 'I've missed you.'

A ripple ran down my back. 'What?' I said sharply, stepping back. 'I haven't heard a word from you.'

He pulled me towards him again. 'Sorry,' he murmured into my neck. 'Really busy. Beijing was full on–' His fingers were stroking my shoulders, trailing across my throat, moving down. 'This silk feels nice ...' I could feel his breaths deepening.

'And what about Lucia?' I enquired.

He carried on stroking. 'I told you. It's been an on-off thing.' He gave a harsh laugh. 'And it's very much off now! She's in a strop with me, so even if I wanted to–'

'Which I'm sure you will in the future,' I said briskly, pulling back from him again.

'No, no. It's you. What about coming over later? I realise I'm not welcome here.' He jerked his head towards the closed kitchen door.

Thoughts of Jinni emboldened me. 'I don't think so,' I said. 'I'm not into one-night stands.'

He stood back too. 'Well, I'm not asking you to marry me!' He gave another laugh and I felt my face flush. 'But I think I would like to see you for more than one night–'

He came closer. 'Jinni's been talking, hasn't she? This is very different, I promise you. You and I will have fun. Don't listen to that bitter old shrew–' There was something in his tone. I looked properly into his eyes for the first time and wondered how many drinks he'd had on the plane.

'Jinni's been a very good friend to me, I said levelly. 'And we're the same age.'

'She looks older.'

'No she doesn't.'

He was running his hands over the silk on my back, but it wasn't filling me with any sort of thrill now. Over his shoulder I saw the kitchen door open and Malcolm appear. He surveyed us impassively then his mouth twisted with disapproval. I felt instant shame.

He walked past us, picked up his jacket from the carved oak newel post and went silently out of the front door. It clunked shut behind him. I stepped right away from David.

'I think you'd better go,' I said. 'Jinni doesn't want you here.'

And, neither, I realised with cold certainty, did I.

They were still chatting and laughing as I went back into the kitchen.

I saw Caroline and Jinni exchange glances as I walked towards them. Caroline raised her eyebrows and I shook my head. 'He's gone,' I said shortly. I felt a strange anxiety pain in my solar plexus as I thought of Malcolm's face. The set of his shoulders as he disappeared through the door.

'Good,' said Jinni.

'Lovely flowers.' Caroline was still scrutinising me.

'They're in the hall. You can have them.'

Jinni and Caroline locked eyes again. 'I'll put them in your room.' Jinni turned to me. 'Come on, I'll show you!' Jinni led me upstairs and along a low-lit landing, freshly painted in white and tasteful shades of grey. She pushed open the door and switched on a lamp.

The room was lovely with stripped floorboards, a huge iron bedstead, crisp white bedding and antique furniture. A single rose sat in a tall glass tube on the marble mantelpiece over the Victorian fireplace. A white embroidered cushion lay plumped in the beautifully restored rocking chair alongside a free-standing full-length looking glass with drawer beneath, which matched the style of the bevelled mirror on the opposite wall. Caroline's smart red-leather holdall sat on the floor by the window.

'Wow,' I said.

She showed me the gleaming grey and white bathroom, with its old-style freestanding bath and piles of fluffy white towels. Then turned and gave me a searching look. 'Are you upset?'

'No.'

'So you and David—?'

'There is no me and David.'

'I'm relieved.'

'Yes, you were right!' I said briskly. 'He does appear to be a commitment-phobe, or whatever you call it, doesn't want *to marry* me, I quote, but will be up for a shag to amuse us both.' I sounded bitter and I tried to smile to soften it, then realised I was simply baring my teeth.

Jinni nodded. 'I was thinking of you. Really.' she said.

'So what did happen with you two?'

'Oh.' She shrugged. 'We met at the open day for this place. He seemed very keen. And I was too, to be honest—' She gave a lopsided smile. 'It had been a while. But it was just an opportunistic leg-over while he found out how much I'd offer.'

'I'm sure he fancied you rotten,' I said honestly. 'You're gorgeous.'

'At first he did. But once he'd got me dangling where he wanted, I saw him wrapped around that dark-haired girl he always goes back to ...'

'Lucia.'

'Yeah, apparently the silly cow is so besotted she puts up with his little away-days. So I told him to fuck off and stay there, and then of course, he was all over me – had a really good go at getting me back—'

Jinni smiled grimly. 'But I got him instead. I objected to his mate's planning application and slapped on a couple of tree preservations right where David wanted to put his conservatory.' Jinni gave one of her dirty laughs.

'Anyway – you won't believe this but the bloke over the back – Mark – is quite a nice guy when you get to know him. He's promised to point his extension windows the other way if I stop kicking up with the council.'

She gave me a grin. 'I think we could have quite a useful

working arrangement. Because – guess what! He's not quite such great mates with Mummy's Boy now – he says David has basically shafted him by–' She broke off as we heard Caroline calling urgently up the stairs.

Back in the hall, my friend looked worried. 'I can't find Malcolm,' she said. 'Have you seen him?'

'He's gone,' I said shortly, walking on into the kitchen, suddenly needing another drink.

Caroline caught up with me just as I was pouring a glass of Prosecco. 'What do you mean, gone?' she demanded, grabbing my arm.

'Left when David was here.'

'Oh, for God's sake.' She looked at Jinni, who had appeared on my other side. Jinni shook her head.

'So what?' I said crossly, although I had a peculiar pain in my solar plexus. 'He's hardly being the life and soul, is he?'

Again, my two friends exchanged looks.

'He bought all the champagne,' said Caroline quietly.

'And paid for the food,' added Jinni.

'OH!' I felt another sharp pang through my middle as I digested this. 'Well, he's still bloody grumpy,' I said defensively. 'And cold-hearted. Look at the way he sacked Gabriel when the poor boy–'

'He didn't!' Jinni cut across me.

'What?'

'Gabriel's still got a job – go and ask him!'

'No – he'd left the paper, I asked Emily. And Malcolm stopped her telling me–'

'That Gabriel was pitching up. It was part of the surprise,'

Caroline interrupted. 'Malcolm's a goodie – he's trying to make it up with you.' She spoke slowly, as if I'd have trouble getting it. 'He – really – likes – you.'

I swallowed, filled with joy and relief and panic that I'd blown it. 'He's got a funny way of showing it.'

Caroline shook her head as if I were beyond help. 'I rather think that's the point ...'

Chapter 42

'He was pretty decent in the end.' Gabriel looked moved all over again. 'He took me to the pub and said I was a total and complete ass. But then he said he'd done stupid things when he was young and that I probably had the makings of a half-functional reporter if I removed my head from my rear.' Gabriel gave a rueful smile.

'He told me to take two weeks off and see my dad and talk to him and then we'd start again. I go back on Monday.'

I realised my mouth was open. 'But he was so angry at all the damage you did–'

Gabriel's smile was small and sad now. 'He said he under-stood. He said we do strange things when–' Gabriel stopped. 'He said a load of stuff. He was decent,' he repeated, his voice breaking.

I put my hand on his arm. 'And how was your dad?'

'He was better when I left.' Gabriel hesitated. 'He doesn't really talk about her either. But I did this time and I think it helped.'

'You can always talk to me,' I said, swallowing hard. 'You and I Gabriel, we can't– but we can– we're still good friends aren't we?' I finished in a rush.

Gabriel nodded. 'Malcolm said if I tried any funny business with you, he'd break my arm.'

I went into a corner of the garden and dialled. His phone went straight to voicemail.

The younger ones were outside too now, grouped around on garden chairs or perched on the low wall. Ben had got hold of a guitar from somewhere and was tuning it.

'He's switched it off,' I said to Caroline.

'Landline number?'

'I'll ask Grace.'

If he had one, Grace had certainly not troubled herself to memorise it, she told me tartly.

'You'll have to go over there,' said Caroline decisively. 'Who can drive? Who's not been drinking?'

We looked blankly around. 'We'll get you an Uber,' said Caroline, tapping at her phone. Jinni snorted. 'Are you kidding? In Northstone? I've got a taxi number but it might take ages.'

I left them ringing it while I ran over the road and changed into jeans and t-shirt. I felt unaccountably anxious now.

'I heard Fran saying a very fulsome thank you to Malcolm for being so kind that night her kid was ill,' said Caroline, when I'd returned.

'Why are you making me feel bad?' I said, upset. 'You were the one who first made me go out with David.'

Caroline took a sip from the flute in her hand. 'That's before I'd realised he was a self-seeking cad and Malcolm was in love with you,' she said calmly.

'Of course he isn't!'

'He put on this party for you, hoping that ...' she stopped and looked reproving. 'Apparently he's invited you to dinner several times and you've always turned him down.'

'Twice,' I said.

'And the last time you saw him you stomped off.'

'What? He was all terse and too busy to–'

'And he didn't push it because he thought you and David–'

'How do you know all this?' I said, thinking uncomfortably of David's arms around me in front of Malcolm earlier.

Caroline gave me a look. 'Apart from the fact that it's bloody obvious, Jinni quizzed him when he came to apologise for Gabriel. She told him it was your birthday–'

'How did she know?'

'Sam told her. She'd planned a tea for you, then Jinni and Malcolm took it over ... He must be so disappointed ...'

'Stop it!' I was feeling terrible now.

'Then tell him how you feel.'

'How DO I feel? Why are you assuming–?'

Caroline looked stern. 'Do you know how much you talked about him when you were staying with me? You might have thought you'd been lusting after David, but I could see where your heart really lay ...'

'Cab's here!' yelled Jinni from the front door. She rolled her eyes towards Caroline as I went past her. 'For someone who's not romantic,' she muttered, 'she doesn't half like a happy ending.'

So did I, I thought, as the taxi sped along the dark country lanes. Caroline was exaggerating how Malcolm felt, but he had been a good friend to me – and an even better one to Gabriel, it transpired – and I had misjudged him.

I would apologise the moment he opened the door. I'd say I appreciated all his generosity in supplying booze for my celebrations and was sad he'd left so early. I would explain that I didn't know then what I knew now, and that if I had I would have given him a big hug. As I thought it, I realised how much I wanted to ... and not just a hug either.

Caroline was right. The way I felt about Malcolm was more than I'd ever felt for David, much more. This was deeper. This was real. I'd been in some sort of denial. But I was out of it now.

My stomach was churning as I paid the driver. The cottage was mostly in darkness, but his car was parked outside. I grasped the knocker and banged it hard. Nobody came. I waited a moment or two and found the bell push on the doorframe.

I heard an old-fashioned ring jangle through the building. Still there was no other sound within and the door remained closed. Was he deliberately ignoring me? Feeling sick, I knocked again.

Suddenly I remembered his young blackbird – maybe he was in the shed. I walked around the side of the house, feeling my way in the dark, ducking under trees and dodging around bushes, finding a wooden side gate set into a wall. I lifted the latch, praying it would not be bolted from the other side. It opened. An outside light shone down on the paving stones in front of the French windows and there, a little further up, was the silhouette of a figure sitting on the same bench we'd shared before. He didn't look round.

Malcolm was staring straight ahead of him down the dark garden. 'It's me,' I said softly, as I came up beside him.

He carried on gazing in front of him. 'Your boyfriend left you already?'

I sat down beside him. 'He's not my boyfriend. He never was,' I said. 'And he won't be now.' I added, disturbed by Malcolm's stony profile still turned away from me.

'And I'm sorry,' I rushed on. 'I'm sorry for calling you a bastard and for not realising you'd helped do the party – well, bought it all, really – and for not knowing you'd been nice to Gabriel when I thought you'd sacked him, and for being very good to me on a number of occasions–'

I stopped. Malcolm hadn't moved.

'I didn't know David was going to turn up,' I went on. 'He didn't stay long. I've realised he's not my type at all,' I finished desperately.

'And I've missed seeing you. I don't want us to fall out because ...' I stopped again as my voice began to wobble.

He put an arm out and closed it around my shoulders.

'Because?' he enquired as he pulled me towards him. He felt warm and solid. I let my head fall against him.

'Because I haven't tried your sausage casserole yet,' I said, attempting to laugh and finding myself choking back tears instead. I gulped and snorted. His arm held me tighter.

'It's not that bad,' he said.

'I was going to make it up with you when I came for lunch. When you cancelled and–'

'I was right up against deadline, you silly woman,' Malcolm sounded entirely unapologetic. 'That was Bill Williams, the

412

leader of the council I had in there, and I was trying to get him to tell me some approximation of the truth or at least a decent lie I could quote. I had only minutes before I needed to send the copy off. We were literally holding the front page.'

As I was silent, he went on. 'Didn't Grace explain? If we miss our slot at the presses all hell breaks loose and it was too good a lead to let go–'

'Why didn't you phone later? Suggest another lunch date?'

'I thought you'd be in a strop. I was going to sort it out tonight. After I'd checked with your friend that you weren't still mooning over the great architect ...'

'I'm not.'

'Have you told him that?'

'Yes. I have now.'

We sat in silence for a minute or two. I wanted to stay there in the warm dark evening, feeling safe and comforted, forever.

'How's your bird?' I said at last.

'Flown off into the big wide world,' said Malcolm. 'I've only got my journalists to spoon feed now. So that twerp of a boy told you he's back, then?'

'He said you were very kind.'

'Pah! Only to stop you wringing your hands.'

'Jinni's forgiven him too.'

'Yeah, she's another bleeding-heart liberal behind that gobby front.'

'Look who's talking!'

I leant into his warmth and listened to the breeze blowing through leaves, the sound of a car in the distance, a sudden burst of laughter from the lane outside.

'I've got a real conspiracy for him now.' Malcolm's tone was conversational. 'Ingrid was right about backhanders. But not at the community centre. I was quizzing Bill after a tip-off that there've been a few brown envelopes doing the rounds over the site of the old swimming pool. The council have sold it off far too cheap and someone is set to make a killing with forty new-builds.' He paused. 'Guess who the architect is behind the development?'

'Not–'

'One Jason Radley. His business partner. So just as well you've seen the light about lover boy,' Malcolm sounded satisfied. 'Because he's going to need to like porridge if this is what I think it is.'

As I stared at him, shocked, Malcolm gave a grim chuckle. 'Irony is Ingrid created merry hell when that pool closed. And has been ranting about corruption at the council ever since. She evidently doesn't know her little boy's up to his neck in it.'

'Are you going to report it?'

'Too bloody right I am.'

'Is that why you gave him that look when he was in my house?'

'I didn't know about it then.'

'Do you think David wrote that horrible note to Jinni? Gabriel swears he didn't.'

'If the spelling was correct.'

'Perhaps he did dye his eyebrows as well.'

We were quiet again. I could feel Malcolm's breaths in rhythm with mine and as I looked up at the clear sky studded with stars I suddenly longed for him to turn and put his arms around me completely. I wondered what it would be like to kiss him and what he would do if I made the first move.

Perhaps if we went indoors and he made coffee. Perhaps I could move towards him naturally, in his kitchen, put *my* arms around *him,* tell him how much I valued his friendship, how I wanted to get to know him better ...

Heart thumping, I stretched out my arm and took his other hand. For a second I felt him tense. 'Shall we–?' I began but he had given my fingers a brisk squeeze and let me go.

'I'd better get you back to the party,' he said, standing up.

My insides shrank in disappointment. 'I'm really not that bothered,' I said, trying to sound blasé.

'I am!' he said firmly.

I followed him through the house. I noticed now he'd changed out of the suit he'd been wearing earlier and had on a pair of dark-green trousers and a soft cotton shirt. I felt touched he'd made an effort to dress up for me and even more guilty that I'd got it all wrong.

'We don't have to–' I tried once more as he picked up car keys from a shelf in the hall.

He turned and gave me a brief, inscrutable smile. 'We do.'

I sat watching his hands as he drove expertly round the twisting lanes. Sick to my stomach that it had taken me so long to realise I wanted him and that it now seemed way too late.

I'd been blinded by my crush on David, like a silly, shallow adolescent. When I was old and ugly enough to know that what really mattered was trust and loyalty. A warm arm around you when things felt grim, pulling you close.

David had me dangling too – on tenterhooks – wanting to choose the right words, make a good impression. With Malcolm I could be me and being me was enough. Or it might have been.

I looked across at his profile, intent on the road ahead. David had only pursued me when he thought I wasn't inter-ested enough. Malcolm had always been there when I needed him. I wished I'd accepted his invitation to dinner, wished I'd sampled his scrambled eggs instead of wasting time on fanta-sies about someone whose speciality was multiple irons in the fire. And making a fast buck. I shuddered at myself. And felt ashamed.

'So here we are!' Malcolm's tone had an air of brittle jollity as we pulled up outside Jinni's once more and crunched across her gravel to the door someone had conveniently left on the latch. He stepped back to let me go first.

The hall was deserted. As we approached, the kitchen door opened a crack, spilling out light and then rapidly closed again. I could hear muffled voices.

As I pushed the door back open, the lights were off. I could see figures moving about in the gloom. Someone giggled.

I swung round to look at Malcolm. What were they plan-ning now?

There was a cry of 'Close your eyes,' and then the soft whoosh of matches being lit and I opened my eyes again to see Caroline and Tilly holding up an enormous cake, alight with a cluster of candles. Guitar chords twanged to my right and half a dozen drunken voices began to sing 'Happy Birthday', as the cake wobbled and yet another champagne cork popped.

I felt Malcolm move up close behind me. 'We couldn't waste that,' he murmured. 'Cost me a fortune.'

'I'm 48,' I said in wonder. 'What will happen when I'm 50?'

'We'll put a ribbon on your Zimmer frame,' said Ben, from a stool beside me, as the lights went back on and they all cheered.

Malcolm was walking away. I swallowed.

'When am I going to meet Maria?' I said brightly. 'She sounds an interesting girl.'

Ben took a swig of beer and moved off, apparently having something pressing to say to Dan on the other side of the room.

'She's 34,' said Tilly in my ear.

'Drink!' cried Jinni, gesturing with the bottle as I stood startled. 'Then I might need to hit the sack.'

'Oh God, me too. I'll help you clear up in the morning.' Caroline caught my eye and cocked an eyebrow towards Malcolm. I gave a small shake of my head.

Sam and Emily were handing round plates of cake. I couldn't swallow. Malcolm was standing next to the Aga munching.

I took a deep breath. 'It's been lovely to see you here, Grace,' I said to his receptionist, who was holding a plate nearby.

She frowned. 'What?'

'Thank you for coming,' I tried again. 'It's very nice of you.'

'Oh.' She still didn't smile. 'Happy Birthday,' she said flatly.

'We signed a card. He's got it somewhere.' She jerked a head at Malcolm.

'I'm not sure she likes me very much,' I said to him as she moved off, glad of a reason to speak. 'I've always tried to be friendly and polite ...'

Malcolm guffawed. 'She's not really Grace,' he said. 'We call her that to be ironic.'

I stared, remembering how many times I'd greeted her by name. No wonder she thought I was peculiar. Malcolm laughed again.

'She's called Shirley ...'

Gabriel was rounding up a party to go to the Fox, announcing it had an extension till one a.m.

'Don't make a racket coming in,' Jinni told Jake and Dan.

'On second thoughts, I think I might get a second wind and go with them,' said Caroline. 'Jake's rather delectable,' she added. 'How old is he?'

Jinni was looking at her phone. 'Twenty-six. I'll give you a key.' She smiled. 'Mark's popping over for a nightcap.'

'We'd better be off, then,' Malcolm put his plate down. I looked at him, heart beating. Did 'we' mean me too?

'Do you need a lift?' he asked Shirley-Grace.

'Can if you want,' she said tersely. 'Save my legs.'

The tight ball inside me tightened further. 'Well, I hope I see you soon.' I said, leaning up to kiss his cheek, willing him to suggest something himself. 'Must be my turn to buy *you* lunch.'

He nodded. 'Okay.'

'And thank you – thank you for the cake. And, er, everything.' I could feel my voice wobbling again and saw Grace-Shirley throw me an odd look.

Malcolm looked at me gravely. I felt my eyes fill and a tear run down my cheek. For a moment neither of us spoke. 'Right, then,' he said heavily and went out into the hall, Shirley-Grace behind him. Jinni pulled a face.

'I'll see you out,' said Caroline cheerily. I could hear a murmur of voices in the hall and hoped she wasn't saying anything cringe-worthy. While I was craning to eavesdrop, Jinni threw an arm around me.

'Hey, I'm glad you moved here, girlfriend,' she hollered in my other ear.

'I am too,' I told her, sniffing hard and grabbing a piece of her kitchen roll. 'Remember that first day we talked, I was feeling so lonely–'

Sam and Alice were leaving.

'Summit meeting about Mother in the morning,' instructed Alice. 'I'll tell you what I've found out and we'll form a strategy.'

'That means *she* will,' I said to Jinni as they disappeared.

Oliver put his glass in the sink. 'I'm going back too,' he said.

'Why didn't you tell me how old Maria was?'

Oliver shrugged. 'It won't last.'

I thought about Malcolm. I wanted something between us to go on and on. I wanted him to hug me to him, to be there when I woke up, with his dear, craggy TV detective face.

I bit my lip and blinked hard. Caroline was holding up her glass.

'A marvellous evening all round,' she declared, looking

pleased with herself and critically at me. 'I've got the most fabulous recovery eye-mask – I'll give you a sachet, darling.'

I began to gather glasses and plates, as around me the pub contingent assembled in the hall.

'That first day–' I continued to Jinni, who was reapplying lipstick and fluffing out her hair, '–the house felt so empty– Now ...'

I stopped as she broke into a wide smile and looked across the room. I turned – expecting my first sighting of her newly re-appraised neighbour.

My heart jumped.

'Just go and say it.' With a sharp shove, Caroline propelled me towards Malcolm.

I came to a halt inches in front of his chest. I looked up. Malcolm was impassive.

'Can I come home with you, please?' I said bravely, heart hammering hard in my chest, aware of Caroline on the edge of my vision, giving me a thumbs-up as she hustled Jinni away.

Malcolm's mouth twitched. 'Are you telling me,' he asked gruffly, 'that after all these bloody months, you have finally fallen for my charms?'

'I have fallen irrevocably and completely,' I confirmed happily, watching his eyes widen. I paused for a mental head count. Taking in my offspring, not forgetting my sister Alice and including Mattie, to whom Tilly was still spot-welded.

'And,' I added, reaching for his hand. 'There's nowhere left to sleep at mine ...'

Family gatherings and how to survive them – Jane's top tips

Christmas, birthdays, weddings and christenings can all be a minefield when today's modern – often blended – families are suddenly brought together. But you can survive them with a little forward thinking...

1. Make a seating plan. Grannies will like sitting next to their grandchildren and can deal with their runny noses and dodgy eating habits. Second wives can be put at the opposite end of the table to the original spouses, and alcoholic uncles placed away from the wine. Make a plan even if it's not your house and enlist an ally to help herd everyone into position.
2. Weigh up the pros and cons of hosting against those of being a guest. If it's your home, you can legitimately spend the evening hiding in the kitchen / popping upstairs to fetch something / searching for the cat in the garden. If it's elsewhere, you can set up a friend to call you with a fake emergency and beat an early retreat.

3. There is a fine art to judging how much alcohol to serve and to whom. As a general rule, for anyone likely to fall asleep - as much as you can get down their necks. Those with grievances to air - hide the whisky!

4. Prime younger members of the family on suitable topics of conversation, and remind them that while they may consider a baah-humbug farting sheep a hilarious centre-piece, Great Aunt Hilda probably won't.

5. Talk of sex, religion and politics can all add spice to the proceedings. Instead, put a ban on discussion of parenting skills, divorce rates or anything that happened 'in my day...'

6. Invite non-family too. Relatives will behave better, and may offer polite chit-chat instead of bickering over the remote control and dragging up what Uncle Roger did in The Great Christmas Row of 1996.

7. Prepare a fund of 'rescue subjects' to distract and divert if tensions are rising. New babies, holiday plans and the shortcomings of other relatives not present, will usually go down well.

8. At funerals remember it is *de rigueur* to declare how much the deceased would have enjoyed the wake. Practise smiling and nodding and do not succumb to the temptation to reply: 'No she wouldn't, she'd have complained about the food and then sat in the corner with a face on.'

9. Serve all food in quantity. It is harder to be argumentative when stuffed to the gills.

10. If you have a cream sofa – cover it.

11. If all else fails, whip out the Trivial Pursuit.

12. Try deep breathing, mindfulness techniques, meditation or yoga. Repeat to yourself: 'I am relaxed, I am calm, I am enjoying this.' Then hit the gin early, grin a lot and remember in a few hours it will all be over.

Acknowledgements

Mum in the Middle was a considerable time in the making and many lovely people helped along the way. I am massively grateful to my good friend and one-time editor, Mike Pearce, for all the wisdom and journalistic know-how he has shared over the years, and for being such an inspiration and encouragement. I couldn't have written this without you!

I'd also like to thank Lynda Wenham-Jones, Rebecca Smith and Janie Millman, for answering my various questions and Matt Bates for being gorgeous. For the entertainment, help, support and fabulous times at Chez-Castillon, I pay tribute to Janie and Mike Wilson, Katie Fforde, Judy Astley, Captain Catherine Jones, Jo Thomas, Clare Mackintosh, and Betty Orme – wonderful friends who have all, in their different ways, given me so much. Along with my dear local pals Janice Biggs, Bill Harris, and Jacqui Cook who unfailingly get me through when the chips are down. My son Tom has provided flashes of brilliance when I've been stuck and also made me laugh like a drain; my agent Teresa Chris has proved once again that beneath that fearsome exterior beats a heart of pure gold, and the marvellous folk at HarperCollins have made it all happen. None more so than my clever, kind, insightful, and clearly discerning editor, Kate Bradley, who I quietly adore. Thank you all xxx